Iten
sho
bor
tele
bar
This
Rene
Fines
incurre
be cha

Leabh

Baile Átha
Dublin Ci

Da

09.

THE CONVERT'S SONG

D0263427

ALSO BY SEBASTIAN ROTELLA

Triple Crossing

Twilight on the Line: Underworlds and Politics
at the U.S.-Mexico Border

THE CONVERT'S SONG

Sebastian Rotella

MULHOLLAND
BOOKS
HODDER

First published in Great Britain in 2014 by Mulholland Books
An imprint of Hodder & Stoughton
An Hachette UK company

1

Copyright © Sebastian Rotella 2014

The right of Sebastian Rotella to be identified as the Author of the Work has been
asserted by him in accordance with the Copyright, Designs and Patents Act 1988.

All rights reserved. No part of this publication may be reproduced, stored in a
retrieval system, or transmitted, in any form or by any means without the prior
written permission of the publisher, nor be otherwise circulated in any form of
binding or cover other than that in which it is published and without a similar
condition being imposed on the subsequent purchaser.

All characters in this publication are fictitious and any resemblance
to real persons, living or dead is purely coincidental.

A CIP catalogue record for this title is available from the British Library

Trade Paperback ISBN 978 1 444 78554 8
eBook ISBN ISBN 978 1 444 78555 5

Printed and bound by Clays Ltd, St Ives plc

Hodder & Stoughton policy is to use papers that are natural, renewable
and recyclable products and made from wood grown in sustainable forests.
The logging and manufacturing processes are expected to conform
to the environmental regulations of the country of origin.

Hodder & Stoughton Ltd
338 Euston Road
London NW1 3BH

www.hodder.co.uk

Para Carmen, mi amor.

"They stay on the fringe of the plot. They are the professionals, the *entrepreneurs,* the links between the businessmen, the politicians who desire the end but are afraid of the means, and the fanatics, the idealists who are prepared to die for their convictions. The important thing to know about an assassination or an attempted assassination is not who fired the shot, but who paid for the bullet. It is the rats like Dimitrios who can best tell you that. They are always ready to talk to save themselves the inconvenience of a prison cell."

— Eric Ambler, *The Mask of Dimitrios*

Dans ce vaste pays qu'il avait tant aimé, il était seul.

— Albert Camus, *L'Hôte*

Pedro Navaja

*R*aymond said tonight was the night.
Raymond said tonight they would make their move. Hit the big time.

Raymond said he kinda hated to bring this up, but he was a little disappointed in Valentín. Felt like he had been fading on him. Making lame excuses: his job, his high-maintenance girlfriend, his folks bitching at him. Raymond felt like maybe Valentín didn't want to make money anymore. Like he was scared. But down deep, he knew Valentín had heart. They were cuates from way back. Tonight was major. Step up, homes. Don't punk out on me now.

Basically, Raymond had talked the usual bullshit.

But if he said he needed backup, he probably meant it.

Valentín ate an Italian beef special at the counter of the sandwich shop, careful to keep the grease off his leather jacket. The sun set on the November streetscape: three-story brick walk-ups behind wrought-iron fences. The Italian-ice stand—red, white and green, draped with decorative lights—closed until May. The grocery across the street where, as a boy, Valentín had accompanied his father on Saturday pilgrimages to Benny the Butcher.

Benny did business in back, his little fort formed by freezers, display cabinets, a chopping block, blades hanging from hooks and arrayed in racks. Benny was squat and grave in black-framed glasses *and meat-stained apron, sweater sleeves rolled up. He had dental problems: chipmunk cheeks, mouth frozen into a mumble. He chopped and sliced and wrapped, talking to Mr. Pescatore and reaching across the scarred wood to hand Valentín slices of mortadella and prosciutto.*

Benny the Butcher had disappeared one day. Just like that. Running from the bookies.

But Vince, the owner of the sandwich shop, was still around. Valentín noticed that a refill cup of Coke had appeared at his elbow. Courtesy of Vince. Valentín looked up. Vince shambled toward a new customer with a grimace. The .45 in the holster on his hip accentuated his limp, which brought to mind Walter Brennan as Stumpy in Rio Bravo. *The neighborhood was on the rebound. Town houses and condominiums were luring back children of old-timers who had run to the suburbs. The Italians, blacks and Mexicans had learned to get along or ignore one another. But good luck convincing Vince to leave his cannon under the register.*

Valentín had an exam the next day. I should be home studying, *he thought.* Instead of waiting on Raymond and whatever catastrophe he's got cooking.

Valentín chugged Coke. He hurried out when the steel-blue BMW pulled up blaring Latin jazz into the dusk. He slid in next to Raymond, who gave him an elaborate handshake and a thump on the chest.

"Cuate," *Raymond boomed.* "Right on time. I likes that in you."

I likes that in you. *Emphasis on the* in. *His latest little catchphrase, acquired from a Latin King who sold him dope. Raymond collected expressions. He repeated them in experimental accents, as if learning a tune. He sounded like an Eighteenth Street Mexican when he said* cuate, *like a Logan Square* cubano *when he said* comemierda.

Driving fast, Raymond lit a joint. He checked his cell phone. He patted the wheel in time to the radio: island drums, percussive piano, rowdy horns.

"*Chano Pozo,*" *Raymond said, passing the joint. " 'Manteca.' "*

"*Old school.*"

"*Nothing wrong with old school.*"

Valentín had stopped smoking weed for the hotel drug test weeks earlier. But he took a hit. And then another.

"*A badass, Chano Pozo,*" *Raymond said.* "*The godfather of the conga. Taught Dizzy Gillespie Afro-Cuban music. A gangster, a cokehead, a tripped-out animal-sacrificing* santero. *Know how he died?*"

Valentín moved his head to the jabbing wail of the trumpets. Ray was an encyclopedia. You always learned something if you listened.

"*In a bar in Harlem,*" *Raymond continued.* "*Dressed sharp. He put a nickel in the jukebox to play 'Manteca,' his big hit. He's singing along, dancing, havin' a great time. That's when they ambushed him. Shot him grooving to his own song.*"

"*Damn.*"

The BMW hit the interchange to Lake Shore Drive. The ramp rose and curved, revealing a panorama of the skyline aglow.

"*So what's up tonight that's so important?*" *Valentín asked.*

Raymond pushed buttons on the CD player. "*Check this out. 'Pedro Navaja.' The Latin 'Mack the Knife.' "*

Head back, driving one-handed, Raymond sang in Spanish. He matched Rubén Blades note for note, nuance for nuance. He had limited technique, but a sweet sound. He was a dead-on mimic: Sinatra, Springsteen. In conversation, he came off as if he was enjoying a private joke at your expense. When he sang, though, he sounded as if he believed every word with all his heart. And it became hard to dislike him.

Raymond wore the leather coat, collar up, that he had bought after seeing Carlito's Way *again. His stubble hinted at plans to grow a trim Carlito-style beard. Raymond was a year older than Valentín: thin, long-armed, and long-backed with straight, slicked-back hair. Valentín was curly-haired, sawed-off, and brawny in the shoulders and chest. Still, people often thought they were related. Raymond used it to tactical advantage: Come on, beautiful, let my cousin here buy you a drink, he's too much of a gentleman to ask you himself.*

The BMW zoomed south between lakefront parkland and train tracks.

"You guys play that cut last night?" Valentín asked. Raymond performed with three bands: rock, Latin, and jazz.

"Nah." After a moment, staring straight ahead, he added: "It was fun, though. College crowd. Fine ladies dancing up front, all frisky."

Raymond steered into an exit. At a stop sign, he thumped Valentín on the shoulder and said: "Been a while, homes. Whaddya hear, whaddya say? How's Dolores treating you? La belle et sympathique *Dolores.*"

Raymond spoke good French thanks to the private school that had finally kicked him out.

"She's okay." Valentín sighed. "Busy. Homework, college applications. You know."

Raymond nodded sagely. "And your folks?"

"Like cats and dogs."

"That's dangerous, Argentine versus Mexican. They giving you shit about college?"

"Well, I'm taking the criminal justice courses. My uncle says that'll help my chances for the PD."

"The PD."

"If the police doesn't work out, my uncle thinks I should apply to the Border Patrol."

"¿La pinche migra?" Raymond whooped. "Those fascist storm troopers?"

"He knows a boss there. They need Spanish speakers."

Valentín's uncle Rocco was a police lieutenant. He disapproved of Raymond even without knowing the extent of his efforts to become a singing gangster. Uncle Rocco had said, "If there's one thing worse than a thug, it's a snotty spoiled lawyer's kid playing thug. Stay away from that jamoke. And don't get me started on his father. He never met a criminal he wouldn't bend over for."

The BMW rolled into a lakeside park. Raymond headed toward a dark corner of the parking lot. He eased into a space with a view of the lot, the traffic, and the columns and cupola of the museum.

"How's the hotel gig?" *Raymond asked.*

Valentín suspected that Raymond had a reason for not telling him about the score until they were in position.

"Pretty good. Had a luggage thief yesterday. Smooth brother in a three-piece suit. Way he works it, he hangs out casing the lobby till he sees a bag he likes. The suitcase was by the bell station; he had a bellhop bring it to a cab. Tipped him a buck, too. I chased the cab on foot, but I lost him."

Raymond chortled. Valentín had known he would love that story.

"He had a bellhop carry the stolen bag? Badass. I likes that in him."

"This big old beat cop, Henry, on Michigan Avenue? Didn't lift a finger. Too busy making money. Everybody's stealing in that hotel: cops, doormen, garage attendants."

"Yeah, well, the biggest thieves are all the fucking executives and bankers and politicians staying up in the rooms, am I right?"

"So Ray: What's the caper?"

Raymond turned toward him for dramatic effect.

"Oh, it's a caper all right. You remember that asshole Wolf? He's meeting us here. Him and his goofy sidekick Alvin. Carrying fifty grand."

Valentín had refused to get involved in Raymond's drug racket on the money end. But Raymond paid him for helping out now and then with security, which basically meant watching Raymond's back and looking mean. As the loads grew, Valentín had done his best to keep his distance.

"Pure profit," *Raymond said.* "Fifty large. I didn't bring any coke."

"What?"

Raymond opened the glove compartment with a ta-dah gesture. There was a pistol inside.

"The Smith and Wesson you like. Nine-millimeter, like the PD.

Me"—he pulled back a lapel to display a shoulder holster—"I got my Beretta."

Valentín blinked, his eyelids heavy. He was not sure if they had been in the lot for five minutes or twenty-five.

"You're gonna take them off? You crazy?"

"What's he gonna do, call the cops? Call his mother?"

Valentín slammed shut the glove compartment. "What if he freaks? What if they're packing? You plan on murdering them?"

"Relax. The minute that punk bitch wannabe sees the cuetes, he's gonna need a new pair of shorts."

"I am not comfortable with this at all."

Valentín slumped. Raymond passed the joint. Valentín waved it off.

"Don't get all worked up, homes," Raymond said. His deep-set, bloodshot eyes gleamed in the lights of the dashboard.

"You can't just jack him and walk away."

"You watch."

"Last time we saw Wolf, you were all friendly, laughing it up."

"A facade." Raymond's brow furrowed. "I can't wait to see that Jew-boy shake in his boots."

"Come on, Raymond. Don't talk that Nazi shit."

Raymond shook his head. "You know my mom's family are Lebanese."

"They moved to Argentina like a hundred years ago."

"Still. We got relatives back home. You know what the Jews have done to Lebanon. To my people. People all over."

"Man, what are you babbling about? You decide to do a drug rip-off, now it's some kinda political thing?"

"You need to smarten up about the world, Valentín."

"Bullshit."

"What's the problem? You're worried because you have this notion you'll be a cop one day? Let me break it to you: the law enforcement thing is not going to work out."

"Why not?"

"You do everything half-assed. You smoke my dope and take my money, then play it off like you're not a drug dealer. You fuck up in school, but you feel bad. You piss off your parents, you worry. Like that Los Lobos song: 'Too weak to live, too strong to die.'"

Valentín checked the dashboard clock.

"Matter of fact," Raymond continued, "Dolores feels the same way."

"Dolores?"

"We were talking about you last night."

Suspicion entered the haze in his head. Raymond always played the big-brotherly gentleman around Dolores. But Raymond was a dog.

"Last night?"

"At my gig."

"She was home studying," Valentín snapped. "We talked on the phone."

"She came to the gig, homes. Dancing, having fun. Looked great too, tight black dress. Está bien buena."

Rage jolted through him. He imagined punching Raymond in the face. He envisioned the mechanics of throwing the punch: swiveling his torso for power, keeping his shoulder low, following through.

Raymond flinched. "What, bro, you gonna hit me now?"

Valentín spoke through gritted teeth. "You're startin' to piss me off."

"I wouldn't mess with your lady, you know that."

Valentín stared out his window. "Listen up, Ray. I'm worried about you. You talk about me not making it as a cop. You're not exactly a bona fide professional criminal."

Raymond busied himself with a joint and lighter. "So?"

"It ain't gonna last. No matter how slick you are, how much shit you talk, it's a game. A bluff. And you're dragging me down with you. You had me buying weight with you up in the projects this summer, man. The fucking projects."

"You handled it fine."

Valentín had carried the Smith & Wesson for the expedition. Except for hard looks from hooded gangbangers in the dim, urine-smelling lobby of the high-rise, the deal had gone smoothly. He had gotten a charge out of it, a gunslinging street adventure. But he wasn't about to admit that now.

"Well, I was plenty scared. You need to cut this shit out before you get killed. Man, you could go to college if you want. Your dad has yank. Or you could get serious about the music. If I could sing like you, that's what I'd be doing. For money and for fun. But you treat it like a big joke. Like you treat everything, basically."

Raymond's expression softened.

"Nobody else disrespects me like you, Valentín."

"Nobody else talks straight to you."

Raymond's cell phone rang. He answered, throaty and brisk.

"What's up, dog? Where you guys at?…That's close…Keep going south five minutes…Yeah, by the lake…I likes that in you. Bye."

He hung up. He rolled his shoulders, the sardonic mask back in place.

"As much as I'm enjoying this deep psychoanalytical dialogue, it's time for business," he announced. "You need to stop fucking around."

Valentín felt sad and relieved. Raymond had given him the opportunity he had wanted for months.

"Tell you what," he said quietly. "I'm gonna walk away."

Raymond made an umph *noise, absorbing the impact.*

"If you were in trouble, I'd step up," Valentín continued. "But this ain't that kind of situation. My advice is, tell Wolf it fell through. Make up something. Drive away. Me, I'm gone."

Raymond checked the clock. He swept his hair back, then looked at the windshield, at Valentín. He cocked his head, as if examining the problem from a new angle. His eyes shone.

Switching to Spanish, Raymond asked, "That's as far as we go, then?"

In Spanish, Valentín answered, "That's right."

Valentín opened the door. A cold breeze swept the lot. His legs ached with accumulated tension. He closed the door behind him.

The window lowered. Raymond leaned toward him, grinning weakly.

"Look, man, it's cool. You made your move. Bad move, but still. I likes that in you."

"Don't do anything crazy, Raymond. Please."

Raymond hesitated. "Sorry about Dolores."

Valentín could not tell if it was an apology or a taunt. Did he mean: Sorry I mentioned Dolores? Sorry you're having problems with Dolores? Sorry I'm fucking Dolores behind your back and you're just now finding out?

He walked fast. Clusters of broken glass glittered on the asphalt. A long low shape scuttled out from under a car into the weeds.

For years, the park had been the spot for soccer, football, hanging out, getting high, talking to girls. People had picnics, walked dogs, sat on the rocks. They looked at the skyline rising from the lake like a science-fiction citadel.

But at night, the park was full of rats. Big bloated galloping rats. You didn't want to look too close or get too comfortable.

He hurried into a dank, graffiti-smeared pedestrian tunnel. The wind wailed around him.

At the end of the tunnel, he stopped. He listened for an echo in his wake: slamming doors, angry shouts, gunshots.

He heard nothing. He kept going. He did not turn back because he wasn't sure if he would end up helping Raymond or beating the shit out of him.

PART I

Cafetín de Buenos Aires

The whole mess started ten years later on a sunny fall day when Valentine Pescatore was feeling at home in Buenos Aires.

He got up and put on a warm-up suit. He took a quick cab ride on Libertador Avenue to the sports club in Palermo Park. At eight a.m., he had the red rubber track to himself. His breath steamed in the morning chill; May was November in Argentina. He was not as fast or strong as he had been while serving as a U.S. Border Patrol agent. Yet he was healthier than during those crazy days at the Line. He had lost the weight he'd acquired eating home-cooked Cuban meals while living in San Diego with Isabel Puente. *Arroz con pollo, ropa vieja,* fried plantains. Washed down with drama and heartbreak.

Leaving the club, he caught a whiff of horse smell on the river wind. A nearby compound of the Argentine federal police housed the stables of the mounted division. Facundo had told him the compound was also the headquarters of the police antiterrorism unit.

Pescatore reclined in the cab, invigorated by the run. The driver was a grandfatherly gent with well-tended white hair encircling his bald spot. His shoulders in the blue sweater-vest moved to the tango classic on the radio, "Cafetín de Buenos

Leabharlanna Poibli Chathair Baile Átha Cliath

Dublin City Public Libraries

Aires" ("Little Café of Buenos Aires"). The cab stopped in front of Pescatore's building on a side street as the song ended in a flourish of bandoneon and violins. It was an homage to a neighborhood café—the best thing in the singer's life except his mother.

"That was great," Pescatore said. "What was that last line? 'In the café I learned philosophy, dice and...'?"

The cabbie studied him over his spectacles. He recited crisply: "'The cruel poetry of thinking of myself no more.'"

Pescatore took the elevator to the tenth floor. He had found the furnished rooftop apartment through Facundo Hyman Bassat, his boss. The landlord had described it as a penthouse. It was cobbled together from a converted maid's quarters and a storage attic. The front door opened into the middle of a narrow hallway that led left to a galley kitchen and living-dining area. A bookshelf held his old collection of compact discs and his new collection of books. At the other end of the hall, a skylight in the low slanted ceiling made the bedroom less claustrophobic. Glass sliding doors opened onto a little balcony-patio.

Rain tended to flood the patio. The sun took no prisoners. The wind was noisy. There were bats. But the apartment was cozy. It got plenty of light. From the railing, you could see the river. Bottom line: he was living in a penthouse in La Recoleta, the swankest neighborhood in town.

Forty minutes later, he hit the street showered and shaved. He wore his Beretta in a shoulder holster under a brown leather jacket. He had let his curly hair grow longer than when he was in the Border Patrol, though he drew the line at slicking it back like the locals. If he didn't talk much, people took him for a local. He preferred it that way.

He turned onto a tree-lined street where a hotel faced a shopping center. Ragged kids from the riverfront slum worked the taxi stand in front of the shopping center, jostling and begging and carrying bags. The high-pitched melodic whistle of a mouth harp echoed among high-rises: the call of the *afilador*, an itinerant Galician knife sharpener in a brimmed cap and blue smock who looked as if he had been pushing his cart for a century.

In the middle of the street, a paunchy police officer stopped traffic so a couple of lean ladies in short fur jackets could jaywalk. Two cops in boots and helmets stood smoking cigarettes near their motorcycle. They were in an anticrime tactical team. Pescatore had seen them zooming the wrong way down Callao Avenue with siren and lights blasting, the driver hunched like a human rocket, the rider with his shotgun at the ready.

The hotel and shopping center had security guards. The doormen of apartment buildings kept watch even on Sundays, which they spent in vertical trances listening to soccer games on earphones. But no one had seen anything on a recent night when a gang robbed the ritzy Italian restaurant next to the shopping center. The robbers were fit, efficient, their hair close-cropped; they barked commands as they relieved diners of valuables. The word on the street: the stickup artists were off-duty cops from the Bonaerense, the police force that patrolled the province of Buenos Aires, an expanse the size of France surrounding the capital. A wave of robberies downtown was part of an ancestral feud between the provincial police and the federal police, who patrolled the city.

The federal beat cop strode to the curb, his cap at a low jaunty angle. He and the motor cops exchanged greetings and kisses on the cheek. Pescatore made his way around them. He was an armed U.S. civilian on foreign soil. Despite the investigator credentials that Facundo had provided for him, despite the rule-breaking he saw at every turn, carrying a gun made him a bit nervous. And he wasn't comfortable with all the kissing. Argentine men kissed each other with alarming frequency. It wasn't some sissified European thing confined to actors and fashion designers. Kissing was a common form of greeting among waiters, garbagemen, bank tellers, soccer players, airport baggage handlers, and, yes, cops.

The hotel had marble columns, plush rugs, and a musty air. Pescatore went up to the suite of the American client. Dr. Block greeted him wearing a suit and tie. They sat in armchairs. Pescatore leaned forward with his elbows on his thighs, fingers interwoven. This was the most delicate assignment that Facundo had given him.

"You doing okay, Dr. Block? Jet-lagged? Want some coffee?"

"I'm fine, Mr. Pescatore," Block responded in a weary monotone. "Just anxious to get this thing done with and go home."

"Please, Doctor, call me Valentine."

Block was a pediatrician from Miami. He had a shiny bald head, a white mustache, a gentleness that came from decades treating little kids. But his blue eyes behind his glasses seemed drained of light. He was the saddest man Pescatore had met in a long time. Block's son had been an engineer married to a Brazilian woman. A public-works project took him to the Triple Border region where Brazil, Paraguay and Argentina meet. He got into a dispute with an Argentine investment partner: a lawsuit, allegations of embezzlement, death threats. During a visit to Paraguay, the younger Block was shot dead at the wheel in a car-to-car ambush.

The Paraguayans hadn't done much of anything about it. Dr. Block hired Facundo, who ran a private investigation agency operating in the tri-border area and Buenos Aires. Facundo helped the FBI identify a hit man and track him to Buenos Aires, where the Argentine police arrested him. The evidence pointed at the former business partner as the shot-caller, but the investigation had stalled. Facundo had warned the U.S. embassy that the killer was likely to be released. Official options had been exhausted.

As Facundo's operative in the capital, Pescatore had been instructed to carry out the unofficial option.

"Doctor, this is the situation," he said. "Bottom line: The judge is gonna cut this guy loose. Unless he gets paid. The figure they named is forty thousand dollars. We recommend paying. It should keep the suspect in jail and get the investigation moving again."

The doctor stared with his defeated eyes. "If I may ask: How did they arrive at that particular price?"

"We think he got thirty thousand from the other side."

"An auction."

"Exactly. I feel terrible about it, but that's the deal. We have an appointment with the judge this morning. If you approve."

"I expected something like this. My in-laws and I agreed to spend what it takes. But Valentine, I don't have forty thousand dollars on me."

"Don't you worry about that, Doctor," Pescatore said. "Long as you got your checkbook, we're fine."

The hired Renault sedan took them down Nueve de Julio Avenue, the pulsing heart of the capital. A dozen lanes, a jam-packed river of traffic. They were en route to a *cueva,* a cave. A clandestine cash house.

"I come here every month to get dollars for my rent," Pescatore said. "It's illegal to use U.S. dollars, but I'm contractually obligated. I give my landlady an envelope full of bills, like a drug deal or something."

The driver, Fabián, negotiated the traffic circle around the Obelisk at the intersection of Nueve de Julio and Corrientes. Fabián was one of Facundo's regulars. He chewed a toothpick and wore the blue and yellow scarf of the Boca Juniors soccer team. Pescatore directed him through the narrow, congested streets of the old business district, the Microcentro, with its faded, 1970s air.

Pescatore and Block got out. Pescatore stayed close behind

19

the client as he walked him across the street. His eyes swept the sidewalk, storefronts, parked and passing cars.

They entered a travel agency. Pescatore went up to a receptionist by a closed door and said the password: "Facundo's American friend."

The receptionist pushed a buzzer. A narrow flight of stairs led to a space enclosed by curtained cubicles. There was a table in the middle of the old brown carpet. The master of ceremonies, a mix of clerk and sergeant with rolled-up sleeves, stood behind the table. Pescatore had privately nicknamed him Mr. Guita, a slang term for money.

"Pescatore," Mr. Guita said.

The establishment prided itself on discretion. Mr. Guita dispensed black-market cash in an atmosphere reminiscent of a church or a hospital. Pescatore wrote down numbers. Mr. Guita gestured at a cubicle. Pescatore held the curtain for Dr. Block, then told him to write a check and leave the payee blank. Mr. Guita entered and put a large reinforced manila envelope on a table. He examined the check. He removed stacks of bills from the envelope, counted them, and put them back. Guita and Pescatore exchanged receipts. The moneyman nodded and disappeared through the curtain.

Before he and the doctor left the cubicle, Pescatore drew his gun. The doctor's eyes widened. Pescatore put the Beretta in the side pocket of his jacket.

"Don't be alarmed, Doctor," he said. "I'm just taking appropriate precautions."

Pescatore carried the envelope in his left hand. He kept the gun gripped in his pocket until they were speeding away. Replacing the gun in the holster, he hefted the envelope. The money made him nervous; he couldn't wait to deliver it. Turning in his seat, he gave Block a reassuring grin.

"Gotta stay alert, Doctor. This city, it feels like Europe or something, right? People are sophisticated, educated, nice clothes and restaurants, beautiful women. But they'll rob you at noon in front of City Hall."

The courthouse was on the other side of the line between the city and the province of Buenos Aires. It was in an uneasy suburb where walled subdivisions, known as "countries," (from the English term "country clubs") abutted feral shantytowns, known as "villas." The courthouse was a modern box that clashed with the cobblestones of the municipal plaza.

On the way up the front steps, Pescatore told Dr. Block that the judge did not speak much English. There was a prearranged signal. If the judge displayed a purple handkerchief, they would hand over the bribe. If he showed a white handkerchief, a problem had arisen that would require further parley.

"Either way, I'll have us outta there as fast as I can," Pescatore whispered. "Apparently this thing with the handkerchief is like the judge's little trademark. The scumbag."

They were received by a middle-aged woman in designer glasses who introduced herself with self-important severity as the judge's secretary. She led them at a hip-swinging, forced-march pace through high-ceilinged hallways. In a busy room with fluorescent lights, they passed two officers in berets—penitentiary police—flanking a prisoner who was being questioned by a civilian at a computer. Personnel talked loudly to one another and into phones. A uniformed waiter went by carrying a tray of steaming coffee cups one-handed. Yellowing file folders bulged on shelves, overflowed a cart, covered desks, and climbed in stacks along the walls.

The atmosphere changed in the judge's office. Muted lighting bathed paneled wood. Tall windows showed greenery. The decorations consisted of crucifixes, religious art—writhing Saint Sebastians riddled with arrows—and photos of the judge with big shots.

The judge was close to fifty, small and trim, a sandy goatee on a boyish face. His ears stuck out from the obligatory gelled and combed-back hair. His suit was double-breasted and snug. He talked through his nose in a sustained whine that blurred words together. He patted Dr. Block on the shoulder, addressing him across the chasm that separates people who speak different languages.

The judge's desk faced three chairs. Pescatore nudged Block into the chair on the left and sat in the middle. He made a slow-motion show of putting the envelope on the chair to his right. The judge saw the envelope but kept talking. Pescatore struggled to translate for Block the verbal salvo about the size of the judge's caseload, his sorrow for the doctor's loss. The judge paused, appraising Pescatore.

"I've seen you before, young man," he said, surprising Pescatore with the informal *vos* appellation. "In the courthouse. You are Argentine, no?"

"No, sir, I—"

"I don't remember the case. Were you an investigator? Or a defendant?" The smile displayed symmetrical, shimmering teeth. "You aren't a crook, are you?"

Pescatore stiffened. "I was a federal police officer in the United States. An agent of the Border Patrol. It's like the Gendarmería here—"

"It was a joke, friend, a joke," the judge said with a chuckle. Then he launched into an explanation of how the calamitous disorder of the legal system was impeding his valiant efforts to keep the accused killer of the doctor's son locked up.

A phone rang on the desk. The judge answered, engaged in animated conversation, laughed, and hung up. He turned to his computer screen and typed, no doubt answering e-mails, while he complained about the do-gooders and human rights activists who had teamed up to install revolving doors for hoodlums in courtrooms across the nation.

Pescatore glanced at Dr. Block, whose face had creased in pain. Pescatore translated for another minute, then stopped.

The judge kept talking. Pescatore brought his palm down on the table, interrupting the monologue. He flashed a head-game grin of his own.

"Lamentably, Your Honor, Dr. Block has to catch a plane this very afternoon," he said. "He's here to express to you how deeply he hopes you can keep the suspect behind bars and move forward with this case. He has full confidence in this court, Your Honor, and in the justice system."

The judge's voice lowered an octave.

"Such a complex case," he intoned. "Many legal subtleties. These mafias, Doctor, they are sinister. But we are doing everything we can. I can only imagine the profound, unbearable agony of losing a son."

The judge shook his head. His eyes welled up. His manicured hand delved into his breast pocket and produced a large purple handkerchief. He dabbed beneath each eye.

"Very sad, very sad," he murmured.

Pescatore got up. Signal received. End of tragicomedy. Dr. Block followed his lead.

"Thank you very much for your time, Your Honor," Pescatore said.

"A lovely chat," the judge declared. "The most important thing, my dear doctor, is to pray. Pray a lot."

Pescatore led Block out before the judge could swoop around the desk for a farewell round of hands-on hypocrisy. They rode back downtown. Pescatore left Block with the car and driver at the hotel, telling him to take the time he needed to pack and check out. Then Pescatore walked to a café called La Biela, the longtime hangout and informal base of operations of his boss, Facundo Hyman Bassat, owner and director of Villa Crespo International Investigations and Security.

Per the dictates of national slang, Facundo was also known as El Ruso (the Russian). He wasn't really Russian. Argentines of Spanish origin were known as *gallegos,* Italians were *tanos,* Arabs *turcos.* And those of Jewish descent were *rusos.*

Facundo divided his time between Buenos Aires and the town of Puerto Iguazú on the Argentine side of the Triple Border with Brazil and Paraguay. His agency did a thriving business with companies and governments. His wife and an adult daughter lived in Buenos Aires; other daughters lived in Miami and Tel Aviv. When in the capital, Facundo held court at Café La Biela. Buenos Aires was full of cafés, ornate as cathedrals, big as ballrooms. La Biela occupied a corner with a view of the Recoleta Cemetery and attracted politicians, executives, journalists, entertainers, intellectuals. The waiters wore bow ties and green vests and moved with speed and pride. The ambience was unpretentious: a well-lit rectangular room with rows of tables, blond-wood paneling, and plants.

Pescatore found Facundo in his usual spot with his back to the wall. The burly Argentine wore a black suit with no tie. He stood with his cell phone at his ear, shaking hands with a sleek-looking, silver-haired man in a blazer and ascot who stopped long enough to say hello and good-bye. When Facundo saw Pescatore, he ended the call, speaking in Hebrew, and put the phone down. Spreading long arms, he advanced wrestler-style, banged Pescatore's shoulder, pumped his hand, and planted a kiss on his cheek that left him with a scratchy sensation and an aroma of cologne and nicotine.

"*¿Cómo te va,* Valentín?"

Facundo's voice rasped from deep in his chest. He sat heavily, wheezing. A waiter slid his usual order onto the table: a double espresso, three sweet mini-croissants known as *medialunas,* and a glass of mineral water.

"My eternal blessing upon you, my son," Facundo told the waiter. Pescatore ordered an espresso. Facundo blissfully contemplated a pastry, which looked flimsy in his hairy mitt of a hand. "Ah, the *medialunas* of La Biela. Did you see that character?"

Brandishing the *medialuna* at the tapered back of the man in the ascot, Facundo continued: "Dario D'Ambrosio. An ex-chief in the SIDE."

The SIDE was the federal intelligence agency of Argentina. Pescatore watched D'Ambrosio stride out as if he were late for a polo match.

"I've heard of him," Pescatore said. "Just retired, right?"

"Supposedly. But he still runs things as far as about thirty percent of the agents are concerned. There you have a spymaster who feels the greatest possible appreciation and gratitude toward this humble servant."

"Why?"

Facundo grinned, his eyes narrowing to slits between stubbled cheeks and furry eyebrows. "Let's say he, eh, ran into trouble with agencies of a very big country that detected his links to an international auto-theft ring and put him on a list of pending indictments. And let's say that someone interceded to convince the agencies in question that, although he is not a saint—and who is?—Dario remains a valuable ally. How did it go today?"

Pescatore sighed. "Fine."

"The judge's secretary called. They are pleased with our 'efficient and professional collaboration.' He will issue an order ensuring detention for trial. So what's the problem?"

Pescatore looked down. After Pescatore had left the Border Patrol and Isabel Puente, Facundo had hired him as a favor to Leo Méndez of Tijuana, a friend from a case they all had worked on at the Triple Border. Méndez had explained to Facundo that the young American wanted to spend time in Argentina and put distance between himself and his troubles. Pescatore knew the Mexican had told Facundo that he was a good kid, tough and reasonably smart. But he also knew the recommendation had come with the warning that the kid had a wild side. Pescatore had overcome Facundo's doubts by proving himself loyal and serious. He didn't want to complain.

"Well, I know it's for a good cause and we didn't have a choice and everything," he said. "But I'm not comfortable being a bagman. I feel much better doing surveillance or executive protection."

"Understandable."

"Also, you were right: The judge is a clown. He told Dr. Block that he needed to pray a lot. That's when I really wanted to slap his face."

"What a *chorro*." Facundo dispatched the last pastry. "Unfortunately, the judge has influence right now with this problematic government. And the American embassy does not. The new FBI attaché has run into so many conflicts he's afraid he might get declared persona non grata."

"Really?"

"Things are not good. Nooo." Facundo shook his head and exhaled audibly. He looked tired. It didn't help that he consumed industrial quantities of steak, coffee, cigarettes and *dulce de leche.* Since Pescatore had met him, he had gone from big to fat. His unruly hair and bushy mustache had grayed. While giving Pescatore pointers on combat skills, Facundo had shown he was in better shape than he looked. But he had five grandchildren. He had to be in his sixties.

"Criminality and terrorism are mixing together," Facundo continued. "Across the region. Along with ideological extremism, anti-Americanism, and hatred of Israel."

Facundo lowered his voice, a rare occurrence. "I was on the phone now with an old friend. A *paisano.*" (For Facundo, that meant an Israeli working for a government agency.) "There is alarming chatter. Unusual movements. Possible preparations for an attack."

"Here?" Pescatore glanced around to ensure no one was listening.

"South America for sure. The Islamic networks see the region as a promising theater of operations. A new frontier."

"Sunni or Shiite networks?"

"I would think the latter. The Iranians and Hezbollah. They are in the hemisphere making money, establishing alliances with mafias and extremists. But it is not clear. The al-Qaedists are looking for unexpected places to strike as well."

Facundo had told him the story of two terrorist attacks in Argentina in the 1990s: the Israeli embassy and the AMIA, a Jewish community center. The car bombings were the work of Iran and Lebanese Hezbollah, whose presence stretched from Buenos Aires to the Triple Border to Venezuela and had grown over the years. No one important had gone to jail. The Jewish community still lived behind bomb barriers, closed circuit cameras and private security, guarding against what people called, with a tone of inevitability, the third attack.

Facundo stood up. Dr. Block had entered La Biela, the door held for him by Fabián the driver. They ordered coffee for Block. Pescatore translated the conversation between the doctor and Facundo and was pleasantly embarrassed when Block praised him.

"I don't ever want to go through an experience like that again," the doctor said. "But if I do, I want this young man with me."

"I'm not surprised to hear that." Facundo beamed. He assured the doctor that he would make his flight on time and sleep well in business class. Then Facundo told a joke: A businessman boards a plane and falls asleep as the meals are being served. His neighbor gobbles his own meal, switches trays, and wolfs down the sleeping businessman's meal too. This makes him nauseated. He throws up all over the businessman, who awakes to find himself covered in vomit and his neighbor dabbing at his face with a napkin and asking, "You feel better now?"

Pescatore translated as best he could. Facundo pantomimed gleefully, delivering the punch line in English with a broad Yiddish accent. For a moment, Block regarded Facundo and Pescatore. His eyes shone behind his glasses. Then he threw his head back and erupted into laughter, rocking in his seat. It was as if he had come out of a stupor. The doctor laughed and laughed, and Pescatore laughed along with him.

Later, Block dozed during the ride to the airport. The good-bye was brief. Watching him clear the security checkpoint, Pescatore thought about the fact that the doctor would always remember him as the young American who had delivered a bribe in Buenos Aires.

That was when someone stepped up close behind him. A hand clapped his shoulder. Two fingers of another hand dug into his back, as if mimicking the barrel of a gun.

He hadn't heard the voice in a long time, but he recognized it instantly. Smooth, jovial, self-aware. A voice that sounded a lot like his own, making the moment even more disorienting. He felt a rush of disbelief, wariness and nostalgia.

"Cuate," Raymond said. "Whaddya hear, whaddya say?"

2

Backstreets

They were drinking rum and Coke, like back in the day.

Pescatore had cut down on liquor. He was out of practice.

Raymond polished off drinks with no visible effect. Like back in the day.

"You look good, bro." Raymond smiled warmly. "I bet you could still hold your own in the ring."

"You too." Pescatore suspected that Raymond had given the compliment to get one. "You been working out?"

"I laid off dope and alcohol. Changed diet. No pork. Cleaned myself up, physically and spiritually."

"Like a born-again thing?"

"Not exactly." Raymond seemed to find this amusing.

"You're drinking now, though."

"This definitely qualifies as a special occasion, Valentín."

Raymond had grown a mustache. His hairline had climbed. He wore his hair short and slicked back, the high forehead and high cheekbones accentuating his hooded eyes. His skin was tight and tanned. He had acquired muscle beneath the black sport jacket and black T-shirt. The outfit and the black Tumi carry-on made him look like a young South American executive. Or a military officer from a wealthy family: aggressive, athletic, urbane. He had said he was on a business trip and happened to spot Pescatore on his way to the check-in counter. He hadn't mentioned his destination or his business.

"Ten years, *cabrón,*" Raymond declared. "Hard to believe."

Ten years since that night at the lakefront—the last time they had talked. Ten years since Raymond had wounded Wolf and gotten arrested. He had disappeared. There were rumors: Jail. A plea bargain. Raymond's father pulling strings.

"I think about that night a lot, man," Raymond said.

"Me too."

The petite waitress deposited drinks. Raymond patted her arm, his nonchalance eliciting a bashful grin. He had always had a thing for waitresses.

"You did right," Raymond told him. "You warned me. You always talked straight to me. I didn't listen. It was my own fault what happened."

"Tell you the truth, I feel kinda bad about it now."

"I was out of control back then. It was inevitable."

"I shouldn'ta just walked away."

"You always looked out for me. I liked that in you."

Although Raymond used the expression nostalgically in that familiar throaty voice, Pescatore saw a change. In the past, Raymond had talked a mile a minute, jiving and gaming, usually half drunk or wasted. Now, he enunciated more clearly, spoke more slowly. It still sounded like patter, though. Like he had settled on this focused, controlled version of his old self.

"What about you, Valentín?" Raymond said. "You're working security?"

"Yep. A bona fide international private investigator." He felt a little thrill when he said it.

"Badass. What about the Border Patrol?"

"Long story. Listen, man, what time is your flight?"

Raymond checked his Rolex. "I'm fine. Worst comes to worst, there's plenty of flights to Miami."

"You live there now?"

"Just connecting. So tell me the story, homes. Your dream came true."

"I don't know about alla that. My dream was to join the Chicago police. Instead, I got in a jam. Almost went to jail myself."

Pescatore recounted his attempt to go undercover on a ring of thieves while working security at the hotel in Chicago. It ended with him getting arrested about two years after Raymond's disappearance. Pescatore's uncle interceded and saved his bacon. Uncle Rocco pressured him to apply to the Border Patrol, calling in favors to make it happen. The Patrol gave him structure. He was good at the work. But the Line was all culture shock and bad company. He got mixed up with a clique of rogue agents.

"That's kind of a recurring thing with you, huh?" Raymond said.

"I got caught chasing a scumbag a few yards across the Line. The OIG—that's like Internal Affairs—they had me *por los cojones*. They recruited me to infiltrate this DTO—drug-trafficking organization. Things got crazy."

"You made headlines, bro. You were a fugitive; they thought you killed a cop. And finally a drug lord got busted, right?"

"Man, I was just hanging on for the ride."

"*Puro* Hollywood."

Pescatore sipped his drink. Telling the story, he had relived the whirl of fear and blood from San Diego to South America and back.

"How come you know about it?" Pescatore asked.

"I Googled you, bro. I wanted to know how you were doing."

"No offense, Raymond, but I'm giving up all kinds of intelligence. Meanwhile, you haven't told me squat."

Raymond leaned back and laughed. "Look at you, all careful and suspicious and whatnot. You're a cop all right."

Pescatore narrowed his eyes. Raymond glanced at his watch. He said, "You're right, homes. There's a lot to talk about. How about this: I'll postpone my flight. We have dinner someplace *piola*, catch up. I'll check back into my hotel and fly out tomorrow."

"You sure?"

"Absolutely. I've done a lot of thinking. I'm thirty. What, a year older than you? The more I travel, the more people I meet in this fucked-up world, the more I realize you're the best friend I ever had. And I treated you like shit. All of a sudden, I run into you down here at the bottom of the world. The land of our ancestors. I get a chance to make it right, reconnect. Everything happens for a reason. It was meant to be."

Raymond spoke in a hoarse voice. His head shook with emotion. The speech sounded sincere but rehearsed. *He can still talk that bullshit,* Pescatore thought. *He acts like he's in a movie. Mr. Drama.*

He said, "Hate to mess up your trip."

"Let me just go deal with the airline. I'll be right back."

On his way out, Raymond murmured to the waitress, whose dark sultry looks made Pescatore think she was from Peru or Bolivia. The waitress smiled uncertainly. *He's still a dog,* Pescatore thought. He considered following Raymond to see if he really did have a ticket and was changing his flight.

Get a grip, he chided himself. *Why would he do some big fake-out setup just to pretend he ran into you at the airport?*

They rode back into the city in Pescatore's hired car. The driver's Boca Juniors scarf got them talking about soccer. Pescatore and Raymond reminisced about their neighborhood team. The Argentine coach knew their parents through immigrant connections. Pescatore was the only kid who went to Catholic school and whose father worked for the county government. Most of their teammates went to Raymond's private school near the university; sons of lawyers, executives, professors. The team traveled the city playing in ethnic fiefdoms.

"There was that Assyrian team, you remember?" Raymond said.

"The Assyrian Eagles. They were cool. Iraqi Christians."

"And that brawl with those fucking Croatians or whatever they were?"

"You decked that humongous Fred Flintstone–looking mug."

"All game he's talking shit. Calling me 'taco' this, 'wetback' that. Finally, I get up in his face. I go, 'Dumbass, I'm not even Mexican.'"

"That's when I came runnin' up," Pescatore exclaimed, the memory flooding back. "You said, 'Now, *he's* Mexican.' Guy goes, 'Fuckin' taco.' Then, *bam!* You did that sweet move where you popped him on the ears."

"He went down like two hundred pounds of Jell-O with an attitude."

They whooped with laughter. Raymond had been a slick and agile fighter. He inflicted pain with cold efficiency and played forward the same way. He did not hesitate to cheat, hiss insults, use elbows and feet to bait opponents into fouls. He showed flashes of brilliance with the ball, though he was lazy, sullen and often wasted. Pescatore was all defense: a competent fullback because of his speed, strength and low center of gravity.

Raymond patted him on the shoulder. "You been to Chez Che?"

"Nope."

"It's great. I used to go all the time when I lived here."

Raymond gave the driver directions. They sped along the elevated highway toward the downtown towers glowing in the sun.

Got that much cleared up, Pescatore thought. *He used to live here.*

At the restaurant, they had finished a bottle of velvety Malbec by the time the food arrived. Raymond ordered a second bottle and gestured at Pescatore's plate of gnocchi.

"That's the payday special right there."

Pescatore strained to hear over the crowd and the speakers cranking U.S. and Latin oldies. Chez Che was in the Palermo Hollywood neighborhood. The walls were adorned with neon signs and murals of buxom ladies in slit dresses dancing tango with *guapos* in fedoras. The clientele was a mix of hip sexy young people and families with dignified grandparents, cavorting kids, and squalling babies.

"Argentines used to eat gnocchi on payday," Raymond explained. "So that's what they call no-show government pay-rollers: gnocchi. They only come to the office to collect their checks."

They were back in the dynamic of Encyclopedia Ray schooling him about one thing or another. Raymond raised a hand. The sound system blared elegiac piano and organ chords. He said: "'Backstreets.' Great song."

Raymond hummed along with Springsteen's soulful growl. His rock band had done Springsteen covers. He had gone through a Springsteen adulation phase, making an effort to emphasize his slight resemblance to the Boss. Pescatore was convinced that Raymond's pensive habit of looking sideways with his fingers over his mouth was an imitation, conscious or not, of the cover photo of *The Wild, the Innocent, and the E Street Shuffle*.

"You still sing, man?" Pescatore asked. "It'd be a shame if you didn't."

Raymond's smile turned melancholy. "You were always pushing me to stick with the music. Ever since we were little."

"I figured it would keep you out of trouble."

"When I first came to BA, I sang for a while. A piano-bar thing. Standards, jazz, tango. Honest money, for a change."

Pescatore gulped wine. Springsteen made him think of Raymond onstage. And Dolores: dancing, smiling, applauding. And now, Isabel. Sweat dampened Pescatore's brow. Springsteen wailed into a guitar solo.

"What's up with you on the personal front?" Raymond asked. "Married?"

"I was engaged for a while."

"Beautiful lady?"

"Like you wouldn't believe."

"A cop too?"

"Yeah."

"Where from?"

"Miami Cuban."

"Oooh, damn." Raymond went into a lascivious riff about *cubanas.* Pescatore looked him in the eye and interrupted.

"So, you still a drug dealer?"

Raymond tilted his head. "No, man, I'm not. Is that important to you?"

"I don't like drug dealers. In fact, I killed a couple of 'em. Mexican cartel guys. Before they could kill me."

Raymond winced. "You still have some rage stored up."

"Look, Ray, you say you're glad to see me." Pescatore strained to keep his voice even. "I'm glad to see you too. The past is past. But I'm waiting for you to fill me in. Instead of talking bullshit."

"There's not that much to tell. You know the Chicago part."

"Just bits and pieces. Is it true you told Wolf not to run or you'd shoot him in the ass? And he ran, so you shot him in the ass?"

"Uh, yeah." Raymond grinned. "I'm not proud of it, mind you."

"Crazy fucker." Pescatore restrained a chuckle. He folded his arms.

Raymond took a deep breath. His eyes were gloomy in the shadows. He explained that, within hours of the shooting, the police tracked him down. They found the Beretta, Wolf's fifty thousand dollars, drugs.

"I was looking at state and federal charges. Enough to put me away till I was a senior citizen. I was in Cook County jail, *cabrón*. I had to move fast."

"They flipped you."

"*Y tanto*. My father, he's an asshole. But he's a helluva lawyer. He said, 'It's strictly a transaction now. Give up everybody and everything.'"

Raymond's father was a criminal defense attorney, slick and youthful despite his gray beard. He specialized in what he called "insurgent" political causes. He defended cop-killers, corrupt politicians. That was why Pescatore's uncle couldn't stand him.

"I went through my BlackBerry and set people up," Raymond continued. "Shit, I gave them Gangster Disciples, North Shore kids, a supplier connected to Sinaloa. A federal task force took over. I convinced them to let me work the streets, use my Spanish. I played *colombiano, mexicano,* whatever. Generating cases. Popping people left and right. The feds loved me. You've worked undercover—you know. The ultimate high."

"When I was undercover, I was pretty terrified the whole time."

Raymond nodded sagely. "I bet you were good at it, but you didn't enjoy it. You don't like lying to people."

And you sure as hell do, Pescatore thought. Out loud, he said, "You skated?"

"I didn't have priors. My father did the deal. One case led to another. They decided to base me in Miami, move me around working Latin America."

Raymond's cell phone rang. He glanced at it and put it away. He was drinking nonstop. They ordered flan with *dulce de leche* for dessert.

"I was a great fucking informant, *un buchón de primera,*

boludo," Raymond said, talking faster now, giving off that old manic energy. "I made money. But I was putting it up my nose. After a couple of years, I was burned out and fucked up. I quit, moved here to stay with relatives. You have people down here?"

"No. My father emigrated alone from Italy when he was eighteen. There was an uncle here, but he died. My dad's brothers were in Chicago. That's why he went there finally."

"I researched my family history. Interesting stuff."

"Like what?"

"Ever see those off-the-boat family photos of Menem, the president in the nineties? The old *turcos*? The women in veils? Our photos look like that. Turns out we were converts."

"Really?"

"We were Muslim in Lebanon. It was the Ottoman Empire, that's why they call Arabs *turcos*. My great-grandparents converted to Catholicism. Like the Menems and a lot of others. So you know what? I converted back."

"You're Muslim now?"

"Yeah." Raymond brightened, his tone earnest. "It helped me center myself. I was intense about it for a while."

"I been studying up about Islam. My boss, he's a real expert. His family came from Turkey."

"Does he go to the King Fahd mosque off Libertador?"

Pescatore opened his mouth to explain that Facundo was Jewish. Then he caught himself.

"No," he said. "That's real interesting, how you converted and everything. Did you do the hajj?"

Raymond was impressed by his knowledge of the term. He said he had done the minor pilgrimage to Mecca, but not the major one known as the hajj. After leaving Buenos Aires a few years before, he had spent time in the Middle East and Europe. He had invested in businesses and property. Things were good.

Raymond's phone rang again. He rolled his eyes apologetically. He had a conversation with a woman, calling her *mamita* and *mi amor.* He told her to calm down and promised to call back. His accent in Spanish was pure *porteño;* he sounded born and bred in Buenos Aires.

Pescatore was thinking about the religious conversion. It had startled him. Still, Facundo had told him that Americans needed to calm down about seeing terrorists everywhere. Pescatore had trouble imagining that Raymond believed in much of anything other than himself and his appetites.

Raymond asked: "What was that Spanish brandy your old man drank?"

"Cardenal Mendoza."

Raymond ordered two snifters of the brandy. He raised his. *"Figli maschi,"* he declaimed. "Male offspring. That was your dad's toast. I remember dinners with you guys when we were kids; he'd make a big deal about breaking out El Cardenal. I always liked your *viejo."*

Raymond rendered Pescatore's father's Italo-Spanish rumble to perfection. Pescatore savored the strong mellow fumes. When, as a teenager, Pescatore complained that his father was strict, Raymond scowled and said that at least he was a stand-up family man. Raymond hated the fact that his own father chased his secretaries and paralegals—and that his mother put up with it.

"I always make that toast." Raymond beamed. "It worked: I have two sons."

"Congratulations."

"Yeah, man, they're cool little guys. Their mom's North African. A princess, a lioness." A text message beeped on his phone. He sighed. "But this Argentine *mina* is a mess. Won't stop calling and texting. She's *rompiéndome las pelotas.* I should go see her tonight, now that I stayed."

"Raymond, where do you live now?"

"Oh, I'm bopping around."

Pescatore's head spun. He thought: *Bopping around? What the fuck is that? This guy wouldn't give a straight answer at gunpoint.*

"So, Valentín." Raymond leaned forward. He seemed sloppy with drink, elbows on the table. "This company you work for. What is that, like security contracting for the U.S. government?"

"Public sector, private sector, different clients."

"I'm just asking, you know. A lot of guys who were in law enforcement go into these companies where they're still working for the feds. Especially overseas. You and this guy Facundo, you're pretty wired up with embassies and whatnot, right?"

"More him than me." Pescatore tried to remember if he had mentioned Facundo by name. "But it's sensitive, Ray. I can't talk about work."

"I know, I know. Just curious." He held both hands aloft in surrender. Spotting the waitress, he transformed the gesture into a signal for the check. He brooded with his hand over his mouth, eyes down: the Springsteen pose. He looked sad and scared.

"Listen, *cuate*." Raymond's tone got husky again. "I need to tell you one thing. About that night."

"Okay."

"Wolf, that *maricón,* the doctors hadn't even dug the bullet out of his butt before he ratted me out. He told the cops you were my partner in the dope business."

"I wasn't your partner in the dope business."

"I know. But your number was in my phone. They had witnesses talking about you sidekicking with me. They wanted me to give you up. My father, he got excited. He said we could build a credible scenario. A guy like me was the follower, a *perejil*. You had the profile of the leader. A tougher background. He said some of your Mexican relatives had criminal records. The more I built up your role, the better off I'd be."

The story had the ring of truth, Pescatore thought. "And?"

"I told him to fuck off." Raymond choked up, paused. "I told them I'd testify against anybody else, set up anybody else. I became a cooperator on the condition that they let you alone. I fucked over a lot of people. But when it came to you, I was a stand-up guy. Because you were a stand-up guy."

Pescatore relived a long-buried dread. He had always wondered why the police hadn't questioned him. He had tried to convince himself that it was because he wasn't that involved. Or because his uncle was a cop.

"What can I say, Raymond? I—"

"Nothing. I just wanted you to know."

Raymond's phone rang again on the table. He ignored it. He put a business card on the wood. The card had his name, an Argentine phone number, and an e-mail address. Pescatore could see the screen of the phone buzzing near the card. The name on the display looked like *Flo*.

"That's how you can reach me, bro. Anytime, anywhere. Got a card?"

"I don't," Pescatore lied, avoiding his gaze. "Sorry."

"Here." Raymond put a notepad and a pen on the table.

Pescatore didn't want to give Raymond contact information related to the investigation agency. He wrote down a personal e-mail address and the number of a local cell phone that he didn't use for work.

"What the hell is this?" Raymond tapped the notepad accusingly.

"What?"

"This Valen*tine* shit." He raised his eyebrows in consternation.

Pescatore chuckled nervously. He explained that when he joined the Border Patrol, a clerical error had added the *e* to his first name. The federal bureaucracy had stuck to the wrong version, so he'd accepted it.

"That's on my passport now too: Valentine. My birth certificate, my school transcripts, they still say Valentín. It's a problem."

"*Qué quilombo.*" Raymond laughed harshly. He drained his brandy. "That's what happens. Governments fuck you around. People fuck you around. By the time they're done, you don't know who you are. Especially if you weren't sure to begin with."

3

Todos Tenemos un Amor

During the next week, uneasiness gnawed at Pescatore about the strange encounter with Raymond.

Although he wasn't enthusiastic about discussing his past, he wanted to tell Facundo about the incident. But he didn't get a chance. He spent most of the week in the city of Rosario setting up security for an Italian client, an executive who had evaded a kidnapping attempt.

Pescatore returned to Buenos Aires Thursday. On Friday morning, he worked on his laptop at his dining room table, bathed in sunlight. He sent a bank transfer to the widow of a California Highway Patrol officer in San Diego. The officer had died in a shootout while Pescatore was in the Border Patrol. Pescatore had been riding undercover at the time with a corrupt Patrol supervisor who opened fire when the CHP officer stopped them en route to Tijuana. Eventually, Pescatore had paid his respects to the widow. She was gracious, but he felt guilty. Despite her protests, he insisted on sending her money for her three children: a hundred dollars a month.

Pescatore spent an hour finishing the latest book Facundo had given him: *Understanding Terror Networks* by Marc Sageman. When Facundo learned of Pescatore's effort to read seriously for the first time in his life, he had taken it upon himself to guide his improvised program of intellectual self-improvement. It had become a ritual: one Friday a month, Facundo helped him pick out a book.

At eleven thirty, Pescatore walked to the bookstore. He ran into Facundo getting out of Fabián's Renault on Santa Fe Avenue. Facundo had his cell phone to his ear, a burning cigarette in his left hand, and a frown on his face. He was natty in a topcoat, pin-striped suit, and pointy black shoes. His neck bulged over the knot of a red tie. He looked like a cross between a bandleader and a bouncer. Neckties caused Facundo to squirm and grimace as if he were in a hangman's noose. He wore ties only for important meetings and on Fridays for temple.

"They dismantled a cell in La Paz yesterday," he said after hanging up. "Three individuals with guns and explosives."

"An Islamic plot in Bolivia?"

"It has become a permissive environment."

"Maybe this plot is what the chatter was about."

"Maybe." Facundo dropped and stomped the cigarette. "The Bolivians aren't talking. But I'm told it was a precise tip."

The bookstore had been a movie theater. The palatial interior retained the cupola, neoclassical murals, statuary, and curving balconies.

"Any target?" Pescatore asked.

"No details yet. What did you think of the Sageman?"

"It was great. Nice concrete examples. His theory makes sense to me: Becoming a terrorist is kind of like joining a gang. It's about hooking up with a bunch of guys who make you feel like a badass."

"Exactly. Religion is important, but not necessarily the driving force. People have trouble understanding that." Facundo shambled among the shelves, hands clasped behind him. "We'll get something in Spanish this time. Let's see…There's a good one by Irujo about the Madrid attacks. Here."

Pescatore heard sirens go by in the street.

Facundo stooped to pull the book from a low shelf, grunting.

"Are you coming to Shabbat?" he asked. "The wife is in Miami, so Esther has taken over the kitchen. Either way, I do what I am told."

"Sure. Thanks."

Friday dinner at Facundo's was part of the monthly book ritual. They were often joined by his divorced daughter, Esther, and her five-year-old, David. Pescatore had hit it off with the boy, and usually ended up reading aloud to him or sitting through demonstrations of his toys.

"I should get David something," Pescatore said. "Would he like *The Cricket in Times Square*?"

"If it's from you, he'll like it." Facundo raised a finger. "I am impressed at how that little ruffian sits still and behaves with you. I think Miss Puente, with all respect, calculated badly: you'd make a good father."

Facundo had said this before; Pescatore was not sure how to respond. He was distracted by more sirens outside. Through a window, he saw police cars speeding west on Santa Fe Avenue. Then an ambulance. Then fire trucks. More police cars, lights flashing, raced by.

Facundo's phone rang. After listening a moment, he exclaimed, "My God. Where?"

He broke into a run, still on the phone, narrowly avoiding a collision with a table of art books. Pescatore followed him out and into Fabián's car.

"El Almacén," Facundo barked. "As fast as you can. And turn up the radio!"

It appeared that all the police and emergency vehicles in the city were swarming in the same direction. Chomping down on his toothpick, Fabián slid into the slipstream of an ambulance and floored it. The radio reported explosions and gunfire at El Almacén, a shopping mall near the garment district. A newscaster described gunmen shooting shoppers, possible suicide bombers, multiple casualties, stampedes. An agitated reporter arriving at the scene shouted over a scratchy phone line about gunmen in police uniforms. She was interrupted by an explosion, followed by screams.

"It's a mixed salad," Facundo bellowed over the noise of the radio, sirens and horns. "A mixed salad!"

"What?" Pescatore asked.

"Gunmen and bombers at the same time." Facundo thumb-punched buttons on his phone. "Complex attack modality… Hello, Dario? Where are you? What is this damned madness? I'll call you from there."

The streets narrowed. Traffic snarled. Emergency vehicles bulled forward. Facundo had a brief phone conversation in Hebrew. Pescatore knew El Almacén was in a traditionally Jewish neighborhood, and the developers of the mall were a wealthy Jewish family. The Israeli embassy advised the community on security matters.

The traffic got so bad that they jumped out. With remarkable agility for his size, Facundo hurtled through a crowd that had two currents: people fleeing the attack, and people rushing toward it. Pescatore kept his hand on his holstered gun in his jacket as he ran. They rounded a corner into bedlam. The street was full of police and fire vehicles. Officers with metal barriers and yellow tape were establishing a haphazard perimeter. Civilians watched, took cover, aided casualties, wandered in a daze.

The mall was an early-twentieth-century behemoth of a building, a former textile warehouse with glass and steel walls set in a design of brick archways. Police holding guns — uniformed, plainclothes, tactical officers in helmets and body armor — crouched behind vehicles and on either side of the main entrance. No shots were audible over the sirens and screams. A contingent of officers from the GEOF — the SWAT team of the federal police — rushed through the entrance into the mall, weapons at the ready. People streamed out in the other direction. A young woman hobbled on one high-heeled shoe. She had sunglasses propped in her hair and clutched shopping bags. Her toreador jacket was streaked with blood.

Pescatore went into crime-scene mode, counting the visible casualties: two dozen corpses on the steps and in the lobby, twice as many wounded. Paramedics, firemen and police tended to the fallen outside but kept back from the entrance. As far as he could tell, the attackers had used guns and grenades. The suicide bombings must have happened inside.

"What a butchery, sons of whores," Facundo snarled, his breath coming in heaves.

It was the worst bloodshed Pescatore had ever seen. As had happened at dangerous moments at the border, a strange calm came over him. A disheveled, hatless police officer intercepted them, saying it was a restricted area and they were going to get killed. Facundo waved some kind of badge.

"Special Investigations!" he exclaimed. "Where's the command post, son?"

The officer stepped back, startled and apologetic, and pointed at police vehicles parked in a sloppy triangle. Pescatore wondered if Facundo had an official credential or had just overwhelmed the cop with bluster. The command post was a scrum. There were chiefs in police uniform and in a kind of plainclothes uniform: scarves, sunglasses, bushy mustaches, slicked-back hair, big-shouldered overcoats spreading around pugilistic necks. The chiefs shouted into radios and telephones and at one another; they huddled around a floor plan spread on the hood of a car. Facundo accosted a plainclothesman who wore a protective vest and a holster strapped to his jean-clad leg. He was tall and hard-faced with shaggy hair like a soccer player's. More a street warrior than a deskbound boss.

"*Che,* Biondani," Facundo hissed. "I'm Facundo the Russian. Dario's pal, remember? How bad is it?"

The mention of Dario D'Ambrosio, the former intelligence

chief who hung out at La Biela, meant that Biondani was not a cop but a spy. He greeted Facundo with instant and respectful warmth.

"Very bad," Biondani said quietly, turning his back on the other chiefs. "A hundred dead, easy. They stormed the front and back with assault rifles and grenades. Apparently suicide bombers too. A massacre."

"Arabs?"

"Some descriptions indicate that. Others do not. They are in police uniforms, which is creating insanity. Officers shooting at each other. Reports of many suspects. I think in reality there are only a few. They have retreated to the upper floors with hostages. They are still shooting and tossing grenades now and then."

"Do they have phones? Someone should check if they are being directed by phone."

"The GEOF is establishing a secondary command post inside. The negotiators are on their way and—"

"The main reason to negotiate is to get a fix on their phones or a line of fire," Facundo interrupted. "The hostages are purely a tool for media coverage. They will kill them all. Also, you should have the bomb squad sweep parked cars in the vicinity. Right away, they could hit out here with a secondary strike."

Facundo's booming voice had drawn attention. Pescatore heard someone in the huddle nearby ask, "Who's that big lug with Biondani?"

"From their embassy," a voice answered knowingly.

It was not the first time Pescatore had seen cops mistakenly presume that Facundo worked for the Israeli embassy. Facundo did not discourage the impression. He had done missions for Israeli and U.S. intelligence in the past, but the relationships now were mostly about access and trading information. The tone of *their embassy* bothered Pescatore. It recalled scenes he had read about after the bombing of the AMIA community center in 1994: emergency personnel looting corpses, commentators differentiating between Jewish victims and "innocent Argentines," anonymous callers taunting survivors.

"Can you get us to the command post inside?" Facundo was on the move, leaving the enclosure formed by the vehicles.

The intelligence officer grabbed his arm. "Facundo, please, it's a madhouse. Dario will never forgive me if something happens to you."

"I don't have to explain to you that I can be useful," Facundo replied. "And I speak Arabic. Do you have many Arabic-speaking negotiators on hand?"

They had reached the fire truck closest to the mall. Two paramedics performed CPR on a victim lying on the asphalt. Facundo flattened himself against the cab of the fire truck and advanced his prowlike profile, peering around the front bumper. He extracted his gun, a Bersa nine-millimeter, from the depths of his coat. Pescatore drew his Beretta. He assumed Facundo was sincere about just wanting to get close enough to help. But if Facundo had decided to shoot it out with terrorists, Pescatore intended to do exactly that. He was with Facundo all the way, to the curb, badge or no badge. At the same time, he was worried. And not just about getting shot or blown up. Facundo was flushed, breathing laboriously. He didn't look like he could withstand much more exertion.

Biondani implored Facundo to come to his senses. He told him he wasn't authorized. Facundo's face filled with rage and sorrow.

"Authorized? Son, for twenty years I have dedicated time and effort to prevent this from happening again. Obviously, I failed. So I am not just going to watch and do nothing. Ready, Valentín?"

"*A todo dar,* boss."

"That's what I want to hear."

Facundo charged in a crouch up the low wide steps and

over a bloody carpet of broken glass. His coat streamed like a cape. Pescatore followed. He found himself hurdling a corpse, a crumpled figure flashing beneath him. Biondani brought up the rear, cursing. They ducked through gaping twisted door frames with the glass blown out of them. The officers flanking the entrance yelled halfhearted orders to stop.

The mall was a four-story atrium. Sunlight streamed into the vault of metal, marble and glass. Biondani took the lead. They careened down a long first-floor hall, staying close to the shops to elude shooters above. They passed more bodies. Scattered bursts of gunfire echoed on the upper levels. The shots were not directed at them. As Biondani had said, the attackers had barricaded themselves in elevated firing positions. In a discussion of tactics, Facundo had once called it "the stronghold option."

About halfway down the hall, Biondani veered into a music store. The three of them huddled in the doorway. Biondani was trying to get his bearings to find the spot where the police were setting up their interior command post. He whispered into his radio. There was movement inside the shop. Pescatore realized people were hiding in the back. He made eye contact with one of them: a salesclerk with guitar-hero hair who crouched behind a display case. Pescatore gave him a reassuring thumbs-up. The salesclerk waved and mouthed words. He wanted to crawl toward them. Clearly, he was hoping that the newcomers with guns had come to evacuate him and the others. Pescatore made a stay-put gesture. Looking out into the hallway, Pescatore realized that a bomb or grenade had gone off here earlier. The area was covered with glass, blood, debris, shoes.

And then he saw an arm.

It was a male arm. It lay on the gleaming linoleum. Bare, olive-skinned, rather well muscled. Stained, perhaps by soot or dirt. The arm looked like it could be from a man in his twenties or thirties. It was bent at the elbow, cleanly severed below the shoulder. There were no other discernible remains nearby, no indication if the limb had been blown off a victim or an attacker. Just an arm.

The sight set off a delayed comprehension of the horror into which he had hurled himself, a kind of hyperawareness. Beyond the arm, sunlight illuminated a rectangular banner advertising a skin product. The ad showed an attractive couple jogging on a beach, tanned and sculpted and sensual. He heard the moans of the wounded, the sobs of the frightened. He noticed that music was still playing in the store. The song was La Mosca's "Todos Tenemos un Amor" ("We All Have a Love"), a good-time party tune heavy on drums and brass.

Facundo and Biondani were conferring in whispers.

"Where to?" Facundo asked. His back was pressed against the wall as he tried to catch his breath. Sweat streamed out of his hair.

Biondani crouched over his police radio. A minute passed. He kept listening. His mouth tightened with disgust.

"What?" Facundo rasped.

"Now a car bomb," Biondani muttered. "At a school."

"Where?"

"Out past Belgrano...a Jewish school."

Facundo bolted upright. "Which one? Which one?"

"I don't know. I just hear transmissions about a car bomb and the explosives squad."

Facundo frantically patted his coat pockets, fumbling for his cell phone. Pescatore remembered that Facundo's grandson went to a school in that general area. Facundo made a choking sound. Pescatore saw with alarm that he had turned deathly pale. The big man's face contorted. His gun slid from his hand. He grabbed his left shoulder. He sagged down the wall, tilting sideways, eyes rolling up, unconscious.

They wrestled off Facundo's overcoat and tie and checked his pulse.

"My God," Biondani said. "It looks like a heart attack."

"We have to get him out of here."

For the first time since arriving on the scene, Pescatore experienced pure fear. He and Biondani organized themselves and retraced their steps to the entrance. Pescatore drag-carried Facundo over his shoulders, thankful that he was in shape and built low to the ground. Biondani backed alongside them with his gun at the ready, watching for threats, helping to the extent he could. Their progress was slow, but they made it.

In the chaos of the street, they realized that Facundo would not be the top priority among multiple casualties mutilated by explosions and shredded by automatic-weapons fire. Biondani managed to commandeer a police sedan, and Pescatore rode with Facundo to a hospital.

Late that night, Pescatore sat in a crowded hospital waiting room with Facundo's grandson.

Facundo had suffered a major heart attack. He was in an intensive care ward jammed with victims of the carnage at the shopping mall. His daughter Esther was at his bedside.

Pescatore was reading to David. He wanted to keep the boy calm and distract him from the nonstop television coverage of the attacks. At the same time, Pescatore was trying to listen to the news. He had chosen seats in the corner farthest from the television, which blared on an overhead mount connected to a pillar. Rummaging in a basket of magazines, he had found a tattered book of comics about a girl named Mafalda, a nationally beloved character.

Although sleepy, David was engrossed in the book. He climbed back and forth between his blue plastic chair and Pescatore's lap. The boy was round-cheeked and sturdily built, and he wore a River Plate soccer jersey. He had his grandfather's unruly hair and alert eyes.

"Mafalda's having a dream," Pescatore explained. "These two little guys with the funny hats, they're aliens on another planet, see? In her dream, they're talking in their language about Earth. That's our planet where we live."

"The *bestiaplaneta*?" David asked, pointing at the word on the page.

"Yes. The aliens call Earth the Beast Planet."

"Why?"

"We're like animals to them."

"Dogs?"

"Well, not exactly animals. Like cavemen. So this alien says: 'They're having a big fight down there on the Beast Planet. Poor Beast Planet.' The aliens feel sorry for us dummies on Earth. Because we're always having some big stupid fight. See?"

A wall clock showed that it was midnight. People in the waiting room congregated below the television. Turning pages, Pescatore listened to the top-of-the-hour headlines. The death toll was in the hundreds. The worst casualties had been caused by two suicide bombers attacking a kosher delicatessen at El Almacén. The authorities had identified half a dozen attackers, all dead. The attempted car bombing at the school had failed. Unsurprisingly, there was confusion and suspicion about basic details.

As he strained to hear the TV, Pescatore realized that David was asking him a question.

"What's up, little guy?" Pescatore asked.

"Did the terrorists kill my grandfather?"

The boy regarded him like a miniature prosecutor. *This kid is too sharp,* Pescatore thought.

"No, David. Don't worry. Your grandfather got sick, that's all. Your mom's with him. Your grandfather's too tough for the terrorists. He's like a big bear. Pretty soon he'll wake up, and he'll be hungry. Like this."

Pescatore mimicked a bear awaking with a sleepy roar. The boy's laugh was bubbly and melodic. Pescatore leaned his head back against the wall and extended his right leg gingerly. The hamstring throbbed with pain. He must have hurt it carrying Facundo. He saw Esther, small-boned and sweet-faced, coming down the hall.

She told him her father was stable. "He'll need cardiac surgery. But he won't be ready for a while. As you can imagine, all the surgeons in the city are occupied anyway. What a barbarity."

"Sounds like he's going to make it."

"He is alive thanks to you. Thanks to you, Valentín. It's late. You should go home and rest."

"I'm fine."

"Please, it makes no sense for you to spend the night here."

Pescatore glanced at the boy. He was reading industriously.

"Esther. Facundo, all of you, have treated me like family since I got here. I don't have anybody else in this city. This is the place I need to be."

In the end, she convinced him to go home. They agreed that he would sleep and return to give her a break the next day. She hugged him, sobbing silently.

"He'll be fine," he said. "This thing had such an impact on Facundo, I think it literally broke his heart. But he's real strong. He'll be fine."

On the way home, Fabián drove him past checkpoints and police convoys. The pedestrians and people in café windows looked stunned: inhabitants of a wounded city.

At his apartment, Pescatore changed into jeans and a green U.S. Border Patrol sweatshirt. He ate a leftover slice of pizza and turned on the television news. There was commentary about the long-dreaded third attack on the Jewish community and the fact that the terrorists had also targeted non-Jews by striking El Almacén. A long-winded politician interviewed in a governmental corridor blamed the United States and Israel for setting the stage for the attacks with draconian policies and imperialistic wars. Pescatore raised his middle finger and held it aloft until the politician was done.

The news reports said that "initial lines of investigation" pointed at al-Qaeda terrorists. Pescatore thought that was strange. Iran and Hezbollah had done the attacks in the 1990s. As far as he knew, their Shiite networks had a far bigger presence in Latin America than the remnants and offshoots of al-Qaeda. And no one had mentioned the arrests in Bolivia that Facundo had told him about. There had to be a link to the attacks in Buenos Aires.

At about four a.m., Pescatore was still wide awake. He remembered that a bottle of Jack Daniel's had been sitting in a cupboard for months. He put ice in a glass and got to work making himself sleepy.

Two drinks later, the television broadcast a report about the failed attack at the school. The rolling bomb was a Renault Trafic van. It had sped past unarmed security guards and up a driveway toward the campus. A federal police officer assigned to guard the school had just finished a coffee break in the cafeteria. He emerged from the building at the top of the hill and saw the onrushing van and the pursuing guards. Instead of running for cover, the police officer walked out into the middle of the driveway. Witnesses described how he planted himself in a firing stance, took aim, and emptied his gun into the approaching van's windshield. The vehicle ran him over before coming to a stop. But the bomb did not go off. The driver died from bullet wounds. The only other casualty was the police officer.

The anchorwoman's voice broke while she read the story. Pescatore got up abruptly, lurching a little. He took his drink out onto the patio, favoring his sore right leg. He leaned on the railing. The wind was cold.

A police helicopter appeared above, rotors clattering, and descended toward the rooftops. He wondered if they were hunt-

ing terrorists in his neighborhood. The helicopter hovered, as-
cended again, and glided north along the riverfront.

The landscape below was shrouded in darkness. He knew it
well: Libertador Avenue, the park, the train tracks, the shanty-
town, the highway, the dock cranes and container yards of the
port, the town of Colonia del Sacramento barely visible on the
Uruguayan coast across the river.

"Oh you motherfuckers," he said into the night above the
city. "You evil motherfuckers."

4

Evil Ways

Thieves from a nearby public housing project once broke into Pescatore's house at night when he was a child. His family slept through the burglary.

A few months later, intruders from the same project armed with baseball bats beat to death a family in their beds near his home. Coincidentally, Pescatore's uncle Rocco led the investigation. During questioning, his detectives threw a suspect out of a second-floor window of the police station. The two cases fused in Pescatore's mind. He became obsessed with the idea that he had heard the burglars but failed to wake up and protect his family from annihilation. His sleep had been troubled ever since. He often shuddered awake, heart pounding, trying to figure out if what he had heard was imaginary or real.

On Saturday, he finally fell asleep before dawn. He collapsed onto his bed, still dressed. When he awoke, gray daylight gleamed in the low skylight and the glass door to the patio. He had slept three or four hours. He stayed on his stomach. He felt obliterated.

He had woken up because he thought he heard something. But he wasn't too worried. The roof was a symphony of flapping, chirping, creaking and dripping caused by birds, bats and the elements. He listened lazily, eager to return to oblivion. He needed more sleep.

Then he heard a distinct noise. A footstep? And another. Maybe metal on metal.

His shoulder holster was on a chair by the patio door. Out of reach. He would have to roll out of bed and lunge for the gun.

Get a grip, he told himself. *Maybe it's nothing.*

Still motionless, he closed his eyes and concentrated. His heart thudded against the mattress. The furtive sounds multiplied. Breathing, rustling, footfalls. No doubt about it. Someone—more than one person—was creeping down the hall toward his bedroom. They must have picked the lock or forced the doorman to give up a key.

Eyes open now, facedown, he visualized his move: roll, lunge, draw.

Interrupting his calculations, a shadow flickered across his peripheral vision on the left. There was someone on the patio too.

Goddamn it, he thought, *they're coming at me from different angles. Like professionals. Like cops…*

The hesitation saved his life. His room erupted in sound and fury.

"Police police police don't move son-of-a-bitch don't move or you're dead your mother's cunt!"

There were half a dozen raiders hulking in body armor and ski masks. Some stormed in the bedroom door, others aimed weapons from the patio, their red laser sights spattering the glass. They screamed orders, curses and threats in a murderous chorus.

"Easy," he declared, his cheek still on the pillow. "I'm an American investigator. Be aware that there's a pistol—"

Gloved hands wrenched him up off the bed. They cuffed his wrists behind his back and slammed him to the floor. They yanked his sweatshirt up over his face like a backward hood, rendering him sightless and helpless. A signature technique. Argentine police routinely covered the faces of suspects with their own shirts or jackets, leaving prisoners to sit at crime scenes trussed in improvised masks. The idea was to preserve the integrity of lineups by concealing suspects' identities. He had always seen it as a badass message: *We caught this sorry bastard. We can do anything we want to him now. Fuck with us and this can happen to you someday.*

Voices and boots invaded his apartment. Radios squawked. Doors banged, drawers crashed, silverware jangled. What the hell was going on?

"Bingo, Commander," a triumphant voice called in the living room. "The phone."

"Well done, *pibe.*"

He could have sworn his phone was on his night table by the bed. He could see variations of light and shadow through the sweatshirt. Someone was standing guard over him. Against his better judgment, Pescatore decided to speak up.

"Excuse me," he said through the fabric over his mouth. "I think there's been some kind of confusion. I am an American citizen. My passport is in the top drawer of the dresser. I am a private investigator and—"

A boot lashed into his left thigh. He writhed in pain. Through clenched teeth he snarled: "Cheap shot monkey-ass punk bitch!"

"Shut your mouth, shitty terrorist."

The owner of the voice sounded large. His breath smelled of coffee, laced perhaps with a finger of pre-raid brandy.

Pescatore was overwhelmed by the kick, the traumatic awakening, and, most of all, disbelief: the officer had called him a terrorist. These guys were door-breakers, head-bashers, trigger-pullers, and, if the target survived, deliverymen. No use engaging in dialogue. After a few minutes, his captors shoved shoes onto his feet. They hustled him downstairs, the air chilling his exposed torso, and into a vehicle. Sirens wailed: a small convoy. They turned left on Libertador Avenue.

The ride was quick and familiar. As the vehicle bounced up a driveway, the smell of stables confirmed his expectations. He had been taken to the federal police site near his running track, the compound that housed the mounted patrol and the antiterrorism unit.

They removed the handcuffs, pulled the sweatshirt down off his face, and left him in a cell. It was dimly lit and had a cement bench built into the wall. The smell of disinfectant was stronger than the smell of urine. He assumed they would let him sit and stew for a while, for both the psychological impact and to give themselves time to examine the material from the search.

Not that he was in a hurry. He wished he did not know as much as he did about the repertoire of tortures utilized by Latin American security forces in general and Argentine ones in particular. Right now, the fear was worse than the pain, but it looked like that equation was about to change. He took deep breaths and tried to focus.

He had become a suspect in the attack at El Almacén. Perhaps a mix-up caused by the fact that he and Facundo had barged into the crime scene with guns in their hands. But they had been with an intelligence officer. It couldn't be that hard to clear things up. Unless there was something more sinister going on.

The terrorists had worn police uniforms. That raised scenarios ranging from an unwitting inside source to direct involvement. Police and soldiers with ultra-right, anti-Jewish ideologies had been implicated in past attacks. And the police were good at framing people by planting guns, concocting decoy conspiracies, coaching false witnesses with case files. An American would be a perfect *perejil*. A fall guy.

At first, he resisted the temptation to sleep. When Pescatore was a kid, Uncle Rocco had told him something that he later confirmed as a Border Patrol agent: the guilty slept like babies in custody. After about an hour, though, he decided to rest a bit. He glanced around for any sign of rats, then slid to a corner of the bench and reclined. His body ached, especially his left thigh and right hamstring.

Stay awake or you'll look guilty, he told himself as he nodded off.

They rousted him right away, as if they had been waiting for him to sleep. In the interrogation room, they cuffed his right wrist to the table.

The interrogator was about what Pescatore had expected. And not in a good way. Barrel chest and hard gut in a navy-blue uniform turtleneck. Balding, moonfaced, long sideburns ending at powerful jaws. An officer in a tactical jumpsuit stood by the door. A youthful plainclothesman with a military-style, side-combed haircut sat behind a laptop. His underfed features and mustache reminded Pescatore of a film character named Ferribotte, a dignified Sicilian thief, from an Italian heist comedy of the 1950s that his father had liked.

Pescatore resisted the impulse to launch into a tirade about how innocent he was. The interrogator studied documents and glanced at his colleague's computer screen. He raised his formidable chin to examine Pescatore from beneath low lids. In a baritone voice that he seemed to enjoy bouncing off the walls, the interrogator started with an overture.

"There's an old policeman's saying: As time passes, the truth flees. I understand you say you were once a police officer. And you claim to be an investigator now. I assume that helps you appreciate my situation. I have two hundred cadavers, hundreds of wounded, a country in shock, enormous repercussions. And you. What I don't have is time. I want you to answer my questions quickly and directly. Do we understand each other?"

"Absolutely. I'm here to help. I don't know why I'm under

arrest, and I haven't done anything wrong, but I want to catch whoever—"

"You see? Already we begin badly." The interrogator rolled his eyes, glancing around like an exasperated headmaster opting for corporal punishment. "I said 'quickly and directly.' Let's start again. My name is Inspector Francisco Mendizábal Wright. Please state your name."

Pescatore gave dutiful answers to basic questions. He fought down panic and anger rising from his stomach. The young sidekick tapped at his keyboard.

"Very well." Mendizábal went back into the jaw-up, slit-eyed pose. "You say you want to help. I give you that opportunity. Explain your role in the terrorist network functioning here, in Bolivia and in France, and everything you know about the preparation and execution of the attacks."

"Inspector, I had nothing to do with it. I have never been to France or Bolivia. I was at the attack scene at El Almacén because I was assisting my employer, Facundo Hyman of Villa Crespo Investigations, and a SIDE officer named Biondani."

The interrogator stared at him. Pescatore considered a problem: *Biondani* might be a code name or an alias, a common practice in spy services. Plus, the relationship between police and intelligence agencies was none too friendly. Even if they tracked down Biondani, he had met Pescatore only once and in chaotic circumstances.

"Look," Pescatore said. "This officer, he was introduced to me as Biondani. He knows my boss, Facundo Hyman. Everybody knows Facundo. The U.S. embassy, the Israeli embassy, your force. How could I be—"

"Shut up!" The baritone echoed in the small room. "You are the worst kind of scum. The coward who makes the plans, who sets it up, but doesn't have the balls to pull a trigger himself."

"You are totally mistaken."

"You come all the way from your shitty country to slaughter

61

people here. Sneaky arrogant American. You think you can get away with anything because of this shitty passport."

Mendizábal picked up and slammed down his passport.

"Inspector, listen: The idea you would accuse me of having anything to do with this makes me physically sick."

Pescatore had a flashback to El Almacén: the bloody broken glass, the fleeing shoppers, the arm. He closed his eyes. He was shaking.

"Spare me your girlish tears. Explain why you were in telephonic contact with the terrorists."

The Ferribotte-looking investigator glanced up from his laptop. Pescatore wondered if Mendizábal was bluffing about the phone calls.

"I haven't phoned any terrorists. Almost all my calls are work-related. Unless someone I have dealt with for work is secretly a terrorist."

Mendizábal sighed operatically.

"To be precise." He put a small silver cell phone on the table and flipped open the display screen. "Your phone shows—"

"That's not my phone! That's not even my—"

Mendizábal shot out of his chair. He grabbed Pescatore by the collar of his sweatshirt and pulled him in to a big descending fist. The punch slammed into his brow, rocking him back, straining his handcuffed arm. The interrogator leaned over the table, his movements measured and precise, to administer a pair of vicious follow-up blows.

Pescatore rode the pain, a roaring noise in his ears, blood in his mouth. The enraged face floated in front of him, distorted and oblong, a moon in a space cloud. His vision blurred. He was going to pass out.

He had fucked up. It *was* his phone.

In his haste, he hadn't recognized it. He had bought the phone on his second or third day in Buenos Aires. He remembered downloading the ringtone: the refrain from "Evil Ways" by Santana. A private joke. While living with Isabel, he had often sung "Evil Ways" when he returned from work, the verse about coming home to a dark house and cold pots.

A week after Pescatore's arrival, Facundo had given him the latest model of the iPhone. Pescatore had stored the cheap local phone in a drawer and rarely used it again.

"I was mistaken," he muttered. "I can confirm that is my phone."

"Where were we?" Mendizábal said. A bead of sweat slid along his temple and down a jowl. "You received three calls from terrorists in France on Tuesday."

"I wasn't here Tuesday," Pescatore said through lacerated and swollen lips. "I was in Rosario on business. That phone never moved. I never knew about any calls; I wasn't here to answer. You can verify that. The phone hasn't been used for months. Hardly anyone has the number…"

He trailed off. He looked down. One person had the number: Raymond. Pescatore had given it to him to avoid giving him a number connected to Facundo's company.

Raymond had the number. The old friend who had materialized out of nowhere. The smooth-singing, fast-talking mystery man. The Muslim convert.

"Yes, no one called that phone for months," Mendizábal snarled. "Radio silence. We have seen it before. The phone is a dedicated secure line. A call is placed to trigger the operation. No conversation, just a call. Three days later, there is an attack. You present yourself at the scene, pretending to help the authorities. We have seen that before too. The pyromaniac fireman. The Carapintadas with an ambulance."

Pescatore was suffocating. He remembered the case of the Carapintadas, or "Painted Faces": they were fascist army commandos who had been caught at the scene of the attack on the Jewish center in 1994 posing as volunteer paramedics with a fake ambulance. Their presence was a mysterious detail in the unsolved case. If someone overseas linked to the attack at El Almacén had called Pescatore's phone, things added up to make him look bad.

"Who called you from France?"

"I have no idea."

He wasn't going to say anything about Raymond unless they asked about him specifically. Scared and suspicious as he was, he didn't know if Raymond had called him. He didn't plan to give him up for no good reason. Especially after what Raymond had said about protecting him in Chicago.

"Who called you from France?"

"I haven't even seen the phone. Show me the number. Tell me whose number it is, maybe I can help you."

Ferribotte put a hand on Mendizábal's arm. They whispered. Ferribotte indicated the computer screen. They were probably getting updates by e-mail. Mendizábal frowned. Pescatore began to think he had misjudged the dynamic of Mendizábal as boss and Ferribotte as underling. He suspected that Ferribotte did not approve of his partner's approach to police work.

"Listen, gentlemen," Pescatore said. He tried to catch Ferribotte's eye, but the investigator hunched over the laptop. "I don't want you to lose time. I think you should contact people who can make it clear I'm not a terrorist. I have a well-documented history of service in law enforcement."

"Who do you know at the U.S. embassy?" Ferribotte asked. His voice was quiet and even.

As Pescatore said the name of an FBI agent he had once met, he remembered that the guy had already finished his tour in Buenos Aires.

"You'll have to do better than that," Ferribotte said.

"I haven't met the new FBI legal attaché. He just got here."

"What about your employer?"

Pescatore didn't even know if Facundo was still alive.

"Mr. Hyman is in intensive care. He wasn't able to talk, last I saw."

"Convenient," Mendizábal growled.

Pescatore regarded him coldly, tasting blood from his cut lip. "He had a heart attack at El Almacén. He was trying to help your GEOF team."

"If this Hyman"—the interrogator pronounced the name as if it were an obscenity—"employs a *chorro* like you, I am not impressed."

"I'll tell you this. He knows there's more to investigative work than acting like a thug and hitting people who can't hit back."

Mendizábal rose. Pescatore crouched behind his free arm, ready for a beat-down. Mendizábal leaned on the table, a wall of blue. His jaws and neck bulged.

He's gonna give another hard-ass speech before he starts dropping bombs, Pescatore thought. *He loves to hear himself talk that shit.*

"Listen carefully, Pescatore. I have orders from the highest levels to do what I must. That includes methods that make Guantánamo look like Disney World. No matter what we do, even if we kill you, there will be no sympathy for you. Not even the loudest, most cretinous human rights faggots will dare complain. On the contrary, I will get a medal. I suggest you start cooperating."

As scary as he sounded, Mendizábal didn't get a chance to deliver. His subsequent questioning was interrupted several times by Ferribotte, who was receiving calls on his BlackBerry. Their rhythm faltered. Something had changed. The guard at the door went out and came back. The three of them huddled. The interrogator and Ferribotte got up and left.

As Pescatore was escorted back to his cell, one thought dominated his mind: From the moment he had seen Raymond at the airport, he had known trouble would follow. He wished that his instincts weren't so frigging accurate.

Minutes later, Ferribotte brought visitors. A man and a woman stood in the dim cell looking down at Pescatore huddled on the bench.

"Mr. Pescatore? I'm Supervisory Special Agent Tony Furukawa of the FBI, the legal attaché at the embassy. This is a colleague from the French police, Commissaire Fatima Belhaj. You're going to be released into my care and custody."

"Good news for me."

"I've worked with Facundo Hyman on some issues. How you doing? Let me get a look at those injuries."

The FBI agent leaned forward, squinting in the bad light. He had a broad Asian face under a graying black buzz cut. He wore a tweed sport jacket, no tie.

"Inspector," the FBI agent said with a dry, side-of-the-mouth delivery. "Somebody's been thumping on my U.S. citizen."

"It is unfortunate, and I apologize in the name of the Argentine federal police," Ferribotte replied in English, neither resentful nor obsequious.

"Is that standard policy for material witnesses?" Furukawa asked sharply. "Give them a few *trancazos* to get their attention?"

Pescatore guessed that the FBI agent had learned his Spanish in or near Mexico. The preferred Argentine term for "punches" was *trompadas*.

"At the moment of his detention, he was considered a suspect, armed and dangerous," Ferribotte responded.

"I don't see how the information in hand justifies that." Furukawa sounded dispassionate and bureaucratic. "You see his shirt? He's a former U.S. federal border agent. And a licensed private investigator. Mr. Pescatore, do you want to file a complaint of excessive force? It is my duty to offer you that option."

"Mainly what I'd like is some Advil," Pescatore said. "This officer isn't the thumper. They got a pumpkin-head gorilla talks like Foghorn Leghorn. They keep him down in the dungeon."

A smile flickered across the woman's face. He saw a mane of curls, striking oval eyes, and that easy smile like a flash in the shadows.

"You wanna file a complaint or not?" Furukawa asked.

"No, man, let it go."

Ferribotte's thin face registered relief. He led them to a squad room and stood across a counter from the FBI agent. They reviewed paperwork related to Pescatore's custody status and the property confiscated at his apartment.

"Listen," Furukawa told Pescatore. "Pending further investigation, they are going to keep your stuff: passport, phones, computer, weapon. If the embassy didn't have a relationship with your firm, it'd be hard to get you released at all."

The Argentine investigator offered Pescatore coffee or water. He declined both. As Pescatore signed forms, Furukawa and the Argentine conferred. Pescatore sensed movement behind him. He turned and saw Mendizábal standing with a couple of officers.

The interrogator sipped from a gourd of *mate* tea. His sleeves were rolled up over brawny forearms. He raised his chin. His expression conveyed amused tolerance.

"Come on, muchacho, it could have been worse," he intoned in Spanish. "We don't have time to play around in these situations."

Pescatore hesitated. Everyone in the room was looking at him.

"I suppose you don't," he said.

"If you were a policeman before, you know how this business works."

"Risks of the profession," Pescatore replied ruefully.

"Exactly."

"These things happen."

"That's what I'm saying."

"I suppose you're right."

Pescatore smiled a conciliatory smile. He stepped forward. He offered his hand.

Mendizábal's eyes hardened. He, too, was aware that they were the center of attention. He appeared to be evaluating risks and assessing contingencies. Slowly, cautiously, he shifted the gourd to his left hand and extended his right.

Pescatore gave him a firm, gentlemanly handshake with sustained eye contact, like his father had taught him. He let the shake linger.

Then he did the most immature, unprofessional, reckless thing he had done in a long time.

He hit him.

His last boxing match had been more than a decade ago. He had not thrown a punch in anger since leaving the Border Patrol. He was overdue. His left fist came up from down low, gathering all the fear and pain and hate and trauma of the past twenty-four hours as it rose. He turned his torso into the punch with plenty of follow-through. The fist hit the head in front of the ear, a dull thunk of bone on bone that sent shock waves back through his arm and shoulder. He grunted with effort and satisfaction.

Mendizábal pitched to his left like a locomotive changing tracks. His *mate* gourd went flying. He and the gourd seemed to hover, suspended in midair, for an unnaturally long time. He belly-flopped to the floor with a resounding crash. The gourd struck and shattered a millisecond later.

Pescatore looked at the stunned Ferribotte.

Pescatore said, "Now that was a cheap shot."

5

Cambalache

Persona non grata," the legal attaché said.

Furukawa's office in the U.S. embassy was decorated with Los Angeles Dodgers and Anaheim Angels posters and paraphernalia. There were photos of college-age kids, but no wife. It was Saturday night. The office glowed in the otherwise empty embassy complex like the command deck of a spacecraft. Pescatore reclined full length on a couch. The FBI agent sat behind his desk. His tone was cheerfully bitter.

"You watch, I'll get PNG'd," Furukawa said. "I'll get kicked out of the country before I'm done unpacking. They won't let me be leeg-att in fucking Zambia. Thanks to you, *pinche baboso cabrón.*"

Pescatore shielded his eyes from the light. His head throbbed. "How come you talk like that?"

"Like what?"

"Like a *vato*. Like you were born in East LA."

"I was born in West LA, actually. Went to school with Mexicans, played baseball with 'em. I worked gangs for the Inglewood police before I joined the Bureau. But enough of my curriculum vitae. We were talking about you pulling that Oscar De La Hoya shit."

During the uproar at the headquarters of the antiterror unit after Pescatore punched the inspector, Mendizábal had struggled to his feet and gone after Pescatore. Staggering like a drunken sailor, shouting: "I'm going to give you a shitstorm of a beating!" Mendizábal's men had wrestled him out of the room. A supervisor threatened to file charges of assaulting an officer. Furukawa threatened to file charges of human rights abuse. Ferribotte and the French female officer played peacemakers and averted a diplomatic incident.

"Look, I'm sorry," Pescatore said from the sofa. "They knew I was law enforcement. They could have reached out, explained. I would've bent over backwards to help. Instead they treat me like a criminal, smack me around, call me a terrorist. Fuck them."

The pouches under Furukawa's eyes gave him a weary air. "Fine. The nasty man hit your facey-wacey. That doesn't—"

"You got that 'nasty man' line from a book."

"What?"

Pescatore pointed at a bookshelf. *The Long Goodbye.*

Furukawa glanced up at the novel and back at Pescatore as if he had just been handed a piece to a puzzle that he thought he had solved.

"My favorite," he said slowly. "Especially the part where the cop says there's no clean way to make a hundred million bucks. You like Chandler?"

"I liked that one. I read more nonfiction, tell you the truth."

"Well—Oh, here's the *commissaire.* I was worried you got lost on the way to the Coke machine."

Fatima Belhaj walked in carrying two cans of Coke. She put one on the low table in front of Pescatore along with a bottle of aspirin. She was with a French counterterrorism agency. She had arrived that morning to investigate the deaths of two French tourists at El Almacén and other French angles of the case. She spoke multiple languages and was a star of her squad, Furukawa had explained.

Belhaj had said she was of Moroccan descent. Pescatore had never met a Moroccan; she looked light-skinned African to him. She sipped her Coke with full lips over small teeth. Her brown curls had a rusty tinge and tumbled around those heavy-lidded eyes. The eyes reminded him of the angel in the da Vinci painting *The Madonna of the Rocks.* Her suede jacket and jeans were no doubt European and expensive and displayed a generous chest, hips and behind. She slid into an armchair by the couch and crossed her long legs.

"*Et votre tête,* Monsieur Valentín?"

Belhaj touched a finger to her own eyebrow. He realized she was asking about his injury. She talked from her throat, a percussive accent separating the syllables. Her voice was like the rest of her: tough, reserved and sexy.

"I'm okay. Thanks." He sat up and took a long grateful swig of Coke.

She peered at him. "You should put a bandage."

"Hey, he's fine," Furukawa interjected. "He's a boxer, he's used to it. We got a first-aid kit, we'll hook him up. I'm the one you should worry about. That burning smell in here is my career going down in flames. Fatima, could you brief us now?"

"Yeah," Pescatore said, opening the aspirin bottle. "What's this they told me about a French terrorist calling my phone?"

"Our Argentine colleagues were, one can say, imprecise," she said. "We have not traced the number to an identified person. It is part of a sequence of stolen SIM cards linked to a gang of Islamo-*braqueurs* in the south of France: radicalized criminals that do armed robberies to finance Islamist groups. The number that called to your phone on Tuesday also called to Bolivia. The call was an anonymous tip that was relayed to the Bolivian authorities and allowed the arrest of a terrorist cell in La Paz before the attack here."

Belhaj produced a pack of Gitanes cigarettes and glanced

conspiratorially at Furukawa. He shook his forefinger back and forth.

"This is a smoke-free United States government facility, young lady."

"Come on, hombre, the place is empty as a tomb," she exclaimed in Spanish. She used the lisping *th* sound, like a Spaniard. One corner of her grin turned down a bit. Pescatore thought that made it more genuine.

"Negative," Furukawa said. "I'm a smoker myself, but rules are rules."

Pescatore had heard nothing yet to implicate Raymond. Things were moving in a strange direction.

"So wait a minute," he said. "The police lied to me. This wasn't a terrorist calling me. This was somebody trying to help the good guys. You think he wanted to warn me that an attack was coming in Buenos Aires?"

"I do," Furukawa said. "And I think whoever it was didn't mind leaving a trail, because he didn't block the number. But some of the locals think the Bolivian cell was a decoy, you were in on the real plot, and the call activated the operation."

"Except I didn't answer the phone. That doesn't make sense."

Furukawa shrugged. "Look at it from their point of view: The Bolivians contacted the French about the tip from a French phone. Fatima's people were already working on the phone lead when the attack happened here. They found the record of calls to your phone and passed the info to the Argentines, who were frantic. Like a one-legged man in an ass-kicking contest. There was phone evidence connecting you to extremist activity in three countries. They had witnesses and closed-circuit footage putting you at the attack scene."

"Jesus Christ." Pescatore put his hands behind his head. He rocked forward and back. "So if I had been using that phone and answered that call, this whole bloodbath wouldn't have happened!"

Belhaj pursed her lips. "Not necessarily."

Furukawa came around his desk, removing the tweed jacket. He had short thick limbs in a white button-down shirt and pleated khaki pants. He sat in the armchair at the other end of the couch.

"Fatima's right," he said. "The bottom line is you weren't using that phone. Whoever called with the warning, if that's what it was, didn't leave you a message. He didn't call anybody else in Argentina. There are a lot of unknowns."

"I'm trying to get my mind around the whole thing."

"Well, get your mind around this. Now's the time to tell us anything you might not have mentioned to *la federal*. It's extremely important if you want this investigation to move forward."

Pescatore glanced from the FBI agent to the French investigator. He had taken a liking to Furukawa. And he not only liked Belhaj but was having trouble keeping his eyes off her. The embassy seemed safe: a mother ship in the night. His status had improved from suspect to witness. But he faced up to a cold certainty: this was another interrogation.

"Hey, listen, I wanna help," he began, stalling for time. "But are we sure this guy was really trying to call me? It could've been a wrong number."

Belhaj stared at him. Furukawa folded his arms.

"What are the odds?" he said. "Do you think it was a wrong number, Valentine?"

Stop bullshitting, Pescatore told himself. *Be a man.*

"All right, I'm gonna tell you some stuff." He took a deep breath. "I'm not sure it means anything, though. Might just be smoke. And I gotta ask you something. I want to play a role in this investigation. I owe it to Facundo. Is that fair?"

The FBI agent frowned. "We'll see. But don't forget: you're my responsibility. So no more *chingaderas*."

"You got it, Agent Furukawa."

Pescatore told them about Raymond. He laid out the whole thing, from the lakefront in Chicago to the restaurant in Palermo Hollywood. It was cathartic. Furukawa's baggy eyes were wide with concentration. Belhaj sipped Coke. Pescatore had their full attention. He felt powerful and vulnerable at the same time.

"Basically, when you get right down to it," he said, "I have a hunch based on certain facts. I run into Raymond. I give him that number, which hardly anybody else has. Then somebody calls that number. Then all this evil shit happens. But I can't tell you it was Raymond who called. I can't claim I understand what's going on."

The questions started. His head swiveled. No, he didn't know where Raymond lived; he had been evasive about that. He had said only that he was changing planes in Miami. No, he didn't know if Raymond had any link to France; he had mentioned spending time in Europe and having a North African wife. Yes, Raymond had said he had been a drug informant in the U.S. and Latin America.

Furukawa seemed interested in the informant angle and in Pescatore's suspicions that the meeting at the airport had been staged.

"Let me get this straight," the agent said. "Why did you think he was lying about running into you?"

"It felt strange. I used to know him pretty good. His mannerisms: he was worried, emotional."

"I'm walking through a scenario where this Ray is the guy who made the calls. He knows you're in BA somehow. He's involved with or aware of the terrorist plots. He finds you, engineers this reunion, couple days later he calls Bolivia—"

"Who got the call in Bolivia, anyway?" Pescatore interjected.

"Unknown. As I was saying: Raymond Mercer hasn't seen you since way back when you booked on him and he got busted. But he reaches out to you. Why?"

"Maybe he trusts me. And maybe what you said: He knew I had law enforcement connections. He asked about Facundo's company, the embassy."

Belhaj toyed with a handful of curls. "Did he explain when and where he converted to Islam? Sunni or Shiite?"

"Argentina. And he's Sunni, I'm pretty sure he said that."

Furukawa jotted notes on a legal pad. "Do you know his mother's maiden name? The Argentine family?"

"Nope. They were originally Lebanese."

Furukawa was scribbling industriously. He glanced at his watch.

"Okay, people," he said. "This is the one angle in the whole case that gives me potential jurisdiction. Believe it or not, there wasn't a single victim who was a U.S. person. Not one. Thanks be to God, knock wood, but still: What are the odds? Fatima, you and I need to hit up our databases on Mercer. We need to tell the federal police right away. What's that look, Valentine? I can't withhold a lead."

"I'm just concerned, you know," Pescatore said. "It could go to the wrong people."

"Despite your experience, their CT squad is pretty good. Professionalized. They learned their lessons from the nineties. I'm more worried about the politics." Furukawa ducked his head confidentially. "There's an agency in this building that thinks this government won't survive these attacks."

"What you need," Pescatore said, "is somebody you trust to run this down. Feed you intel on the side. To know if they play the case straight."

Furukawa nodded. "A back channel. But my go-to source for that kind of thing, your boss, is in the hospital. Any suggestions?"

"I think I got a guy."

The next day, Belhaj picked up Pescatore in a French embassy vehicle. She showed him a headline in a newspaper: "From Policeman to Terrorist." The investigation had identified a chief suspect, a former narcotics officer of the provincial police of Buenos Aires. A Muslim convert. His body had been found, surrounded by dead hostages, on the top floor of El Almacén. His name was Belisario Ortega. The newspaper showed a photo of a youthful man in uniform, a stern dark face. Some newspapers said the terrorists appeared to be a mix of Argentines and foreigners, but the police had not made conclusive identifications.

Belhaj told him that French record checks on Raymond had turned up nothing.

"If Mercer has been there, he entered from another country or with a different name. We are asking other European countries, but Sunday, the things do not move very fast. Tony said the American records did not find much either."

"Can I use your cell phone? I don't have one anymore. Or a gun, or a computer, or a passport. This sucks."

"An orphan in the modern world," Belhaj said.

Pescatore remembered her dusky eyes hovering above him the night before while she bandaged his forehead at the embassy. She had insisted on doing it. Her touch was gentle and efficient. Images of her had nagged him overnight, along with the conundrum of Raymond's role—tipster, terrorist, double agent?—in the eruption of catastrophe in his life.

Pescatore called Café La Biela. He talked to a waiter he knew, a Galician immigrant named Modesto. He was an old-school *gallego*: wary, courtly, talkative. After thirty years in Argentina, he retained the rustic accent of his mountain village.

"Is he there?" Pescatore asked Modesto.

"He just asked for the check," the waiter reported. "This one doesn't stay too long on Sundays."

"Modesto, I'm on my way." Pescatore gestured at Belhaj to have the driver go faster. "There's fifty pesos in it for you. Keep him there."

"How?"

"Talk to him!"

"About what?"

"Soccer, women, I don't know. Has Televisión Española done any programs on Galicia lately?"

"Well, now that you mention it, there was an interesting report the other day about the region of the Rías Baixas. Apparently the marine currents—"

"Perfect. Go tell him about that. We'll be there in a minute."

Pescatore hoped for the best. If Modesto was inspired, he could talk a customer's ear off. He liked to describe in detail the interminable documentaries with which Spain's television network fed the nostalgia of the Galician diaspora overseas.

Pescatore had decided that Dario D'Ambrosio, the former spy chief who hung out at La Biela, was his best prospect for a hip-pocket ally among Facundo's many contacts. Facundo had said D'Ambrosio owed him and still pulled strings in the intelligence service. Pescatore and Belhaj were making the initial approach.

"I'm not real presentable," Pescatore told her in the vehicle, touching the bandage and his swollen upper lip. "I hate to go in there looking like Raging Bull."

"It is not grave," she said. "You have the body of a boxer, and now the face of a boxer."

Pescatore digested that comment. The vehicle stopped on Quintana Avenue by the green-and-white awnings of the café. He glanced at Belhaj, who was looking out the drizzle-streaked window.

"So when you say that about the, uh, body of a boxer, is that a good thing?"

"C'est une question de goût," she said, opening her door. "A question of taste."

She's messing with me, he thought. *She's smart and hot and French and she's messing with me.*

They found D'Ambrosio sitting at a corner table in the glass-partitioned smoking section of La Biela. Modesto the waiter stood in front of the table like a soccer goalie poised for a penalty kick, tray in hand and dish towel over his arm. He was deep in a monologue. He stopped midsentence and slid aside when Pescatore strode up out of the smoke and introduced himself as Facundo Hyman's right-hand man and dear friend.

"Yes, of course, I know who you are," D'Ambrosio said, startled but suave.

Pescatore spotted money on the table; they had arrived just in time.

D'Ambrosio eyed the damage to Pescatore's face. He asked: "How is our friend Facundo? The hospital said he was not ready for visitors yet."

"I checked this morning and his condition is stable, thank God."

The spymaster was the first person Pescatore had ever seen use a cigarette holder. The lanky D'Ambrosio had silver hair. His burgundy ascot and corduroy sport jacket gave him a rugged patrician air: an outfit for relaxing at a country home after a day of hunting. When Pescatore introduced Belhaj as a French counterterrorism chief, D'Ambrosio rose to his full height, squared his shoulders, and said he was enchanted. He invited them to sit down while glancing appreciatively at the contours of Belhaj's tight sweater. Pescatore congratulated himself. Furukawa had wanted him to meet the Argentine one-on-one to maintain deniability. Pescatore had insisted that Fatima Belhaj at least should come along to prove he was working with a bona fide police force. He hadn't mentioned his other reason: the presence of this particular Frenchwoman would weaken D'Ambrosio's defenses.

Pescatore dove in. He described his arrest by the federal police.

"I heard about a misunderstanding with an American," D'Ambrosio said.

"They misunderstood that my head wasn't a punching bag."

D'Ambrosio smiled. Pescatore said he needed urgent help on a delicate matter. D'Ambrosio dragged on the cigarette holder, squinting.

"In reality, then, this is an ambush." His tone suggested that he was being a good sport—for the moment.

"A friendly ambush," Pescatore said. "With Facundo in such bad condition, I didn't know where to turn. I know he would want me, and you, sir, to help the *commissaire* and the FBI. I am in the middle of this thing."

Pescatore asked about the feasibility of making discreet inquiries about another American who had surfaced in the case.

"You put me in a complicated position," D'Ambrosio replied. "Don't forget, I am retired." He turned to Belhaj. "I retired early, you see. Mademoiselle, how old do you think I am?"

Sixty, but say fifty-five, Pescatore thought.

"Fifty?" She said it with her eyes extra-wide.

"You are flattering me, mademoiselle!" D'Ambrosio had the toothy debonair laugh of a talk-show host. "The point is, I cannot go poking my nose into this."

"Dr. D'Ambrosio," Pescatore said softly, figuring that the spy chief might have a law degree (which in Argentina made him *Doctor*) and that in any case, the title was appropriately deferential. "Facundo has explained to me that you still have great influence in your former service, and that you are a force for good."

"As dear friends will do, Facundo exaggerates my merits." He beamed at the woman before shaking his head at Pescatore. "I am afraid I cannot help you, son."

"Maybe I am not being clear, Doctor," Pescatore said.

"You are being very clear."

"But Doctor, I—"

"Now if you'll excuse me, I have a pressing engagement."

D'Ambrosio started to get up. Pescatore decided to drop the *Doctor* crap.

"Listen," he said through clenched teeth. "It happens that I know Facundo Hyman did you a big and specific favor. I know that he saved you from an embarrassing and unpleasant situation with my government. You owe him, which at this moment means you owe me. I need you to repay the favor. Right now. Understood?"

D'Ambrosio's scowl made him look less country-house and more street.

"Muchacho, you are leaning on me," he hissed. "And I don't like it."

Although Pescatore returned the stare, he was concerned that he had overplayed his hand. Belhaj intervened. With a high-voltage smile, she asked for a cigarette. D'Ambrosio handed her one and gallantly proffered his lighter. She pushed back her hair and blew smoke.

"Monsieur, you must remember that Monsieur Valentín has had a traumatic experience," she said earnestly in her Castilian-style Spanish. "He was at the scene of the attack, he was wrongly accused. He is understandably upset. We want to seek justice for this terrible crime. You are the only person who can help us."

D'Ambrosio concentrated on a new cigarette, avoiding eye contact, flustered.

Pescatore offered an olive branch. "I apologize if I spoke harshly."

"Perhaps we both got a bit tense," D'Ambrosio muttered. "These are days of great tension. I imagine Facundo would want me to lend a hand. I am going to order a cognac. Why don't we have a cognac and chat?"

As Pescatore sketched out Raymond's visit and his possible

link to the terrorist attack, the veteran spy chief listened with increasing zeal. He asked incisive questions.

This guy is good, Pescatore thought. He handed over a print-out with basic data, including the Argentine phone number and e-mail address that Raymond had given him. The spymaster waved off the papers, pulling out a Moleskine notebook and a Montblanc pen to take notes instead.

"Better to avoid exchanging documents," he said. "You were shrewd to come to me. I can steer this data to the right operators. The investigation is being distorted and damaged by competing interests. Both the federal and provincial police are implicated in the plot at some level. And the politicians are affected by domestic and foreign issues. A real *cambalache*."

Pescatore told the woman, "That's a tango about how everything is so corrupt and upside down, you can't tell who's a crook and who's a saint."

"Exactly," D'Ambrosio said. "*Mademoiselle la commissaire,* do you really think this was the work of an al-Qaedist organization, as the official version asserts?" He asked the question with sudden sharpness.

He has trouble believing a Moroccan chick could be a hotshot cop, Pescatore thought.

"The thesis is not excluded," she replied. "The French phone number connects to networks sending extremists to Pakistan and Syria. The universe of al-Qaeda. South America would be new territory for them, but these days, they are looking for opportunities. Cells form spontaneously and strike where they can."

"In my view, this was an unusually professional operation. It is inconsistent with the signature of al-Qaeda in recent years, which has been clumsiness and failure outside its traditional strongholds. I will share with you something that is not public." D'Ambrosio lowered his voice. They leaned forward. "The forensics people found the detonators of the two bombers who blew themselves to bits at the delicatessen in the mall. Each detonator was still gripped in a hand: one right hand, one left hand. The investigators realized that they were the hands of the same person. What does that tell you?"

Another flirtatious jab at Belhaj. She tilted up her face and inhaled serenely from her cigarette. She was enjoying herself.

"It suggests the masterminds studied the psychology of the bombers," she said. "They probably had doubts that one would go through with it. The more resolute kamikaze, the one whom they trusted, was responsible for his comrade. He detonated both bombs. Expert planning."

"An excellent analysis, and one that reinforces my view of mysterious powers at work. Pescatore, anything else?"

"Yes. An Argentine woman phoned Raymond Mercer while I was with him. He talked as if it was a romantic relationship. It sounded like she was upset. He said he was going to visit her that night. I think her name was Flo, maybe short for Flora or Florencia."

Belhaj stared with surprise at Pescatore, who avoided her gaze. He had kept a card up his sleeve. He had forgotten to mention Flo at the embassy the night before, which meant Furukawa had not told the federal police about that detail. By the time Pescatore remembered, they were already planning to go to D'Ambrosio. He had decided to share the lead exclusively with the SIDE. If the spy agency had ammunition to compete with the police, it would help keep everybody honest. Not to mention giving leverage to the Americans, the French, and Pescatore himself.

The move had been risky and sneaky. But necessary.

6

Sophisticated Lady

The building was one of the most exclusive high-rises in the city. A celestial refuge for magnates, politicos, soccer stars, television personalities and other fashionable fauna.

The service elevator climbed in its vertical cage. The narrow windows of back-door landings gave glimpses of the Puerto Madero district, the waterfront of old docks and brick granaries transformed into boardwalks lined with restaurants.

"You see how many fancy dogs that poor bastard was hauling downstairs?" Furukawa whispered. "Couple thousand dollars a dog, a dozen leashes: thirty grand worth of pooch."

"Flo did good," Pescatore whispered back. "Nobody in the immigration service back home lives like this. Even the ones who steal."

The investigation had advanced on two tracks during the three days since the meet at La Biela. The official version now depicted a homegrown Islamic terrorist plot—an unprecedented event in Latin America. The radicalized former drug cop Belisario Ortega had traveled to Pakistan and trained with terrorists there. He had returned home and assembled a misfit band of Argentines of Middle Eastern descent and criminals who had converted to Islam. His group's ideology mixed the influences of al-Qaeda and neo-Nazis. The authorities insisted that the ex-cop had trained, armed and led the plotters on his own. The attackers' federal police uniforms were declared to be fakes. Spokesmen proclaimed that initial reports of foreigners among the terrorists were wrong and dismissed talk of overseas masterminds.

"The more local they say it is, the easier it is to control," D'Ambrosio had explained during a second meeting at La Biela, wreathed in a smoke cloud that he and Belhaj had created. "This new government doesn't get along with the Americans, the Europeans or the Israelis. It does big business with the Middle East. This way, there is no sharing with pesky foreign espionage services, no pointing fingers in dangerous directions. In Mumbai in 2008, an attack like this took two years of external planning, a high-level operation by a terrorist group and Pakistani intelligence working together. Here, they claim these *pelotudos* pulled it off alone, and they expect the rest of us *pelotudos* to believe it."

D'Ambrosio's crew at the spy agency had leaped on Pescatore's lead. They had tracked Raymond's trail in Buenos Aires and identified his woman friend as Florencia Pucinski Rodriguez, also known as La Gorda Flo (Fat Flo), a section chief in the national immigration service. The spy agency had put her under house arrest, and she had cooperated, providing a wealth of information. D'Ambrosio had offered the Americans and French secret access to the star source.

"I haven't had this much fun in years," a beaming D'Ambrosio had told Pescatore at the café. "Thanks to you, I'm going to flunk retirement."

The elevator stopped at the twenty-sixth floor. The metal gate clattered open to reveal a familiar face: Biondani, the shaggy-haired intelligence officer who had been at El Almacén during the attack.

"The lady of the house was working out at the gym upstairs," he said. "She is grooming herself and will be at your disposal shortly."

Biondani led them through a sunny kitchen past plain-clothesmen at a table covered with breakfast and a mean-looking MP5 machine pistol. The apartment occupied the entire floor and offered panoramic views. It had the air of a showroom: a grand piano, lush carpeting, sumptuous sofas.

"Hello, everyone!"

Florencia greeted them like a perky hostess, not a prisoner in gilded limbo. She was trailed by a weary-looking female officer in jeans and a wearier-looking maid in uniform. Biondani made introductions.

"The famous Valentín from Chicago!" Florencia kissed him on both cheeks. "I've heard all about you."

As she bustled around getting them seated, Pescatore decided that, despite her ungentlemanly nickname, La Gorda Flo wasn't that fat. She reclined on her side next to him on the couch, her movements creating hills and valleys in her low-cut, leopard-skin top and electric-blue leather pants. She was over forty, at least ten years older than Raymond. Her helmet-style hairdo reminded him of the suburban molls in *The Sopranos*. Below the bangs, the perpetually startled eyes and oddly up-turned nose reflected a vicious cycle of cosmetic surgery.

"My goodness, that one looks like Beyoncé," Florencia chirped. "At least from the back. And the hair."

She was appraising Belhaj as the French investigator removed her coat and draped it over a chair. The comment was marginally accurate, at best. It confirmed his impression that Florencia expressed her thoughts as they crossed her mind, unconcerned about saying something politically incorrect or wildly inappropriate.

"So you want to talk about Ramón." She turned to Pescatore. Her smile was a mask of makeup strained by fear. "Your old and dear friend. The love of my life. The curse of my life."

"I always called him Raymond," he replied. "Don't tell me his name was really Ramón all this time."

"No, that was what I called him. He started using it himself. It was part of his discovery of where he came from, he said."

Pescatore had planned to defer to the others. But he sensed that Florencia felt a connection to him. He glanced at Furukawa, who nodded.

"You said he talked about me?" Pescatore continued.

"A lot." She put her hand on his arm. He smelled coconut perfume. "He had great fondness for you. His best friend from childhood. You could have been a good influence on him. Instead, he was a bad influence on you. He regretted it very much. As if it were the cause of all his troubles."

Pescatore's hopes that Raymond would somehow turn out to be one of the good guys had been waning. Now, the first thing out of her mouth amounted to a heartfelt apology from Raymond.

"How did you come to meet him?"

"It was about eight years ago. I used to do favors for some rich *turquitos:* residency papers, bureaucratic troubles. They would throw me some mangoes for my help. Ramón had a relative who sent him to me through a family named Kharroubi. Ramón wanted Argentine citizenship."

He qualified for citizenship because of his Argentine mother, Florencia explained. She expedited the process for a private fee. Raymond invited her to see him sing at a hole-in-the-wall club in the San Telmo neighborhood. He performed several times a week, accompanying himself on piano or teaming with a rhythm section.

"The first time I went, he dedicated a song to me: 'Sophisticated Lady,'" she said wistfully. "From then on, he always sang it for me. What a song. What a voice. I didn't understand half the words, but it didn't matter."

A memory came to Pescatore. He was getting high with Raymond and listening to jazz, a Tony Bennett version of "Sophisticated Lady." Raymond called it one of the best songs ever.

He said no woman was going to turn down Tony Benedetto with lines like that.

"He told me I was his sophisticated lady," Florencia said. "I felt like the queen of the world. He shot an arrow right through my heart. Ay."

She pressed a hand over the afflicted organ and addressed Belhaj in a sisterly tone. "What a romance. First class all the way: champagne, restaurants, hotels. Very physical. The age difference made it better. A vigorous, passionate young man!"

Please God no details, Pescatore thought. She described romantic getaways to the beach resorts of Uruguay.

"He loved that coast. I told him the old joke: If the Apocalypse comes, move to Uruguay: everything there happens fifty years later. He said he would be perfectly content to find a little club on the beach and play the piano waiting for the Apocalypse. He liked how calm and slow Uruguay was. It soothed him. Remember, he was still recovering from his cocaine addiction. Very tormented. I took care of him. I cured him."

She explained that Raymond grew close to Suleiman Kharroubi, who was in his thirties and owned car lots and import/export companies that did business with Bolivia.

"Well connected in the Arab community, the Kharroubis," she said. "A used-car empire. Half gangsters. Well, to tell the truth, total gangsters."

Raymond told Flo they had an opportunity to make serious money. He began bringing her "clients" for illegal help with documents.

"Turquitos, chinitos, bolitas," she said.

Arabs, Asians, Bolivians, Pescatore translated to himself as she threw around impolite ethnic labels.

"Also Indians, Pakistanis, Mexicans. An American or two. Some bought new identities. Some left with their Argentine passports and visas for the United States or Europe. I wanted to stay low-key, not overdo it, but Ramón kept pushing. He was so charming and persuasive. I was drunk on him. And the money was incredible. Even before the drug aspect began. We were *The Bold and the Beautiful.* Pardon me, I am dying for a cigarette. You don't mind, Valentín?"

He minded. Belhaj had been smoking in his face for days. But he wasn't going to complain. Florencia's plump hands fumbled with the lighter.

"The drug aspect is where Belisario Ortega comes in, the leader of the terrorist cell," Biondani interjected. He was perched on the edge of an armchair, as if getting comfortable might implicate him in the acquisition of ill-gotten goods.

"I only met Ortega a few times." Florencia wrinkled her nose. "I never liked that one. *Un negro de la provincia.*"

The commonly used, casually racist term meant "a black from the province." It referred to dark-skinned, working-class people living in the hinterland around the capital. Pescatore wondered if the maid hovering in the next room had heard it. He wondered what Florencia would have called his mother.

Cocaine smuggling grew out of the human trafficking, she said. The ring moved migrants with strategically placed officials in ports, airports and border posts. They started using the same pipelines for drugs: inbound from suppliers in Bolivia, outbound to Europe through Africa. At first, couriers carried the cocaine. As the volume grew, loads were hidden in shipments of cargo, mainly used cars, using the cover of Kharroubi's firms.

"Ramón brought in Ortega, who was a narcotics chief in the Bonaerense. His men in the police escorted loads, protected distribution. Soon we were swimming in cash. You can't imagine. I couldn't spend it fast enough. I bought this home. I bought that piano for Raymond."

Her languid wave took in the piano, the apartment, the city below, the horizon beyond. As if to say: *Behold all I am about to lose.*

"It's a lovely home," Pescatore said, sensing that she expected a compliment. "Life was good."

She sighed. "Yes and no, dear. Yes and no. Frankly, I was frightened. We were playing in a heavyweight world. Ramón told me he knew what he was doing. He had contacts: the police, the Americans. He had worked for American agents, and he still had connections. He threw them something once in a while, little tips. Meanwhile, our romantic—"

"Which Americans?" Furukawa looked as if his breakfast had disagreed with him. "Agencies? Names? Did you meet Americans?"

"No." She rearranged herself into a childlike, cross-legged pose. "Our relationship deteriorated. I knew he had other women. Younger women. Then he got all caught up in the Islamic thing. Because of his family history. The *turquitos* took him to their mosque. They were always going on about Muslims, Israel, Palestine. I could care less about politics. Ramón was obsessed. He converted. That beast Ortega converted. You know what a talker Ramón is. He said they were becoming international warriors."

Raymond went through intensely devout periods when he grew a beard, prayed constantly, and shunned pleasure, Florencia said.

"He was driving me crazy. He became abusive. Verbally and physically. Telling me I dressed like a whore, acted like a whore. Then, after a few weeks, he would return to his old self: shave, spend money, carouse. Like the religious thing was a joke. The drug smuggling kept growing. I told him we should slow down. How much money did we need? He got angry. He said it was about 'the cause.' Whatever that meant."

Disaster struck. Federal police intercepted a truckload of cocaine in the province of Buenos Aires. There were rumors of DEA involvement in the bust. Raymond visited Florencia, agitated and intense. He said he was leaving for Bolivia to lie low.

"A week went by. Kharroubi came to see me. He said I had nothing to worry about. My people were not touched. Ramón used his allies to protect us. Kharroubi said Ramón would be back soon."

She took a deep breath. Pescatore noticed that Biondani was texting on his BlackBerry.

"I never heard from him. For months, I called. I sent e-mails. Not a word. I wanted to go to Bolivia. They told me to be patient, things were delicate. The man vanished from my life. It was absolutely brutal. Like a kick in the stomach. Like…"

She stopped. Her fleshy shoulders hunched. She began to cry soundlessly, sobs shuddering through her, tears jumping from her eyes. Pescatore glanced at the others; apparently, the next move was up to him. He patted her tentatively on the back. Although her snobbery annoyed him, now he felt sorry for her.

"It's all right, Flo," he said. "You take your time."

He gave her Kleenex from a box on the coffee table.

"Me van a limpiar," she wailed. Underworld slang: "They are going to clean me." Meaning: "They are going to kill me."

"Please, Florencia," Biondani said, looking up grumpily from his BlackBerry. "We are here protecting you around the clock."

"Soy boleta," she sobbed. More gangster talk: "My ticket's going to get punched."

"For the love of God, who wants to kill you?" Biondani demanded.

"Who doesn't?" Her wet mascaraed eyes stared over the handful of Kleenex. "The narcos. The terrorists. The police. Everybody!"

"What melodrama."

"It might be melodrama, but it's true."

Biondani reminded her that, as a condition of her comfortable detention, she had agreed to cooperate fully. She composed herself and went on. A year ago, Raymond had resurfaced. He showed up at her door with a bottle of champagne and an apology. He said he had been forced to go underground. He alluded to intrigues, mafias, governments. Now, however, his wild ways were behind him. He had used his drug fortune to invest well. He was back in Argentina on business.

"He had changed, physically and in personality," she said. "Colder. More mature."

"Where was he living?" Belhaj asked.

"He was vague. Perhaps Europe."

"What about his religious activity?"

"He was still Muslim. But he said he had gotten the fanaticism out of his system. He had put his faith in perspective."

"Did you believe him?"

"Based on the way he looked and acted, yes. I had sworn I would never forgive him. But of course, I did. He left a few days later. He visited again several times. And of course, a few months ago it turned out he wanted something: two passports."

"We believe they were for the attackers last week," Biondani told the visitors. "The suicide bomber with the two detonators at El Almacén. And the driver of the car bomb at the school."

"I know nothing about that," Florencia declared. "I never met them. I sent Ramón to a specialist we used in the passport department."

Furukawa asked, "So these were fake passports?"

"Absolutely not," she responded huffily. "Authentic and official."

Pescatore could see how the authorities were able to squelch word of foreign involvement. For the official record, the attackers were all Argentines, with documents to prove it.

"The two Arabs were not in the country yet," she continued. "A couple of weeks ago, Ramón came to town once more. His friends were in Bolivia about to fly to Buenos Aires. They had the passports, but Ramón wanted to make sure they wouldn't have problems. I said I didn't want anything to do with it. He sweet-talked and manipulated and browbeat me. Fool that I am, I agreed to have them fly in at a time when I had a trusted inspector on duty. Just for insurance; no one had to do anything. And that was all."

There was a pause.

"Do you know if he was familiar with the Almacén mall?" Furukawa asked quietly. Pescatore was impressed at the FBI agent's restraint. The guy was good at listening. "Did he ever shoot video or photos there, anything that might be considered surveillance or reconnaissance?"

Florencia stared at him with a kind of muted horror.

"Reconnaissance? Surveillance?" she exclaimed. "He knew El Almacén like the back of his hand. It was one of the first places I took him to show him the city. We went all the time. Shopping, movies, coffee. It was where he bought me clothes and jewelry. And now, when I think what happened…"

Furukawa nodded patiently. New tears slid down Florencia's cheeks.

"We used to eat at the delicatessen, the one that was bombed," she said plaintively. "Raymond was friendly with the waiters, he knew their names. The food reminded him of a place in Chicago. Moro, Mauri, something like that. When he became very religious, though, we stopped going."

Morry's, Pescatore realized, gritting his teeth. He had a vivid flashback of buying corned beef sandwiches at the deli on the South Side, of Raymond clowning around with the countermen.

Cold-blooded bastard, he thought.

Furukawa and Belhaj asked more questions. Florencia told them she believed Raymond had been in touch with Kharroubi in recent months.

"I haven't heard from Kharroubi in a while, but he knows a lot," she said. "A heavyweight mafioso."

She opened a folder on the coffee table. She showed them a photo of Raymond with Kharroubi, who was round-faced and arrogant-looking, and Ortega, the ex-cop turned terrorist. All three had beards. There was a photocopy of Raymond's original Argentine passport. He was clean-shaven and wore his hair long and slicked back. He had the haggard air of a recovering addict. The name on the passport was Ramón Verdugo. The word *verdugo* meant "executioner" in Spanish.

Raymond would think that was cool, Pescatore told himself.

"His mother's family name was Takiedinne Verdugo," Florencia said. "He chose the second last name. He said the Arab name would cause him trouble traveling. But remember: He dealt directly with my document people and obtained passports under other names. For himself and others. These colleagues"—she gestured at Biondani—"are looking into that, I am sure."

Biondani nodded impatiently. He seemed eager to wrap things up.

Florencia hugged her pillow, looking drained and forlorn. She reached over and patted Pescatore on the cheek.

"Ay, Valentín. In what an inferno your friend has left me. And to think, in spite of it all, I still love him. If you find him, you tell him that for me."

She examined him for a moment.

"It's curious," she said. "You are different than Ramón. But at the same time, the way you talk, the way you carry yourself—you remind me of him."

"I don't know if that's a good thing."

Biondani rode down with them in the elevator. He had news. The spy agency was closing in on Raymond's friend Kharroubi. After learning that the SIDE was onto him, the businessman had fled his home with bodyguards, planning to take a private plane to Bolivia. SIDE officers arrived at the airfield at the same time, but Kharroubi escaped by car. Officers had been tracking him overnight. They had identified a safe house in the industrial suburbs west of the city.

"We are convinced Kharroubi was involved in the attacks," Biondani said excitedly, standing in the street outside the high-rise. "He is implicated by evidence from the searches of the homes of Ortega and the others, their phones and e-mails. Kharroubi was the logistics man for guns, vehicles, explosives, police uniforms—which were authentic, no matter what the media says. We are putting together an operation to capture him now. If you follow me, we can be there for the show."

As they sped off, Belhaj and Furukawa called their embassies and relayed the information on Raymond's new identity. Pescatore pulled out the iPhone he had bought that morning. He called the hospital and learned that Facundo was doing better and would be ready for visitors soon.

"So," Furukawa said grimly. "What did we think of that *telenovela* up there?"

"I think she essentially told the truth," Belhaj said. "She exaggerates her role as a victim. His arc of radicalization is familiar. Crime evolves into extremism. They justify drugs as jihad. *Gangsterrorisme.*"

"The passports for the suicide bombers fit your theory," Furukawa told her. "They weren't sure the locals were committed to blowing themselves to kingdom come. So they brought in outsiders with *cojones.*"

Belhaj turned in the front seat to look at Pescatore. "And Monsieur Valentín, what did you think? You are our expert on Raymond/Ramón."

He liked her calling him Monsieur Valentín in her throaty voice.

"The way he treated Flo rings true," he replied. "He was always a dog. The U.S. agency stuff was weird."

"Damn right," Furukawa said. "I didn't like that one bit."

"Explain something to me," Pescatore said. "Sounds like Raymond was a player. He got documents, got the bombers into the country. Had to be involved in the Bolivian cell too. Why would he do all that, then turn around and blow the whistle at the last minute? I know he likes to play both sides, but does that make sense?"

"Your homeboy is bad news."

"Maybe now we can figure out where he is and what the hell he's doing."

Morning mist rose off roadside meadows. The highway led out of the city into a bleak landscape dominated by the spires of a Mormon temple. Atop the tallest tower, the statue of a golden angel with a trumpet glinted in the pale sun.

"What is the name of the area where we are going?" asked Belhaj.

"La Matanza," Furukawa said.

"That means…"

"'The Massacre,'" Pescatore said. "A bunch of Spaniards got killed there by Indians in the 1500s. I've been there a couple times on cases. No need to change the name."

7

Modern Major General

The commander ate steak every day.

The commander was a throw-down individual. You could tell from his thick-veined hands working the knife and fork, the set of his shoulders, the edge in his voice. Like he was chewing rocks. He wore a blue blazer over a wool vest in the chill of the station house dining room. The district headquarters had defective heating. Officers wore scarves and coats indoors. Several had hacking coughs.

The commander's name was Saladino. There was a statuette on a shelf above him: the Virgin of Luján, the patron of the provincial police. It was the only decoration on the peeling green walls other than the flags of Argentina and the province.

"I was in New York once on a mission," the commander said, eyeing Furukawa through square glasses. "Dirty. Noisy. Lunatics. Savages. The Americans didn't know anything about us. They expected Indians with feathers. They invited us to eat raw fish, Chinese vegetables. Girl food. There's nothing like our Argentine meat. I eat steak every day."

The deputies flanking him nodded, crew cuts bobbing above necks that resembled the slabs of beef on platters served by uniformed cops. The provincial police were the biggest armed force in the country. They averaged a shootout a day.

Pescatore took a sip of red wine that warmed his insides. The hunt for Raymond's associate had detoured into an epic meal, courtesy of the police in La Matanza. Upon arriving at the headquarters, a ranchlike facility with a muddy courtyard, Biondani had given them a quick briefing in the vehicle. The spy agency had located Kharroubi's hideout in La Matanza, where he owned used-car lots and other property. Biondani had a dilemma. His agency was doing a parallel investigation of the terrorist attack; he didn't want to involve the federal police. So he had enlisted the help of the provincial police, bitter enemies of the federal force. Commander Saladino oversaw a district with almost a million residents. A sea of mafias, civilian and uniformed.

"The provincial police own the turf," Biondani said. "If we tried a raid on our own, they would mess it up one way or another. We will take the risk of working with them. Saladino is relatively trustworthy."

Pescatore had his doubts. They had put themselves in the hands of a notorious force involved in a crossfire of feuds.

"I've heard about Saladino," Pescatore said. "A specialist in operettas, no?"

"Correct," Biondani responded curtly. "We work with what we have."

Biondani got out of the vehicle.

Belhaj asked: "Operettas? Like *The Pirates of Penzance*? 'Modern Major General'?"

"Not exactly." Pescatore felt a glow of confidence. His trips into the province with Facundo, the solo missions to remote police outposts, soaking up details: it had all paid off. He was an expert now.

"An operetta works like this," he said. "The police go partners with a stickup gang. They help choose the target, a store or a bank, secure the perimeter. A 'liberated zone.' They make sure the robbers get in and out. They split the loot. They do it a few times, everybody gets comfortable. Then there's another robbery. But this time, the police set up an ambush outside. When the robbers come out, they kill them. And announce another victory against crime."

The commander had welcomed his visitors with the news that they were in luck: on Wednesdays, he and his staff ate an *asado,* a carnivorous extravaganza prepared in a barbecue pit of industrial dimensions. The raid could wait until after lunch.

Belhaj took it in stride. Furukawa reacted like an uptight American. He was climbing the walls. For the second time, the FBI agent cleared his throat and said that, while he was really enjoying the food and the company, he was concerned that they needed to focus on the fugitive.

"No hurry," the commander responded. "We are putting the operation in place. Things are under control. Have a glass of wine."

The commander and his deputies sat facing Furukawa, Biondani and Belhaj. Pescatore was on one end, the odd man out. He stayed quiet and ate. He stole a glance at Belhaj, next to him. She was looking good in black: boots, jeans, blouse, and a sleeved garment over the shoulders that, as a result of intel acquired during his engagement to Isabel, he knew was called a shrug. He was having trouble figuring out Belhaj. Although a stickler for formalities, she had little time for small talk. Her silences bordered on aloofness. Yet she had a sense of humor and turned on the charm in a flash. She clearly enjoyed the team spirit that had developed with Furukawa and Pescatore.

After coffee, the commander got down to business. The safe house was twenty minutes away. Kharroubi had two armed bodyguards. Police and intelligence officers had surrounded the hideout.

"Let's go see if we can find some trouble," the commander said.

The day had clouded over. The fog had thickened. A line of

police vehicles idled in the courtyard. Two pickup trucks carried a tactical team in baseball caps and paramilitary jumpsuits. They had assault rifles and machete-type weapons in their belts. A small helicopter with a bubble-shaped cockpit whirred to life on a nearby pad.

Biondani and Furukawa got in one police sedan, Pescatore and Belhaj in another. Their minder was named Aldo: a mustachioed, weather-beaten supervisor in a down coat that accentuated his width. He toted a shotgun. He acted delighted about having to babysit dignitaries. He helped them strap on armored vests, held the door of the aging blue sedan for Belhaj, and clapped Pescatore on the back as he got in.

The convoy drove past rows of well-kept brick homes with barred windows, security cameras, spiked ornamental fences. The neighborhood ended abruptly in a prairie of muddy lots where multicolored buses, vans and taxis picked up and dropped off passengers. The commuters hunched against the wind, silhouettes plodding over misty terrain. Many of them were Bolivian and Paraguayan immigrants coming off morning work shifts. Their breath steamed beneath hoods and wool caps. They watched the police go by. The city limit of Buenos Aires was the border between illusions of Europe and the reality of Latin America.

Aldo had his front passenger-side window open, unbothered by the icy wind. He alternated between talking into a handheld radio and the microphone of the dashboard radio. They entered a slum. The streets turned narrow and dusty; many were unpaved. The sidewalks were high and the buildings low, a dense patchwork of brick, wood, stucco and tin. They passed a grocery with hand-painted signs announcing empanadas, and an automotive-repair complex where a gaunt Doberman paced the roof.

The safe house was a narrow bungalow with barred windows. There was a yard and a warren of sheds and huts visible behind it. By the time Pescatore's car pulled up, armed officers had stormed the bungalow, but their stances were relaxed. The chief of the tactical team stood talking to his men in the open front doorway. The helicopter appeared. Neighbors stuck heads out of windows.

Pescatore went up to Furukawa and asked what was going on.

"They hit the place, but no one was home."

Just then, a dozen radios erupted in vehicles, belts and hands: the sounds of a siren, gunfire, a distorted voice shouting about pulling a trigger.

Everybody whirled. The crisp urgent tone of a female radio dispatcher cut through the racket: "*¡Enfrentamiento a mano armada! ¡Enfrentamiento a mano armada!*"

A shootout. They scrambled back into the vehicles and took off in an uproar of sirens and brakes and tires. The speeding caravan churned sheets of dust into the fog.

The three suspects were in a Ford Falcon. They had rammed a squad car a few blocks away, opened fire, and fled. Ear to the radio, Aldo exclaimed gleefully: "*Epah!* How about that! They have a FAL!"

The speed and rough terrain sent Pescatore sliding into Belhaj. He clung to an overhead handle. The caravan split up, taking different routes. The police sedan careened uphill out of the slum onto a major paved road, skidded wildly, and almost got broadsided by a rusty tow truck. The tow truck went into a spin, horn blaring. Aldo pounded his driver's arm, urging him to go faster. The two-lane road had no divider. Traffic slowed ahead. Instead of braking, the driver whipped into the wrong lane and stomped the gas. It felt as if the back wheels were lifting off the pavement. Oncoming cars swerved desperately to get out of the way, lurching onto the shoulder, fleeting glimpses of faces congealed in fear and anger behind windshields. The sedan hit a pothole with a resounding bang. The jaw-jarring impact knocked the police radio right off the dashboard. Aldo whooped and thumped the driver again.

Crazy fuckers, Pescatore thought. *Either we crash or they drive us right into a volley of machine-gun fire.*

The sedan rattled. The driver slalomed back and forth, cursing and blasting the siren. The traffic got worse. The civilian drivers pulled over slowly and resentfully.

Pescatore told Belhaj, "You'd think with the sirens and everything, they'd get out of the way."

Overhearing the comment, Aldo spun around. He was holding the shotgun with the barrel out the window. Tendons bulged in his neck.

"You see?" he demanded furiously. "You see how they don't give us the ball?"

The next thing Pescatore knew, Aldo had lunged halfway out his window. He brandished his shotgun at cars. He banged a fist on the side of a van. His hair streamed in the wind.

"Get out of the way, sons of whores!" he bellowed. "Move, move, your mother's cunt!"

Pescatore saw the helicopter whiz overhead. The driver hunched over the wheel to keep it in sight. The sedan followed other police vehicles swinging off the main road. They barreled across a wooden bridge over a filthy creek bed. Clumps of trees and overgrown fields ended at the walls of an abandoned factory. It had tall shattered windows and rusty cylindrical tanks: a ghost hulk in the fog. The driver hit the brakes. Pescatore and Belhaj were tossed against the front seat.

"Everybody fine?" Aldo demanded. "Let's go!"

They tumbled out. The fugitives had abandoned the Ford Falcon in a ditch, its tail fins sticking up at an angle, and taken off in three directions. Cops gave chase on foot. Pescatore heard gunfire near the factory gates, where the helicopter was circling.

Aldo plunged left into the tangled vegetation of a field. Pescatore and Belhaj followed. They crashed through waist-high weeds wreathed in fog. Cold air slammed Pescatore's lungs. He ran stiffly in the heavy armored vest, puffing breath clouds.

Shots echoed in the distance. He thought he heard the chatter of the FAL automatic rifle. He kept going, head low. He cursed the federal police once again for confiscating his gun. Aldo veered toward a stand of trees in the distance by a stone wall, converging with other officers. They were hot on the trail of a suspect.

"Careful, careful," a voice said. "He's right here somewhere."

The officers slowed. They advanced in crouches behind their guns. Aldo scanned the high weeds like a duck hunter, shotgun poised. The underbrush made Pescatore wish for one of the machetes the tactical boys carried. He saw Belhaj on his right, moving gracefully in her high boots. She was also unarmed.

Pescatore had an unpleasant epiphany. In his vest, he looked like a cop. Their quarry was hiding in the weeds, so close they might step on him. If the gunman had any street savvy, he knew the officers would open fire no matter what his intentions. His only chance of survival was to take a hostage, a frequent underworld tactic fomented by the trigger-happy tendencies of the police. And he would grab the closest dumbass without a gun.

Sure enough, it happened.

To Belhaj.

Pescatore saw a blur of motion on his right. The gunman erupted out of the weeds like a diver coming up for air. He pounced on Belhaj and got her in a choke hold. He had a broken nose, a goatee, and a shaven brown pate—one of Kharroubi's bodyguards. He crouched behind Belhaj and jammed his pistol against her head.

"Get back or I clean this *rati* whore!" the gunman screamed. "I'll blow her brains out."

Aldo and the other officers took aim from three sides. Pescatore was the closest to Belhaj and the gunman, only about ten feet away. He spread his hands so the gunman could see they were empty.

Aldo ordered the gunman to drop his weapon. The gunman told Aldo to fuck himself. He tightened his forearm against Belhaj's throat.

"Get back, *ratis*!"

Pescatore knew that if he didn't act fast, Belhaj would die at the hands of the gunman or the police or both.

He stepped forward, arms high in surrender.

"Look at me," he told the gunman. "I'm not armed. Listen to me. Don't shoot, whatever you do. Listen to me, I'm your only chance."

Terror distorted the gunman's face. He jammed the pistol into her neck.

"Get back or she's dead!"

"Don't do it," Pescatore said. He took another step forward. His goal was to get him to point the pistol away from Belhaj. "Look at me, man, I'm trying to save your life!"

Pescatore saw more cops closing in and, as if he didn't have enough problems, creating a potential crossfire.

"Don't shoot," he implored them. "Give this man room. He's going to do the right thing if we let him."

Pescatore took another step. The helicopter swooped above them, whining like a big angry insect. The rotor wind whipped the weeds. The gunman glanced up in panic, eyes bulging in their sockets.

Come on, aim at me, you skull-faced psycho, Pescatore thought. *You can do it.*

He edged to his left. He calculated that the gunman would shoot at him before Belhaj in order to preserve his human shield. He caught Belhaj's eye. Her look told him she was going to make a move.

"Listen to me now!" Pescatore roared, taking one more step.

The pistol shifted to point at Pescatore. Belhaj threw an elbow in her captor's face, staggering him, and broke free. Pescatore lunged. He saw the barrel spew flame and felt a sledgehammer blow against his chest and then he was tackling Belhaj and driving her down into the weeds. Shots rang out as the two of them hit the mud. They rolled twice and he landed heavily on top of her and stayed there, shielding her.

The barrage lasted awhile. When the shooting and the shouting finally stopped, when the roar of the helicopter receded, Pescatore came to the conclusion that they were still alive.

His mouth was full of Belhaj's hair. He had gotten involuntary intimate confirmation that she was firm as well as curvaceous. He untangled himself from her.

"You all right?" he asked, sitting up.

Kneeling, she pulled matted curls back from her face. She was breathing fast. Her eyes were huge. Her clothes were smeared with mud. When she spoke, however, her voice was pretty steady.

"I am fine. And you?"

He followed her gaze to his own torso. It was as if he were looking down from a great height. Slowly, his fingers probed the spot where the bullet had hit him. He touched the mangled slug encrusted in the vest. He could not find blood or damage. Pain flared in his midsection. The impact would no doubt leave a bruise. But the body armor had done its job.

"Got me right in the ten ring." His laugh was shaky. "That's what vests are for, right?"

Moving slowly, tentatively, he and Belhaj helped each other to their feet. They swayed together like drunkards. She put an arm around his neck and gave him a brief hard hug. She spoke in his ear as if telling him a secret.

"Thank you."

"Thank you too," he said, feeling dizzy and warm. "You played it just right. And we got lucky."

The gunman had staggered several yards and fallen at the

edge of the trees. Cops surrounded the body. A youthful officer in a uniform sweater walked in circles, hands on narrow hips, looking up at the sky and then bending over. He was trying not to throw up. Aldo stood examining the corpse with workmanlike nonchalance, his shotgun over his shoulder. He greeted a pudgy uniformed sergeant who held a revolver.

"Che, polaco," Aldo said to the sergeant. "All good?"

"All good."

The two officers leaned over the corpse and exchanged kisses on the cheek.

Pescatore and Belhaj approached the dead gunman. He lay sprawled on his back, a long arm flung up above his head. He wore a tracksuit and mud-stained high-tops with no socks. An extra ammunition magazine for his pistol protruded from one of his shoes. The body was a mess, but the corpse's face was relatively unscathed.

The gunman's voice echoed in Pescatore's head. He had called them *ratis*. Pescatore remembered what the word meant. The origin was *tira,* a strap once worn on police uniforms. Jailhouse slang scrambled letters; *tira* became *rati*.

"See that on his forehead?" he asked Belhaj. "A prayer mark?"

She crouched. *"Oui. Une zebiba."*

"He looks Argentine. No beard."

"But the *zebiba* suggests a devout Islamist. A convert."

"That's what I'm thinking. By way of prison, maybe."

The officers made a fuss over Pescatore and Belhaj. They put a lot of ceremony into making sure their guests were unharmed. They dusted them off, praising their bravery and professionalism. The group trudged back through the field to the road. Pescatore lay down on the hood of a squad car. A dull ache expanded in his chest and ribs.

I just got the bandage off my head and now this, he thought. *Raymond's going to be the death of me.*

105

Furukawa hurried up. He turned pale when he heard their story.

"You know what kind of international interagency cluster fuck I'd have to go through if you got killed?" he declared. "You two need to cut that shit out."

"Did they catch Kharroubi?" Pescatore asked.

"The SWAT team smoked them both."

"There goes the best lead, right? Except for Raymond, everybody we know about who's connected to the attack is dead."

Belhaj got a ferocious look on her face. She was coming to grips with what had just happened—and almost happened.

"Was this what you call an operetta?" she asked. "They have silenced them intentionally?"

She had a point. The commander had said the safe house was under surveillance and the area was surrounded. Yet Kharroubi and his men had managed to get to their car and break through the perimeter. The police could have engineered it to finish them off during hot pursuit.

"Biondani said these guys were helping in good faith," Furukawa muttered uneasily. "I'd like to believe him. But you're getting the hang of how things work around here."

Ansiedad

When Pescatore showed up at the U.S. embassy the next morning, Belhaj called him Valentín instead of Monsieur Valentín. She didn't say much else, but her smile was enough to make his day.

Furukawa, meanwhile, looked glum. Kharroubi's death had been a setback. The SIDE spy agency was convinced that Raymond had been the conduit between foreign masterminds and the local cell. Other than Florencia's account, however, there was little evidence to rebut the official version of a homegrown plot.

Furukawa announced that he wanted to try a long shot. He asked Pescatore to write an e-mail to the Argentine address that Raymond had given him. Stepping aside to let Pescatore sit at his desktop computer, he said to keep the note short and general.

In the e-mail, Pescatore told Raymond that he hoped he was all right and urged him to get in touch as soon as possible. He wanted to help Raymond and was working with people who could lend a hand, but Raymond had to make contact if he wanted that to happen. Pescatore gave him all his phone numbers.

Reading over his shoulder, Furukawa suggested adding a personal touch.

"Like what?"

"Something only you would know. To prove it's you writing."

Pescatore thought for a minute.

"We both liked old movies when we were kids. Gangster films, Westerns. We saw *Rio Bravo* a dozen times."

"Mention that, *órale*."

Pescatore remembered the movie: John Wayne played Sheriff John T. Chance. Dean Martin played Dude, his alcoholic deputy. They holed up in the local jail and fought off a town full of enemies.

I figure you're probably feeling like John T. alone in the jail right now, Pescatore wrote. *Or maybe more like Dude; he was the singer. Anyway, bro, you need some backup.*

Furukawa nodded. Pescatore hit the Send button. He said, "There you go. It's a long shot, all right."

"Hey, if the guy really reached out to you before, there's always the chance he'll do it again."

The next item on the agenda was a meeting with one of Raymond's cousins: Professor Jorge Takiedinne. Although Takiedinne had already been interviewed by the SIDE, Furukawa and Belhaj wanted to hear his account firsthand. Takiedinne received them at home in the Belgrano neighborhood. The somber apartment was crammed with antiques and carved wood furniture. Takiedinne did research on infectious diseases. The walls of his study displayed awards, diplomas, and a large glass case containing specimens of tropical parasites: a nightmare gallery of miniature monsters—with antennae, tentacles, shells—that had apparently been removed from people's guts.

The professor's courtesy did not conceal his resentment. He had a glossy head of hair and a handlebar mustache. He was a younger cousin of Raymond's mother. There was a family resemblance in the hard, intelligent eyes above high cheekbones. Raymond had lived with the professor and his wife for a few months before finding his own place. Takiedinne acknowledged sending Raymond to the Kharroubi family for help with immigration issues. He knew the Kharroubis because they had once consulted him about a medical issue. The professor said that Raymond was pleasant but private. After Raymond moved out, his relatives saw him for occasional meals and visits and eventually lost contact with him. When the FBI agent interrupted to ask about Raymond's religious conversion, Takiedinne got riled up.

"All I know is that he converted," he declared. "A legitimate decision by a restless young man with an impressive intellect. I am doing my civic duty and answering your questions. I was horrified by the attacks. I personally know someone who was hurt. Yet it seems that terrorism is in the eye of the beholder. The rich and powerful nations decide who the terrorists are, who the war criminals are, who can plant bombs and commit assassinations. As I tell my Jewish colleagues: If you are Jewish and support Israel, that's fine. If you are Lebanese, and you mention that Hezbollah has defended the nation and helped the poor, you are a terrorist, a fiend."

"No one is saying anything like that, Professor," Furukawa said. "We're trying to understand who or what might have driven this young man to become radicalized."

"I am not an expert on Islam. I am a nonpracticing Catholic. That does not stop your airport police from asking tiresome, stupid, insulting questions every time I go to an academic conference in the United States. Apparently, there are few offenses more grave in your country than having an Arab name."

Furukawa expressed his disappointment that terrorism had forced the United States, a country of immigrants, to become less welcoming.

"Have those elements ever caught a real terrorist?" Takiedinne snorted. "Have you seen that science-fiction movie

Brazil? Those brutes barking at people and arresting the innocent? That's what your airports are like. The gates of an empire
in decay."

Pescatore's abdomen still hurt from getting shot in the vest.
He was in no mood to listen to disrespect of the U.S.A., not to
mention of his former coworkers at Customs and Border Protection. He interrupted to point out that, as a matter of fact,
U.S. airport inspectors had been instrumental in catching terrorists: from the would-be twentieth hijacker in the September
11 plot to the Times Square bomber.

"And who are you, exactly, young man?" Takiedinne demanded, his nostrils flaring over the formidable mustache.

"I'm an old friend of Raymond's from Chicago," Pescatore
said, returning the stare. "I've known him since I was little. His
parents too. We think Raymond is in serious danger. We want
to find him before it's too late."

Takiedinne frowned. "You know Lydia?"

"When I was a kid, I spent a lot of time running in and out of
her kitchen." Pescatore allowed himself a grin. "The best empanadas I ever ate."

The professor's eyes softened. He asked questions about Raymond's childhood. Pescatore was pretty sure he was being
tested to see if he was telling the truth. Takiedinne sighed.

"I wish I could help," he said. "At a certain point, Raymond
made a decision to distance himself from us. We had a warm
rapport. He went in a different and unfortunate direction."

"Do you mean his friendship with Kharroubi?" Pescatore
said. "And Florencia Pucinski?"

"In general. I have not seen Raymond since he moved away."

"But it sounds like he cared too much about you to just dis-
appear. You never heard from him again, sir? A phone call? An
e-mail?"

"A postcard," Takiedinne said at last. "About two years ago.
From Lebanon. He had visited the village near Tripoli, in the

north, where our family comes from originally. He sent a card with a brief greeting. I no longer have it, I am afraid."

The summary of the SIDE interview had not mentioned a postcard from Lebanon. Not the kind of thing they would leave out. Takiedinne turned to Furukawa, showing his teeth without smiling.

"That detail slipped my mind during my conversation with the authorities," he said. "Something about the way your colleague asked me just now stirred my memory. Strange, no?"

Takiedinne did not give up any other nuggets. After the interview, Furukawa and Belhaj held a brief whispered conference on the street. Then they told Pescatore they had business to attend to at their embassies. They needed him to make himself scarce.

He didn't mind. He was tired and sore and wanted to think. He went to a café and ordered a *milanesa a la napolitana:* a breaded steak with ham and melted mozzarella cheese on top. Comfort food. His father had joked about the irony of the Argentines coming up with a dish that united northern snobby Milan and southern rowdy Naples.

Pescatore ate slowly and thought about what he'd learned so far. If the Buenos Aires plot was not homegrown, where did Raymond fit in? Did his visit to Lebanon mean anything? Though Shiite Hezbollah dominated Lebanon, Sunni al-Qaedist groups operated in the north of the country and in Syria and Iraq. Raymond was Sunni—as were the others in the Buenos Aires terrorist cell. But Kharroubi had been a Shiite.

Pescatore went home, put an ice pack on his midsection, and dozed. When he woke up, he decided to check out the club in San Telmo where Raymond had wooed Florencia. Not because he expected to turn up hot leads; he just hoped for more details of Raymond's life in the city.

Pescatore spent the cab ride scanning the traffic for surveillance. He spotted a motorcycle and a Renault sedan that might or might not have been tails. The federal police were probably shadowing him. Maybe the Americans and the French too, hedging their bets about his reliability. And, what the heck, why not the Israelis for good measure.

He remembered reading a quote by an author named Taibo: "A paranoid Mexican is someone who is sure he is being followed, and about to get screwed, and he is right."

That's me, homes, Pescatore thought, slumped in the seat, his head low in the collar of the leather jacket. *A paranoid half Mexican. And the other half is paranoid too.*

The corner club was on the fringe of the cobblestoned historic district of San Telmo. The heart of the area was Plaza Dorrego, where vintage nightspots offered tango revues with orchestras and dance troupes. This club was more modest. A step-down entrance led to a narrow, smoky interior half a floor below street level. Overhead fans and a titanic espresso machine with an eagle statue on top made it feel like a neighborhood joint.

The place was almost empty. A pianist and bandoneon player warmed up onstage playing a lazy version of "Libertango," the Astor Piazzolla classic. Jazzy piano chords anchored the lament of the bandoneon. Pescatore listened, savoring his rum and Coke.

The waitress wore her multitinted hair Rasta-style. Her T-shirt depicted Che Guevara wearing a Che Guevara T-shirt and exposed her flat belly. After ordering a second drink, Pescatore told her he was looking for an old friend, a singer who had performed at the club seven or eight years ago.

"Before my time, *gordo*." She called him "fats" in the Argentine way, a term of endearment rather than an insult. "I'll ask the muchachos. They've been around for years."

The muchachos were the musicians. Within a couple of minutes, they wrapped up their rehearsal, sat down at Pescatore's table, and accepted his offer of drinks. They gave no indication that the police or the SIDE had come by asking about Raymond. By now, Pescatore was used to the name causing people to get pained, angry or frightened looks on their faces, yet the musicians reacted with enthusiasm. They had played gigs with Raymond and seen him often at the club.

"What a great guy," exclaimed Nestor, the bandoneon player, tossing back long hair. "We used to have fun with his imitations. Bocha, remember when he would do Nat King Cole? 'Ansiedad'?"

"Of course, *loco,*" said the pianist, a chunky, sleepy-eyed mulatto from Uruguay. "A genius."

Bocha crooned a verse of "Ansiedad" ("Anxiety"), approximating the velvet tone in which Cole had mispronounced Spanish—especially the *o*'s—so beautifully. Bocha and Nestor broke up laughing. Pescatore joined in. He liked these guys, and he wanted to keep the conversation going.

"That Raymond was something," Nestor said. "Very talented."

"Perhaps not the best pianist." Bocha grimaced apologetically, as if compelled to put that evaluation on the record.

"He used to tell me he was basically faking it on the piano," Pescatore said. "He said he played just well enough to get into trouble."

Bocha chuckled. "That's about right. What is he up to these days?"

"I don't know," Pescatore said. "I was hoping you could help me."

Pescatore explained that Raymond's family had lost touch with him. Because of Pescatore's Argentine connections and investigative experience, he had agreed to help look for Raymond. He was worried about his friend. Although all that was technically true, Pescatore felt sneaky. Once he mentioned law enforcement, he expected the musicians to get nervous. They didn't. He realized that they lived in a simpler, more civilized world than he did. They were cool and open-minded and presumed others were the same way.

The musicians said Raymond had been a fixture at the club, performing or hanging out, during his first two years in town. His onstage persona was a hit—he introduced numbers in *porteño* Spanish, then sang in bona fide American—and he became a minor celebrity. He was affectionate and generous. Bocha told an anecdote about Raymond loaning money to a waitress who had gotten evicted then refusing to let her repay him.

"He probably ended up hitting on her, though, right?" Pescatore asked cautiously.

"No, *che,* he was a real gentleman," Bocha said. "He told her this place was like home for him, we were like family. He didn't talk about it much, but he was recovering from a drug problem. The music helped him get clean."

The musicians recalled Flo Pucinski vividly and Kharroubi vaguely. The more Florencia and Kharroubi came around, the less Raymond played regular gigs. He said he was traveling a lot on business. Eventually, he stopped playing any gigs at all. On rare visits to the club, he talked about having discovered Islam.

"He said he loved music, but he also loved his religion," Nestor said, shrugging. "A personal issue, of course, so you don't interfere. It was a shame he had to make that kind of choice."

Bocha had been rubbing his goatee. He opened and closed his mouth. He sipped beer. He rubbed the goatee again. Pescatore waited.

"You know," Bocha said at last. "I can't be sure, but this year I thought I saw him. A strange thing."

Bocha paused. Pescatore got impatient and said, "Really?"

"I hadn't thought about it for a while," Bocha said. "I remember I was on a break between sets. I was out on the sidewalk, having, eh, a smoke."

Nestor grinned. Assessing Bocha's watery gaze, it occurred to Pescatore that the pianist had gone outside to smoke a joint.

"It was drizzling," Bocha continued. "I was about to go back inside. Then I had that sensation, you know, when someone is looking at you? There was a car across the street, a guy at the wheel. Watching. It startled me. It was dark, but the face was familiar. I thought, *Che, I know who that looks like: Raymond, the American singer.* I took a step forward. I might have waved. But the car started up and took off fast."

"So you are pretty sure it was him?"

"Hard to say. The dark, the reflection, the rain. If it was Raymond, I think he would have acknowledged me."

Pescatore tried to pin down the date. He asked Bocha to remember gigs, travel, holidays. The conclusion: the possible sighting of Raymond had happened between six weeks and three months ago.

After another round, the musicians thanked him and returned to the stage. Pescatore had been expecting them to tell him about hustles, drug deals, seductions. But Raymond had been a model citizen at the club. He had shown his good side, had even kept his mitts off the waitresses. At least for a while, he had done what Pescatore had always urged him to do: stick to the music. Maybe Raymond wasn't good enough to get rich, but he certainly could have made a living.

If I could sing, Pescatore told himself, *I'd be happy in joints like this.*

He had no doubt that the man whom the pianist had seen in the car was Raymond. The timing matched Florencia's story. Pescatore could see the scene: Raymond comes back to Buenos Aires. He's operational, deep into a terrorist plot, whether as an accomplice or an agent for somebody. But he can't resist passing by the club one night. Raymond sits in the car. He thinks about going inside, looking for old friends, listening for a while.

115

He sees Bocha, which brings back memories. Bocha spots him. Raymond panics and drives away.

Pescatore was now more inclined to believe that Raymond might not have wanted to go through with the plot. Maybe he had been wrestling with doubt and guilt.

Pescatore gulped rum and Coke. He was drinking too much these days.

His cell phone buzzed on his hip. A text message. Furukawa.

The FBI agent wanted to see him right away. He named a location. It was urgent.

Pescatore doubted that a sudden street meeting at eleven p.m. could involve good news.

9

Heart Won't Tell a Lie

The night had turned cold.

Closing the door of the taxi, he shivered. The air was clearing the rum out of his head.

Furukawa was waiting for him at a downtown corner next to an illegally parked Chevrolet Suburban with diplomatic plates. The FBI agent wore a belted coat over a turtleneck. He greeted Pescatore, jerked his head, and started walking. He didn't say anything for three blocks. He walked fast, turning left onto Nueve de Julio Avenue. His driver, a crew-cut Special Forces–looking guy, followed them on foot at a distance.

Furukawa stopped to light a cigarette, eyes narrow. He headed south toward the Obelisk, back toward where they had started.

The whole deal was weird. The hour. Furukawa's silence. Belhaj's absence.

"I got your passport back," Furukawa said. Without breaking stride, he handed over an envelope.

"Thanks, Tony."

Pescatore stuck the envelope in an inside pocket of his jacket. With profound relief, he zipped shut the pocket. He was no longer, as Belhaj had put it, an orphan in the modern world.

"Think seriously about using it." The agent's voice was dry.

"Like leave the country?"

Furukawa kept walking, smoking, staring straight ahead.

"Yep. Things are getting complicated. The local level and the Washington level. D.C. headquarters is going to take over the Ray Mercer aspect. I'm going to restrict myself to liaison duties. That's what leeg-atts are supposed to do. That ends your involvement."

"Why?"

Furukawa took a fierce drag on the cigarette. "I need to spell it out?"

"Um…I guess I have a theory."

"Which is?"

"I figure the more you guys find out about Raymond, the more sensitive it gets. Because he used to work for the U.S. government."

"I've dealt with guys like him." Furukawa sighed in disgust. "A disaster waiting to happen. The better an informant is, the more he gets into the shit. The more you worry. If he was my snitch, I'd have his deactivation papers all written up. He gets arrested for some outrageous nonsense at midnight, I'm good to go: I type in he was deactivated at noon."

"So am I right?"

"Mercer's narcotics cooperation evolved. Several agencies had contact."

"Maybe he still has connections now."

"If he does, why did he call you?"

"Good point."

"His whole file is under review. Multiagency. Who knew what when, who signed what agreement, all those career-killer-type questions."

They neared the circular plaza where the Obelisk rose above the epic urban event that was the convergence of Corrientes and Nueve de Julio Avenues. Light emanated from the stores, the giant video screens, and the neon brand names scrawled across facades and roofs. The sidewalk was almost as bright as day. Traffic roared in the roundabout; crowds filled the sidewalks; music spilled out of doorways.

Pescatore heard distant guitar chords from a store. It sounded like "Heart Won't Tell a Lie," by Los Lonely Boys. He had discovered the Texican band after joining the Border Patrol. Los Lonely Boys made him homesick for San Diego. Where he had been homesick for Chicago. Apparently, another city was about to join the list of former places of residence.

Take a good look around, he thought with disbelief. *Say good-bye. The man just delivered the news. Buenos Aires is over.*

Pescatore asked: "Do they know where Raymond is?"

"Nope."

"We should keep working this. We're a great team. Just tonight I—"

"*Se acabó.* No more Three Amigos."

"What if he reaches out again?"

Furukawa fired a sidelong look at him.

Of course they'll know, and fast, Pescatore thought, chiding himself. *No doubt they've opened up on me. Monitoring my phones, e-mails. I thought I was paranoid before.*

"If they need you, they'll find you," Furukawa said. "I put my contact info in that envelope. You hear from Raymond, call me right away."

The agent turned left, back onto Roque Sáenz Peña, which ran on a diagonal toward the Plaza de Mayo, the site of the presidential palace. They left the lights and noise behind. Pescatore checked to make sure no one was within earshot.

"You mind explaining why I need to leave town all of a sudden?" He hated the tremor he heard in his own voice. "I can understand you want me to back off, but this is kinda drastic."

"It's getting ugly. Political. The SIDE wants to take over the case. The police want to shut it down, squash the Raymond and Florencia angle. It might end up with two judges fighting

119

over the investigation. The government is shaky. You'd be in the middle of a political war."

"I could help the intel guys. Testify about Raymond."

"Chances are you'll get stomped."

"I don't like the idea of running."

"Did you like getting locked up?" Furukawa snapped. "You clocked an investigator, remember that bright little move? They're still looking for an excuse to charge you. Nothing has changed that."

"But I explained the French phone calls. There's no evidence—"

"Yeah, uh-huh. Big obstacle if they need a fall guy. Especially an American. We're losing popularity in this part of the world, case you hadn't noticed."

They had reached the parked Suburban. The driver slid behind the wheel. Furukawa opened a door.

"And my job?" Pescatore asked. "I got responsibilities. A life here."

"Facundo will understand."

"What does Fatima say?"

Furukawa rolled his eyes. His oval face shimmered in the glow of the streetlights. "She's disappointed. She thinks you're our best shot at Raymond Mercer, we should stick close to you. I don't disagree. But I have orders."

"Where is she?"

"Bolivia. As far as I know."

"Bolivia?"

"Chasing a lead."

"I'd like to talk—"

"Don't think I didn't notice the vibe between you two."

Pescatore's eyes widened. He was surprised, a bit offended, and ultimately pleased that Furukawa perceived a vibe from Belhaj directed at him. Pescatore thought she must have left for Bolivia right after the interview with the cousin. She hadn't given any hint. Her manner had led him to think there was a trust, a friendship, an attraction—something—between them.

"You're adults," Furukawa continued. "It's your business. But I think you should let it go. Your life is complicated enough right now. Go home, *vato*."

The FBI agent tossed away his cigarette. Pescatore had the premonition that he would never see him again. He was being abandoned on a cold, dark street to fend for himself.

"Listen, I'm sorry I had to drop a bomb on you like this, Valentine," Furukawa said. "You're a nice kid. But your boy has pulled you down into the shit. I need to step back. I suggest you do the same."

Furukawa shook his hand, got in the Suburban, and left.

Back at his apartment, Pescatore paced. He looked at airline schedules on his iPhone. Flights to Miami, to Los Angeles via Lima. His clothes would fit in a couple of suitcases. His mind spun through scenarios. If the federal police had issued an immigration lookout for him, he would walk into their clutches at the airport. He thought about asking Furukawa to ensure safe passage. Or maybe better just to slip out another way: take a hydrofoil ferry across the river to Uruguay, or leave overland to Chile.

He started getting mad. At the cops, Furukawa, Raymond, himself. He felt a responsibility to help. His work history for the federal government and Facundo qualified him as a trusted operative, a known player to U.S. authorities. His information had helped Furukawa and Belhaj. They needed him. He thought about how determined—in his grumpy way—Furukawa had been during the investigation. He had reversed direction fast. His D.C. bosses must have dropped a bomb of their own on him.

Pescatore decided to go to bed. To make up for the loss of his gun, he had bought a hunting knife and a baseball bat. He checked his home-defense arsenal. The knife was on the night table. The bat lay within arm's reach under the bed. Not that the weapons would be much use in another raid. Except to give the raiders an excuse to shoot him.

He lay awake, imagining a reunion with Inspector Neanderthal. Who could help if he got arrested again? Facundo's best connections were with the SIDE, the Israelis, and the Americans. Biondani's group in the SIDE would back Pescatore, but they were busy feuding with the police. Even if the Israelis stuck their necks out for him, they didn't have much clout. Worst of all, Furukawa had implied that he shouldn't count on the U.S. embassy.

For the first time in days, Pescatore thought about Isabel Puente. His ex-fiancée was probably the most powerful person he knew. She had a high-up job at Homeland Security. Probably enough juice to spring him from an Argentine prison. Isabel knew about his wild Chicago days, but he had never mentioned Raymond specifically. He could not imagine swallowing his pride and going to her for help.

As he drifted off, he told himself: *Face it. You're on your own, bro. If you stick around, you aren't going to help anybody. You'll make it worse. You'll end up where Uncle Rocco always worried you'd end up: the joint.*

He had intended to reserve a flight before visiting Facundo, but he overslept. He hadn't done that for a long time. Shortly before noon, he hurried to the hospital. Sawhorses blocked streets; police lined up on foot and in cars. Something was going on. As he crossed a plaza, a polite young couple handed him a flyer. The guy wore a Star of David on a gold chain; the woman wore little designer glasses and called him *compañero*. They urged him to attend a combined memorial and protest for the one-week anniversary of the attacks. He explained that he was going to visit one of the victims in the hospital.

Esther met him outside her father's room, dressed for work.

"I know you two will talk about business, even though he's not supposed to," she said. "Please remember he remains in a delicate state. He shouldn't get agitated. He's going to have surgery in a few days."

"Of course."

When talking about Facundo to his grandson, Pescatore had compared him to a bear. The resemblance—to a graying, bedraggled, Sephardic bear—had intensified. Facundo sat in bed propped against pillows, sniping at the television with a remote control. A new salt-and-pepper beard complemented his unkempt hair. His sleeveless green gown revealed the forest on his chest and arms.

"Valentín," Facundo said, his voice at about half the usual power. "Son."

Pescatore bent to give him a clumsy hug. It was hard to see Facundo laid low. And to know this was probably good-bye. Pescatore forced a smile.

"How are you, boss?"

"As you see." Facundo emitted a morose growling noise.

"To tell the truth, better than I expected," Pescatore said.

Facundo's gestures and expressions had a torpid quality. He was disturbingly pale.

"The doctors are compiling a list of all the things that are prohibited to me from now on," he rasped. "Cigarettes, coffee, alcohol, ice cream, *medialunas, dulce de leche*—in short, every decent kind of food—talking excessively, getting upset or excited. They didn't mention sex, but since it is a good thing, I fear the worst. Meanwhile, my sweet little daughter, I discover to my amazement, has a future as a prison warden if she ever gets bored with architecture. She won't even let me talk on the phone."

"They are taking care of you. You had a massive heart attack."

"A massive indignity, is what it is. Who wants an existence like this? Nooo. From what I understand, I am alive and kvetching because of you. I have to thank—"

"Don't mention it. Biondani and me teamed up."

Facundo drank water from a plastic cup. His head sagged back. He stared past Pescatore at the television, which was on mute.

"A memorial," Facundo muttered. "Can you believe a week went by?"

"Feels like yesterday."

"I have lost my sense of time. Most of what I know about the case is from the news. An extremely unsatisfactory source. Lamentably low level. Nooo. For mental hygiene, almost better not to watch."

"You'll catch up when you're stronger."

"During a lapse on the part of my jailers, I managed to call my friend at La Biela. A brief conversation. I gather you have played an important role. Dario D'Ambrosio is impressed. But there are a million things I don't know or understand."

"You're not supposed to talk about work stuff. I promised Esther."

"*Et tu,* Valentín? Do you think it puts more strain on my heart to receive credible, helpful, specific information, or to continue like this—totally frustrated, depressed, and in the dark like a useless cretin?"

"It's a long story."

"Fortunately, I was able to clear my busy schedule for you. Have a seat, for the love of God. Take off your jacket."

Pescatore sat. He did not take off his jacket. He positioned his chair so they could both see the television. The screen showed images of a covered outdoor podium surrounded by a blue wall of police officers. Dignitaries wore black armbands. Umbrellas and signs sprouted from the crowd. The memorial service had begun, along with the rain.

"Please don't get worked up," Pescatore said.

"Go ahead!" Facundo exclaimed.

In Pescatore's experience, loud and talkative people tended to be bad listeners. Facundo was an exception. He could cut off the verbal torrent as if shutting a faucet. He sat very still. His barrel chest rose and fell with his labored breathing. Pescatore started with the prologue: the strange reunion with Raymond.

"Your friend sounds like a bit of a *chanta,*" Facundo commented mildly.

"*Chanta, chorro, atorrante,* all of that. I'll never forgive myself for not calling right away to tell you about him. If I had—"

"It would have made no difference."

"Still. I'm embarrassed I even knew a guy like him."

"We all have had inconvenient friends."

The response comforted Pescatore. For the first time in a week, he felt safe. His words would not be used against him. The story came pouring out: his arrest, the FBI and the French police, Flo, La Matanza, the club.

Facundo nodded. His furry eyebrows rose. He closed his eyes to concentrate. He murmured "How about that" and *"Epah."*

Pescatore ended with the warning from the FBI attaché.

"Out of the blue, boom! He tells me to shut it down or I'm going to jail," Pescatore said. Averting his gaze from Facundo, he added, "I'm thinking I need to take his advice and leave town for a while."

Facundo sighed. "Tony is a good man. He has had bad experiences with his bureaucracy. It sounds like he's following orders and trying to reduce any focus on Americans. I don't think they would arrest you. At worst, they might haul you in for another interrogation."

"I'm not looking forward to that."

"What I find interesting is the authorities have succeeded in keeping this business about Raymond a total secret. Let me understand: We do not know for a fact that it was your friend who called from the French phone?"

"No. But hardly anybody else had that number except you."

"What do we know about the dismantled cell in Bolivia?"

"Me, nothing. Furukawa said the Bolivian government barely talks to the Bureau. Or the Agency."

Facundo closed his eyes. He seemed winded. Pescatore waited until he opened them to pour him a glass of water. Facundo drank gratefully. He said, "And you think Raymond's purpose in calling you was…"

Pescatore folded his arms and crossed his legs at the ankles. "I'd like to think he called to warn me about what was going to happen. And I'm not saying that just because he used to be my best friend."

"You have mixed feelings now."

"Very mixed. Thanks to him, I've gotten locked up, beat down, shot, threatened, and practically kicked out of Argentina. But I'm trying to analyze it like you would. First of all, I assume it was Raymond who alerted somebody in Bolivia and called me. The night I saw him, he was torn up about something. Whether he ran into me on purpose or by accident, maybe he was sizing me up. Figuring out if he could use me to get out of his predicament. With Raymond, it's pretty much all about Raymond."

"If he is still an informant, someone could have pushed him forward."

"Like Tony said, if he's working for the Americans, why bother with me?"

"Individuals like this often have relationships with more than one government. There are intelligence services that for reasons of politics or tradecraft would want to sound the alarm indirectly. Using someone like Raymond."

Pescatore's gaze strayed to the television. An elderly bearded man in a yarmulke spoke into the microphones.

"Your assessment is largely psychological," Facundo said. "You have a unique knowledge of the subject. It is valuable and raises larger questions: Who is this interesting personage? Who is he affiliated with?"

"At first I thought Hezbollah and Iran did it and he's with them," Pescatore said. "After all, they hit Argentina twice before. Iran was the prime suspect for me. But I'm starting to wonder."

"Why?" Facundo's expression was approving but noncommittal.

"For one thing, he's Lebanese Sunni, not Shiite."

"There have been Sunnis recruited or manipulated by Iran."

"But Ortega, the cop, was in Pakistan with the Sunni al-Qaeda-type networks."

"Go on."

"This attack was big, like the Iranian Quds Force would do. But the style seems different. Taking over a soft target, shooting everybody up all crazy. That's more like al-Qaeda. And the car bomb failed. And they brought in suicide bombers at the last minute. For a state-sponsored op, that's a lot of hiccups."

"The Iranians have global reach, but in many cases they are inept and undisciplined. If it wasn't them, who was it?"

Pescatore was reminded of the times he had testified in court, gaining confidence as the questions gathered momentum. He answered, "Like you've told me: Most attacks are simpler and more amateurish than people think. So couldn't it be a bunch of radicalized criminals who come together on their own? They develop the plot, and then Ortega, and maybe Raymond, get them help and personnel from al-Qaeda groups overseas."

"And why do they strike in Bolivia and Argentina, of all places?"

"This is the territory they know. Opportunism."

"I like your analysis, the way you look at all the angles. But for me, Iran and Hezbollah are the ones who did it. They have the history, the regional infrastructure, the—"

Esther walked into the room. Her high heels clicked. She stared at Pescatore and her father, tight-lipped. Facundo gazed skyward.

"I know what you are going to say, dear," he said. "I feel stupendous."

"Valentín, he really needs to eat his lunch and rest." Esther ignored her father in a burlesque of exasperation.

"Absolutely," Pescatore said.

"Thank you for your eternal vigilance, my dear," Facundo murmured.

She blew him a stone-faced kiss and left.

"So Facundo," Pescatore began. "About what Furukawa said. I've been thinking, maybe a leave of absence—"

"Where's the damned remote?" Facundo pawed the sheets around him. "I know that girl, her family. Claudia Rabinovich. She lost her father and her son, poor thing."

Pescatore noticed that a dark-haired woman had taken the speaker's podium at the memorial service on television. He recognized her—in her forties, long bony features, a frozen stare—from TV and newspaper reports. Her family owned the delicatessen in the Almacén mall. On the morning of the attack, her teenage son had been working at the entrance, seating customers. Claudia Rabinovich had been with her father in a back office doing the books. She tried to send a fax from the office, but the machine malfunctioned. She left to send the fax from a nearby store. Her father went out to the front to help his grandson with the Friday lunch rush. The two suicide bombers charged in minutes later.

Facundo grunted, leaning perilously sideways to retrieve the remote control. People around Rabinovich wiped their eyes. A contingent of government officials on the stage, huddling together as if for warmth or safety, looked uncomfortable. The volume came up.

"I find myself here today, on this stage, surrounded by the police," the woman thundered. "Surrounded by all these representatives of the Interior Ministry, the security services, the presidential palace, the judiciary, the congress. But I do not feel safe. *We* do not feel safe. Listen to me well, ladies and gentlemen of the government. *We do not feel safe.*"

Applause. Insults shouted at politicians. Rabinovich pointed at the cordon of uniforms, at officials. She zeroed in on a Cabinet minister in charge of national security. He wore a trench coat. He had a ski tan, puffy lips and reinforced cheekbones supplied by a cosmetic surgeon, the thick sideburns favored by provincial politicos. He looked solemnly into the middle distance, as if he were giving her words deep thought. But his eyelids fluttered. Clearly, he was wishing for an escape hatch. The camera zoomed in on Rabinovich.

"We do not feel safe, because you are liars! We do not feel safe, because you are traitors! We do not feel safe, because you are criminals!"

Her wounded eloquence sent a chill through Pescatore. She recited a catalog of notorious crimes and cover-ups, including the unsolved attacks of the 1990s, and listed the contradictions and mysteries surrounding the attack at El Almacén: Were the police uniforms worn by the terrorists real or fake? Was the plot foreign or domestic? Pescatore marveled once again at what great speakers the Argentines were, regardless of age, class or education. They were fast, sharp, theatrical, funny, merciless. He loved to hear them talk.

The crowd echoed the refrain: "We do not feel safe!"

A man in a fedora, a leader of the Jewish community, leaned out of the crush of dignitaries. He patted the woman's shoulder and whispered.

"Oh, leave her in peace, you stooge," Facundo hissed. "Go tend your sleazy bank."

Rabinovich shook the man off, eyes blazing, voice reverberating.

"We do not feel safe! Because, by commission or omission, one way or another, you are all part of a monstrous system of corruption, impunity, cruelty, hatred, and, finally, terrorism! We do not feel safe! Because you have the blood of my father and my son, of our fathers and sons, our mothers and daughters, on your hands!"

She turned away abruptly. She wavered on her feet, steadied by people around her. The applause went on and on.

"God," Pescatore said. "She called those goons everything except pretty. I hope she has security."

Facundo killed the volume. "No one is going to hurt her."

The strangled disgust in his tone surprised Pescatore. "No?"

"No one is going to hurt her. You know why? She's brave, magnificent. But she's impotent. Next year, and the year after, and the year after that, there will be more anniversaries. More rallies. And she will speak. The same speech, more or less. Because nothing will have changed. At best, tangential arrests, meaningless indictments. Every year, she will give that speech. And nothing will change. For the people who did it, for the system that permitted it, she is a symbol of their impunity."

Facundo glowered. Pescatore raised a soothing hand.

"Who's going to solve it?" Facundo demanded. "Who cares? Dario is trying, but there's only so far he can go. The official version is written."

"Maybe the Americans, the Israelis…"

"There were no American victims. The Americans care only because of this Raymond matter. The Israelis will do what they can, but it is not their top priority, I assure you. Listen to me, Valentín. Unless someone does something extraordinary, in twenty years Claudia Rabinovich will be like the families of the

AMIA. Or like the Mothers of the Plaza de Mayo. Walking in circles, looking for justice, losing their way."

Pescatore imagined a gray-haired, bent-over Claudia Rabinovich at the microphones.

"That's terrible," he said.

Facundo had run out of steam. He took a catnap. Pescatore watched the rain falling outside the windows and on the screen.

Facundo stirred.

"What did you say before?" he asked hoarsely. "About Furukawa?"

"He wants me to get on a plane right away. Go home."

"Ah."

"He was pretty insistent."

"Ah."

"Made it sound like I'm in big trouble if I don't."

Facundo's eyes fastened on him. "And what do you want to do?"

Tell him, Pescatore thought. *Tell him you made up your mind. Time to get out of Dodge. You're real sorry, but you need to put serious distance between you and Raymond and this god-awful mess. You hereby resign. You turn in your badge. Tell him.*

Pescatore heard himself answer: "I'm not going home."

Facundo waited. Pescatore continued, "I know Raymond better than anybody. Sooner or later, I'll find him. Or he'll find me. Meanwhile, I want to reconstruct the parts of his life I don't know about. That will help explain the attacks. I'm not gonna sit waiting for the FBI to throw me a bone. I want to work this case."

Pescatore concluded that his decision had been worth it just to see the elation on Facundo's face. Still, he had the distinct notion that he had run to the edge of a cliff, stopped in time to save himself, then jumped anyway.

Facundo rubbed his hands together.

"And how," he asked, "do you propose we go about doing that?"

131

PART II

10

Gibraltar

They left for the jungle before dawn.

Belhaj slept. Enclosed in a sensory cocoon of sunglasses and the earbuds of her iPhone, she curled up against her door behind the driver's seat. The pose brought out her curves encased in a fitted fatigue jacket. Pescatore dozed intermittently against the opposite window.

The ride unfolded as if in a dream. The road climbed through the mountains toward the sunrise. Then it descended rapidly into the rain forest. The tapestry of hallucinatory beauty came alive with the day. The Toyota Land Cruiser raced downhill through cloud banks and sunshine, drizzle and rainbows. The asphalt got bumpier. The vehicle rattled and whined. The heat and humidity rose. The vegetation turned tropical: vines, spatters of flowers, canopies of green.

The spry little driver turned up the air conditioner. He pointed across the security officer from the French embassy, a fellow Bolivian with a razor-sharp part in his hair and a machine gun worn on a strap.

"Coca," the driver said.

Pescatore saw a tarpaulin covered with kelly-green leaves go by. He assumed that coca drying in the sun right by the road had to be the legal variety; the drug laws were complex in Bolivia.

The past twenty hours had been a blur. At the hospital in Buenos Aires, Pescatore and Facundo had agreed that Pescatore would continue the investigation however he could. Facundo would work sources by phone and e-mail after his surgery. His daughter in Miami, who handled his agency's finances, would keep paying Pescatore with the usual transfers to the bank in San Diego and wire him expense money if necessary. In addition, Facundo told him to go to the *cueva* and collect eight thousand dollars. Pescatore now carried the cash stuffed into the pockets of his black military-style vest like a smuggler.

"Be careful, Valentín," Facundo had said. "There are generally two kinds of terrorists: furious madmen and cold mercenaries. I think we are dealing with both."

As Pescatore left the hospital, it occurred to him that Tony Furukawa, like Pescatore himself, was not comfortable telling outright lies. The FBI agent had said that Fatima Belhaj was in Bolivia—"as far as I know." Pescatore jumped in a cab. Sure enough, he found the French investigator at her hotel preparing to check out; her flight to Bolivia was not scheduled to leave until that evening. His breathless arrival did not faze her. They talked over coffee on the hotel's executive floor overlooking Plaza San Martin and La Torre de los Ingleses, the Big Ben–style clock tower that—like polo and rugby—was a relic of British influence.

Pescatore had rehearsed a pitch in his head. He expected rebuttals and counterattacks. Belhaj surprised him by accepting on the spot.

"An excellent idea," she said. "We keep working together. I do not understand the logic of the FBI. I told Tony you are a resource that must not be discarded."

She told Pescatore why she was rushing to Bolivia. Although the Bolivians were keeping things quiet, the French embassy in La Paz had identified the tipster who had alerted authorities about the terrorist cell after receiving a call from France. The tipster had agreed to talk to Belhaj.

Pescatore blinked awake. The Land Cruiser had stopped in a police checkpoint beneath a wooden structure bridging the highway. The officers searching vehicles seemed cast from a toy-soldier mold: warrior faces, compact bodies in fatigues. They surrounded an ancient truck piled high with pineapples. The hood and doors were open. The officers appeared to be tearing the innards out of the dashboard. A group of female passengers stood to one side. They were Quechuas or Aymaras. They wore long dresses and straw hats decorated with ribbons.

An officer in a crisp uniform approached the Land Cruiser. The brim of his cap was low. After glancing at the foreign passports and embassy credentials, he waved them on. The driver and the embassy security man exchanged sotto voce comments about how only a fool would cross the police antidrug commandos known as the Leopards; they didn't play games and they could chase you through the jungle forever.

"Refreshed?" Belhaj asked Pescatore with a demure yawn. She pushed her sunglasses up into her hair.

"All good. Does this lady know I'm coming along, and who I am?"

"You are a colleague from Buenos Aires, *tout court*. If she asks your nationality, tell her. Otherwise, discretion is best."

"Okay," he said. "What are you listening to?"

"Abd al Malik. An enlightened French Muslim rap artist." She offered the earbuds. "The song is called 'Gibraltar.'"

He listened. "Cool. With that fast piano and drum, it's like spoken-word jazz."

"It is about a young man at the Strait of Gibraltar."

"Yeah, I think I got it. A black guy. He's going through all kinds of changes. First he's crying, then he's singing in a bar, right? Then he's yelling, all happy. He goes to the beautiful kingdom of Morocco."

She nodded, studying him quizzically. "Now you tell me you secretly speak French?"

"Not really. But I did take it in school. Ten years. I spoke Spanish already. My father, he thought French was classy. Raymond speaks it better than I do."

"Valentín Pescatore," she said, shaking her curls, accentuating the last syllable of the last name. *"Toujours plein de surprises."*

They had barely talked since Buenos Aires, where she had cut short the conversation to catch her flight. Pescatore had flown out hours later, entrusting the care of his apartment to Facundo's daughter. He tensed up in the immigration departure line at the Ezeiza airport, but the inspectors didn't give him a second look. He didn't know if that meant Furukawa had exaggerated, that someone had put in a good word, or neither of the above. He was so relieved about not getting arrested—and exhilarated about being back in the game—that it took a while to realize that his prospects for returning to Argentina were uncertain. In the Bolivian city of Cochabamba, he had found a note from Belhaj at the hotel instructing him to be ready at five a.m.

Belhaj lowered her sunglasses and gazed out the window. She asked, "Do you know Bolivia?"

"Not really," Pescatore said. "I did a case with Facundo. We spent a couple of days guarding a guy, a Bolivian on the run from dopers. He told me this jungle produces like a quarter of the cocaine in the world. I guess that's how most people around here make a living."

Belhaj nodded. "Our police services keep an eye because most of the cocaine goes to Europe. Through Argentina or Brazil."

"The president of the country used to be a coca farmer. He kicked out the DEA, so that pretty much tells you what you need to know about him."

Eventually, the Land Cruiser turned off the main highway. A narrow, semi-paved road became a tunnel through dense foliage. The vehicle slithered in a yellow slop of puddles, gravel and mud. They passed huts, a tethered cow, women washing laundry in a stream. It rained. The driver rounded a curve and came to an abrupt halt. Pescatore saw police officers in the uniforms of the Leopards. They stood with rifles at the ready, covering officers holding machetes who swarmed on a hillside. The Leopards clambered up and down the steep slope with casual agility, using vines and trees as handholds, steadying their comrades in rough spots. Smoke and flames rose from the tree-tops at the crest of the hill.

The security man said the police had set fire to a clandestine lab for producing coca base paste. The Land Cruiser advanced slowly. Three handcuffed prisoners sat at the roadside. Two were barefoot, unkempt and emaciated, their cheeks distended by wads of coca.

"I think they are *pisacocas,*" Belhaj said in Pescatore's ear. She had slid over to look through his window. "The ones who step on the coca to make paste. Like they used to make the wine in France."

The third prisoner looked meaner and better fed and wore boots. He glared at a police officer who was inspecting an old rifle. The police and the suspects were all stained with yellow mud. The security man said the prisoner in boots had probably been a sentry guarding the lab with the rifle.

"A Mauser," the security man said. "Durable weapon. Accurate. The favorite of the *cocaleros.* Along with dynamite."

"Dynamite?" Pescatore asked.

"They throw dynamite around like firecrackers. Many of them were miners before. They migrated from the mountains. From tin to coca."

The sun was shining by the time they reached their destination, a village with wide muddy streets and low wooden buildings. Pescatore climbed out of the vehicle into a murk of heat. He imagined Raymond walking these streets where pigs rooted in gutters, where clouds of flies hovered over jumbo bottles of Coke and Fanta on the tables of outdoor eateries. Raymond had established alliances, set up deals, and made a lot of money in the Chapare jungle. What a place. Raymond was leading him a long way from home.

They entered an open-air meeting hall with a corrugated metal roof on poles. A rally was in progress: a meeting of a union representing coca growers, the *cocaleros*. The speakers stood on a stage adorned with banners and a poster of the Bolivian president, the former *cocalero* leader, smiling in indigenous ceremonial garb, his chest swathed with flower necklaces. The audience stood or sat in folding chairs. Children wandered, played and slept. The security man went toward the stage. Belhaj and Pescatore waited by a waist-high wall. Men squatted or leaned along the wall, faces stolid beneath caps. They chewed coca, the wads swelling their cheeks. Their knockoff windbreakers and warm-up jackets were adorned with the names of European soccer teams or English phrases such as *Daytona City* and *Western Traditional*.

A stocky woman was giving a speech. Her black hair was intricately braided, her skirt red, purple and orange. She spoke in Quechua. Her high, reedy cadence built to a crescendo, eliciting dutiful cheers. She pumped her fist in the air.

Shifting to accented Spanish, the woman shouted: *"¡Viva la coca! ¡Muerte a los Yanquis! ¡Viva la coca! ¡Muerte a los Yanquis!"*

The crowd echoed the chant. Pescatore leaned close to Belhaj.

"I understood that," he muttered. "'Death to the Americans.' You hear that shit?"

Belhaj made an impatient clicking noise with her mouth. She wanted him to keep his patriotic indignation to himself.

Pescatore looked around again. As he had watched them trudging beneath bales and pedaling rusty bikes, he had felt sympathy for the people of the Chapare. Although many were involved in the drug racket at some level, it was hard to compare them to the psycho cartel gunslingers he had tangled with in the past. Bolivia seemed pretty medieval; the coca farmers were literally peons. But the chant had annoyed and alarmed him. He was the only Yanqui in the vicinity.

Okay, coca lady, I see what time it is, he thought. *I need to get myself a gun.*

The embassy security man returned with a willowy brown-haired woman in her thirties. She did not look like a migrant from the mountains—unless her family had owned a mine. As she walked through the crowd, she exchanged smiles and pleasantries. She greeted Belhaj quietly and hurried them to the Land Cruiser. They rode to a small compound that a sign announced was the headquarters of the Legal Center for Conflict Mediation and Social Justice.

The sweaty office had windows with bars but no glass, and cinder-block walls. Their host was named Amélie Hidalgo Florian. Belhaj had told Pescatore that she was a lawyer who directed the nonprofit funded by the United Nations and the European Union. Her center provided free legal services and mediated between the *cocaleros* and the government. Hidalgo served tea. She poured herself a cup from a different pitcher.

"Mine is coca tea," she said in French, adding sardonically, "I wouldn't want you to fail a drug test and cause a scandal in the French police."

Hidalgo continued in Spanish. Pescatore was not surprised to learn that she was half Belgian. It explained her name, the light complexion combined with strong-lined Andean features, the connection to the French embassy. She cultivated a down-to-earth look. No makeup. She wore sandals, torn jeans, a white cotton shirt. She had the bearing of a dancer or a model. Her hand rested at the base of her throat, fingers touching her chiseled collarbone, as she answered questions. Her straight hair was pulled back in a short ponytail. She came from money and privilege and was attractive in a hard-bitten way. He could see her appealing to Raymond's appetites.

It's a girl in every port with this guy, Pescatore thought.

Hidalgo had met Raymond seven years ago, when his drug business was taking off. He had come up to her at a coffee bar in Cochabamba and introduced himself as Ramón Verdugo, an Argentine businessman.

"I live here," Hidalgo told them, gesturing over her shoulder at the compound. "But now and then I spend weekends in Cochabamba. This character sat next to me and struck up a conversation. Something about the best cappuccino in Bolivia. Smooth and sleazy. Then Suleiman Kharroubi, a bona fide gangster, comes in to meet him. Ramón invited me to dinner with them. I told him that was impossible. I didn't know who he was, but I knew what he was. He found that amusing."

Hidalgo knew a lot about the drug traffickers who operated in the jungle and Cochabamba and Santa Cruz, the cities flanking the Chapare. The mafias regarded her as a useful player on the chessboard because of her legal assistance to coca growers and her probes of abuse by the security forces. Although she made a point of criticizing the drug lords too, they left her alone. The drug lords, coca growers and government all considered her a neutral arbiter.

During the next two years, Hidalgo ran into Raymond at places popular with foreigners and the elite in Cochabamba. He visited her office in the Chapare. It became a ritual. He always asked her out; she always fended him off.

"He called me the queen of the jungle," she said. "What a talker. Intelligent, yes. He liked music and literature and film. I don't think he had anyone else to talk to about such things. When he found out my mother was Belgian, he would sometimes speak French. And he told me about the underworld. He liked to drop hints, show off. His group was muscling in. The traditional smuggling strategy is a shotgun approach: peasants carry loads of base paste on remote trails or in hidden compartments. Enough make it out of the valley for the bosses to profit. Ramón's gang changed that. They went industrial. They did their own refining. They paid off police chiefs and moved truckloads straight down the main highway."

"I understand the network had Middle Eastern links," Belhaj said.

The information came from her briefing at the French embassy in La Paz. She had told Pescatore that Hidalgo was the best source they would find; the Bolivian authorities were not cooperating.

The lawyer frowned.

"I should make something clear," she said. "I have my hands full. Two hundred thousand people live in the Chapare. It is a labyrinth, geographically and otherwise. The *cocalero* unions, the political parties, the police and military, the drug mafias—local, Brazilian, Colombian, Argentine. My reputation is based on absolute neutrality. I am not an informant for anyone."

"I want to protect your reputation," Belhaj said.

"I resent being dragged into an affair of international terrorism. That's the only reason I am talking to you. And why I receive you here in the open, on my territory, which is crawling with spies."

Hidalgo resumed her story. She said that Kharroubi's companies shipped cars, pineapples and other products to Argentina and overseas. The firms were thought to be screens for cocaine smuggling to Europe, Africa and the Middle East.

"There was a foreigner. Hardly anyone saw him in person or knew his real name. An influential partner of Ramón's gang, people said. People called him Ali Baba."

"Was he from the Arab world? Or possibly a Latin American of Middle Eastern origin?"

"I have no idea. I never met him myself."

"Did Ramón talk about Islam?"

"He mentioned he was Muslim the way I could tell you I am Catholic. He talked more about world politics, feminist issues, things he thought would impress me. He wanted me to understand the Islamic movements in the context of the anti-imperialist struggle. In fact…"

The lawyer unlocked a cabinet, removed a book, and, holding it as if it were toxic, gave it to Belhaj. Pescatore saw the word CARLOS in block letters on a black cover. The title was French: *L'Islam Révolutionnaire.*

"Written in prison," Hidalgo said. "The author is Carlos the Jackal, the Venezuelan terrorist from the eighties. His ode to bin Laden. He wants the leftists and revolutionaries of the world to rally behind al-Qaeda. Pure and absolute shit. Please keep it for evidence, fingerprints, whatever."

Raymond had given her the book during what turned out to be his last visit to her office. A turf war broke out between his trafficking group and rival mafias. She did not see him again.

Belhaj opened the book to the title page and passed it to Pescatore. He saw the initial *R* below a handwritten inscription in French: "To Amélie, the loveliest revolutionary."

Raymond's ornate loops and swirls hadn't changed much. Pescatore nodded to indicate that he recognized the handwriting.

"How about the phone call, the terrorism warning?" Belhaj asked.

"It was two weeks ago," Hidalgo said. "Ramón telephoned me here. He asked if I remembered him. I was surprised. He said he had always trusted and respected me. He needed to transmit sensitive information to the government."

Raymond had told her that an Islamic terrorist cell was in Bolivia preparing an attack. He gave her a name and the address of a safe house in La Paz. He declined to say where he was or answer questions.

"He said I needed to advise the authorities right away. Like he was reading from a script. Lives at risk. Not a moment to lose. Before he hung up, he joked in a creepy way. He called me the queen of the jungle again. He said: 'You see how strong my sentiments are, my queen? Even though you rejected me, I haven't stopped thinking about you.' As if he were doing me an honor. I called a friend in the Justice Ministry. The police tracked down the group. The terrorism angle was kept secret."

The two main suspects were a Spanish convert and a Bolivian convert who had studied in Madrid. The third suspect was a local criminal who owned the safe house where police found AK-47s, pistols, grenades, and a computer containing extremist literature and videos. The converts had visited a shopping mall in La Paz and driven around embassies, diplomatic residences, and other places frequented by foreigners. They had shot a lot of video. But there was no hard evidence of a specific plot.

Pescatore wiped sweat from his face. Any shred of doubt had vanished. It was Raymond who had called Pescatore's phone, just as he had called Amélie Hidalgo. Once again he couldn't help thinking, with a hollowness in the pit of his stomach, that things might have turned out better in Buenos Aires if he had handled Raymond differently.

Hidalgo poured more tea. Belhaj thanked her and said, "There is something I don't understand, if you permit me. Why did you keep Ramón's identity secret at first?"

Hidalgo nodded as if she had been expecting the question.

"The authorities and the traffickers know my rules. I may pass on information, but I protect my sources. Beyond whatever annoying infatuation Ramón may have had, that is why he chose me. My friend at the Justice Ministry implored me to tell him more. At that point, no one had died. The suspects in La Paz were captured. So I told my friend only that I had received the information from overseas. I assume the security services, who monitor me rather brazenly, retrieved the number from my phone records and traced it to France."

"Then the attack in Buenos Aires happened."

"Exactly." Hidalgo's eyes smoldered. "All bets were off. I wasn't sure if Ramón was involved, but I had to do something. I identified him to the Bolivians and made myself available to you."

Pescatore decided to ask a question. In his best Argentine accent, he said, "Ms. Hidalgo, did Ramón talk about where he was from or his childhood?"

"No. He lived in Buenos Aires and I assumed he was from there."

"Ma'am, you said 'hardly anyone' saw Ali Baba. Someone did see him?"

Hidalgo returned his gaze. Her fingers tapped at the base of her throat.

"I know of one instance," she said slowly. "About six years ago, not long after Ramón gave me the book."

It was a violent period, the lawyer explained. Brazilian traffickers were fighting Raymond's group. There were shootings. The warring factions manipulated the police, tipping them off about enemy activity. One night, a special investigative team busted two SUVs on the highway en route to Santa Cruz. The vehicles were full of weapons, cash and cocaine.

"They detained Ramón and a man with a Middle Eastern name," she said. "I think it was this Ali Baba, his mysterious partner. The police questioned them. There was haggling. My understanding is that it got very tense, because the Brazilian narcos put pressure on the police. They wanted Ramón dead. But a large bribe was paid. Everyone shook hands and the police sent the two of them on their way. That kind of thing is not unusual. What stands out is this: The man they called Ali Baba was carrying a foreign passport. A diplomatic passport."

11

Angelina

The original plan, dictated by the security concerns of the French embassy, had been to get out of the Chapare before dark.

Yet here they were: sitting after dinner at a hotel in the jungle. Rain pattered on the thatched roof of the outdoor dining area, a candlelit island in the encroaching blackness. Pescatore and Belhaj were the only diners. The hotel had been recommended, grudgingly, by the embassy security man after he finished complaining about the risks. The low-slung complex off the main highway offered a swimming pool, rustic decor, two dozen cabins for guests. It survived on a clientele of government visitors, foreign-aid workers, and adventure tourists.

The security man and the driver had gone to their cabins after dinner. Pescatore had expected Fatima Belhaj to call it a night as well. Instead, the two of them worked their way through a second bottle of wine while discussing the day's developments. The official language between them slid gradually from Spanish to English.

"Do you think we'll hear from Amélie tonight?" Pescatore asked.

"I doubt it." Belhaj held out her glass for him to pour the last of the Chilean red. "I hope tomorrow."

"You were nice about it, but you worked her over pretty good."

"We have come upon something important with this *type* Ali Baba."

After Hidalgo dropped her bombshell, Belhaj had coaxed the lawyer to tell them more about Ali Baba and his diplomatic passport. Hidalgo resisted. She had told them everything she knew. She refused to endanger her source. Belhaj warned that there was grave danger of terrorist attacks as long as Raymond was at large. They had to find him—and find out as much as they could about him. Pescatore chimed in to explain that he had been at the scene of the carnage in Buenos Aires. He described the suicide bombing at the delicatessen, how fate had saved Claudia Rabinovich and wiped out her father and son.

Amélie Hidalgo grumbled and relented. She said she would do what she could. But she couldn't promise anything. They would have to wait.

Pescatore listened to the noises of the night: birds, frogs, insects, monkeys, an unsettling shriek of indeterminate provenance.

"What a racket," Pescatore said. "Are you a city person like me?"

"Yes," Belhaj said. "I grew up in an HLM, public residences outside Paris. Pure cement."

"Like the housing projects where they have the riots?"

"Exactly. I find this place beautiful."

"Yeah, but it's narco-land. I'd be more comfortable if we were armed."

The candle was enclosed in a red glass square. When Belhaj turned toward him, the light flickered in her heavy-lidded eyes and played across her deep cleavage. At some point during the oppressively hot day, she had undone the top buttons of her olive-colored work shirt.

"Our guard is armed," she said. "I am prohibited from carrying a gun overseas."

"You don't seem disappointed."

"Except during operations, I have rarely drawn my gun. Often I don't carry it."

That was a difference between Belhaj and Isabel Puente. Isabel felt naked without her sidearm. She trained religiously at the range and had been in two shootouts that he knew of. Pescatore found himself comparing the women. Belhaj was less talkative and more relaxed than Isabel, whose in-your-face style was alternately engaging and fierce. Physically, Isabel was petite if proportionately voluptuous. Belhaj had a high waist and those long legs; she was bigger all over.

The manager, a woman with a bespectacled outdoorsy look who had served the meal, inquired about an after-dinner drink. Belhaj raised her eyebrows at Pescatore. They ordered Baileys Irish Cream on the rocks. The manager left the bottle and an ice bucket and bade them good night. The light soon went out in the reception building.

Pescatore swirled his glass, ice cubes clinking, the caramel color aflame in the candlelight. He said, "Ali Baba's passport, what do you think? Iranian? The Quds Force uses diplomatic cover. They're in the region causing trouble, making money. Of course, if it's Iranian, I'm confused, because Raymond's network was Sunni, not Shiite."

"I don't exclude the possibility. But she did not say it was a Middle Eastern passport. And it could have been false."

"That's true. You can buy documents in Venezuela, Honduras, Belize. Or Raymond could have hooked him up with Florencia. A diplomatic passport, though—that's hard to score. Your people can't find a trace of Ray in France?"

"Not yet. It takes time pursuing aliases, requesting data to the European Union."

"Slick as he is, I don't think Raymond could stay invisible in Europe."

"The enigmatic Raymond." She used the candle to light a cigarette. "How did you become friends?"

"Do you have brothers and sisters?"

"Eight."

"Eight? Jeez. Well, I don't have any. Raymond either. There was the Argentine thing in common, his mom and my dad. Our families had us play together. Ever since I can remember, he was around and we were friends."

"Like brothers."

"When we were little, he was funny, smart, generous. A year older too, so I learned a lot from him. Like it or not, he influenced the sports I played, the music and movies I liked, how I talked. And he was one of those guys who everybody wanted to be like, be around. Especially once he started singing. He was a star. When he sang, the bad side of him kind of melted away. You wanted to believe in him."

Flashes of lightning illuminated the treeline, accompanied by a sustained hiss and crackle. Thunder followed. The rain gathered force.

"But why is it he still feels this connection to you, this confidence?" she asked.

"I wonder about that. His family had more money: he went to private school, lived in a better neighborhood. But he said my neighborhood was where 'the real people' lived, whatever that meant. I was closer to the street, I guess, and he wished he was from the street. Of course, he did more crazy illegal stuff than I ever dreamed of."

"He romanticized gangsterism."

"But he had this weird attitude with me. Florencia mentioned it, remember? He said I was the one person he could trust. He told me: 'Things are so simple with you. You say something and you mean it.'"

Belhaj puffed smoke. He liked watching her alternate the cigarette and the drink. The languid grace with which she crossed her thighs. Her curls swirling.

"Do you think Raymond is bisexual?" she asked.

He bobbed his head back as if avoiding a punch. "Excuse me?"

"If he sleeps with men as well as women."

"I understand the question. I'm trying to figure out why you would ask that."

She flashed the slightly lopsided grin. "I know his type. Professional informants, double agents. Selling information, changing sides. They seduce and betray. They use sex for that, even with other men."

The idea irked him. If you're asking a guy about his relationship with his oldest friend, and then you ask if that oldest friend is bisexual, there's an implication. He wondered if she was messing with him again. She sounded sincere.

"I never considered that," he said. "When I hung out with him, he chased women nonstop and bragged about how much he got over. Looks like that hasn't changed."

He considered telling her about Raymond stealing his girlfriend, but chose not to open that particular Pandora's box. He finished his drink, enjoying the sweet tang of the Baileys, feeling mellow. Belhaj did not appear to be tipsy, though he had never heard her talk so much. Her percussive North African accent had gotten stronger.

"A Casanova type," she said.

"A dog. He had this habit of hitting on waitresses. It was a game to him. If the waitress was halfway pretty, he'd go into his sweet-talk routine. He'd sing her 'Angelina,' by Louis Prima."

Belhaj looked at him blankly.

"You know, Louis Prima," he said. "'Just a Gigolo'? 'Banana Split for My Baby'? You never heard of him?"

"No."

"Oh, man, he's great. New Orleans Sicilian. A mix of Louis Armstrong and Dean Martin. You don't know that song 'Angelina,' about the waitress at the pizzeria?"

"I promise you, I do not."

Pescatore chuckled. "I've had enough to drink to the point where I might just sing it."

She widened her eyes in jovial expectation. "Please."

The impulse took over. Tapping out the bouncy rhythm on the wood, he belted out the song with gusto—even the words in Italian. Belhaj laughed and applauded.

"A positive influence of Raymond," she said. "And good pronunciation."

"My old man's really Italian, he basically passed through Argentina."

"You are Mexican too, no?"

"Yep. You keep pouring that, I'll start with the *rancheras*."

Belhaj topped off his drink.

"So, Fatima," he said. "Now that I've told you about my childhood, and I've done my goofy Louis Prima imitation, and you questioned my sexual orientation and everything—"

She laughed again. "His orientation, not yours."

"Anyway. I gotta ask you. I don't know about Paris, but in Chicago you don't meet a lotta big-time federal counterterrorism investigators who grew up in public housing projects. How did you come to be a cop?"

She lowered her brows, feigning wariness. "A biographical question."

"Yep."

She shrugged. "The main reason is my father."

Her father had emigrated to France from the Moroccan countryside—*le bled,* she called it. People in his village pitched in to buy him a suit for the journey. In France, her father built a life thanks to a job that was the source of his pride and dignity: he drove a municipal bus.

"The bus was his ship." Belhaj spoke with a tenderness that Pescatore had not seen before. "He was the captain. He kept it impeccable. He knew the passengers' names. They gave him gifts for his children. One passenger was a chief in the police intelligence service. This man was a legend. He investigated big dossiers of terrorism. Lebanon, Algeria, Pakistan. *Arabisant:* he spoke Arabic. At this time he was older, a chief of the analysts in the service. One day he saw my father very sad. My father explained he had a problem with his daughter."

Pescatore leaned forward, forearms on thighs. He said, "Which was you."

"Which was me."

Belhaj sipped her drink. Her voice slowed, lingering on the memories. Thunder boomed. Rain fell in sheets.

Her childhood had been difficult. Older brothers slid into crime and drugs, consuming her parents' energies. She was an excellent student, but solitary and moody. When she was an adolescent, her braininess and taste for revealing outfits brought constant harassment from the two groups that dominated the housing project: Islamic fundamentalists and street gangs.

"I was miserable," she said. "I hated to go anywhere, they were always waiting to abuse me. At school too. I spent more and more time hiding at home. Reading, eating. I had the very bad depression. I was fat also."

"Hard to believe," Pescatore said.

"I weighed twenty-five kilos more than now. Fifty pounds?"

He could see it now. She had reinvented herself. She had sculpted her beauty out of excess and trauma. She carried herself with the awareness, the daily joy, of that achievement.

By the time she was seventeen, her grades had plummeted. Her father was devastated. Her teachers had always told him that she was bright, that she would go far if her attitude didn't interfere. When the veteran intelligence officer heard the story on the bus, he offered to help.

"He came to our apartment Sunday for couscous," she said. "For my father, it was like a presidential visit. We talked. About his travels, cases, Islam, espionage. I was fascinated. He was so cerebral. And *raffiné*."

"Refined?"

"Yes. The policemen I had known were alcoholic brutes or frightened boys from the provinces—they never saw so many blacks and Arabs. The chief became my, eh, mentor. I went to the university and he helped me to join the service. I started as an analyst and translator. Interesting, but too much wearing the headphones, transcription. I changed to investigator."

"I bet you put the fear a' God into those assholes in the projects when they saw you in uniform."

Her teeth gleamed in the shadows. "That was a good day."

"A real French success story, huh?"

"*C'est vrai.* In this aspect, France is improving. I told Jean-Louis, my mentor, 'The police don't want me. They don't even consider me French.' He said, '*Au contraire, chérie.* You are a Frenchwoman. You will be a French policewoman. And you will command a great respect.' Many women from the *banlieue* join the police or the military. It helps them break with the projects, the fundamentalists, their families. What you comprehend with the Islamist networks is that the extremist is searching for an identity. I was too, but I found it on the other side."

"Lucky for the good guys," Pescatore said.

He raised his glass. She clinked it with hers. They watched the downpour. He glanced over at her. She held his gaze. He thought again about the resemblance, in the eyes, to the angel in *The Madonna of the Rocks*.

"What?" she asked finally.

"I was thinking," he said. "Right now, the smugglers are out there moving dope and cash and chemicals. The narcos are running their labs and coca pits. Cops and soldiers prowling around. Everybody getting real wet. You and me, we're sitting here nice and dry with our Baileys in this beautiful spot. I could sit here all night."

"Moi aussi," she said.

After a moment, she rose. "But let's go."

Caught off guard, he got up. They stood at the edge of the dining area. The rain hammered the roof and the grass. A path of flat stones, vaguely visible, led to the cluster of cabins several hundred feet away.

"I do not think it will stop," she said.

"I think you're right."

He extended his hand. She took it. Confidence and desire flooded him.

They bolted onto the path and ran silently, holding hands, splashing through puddles, charging through curtains of water. The guest quarters were organized in units of three attached cabins enclosing an entrance porch. Pescatore and Belhaj had cabins facing each other. They stumbled into the shelter of the porch area, dripping wet. They caught their breath, smiling at each other. She tossed her head back, shaking out her mane of curls in a halo of water.

A wild woman, he thought. They were still holding hands.

"You know, I noticed something," he said softly. "These cabin doors don't lock. It's bad enough we don't have guns. We don't even have locks."

"Alarming." She made a solemn face. She was standing very close to him.

"Yeah. The thing to do is wedge a chair under the doorknob. Put keys on it, they fall and make noise if someone opens the door."

"Good idea," she whispered. Her free hand gripped his left triceps, fingers digging into the taut muscle. "Maybe you should show me."

"Maybe I should."

They went into her cabin. The door slammed. Their bodies slammed together in the dark. His head whirled. A bombardment of sensations: her mouth and skin tasting like Baileys and nicotine and rain, her breasts bursting free when he pulled apart the soaked shirt, her hair in his face when he turned her around. They peeled off each other's clothes, water everywhere. They grappled and contorted and banged against the door and the wall.

She led him to the bed. They slowed down, enjoying each other, intoxicated by each other. At one point, he said he hoped she didn't think he presumed he was entitled to anything because of the shooting incident in La Matanza. She assured him that she didn't, then kissed the bruise on his chest and said she wanted to express her gratitude for La Matanza. Sometime later, she informed him that from now on, he would speak French in her bed. He responded, in French, that there were several terms he hoped to learn.

The rain fell. The narco-jungle growled and whispered and moaned.

12

El Baile del Sua-Sua

A mélie Hidalgo showed up at breakfast with a proposition. The lawyer joined Pescatore and Fatima at the table where they had dined the night before. The soggy verdant landscape shimmered in the sun.

The hotel didn't have espresso. Pescatore downed cups of foul coffee. He was gloriously tired. He had expected that he would feel guilty. He didn't see a problem in joining forces with the French police after the FBI kicked him to the curb. But it was unprofessional and unwise to sleep with the lead investigator. Nonetheless, he couldn't work up much regret about it. As far as he could tell, neither could Fatima. This morning, she had retreated into serene silence.

"He won't see you and he won't talk to you," Amélie Hidalgo declared. "Not here, not in Cochabamba, not in Timbuktu."

The lawyer sipped coffee and frowned. She wore a long white dress. Her fingers toyed with a necklace of red wayruro seeds. She clearly disliked playing the role of go-between. Pescatore was convinced that her secret source was a Bolivian police officer who had taken part in the shakedown of Raymond and his crony Ali Baba.

"He won't communicate with you by phone or e-mail," she continued. "He offers one thing. He has a photo for sale."

"Of Ali Baba?" Pescatore asked.

"A photo that he knows you will find interesting."

After conferring, Pescatore and Belhaj offered one thousand dollars for the photo. The lawyer sent a one-word text message. The response was a demand for five thousand dollars. They settled on three thousand. The French government was picking up the tab.

"Now listen," Hidalgo said. "He gave me very specific instructions. I will explain. And then, at his insistence as well as mine, I withdraw from this sordid episode."

The plan for the exchange was elaborate. The main virtue was that it gave Pescatore a chance to return to his preferred operational status: packing heat.

Ten hours later, as they sat in the Land Cruiser, the embassy security man handed Pescatore a SIG Sauer SP2022 nine-millimeter semiautomatic. The pistol was in a shoulder holster. Pescatore strapped the holster over his black T-shirt and put on his black travel vest. He patted the gun.

"Much better," he said.

Fatima winked at him. She and the security man, whose name was Wenceslao, had argued. Wenceslao had suggested demanding an alternative plan, delaying the rendezvous in order to request reinforcements, or returning immediately to the embassy in La Paz—his preference. He balked at providing Pescatore with the gun from a small arsenal in a locked case in the Land Cruiser. Fatima stood firm. The security man kept saying *"C'est pas bon."* She finally cut him off with a phrase that sounded like French for "Shut the fuck up."

The Land Cruiser was parked in the ramshackle business district of Villa Tunari, the biggest town in the Chapare. They were two blocks from the site designated for the meet. Pescatore and Belhaj went over instructions, code words and contingencies.

"Please be careful," she said.

It was dusk. A breeze stirred stagnant heat. Pescatore walked along a row of brick and wood facades. Awnings and corrugated metal roofs overhung the sidewalk, dripping rainwater. The storefronts were pale green, bold blue, hot pink in the fading light. He passed a general store, an Internet café full of Scandinavian-looking backpackers, an outdoor bar where two Quechua men sat zombie-like in red plastic chairs, their table lined with beer bottles. Motor scooters whined by. A dog drank from a puddle. Pescatore made way for three women vendors hauling sacks, tent-shaped silhouettes topped by tall hats.

The Pensión Lola was on a dimly lit stretch where palm trees began to reclaim the street. Pescatore entered the small hotel, parting a curtain of beads beneath an ad for Cerveza Taquiña depicting Andean peaks. The clerk behind the caged front desk had a pulverized nose, lank gray hair, and an air of dazed hostility. Pescatore asked for room 205 and paid thirty-eight dollars.

The dim staircase led up into a pall of heat and smells: cigarettes, plumbing, incense, ammonia, and pervasive, ancestral mold. He heard a television, a raucous female laugh. He drew his gun, let himself into room 205, and checked the closet and the bathroom. He sat in a lumpy leather armchair. The flatscreen television was the only thing in the room that didn't look older than him.

Night fell outside. Catching sight of himself in a wall mirror, he ran a hand through his curly hair. His reflection was dirty and distorted. He looked grim sitting in the gloom in the black outfit in the black chair. Like a specter.

The Pensión Lola was a flophouse that catered to prostitutes whose clients were denizens of the drug trade and grunts from military and police bases. Pescatore's dislike for brothels went beyond an aversion to sleaze and disease. While in the Border Patrol, he had worked cases and heard stories involving migrant women and children forced into service as prostitutes on both sides of the border. Stories full of cruelty, perversion and despair. Stories that had burned foul images into his brain.

There was a knock on the door. The woman said her name was Yennifer. His gun low by his leg, he glanced down the narrow hall before stepping aside. She flounced past him in a tight green cotton minidress that ended at her upper thighs, outlining a diminutive, short-armed, cartoonishly abundant figure. Her perfume invaded the room, a chemical cloud that stung his throat.

"My friend sent me," she said.

Yennifer looked about Pescatore's age, though her round face showed wear. Her black hair was arranged with clips in the shapes of Mickey and Minnie Mouse. She plunked her purse onto the bed and propped a hand on a robust hip.

"So?" she asked.

Pescatore gave her the three thousand dollars. She counted it, then handed him a sealed envelope and announced that she was going to use the facilities. When the bathroom door closed, he opened the envelope.

The photo had apparently been taken with a cell phone. The quality was decent. It showed Raymond and another man sitting on a wooden bench. Neither was handcuffed, but it was not hard to see that they were prisoners. A uniformed arm and shoulder were visible on one side of the frame, and a row of walkie-talkies stood in a rack next to the bench.

Raymond looked as if he was working an audience, as usual. His legs were crossed, his right foot dangling in a hiking boot over his left knee. His arms were spread wide in an expansive gesture, as if he were telling an anecdote at a party. His eyes, however, were tense and watchful. He wore a Chicago Bulls sweatshirt.

Clenching his fist victoriously, Pescatore saw that the image of the man next to Raymond was clear and sharp. Ali Baba sat with folded arms, letting Raymond handle the public relations. He gazed at the camera. His stern face reminded Pescatore of an Arabic proverb that Facundo had told him: "Sit in your doorway and wait for the coffin of your enemy to go by."

Pescatore put Ali Baba at over forty and in good shape. He had broad shoulders, his beard was trim and black, his head conical and balding. A white button-down shirt emerged from his V-neck sweater.

Whoever he is, he looks like serious business, Pescatore thought.

He used his iPhone to snap a photo of the photo and e-mail it to Fatima. They had agreed he would do this for security and as a signal that he would be done shortly. Next, he sent the photo in a separate e-mail to Facundo with a message: *Can you ID? Will explain.*

Pescatore put the photo in a vest pocket. Yennifer emerged from the bathroom. Her hair now tumbled to her shoulders. She placed the Mickey and Minnie Mouse clips on the night-stand. She was even shorter than before; she had removed her red platform shoes. He needed to make clear to her that the transaction was over.

"Well, señorita, everything seems fine," he said quickly, rising. "Many thanks. I know you've already been compensated, but here's a token of appreciation."

He pressed the equivalent of twenty dollars into her hand. He wished her a good evening and started to usher her toward the door.

Yennifer's eyebrows arched. Her heavily painted eyes had a liquid sheen, as if she had been drinking or doing drugs.

"What are you talking about?" she said.

"We're done. I need to get going."

"None of that, friend," she declared. "I was told to spend an hour here. As part of the cover story. To make it realistic."

He said that was unnecessary. She responded that she had been paid handsomely and given strict orders. She needed to obey in case anyone was watching. Whatever they did or didn't do, she had to stay in the room with him.

"You sure?" he asked.

"I'm sure."

He slumped into the armchair. He didn't want to spend any more time in this dump. Fatima and the others were waiting down the street.

Yennifer cocked her head. "What's your name?"

"Valentín."

"You look like that singer."

Startled, he asked, "What singer?"

"He's an actor too." Her smile was bleary. "A bad guy on a *telenovela*."

She approached and stood over him.

"Listen, Valentín," she said. "If you want, we could make it really realistic."

Her body strained every fiber of the minidress. She lowered herself into his lap. The force of her perfume made him blink. Her arms encircled his neck. Her bosom filled his face.

His body, still charged up after the night with Fatima, responded. Here he was, a night later: another woman, another hotel room. The danger and raunchiness and craziness of it excited him.

His hand slid up the back of her meaty thigh to discover she was wearing nothing but the dress. She stuck her tongue in his ear. He cupped her haunches and pulled her against him.

This kind of shit doesn't happen to me, he thought. *This is a Raymond-type situation.*

That stopped him cold. He gripped her fleshy shoulders. Gently, he pushed her back and away.

"Señorita." His voice was hoarse. "Yennifer. Please. Not a good idea."

"You sure?"

"I'm sure."

He kept pushing. She slid off and straightened. Flushed and disheveled, she tucked herself back into the top of her dress. He exhaled, mortified by his descent to sleaze-dog level. He was covered in sweat.

"If you really don't want to..." she said. Her tone said, *If you're really that gay...*

She demanded to know what they were going to do for an hour. He suggested turning on the television. She flopped onto the bed. He called Fatima and explained the situation tersely.

Fatima said they would adapt to the delay. In forty-five minutes, their vehicle would advance to a prearranged point with a view of the hotel.

"We will be in position," Fatima said. Wenceslao's voice was audible in the background, no doubt giving her grief.

Pescatore and Yennifer watched a music-video program. She cheered when they played one of her favorites, "El Baile del Sua-Sua," by Kinito Méndez. She hopped off the bed and danced to the merengue along with the cheerful, sexy Dominicans undulating onscreen. Chanting the moves in unison with the singer, she demonstrated: Divide the body. From the waist up, do nothing. From the waist down, you go sua-sua-sua. Pescatore applauded, but declined her invitation to join in.

When the hour was up, she shook his hand. She said it had been an immense pleasure. He said the feeling was mutual. He closed the door behind her and called Fatima.

"Five minutes," he said.

"Hurry up," Fatima said.

Pescatore had intended to wait long enough for Yennifer to get clear of the hotel. But then he noticed that she had forgotten the Mickey and Minnie Mouse barrettes on the nightstand. He scooped them up and hurried downstairs to catch her. As he reached the lobby, he heard a screech of tires, a commotion, and a woman's scream outside.

The battered desk clerk did not react; maybe he heard

screams like that all the time. Pescatore drew his gun and peered out through the curtain of beads.

He saw the prostitute in the street struggling with two men near a GMC Yukon. The assailants were burly and military-looking. One man held Yennifer by the hair and pointed a pistol at her face, threatening to shoot her if she didn't stop scratching. She cursed and twisted and slashed at him. The other man rummaged in her purse.

This was not a coincidental street robbery, Pescatore thought. The duo knew about the photo, or at least that Yennifer was involved in some kind of exchange. The struggle was taking place a few yards to the left of the hotel entrance. Pescatore's getaway vehicle waited down the street to the right. If he slipped out while they were distracted with Yennifer, he had a good chance of escaping in the dark.

A slap knocked Yennifer down. She tried to crawl away in the mud. The gunman strode forward to kick her. As Pescatore watched the cowboy boot swing back, he chided himself for considering the escape option. He had a single, brutal alternative.

He stepped through the bead curtain and went into a combat stance. He shouted, *"Policía!"*

But he wasn't the police. Unless they surrendered on the spot, he didn't plan to attempt some kind of citizen's arrest of two armed, meat-eating, woman-kicking gangsters on their own turf. He had no badge, no jurisdiction, no reason to play fair.

The gunman wheeled. Pescatore fired three shots at him, aiming for the center of the body mass, and three at the sidekick. The gunman spun in a circle and dropped. The sidekick tottered toward the Yukon and sank to his knees. Yennifer screamed. Pescatore yelled at her to stay down.

A flash lit up the interior of the Yukon. Pescatore realized, painfully late, that there was a third man behind the wheel. The third man was firing at him through his own windshield.

Pescatore fled, hearing slugs break glass. He twisted to shoot back wildly on the run, tripped, and fell hard. The impact knocked the breath out of him. He flopped onto his stomach, cringing as bullets whined overhead.

A vehicle roared up. Pescatore saw Wenceslao hanging out of the passenger window of the speeding Land Cruiser. The security man aimed the machine gun, steady as a surgeon. His volley chewed up the windshield of the Yukon. The gunman behind the wheel bounced around like a crash dummy and slumped out of view. The Land Cruiser swerved up onto the sidewalk, skidding to a halt next to Pescatore. Wenceslao sprayed an insurance volley at the two men lying in the gutter. Pescatore hauled himself into the backseat next to Fatima.

Glancing back, he saw Yennifer running away down the middle of the street on broad stubby legs and bare feet, a platform shoe in each hand.

"What happened?" Fatima asked.

Pescatore struggled to catch his breath. "Somebody found out about our little transaction."

He leaned forward to pat Wenceslao gratefully on the shoulder. The security man nodded. *The dude might be a complainer, but he's not shy about pulling a trigger,* Pescatore thought.

Fatima lit a cigarette. She gave the order to go to Santa Cruz, which had an international airport. She had no intention of sticking around to explain to the authorities the chain of events that had deposited three casualties on the doorstep of the Pensión Lola. The Land Cruiser hurtled down the two-lane highway. The driver cursed the occasional vehicles, cyclists, pedestrians and animals that flashed by like apparitions in the corridor bisecting the pitch-black rain forest.

About a half hour later, the driver said a Nissan Frontier was following them. He slowed down; the Nissan slowed down. When he sped up, the Nissan matched his pace. A red light began flashing on its roof.

There was a conversation about whether the unmarked Nissan was really the police, whether that was good or bad, and whether they should stop.

"I hate to bring this up," Pescatore said, "but those guys we shot mighta been cops. Plainclothes or off duty. They had that look."

Fatima told the driver: "Go faster."

She lit another cigarette. Pescatore reloaded. The security officer used his phone to report an emergency, presumably to the French embassy in the Bolivian capital hundreds of miles away. He described their location. Pescatore thought, *Just tell them it's so deep in the jungle that the cavalry will get here in time to tag our toes.*

Ten minutes later, more flashing red lights appeared up ahead. Two vehicles blocked the road. Silhouettes with long guns took shape. Belhaj, Pescatore and Wenceslao had a rushed conversation about strategy. Pescatore voted for blasting through the roadblock.

"What do we do, Commissaire?" Wenceslao demanded.

Fatima angled her head to blow smoke, as if she were sitting in a sidewalk café with someone who had made an annoying comment.

"This is a vehicle of the embassy of France carrying representatives of the government of France on official business," she said. "We will stop as requested."

By now, silhouettes at the roadblock were flashing headlights in a signal to stop and scurrying to take cover. The driver hit the brakes on the Land Cruiser. After the howl of the engine and the shriek of the tires, the quiet was startling.

Pescatore gripped his pistol. The Nissan behind them disgorged two gunmen. *We're good and surrounded now,* he thought. *I hope Fatima has a plan.*

A half dozen gunmen at the roadblock took aim at the Land Cruiser. But Pescatore wasn't convinced they were confederates of the guys he had just shot. They seemed too calm. Unless they were real cold-blooded.

The lean, bespectacled man who approached the vehicle made a show of holstering his pistol as he walked. He wore a uniform-style cap, a fatigue jacket, and khaki pants—an outfit that left some ambiguity about his affiliation with law enforcement. He carried a satellite phone.

Wenceslao lowered his window, talked with the man, and turned in his seat.

"The gentleman identifies himself as a police lieutenant," Wenceslao said, his voice full of disbelief. "He says he has a phone call for Mr. Valentín."

"What?" Pescatore demanded.

Wenceslao handed Pescatore the lieutenant's phone. Because his life was getting stranger every day, Pescatore wasn't altogether surprised to hear Raymond's voice on the other end of the line.

"Cuate," Raymond said. "Whaddya hear, whaddya say?"

13

I Love Paris

The line was from *Angels with Dirty Faces,* a 1930s gangster film they had liked as kids. James Cagney and Pat O'Brien are boyhood pals in a tough neighborhood. One day the police chase them. Cagney gets caught and becomes a gangster; O'Brien escapes and becomes a priest. The gangster goes to the electric chair after helping the priest reform a bunch of punks played by the Bowery Boys. Raymond liked to mimic the nasal delivery of the pals greeting each other: "Whaddya hear, whaddya say?"

"Raymond." Pescatore spoke into the phone through clenched teeth. He saw an incredulous look on Fatima's face. "You think this is some kinda joke? I got guys pointing guns at me over here."

"Just getting your attention, bro." Raymond sounded jovial. "Bringing the drama."

"Where you calling from?"

"Far away. What're you doing in the Chapare? That's a bad place to cause trouble. And you're sidekicking with a lady fed. African American babe. What is she, FBI?"

Raymond had enough clout in the area to track their movements and sic the cops on them. Someone had given him a description or photo of Fatima Belhaj. Yet his sources weren't that great; he was under the impression that she was a U.S. agent. Pescatore wondered if Raymond had sent the gunmen to the Pensión Lola.

Raymond asked, "So, homes, are you tapping that?"

"Man, *fuck* you!" Pescatore's exclamation made the others jump in their seats. "You and your goddamn head games."

"You're lucky I heard what was going on and got involved." Raymond's voice hardened. "You're messing with heavy-weights."

"Oh yeah, I forgot, that's your specialty now: long-distance murder." He trembled with rage. "I was at El Almacén, Ray. I saw those people with their arms and legs blown off, guts all over the floor. God rest their souls. You proud of yourself, scumbag?"

A long pause. Finally, Raymond asked, "You were at El Almacén?"

"Goddamn right."

"How—"

"That was the worst shit I ever saw."

Raymond's voice faltered. "I'm sorry, Valentín, I hope you—"

"Sorry I was there? Or sorry two hundred people got massacred?"

"The whole thing."

Outgunned or not, Pescatore pressed his apparent advantage.

"Bullshit," he snarled. "Next you're gonna say you had nothing to do with it."

"Less than you think. And don't forget, I called you. When I found out something was coming down in Buenos Aires, I tried to warn you."

"Didn't try too hard."

"You gave me a fucked-up number."

"You could've kept calling, or dialed fucking Argentine 911."

"It's not that simple. I took a big risk. Like I'm taking right now."

Pescatore was aware of Fatima, the security man, and the driver listening in consternation: his audience for a conversation at gunpoint. He took a breath.

"Raymond, I appreciate that," he said. "What you need to do is step up and turn yourself in. Before it's too late. Before more people get killed."

He looked at Fatima, who nodded encouragingly.

"Unfortunately, that's not possible at this time." Raymond spoke mechanically, as if for the record.

Maybe he thinks U.S. intelligence is monitoring the conversation, Pescatore thought. *Maybe he's right.*

"Come on, man," Pescatore insisted. "You and me need to figure something out."

"If the time comes, you'll be the one I deal with, believe me."

"At least tell me if there's any more attacks out there getting ready to happen."

"All I can say is keep an eye on Europe. That's where it's gonna hit the fan."

"Where in Europe?"

"*Escuchame, fiera,* you're not exactly in a position to be interrogating me right this minute." Raymond chuckled harshly. He had regained control.

"Guess not." Pescatore glanced at the roadblock. "You gonna call off your monkeys?"

"Yes. But get your ass out of Bolivia."

"Okay." And then, "Thanks."

"Pass me the *teniente.*"

"Think about what I said, Raymond. I'll be waiting on your call."

No response. Pescatore reached around Wenceslao and handed the phone back through the window.

"My friend wants to talk to you about giving us safe passage," Pescatore told the lieutenant in a voice intended to convey that he didn't take any shit.

After listening briefly to the phone, the lieutenant stepped back. The officers cleared the road. The Land Cruiser lunged forward as if heading for takeoff. The occupants relaxed in their seats as the danger faded in the rearview mirror.

Pescatore told Fatima about Raymond's end of the conversation.

"Here we been chasing this guy's shadow," he said. "And all of a sudden he's on the phone, calling the shots."

"Incredible," she said, shaking her head.

"I think Raymond might've just saved our lives."

"That is certainly one interpretation."

Fatima and the embassy security man conferred, then talked on their phones. Resting next to her with his eyes closed, their legs touching, Pescatore heard bits and pieces. The talk was about hustling Pescatore and Belhaj out of the country before the Bolivian authorities could trace the shooting and intercept them. Pescatore added Bolivia to the list of nations where he had worn out his welcome. His mind wandered; he relived the gunplay in Villa Tunari. He had most probably killed two men. Things had happened so fast he hadn't had time to dwell on it. He wasn't sure what to feel. The conversation with Raymond had freaked him out. Raymond had seemed self-confident but fragile. He relished playing the puppeteer, with the power to take or spare lives by phone. But he had sounded genuinely distraught about the news that Pescatore had been at the scene of the attack in Buenos Aires.

At the Santa Cruz airport, they were met by a local security team dispatched by the embassy: a Frenchman and three Bolivians. Wenceslao and the new guards brought in the luggage. They escorted Belhaj and Pescatore, who grudgingly handed over the SIG Sauer, through immigration and security checkpoints to a VIP lounge. The guards hovered near the door.

"These guys look like they expect the police to charge in any minute," Pescatore said.

171

Typing one-handed on her phone, Fatima said, "They will be happy when we are in the air."

"Why are we going to Miami?"

"It is the first available international flight."

"Oh. Then what?"

She looked up. "I want to go to Paris to push the investigation. Especially after what Raymond told you about possible attacks in Europe."

"And me?"

"It is up to you."

"What do you want me to do?"

"I would like you to come with me and continue our work."

Pescatore leaned closer in his armchair, glancing around. "In what capacity?"

"What?"

"For professional or personal reasons?"

She mimicked his pose with a conspiratorial grin. He felt as if he were drowning in her eyes. She kept her voice down.

"Both."

"Let's go to Paris," he said.

"Good."

"One thing, though. I pay my own way, my company's covering the expenses."

"We can discuss the accounts later." She made a dismissive noise. "Now I have something for you to help me."

She had received an e-mail with a list of names the French police had generated in the hunt for Raymond. They were mostly Argentines residing in France: legal and illegal immigrants, criminal records and clean. The theory was that Raymond was using a fake identity with a real Argentine passport obtained through Florencia. Fatima said it was her experience that people didn't make up aliases out of the blue, but chose names that had some significance.

"Tell me if you see anything that could be relevant for him."

She handed him her phone. He scanned the two dozen names in the e-mail.

"Why are these five in a separate list at the end?"

"They are not probably in France. Little information. No photos."

"Well, this one is interesting. Alberto Francisco."

"Why?"

"Turn it around and make it English. Or French."

"Francis Albert."

"It could be a coincidence. But it's the first two names of a singer. One of Raymond's idols." He smiled. "I'll give you a hint: he loved Paris."

"Sinatra."

"Yep. I figure if I'm Raymond playing around with aliases, that's the kind of thing I'd come up with."

"Excellent." She started tapping out an e-mail.

Pescatore called Facundo, who had been asleep but was happy to hear from him. Pescatore briefed him on events in Bolivia and the story behind the photo that he had e-mailed him. Facundo did not recognize Ali Baba, but he promised to make inquiries. Pescatore told him Fatima Belhaj had sent the photo to the FBI as well.

"We'll find out who the rascal is." Facundo sounded groggy. "I'm having the surgery tomorrow. I might be woozy for a couple of days."

Facundo played it casual, but the surgery was not a small matter. Pescatore knocked the wood of a side table, hoping he would pull through.

"Okay, boss," he said, keeping his voice warm and upbeat. "Hurry up and get better. You'll be taking care of business at La Biela in no time."

"I can't wait to watch other people have coffee and *medialunas*," Facundo replied. Pescatore wished him luck and they hung up.

Pescatore and Belhaj caught their flight. A long layover gave Pescatore a chance to play tour guide at the Miami airport, which combined U.S. infrastructure and Latin personality. He took Fatima for Cuban coffee at a counter where the workers addressed him in Spanish. They wandered boutiques where the salespeople and customers represented Ibero-America: Caracas, Madrid, São Paulo, Santo Domingo. At La Carreta diner, he introduced her to fried plantains, guanabana shakes, and a rice and beans dish whose name provoked a wry smile from Fatima: Moors and Christians.

He didn't mention that he also liked the Miami airport because of the high proportion of good-looking women who reminded him of Isabel Puente. But when Fatima asked how he knew Florida, he said his ex-girlfriend was from Miami. He found himself telling her about Isabel: a love story intertwined with a crime story. He explained that Isabel, then an internal affairs agent, had recruited him as an informant in a case that led to the Triple Border. Back in San Diego, they got engaged. It lasted three years.

Fatima said that romances between handlers and informants were problematic.

"You got that right," he said. "The relationship was all about danger, excitement, adrenaline. Us against the world. It was hard to adjust to a nine-to-five life. We were hot or cold, no in between. Isabel is real organized, ambitious. Me, uh, you know, I'm more of an improviser. I see you smiling over there behind your hand, Commissaire. Anyway, the bosses didn't want me working the Line anymore. There was intel that the mafia in Tijuana wanted to retaliate against me. I bounced around — the anti-smuggling unit, details in Arizona and Texas. More tension at home. We were like cats and dogs. Finally, she got a promotion to Washington. And it ended."

"But you still care about her." Her tone was soft.

"I guess you're right. But listen: I moved to Buenos Aires

partly to get away from her. I couldn't get her off my mind for months. Then I met you. And I've been thinking about you nonstop."

She smiled. She didn't say anything. He was comfortable with that. He had done enough talking.

They arrived in Paris on another overnight flight. The taxi sped through a gray dawn. He had never been to France, and he didn't spot any landmarks before Belhaj dropped him at a hotel on Porte Maillot, the city's northwest edge, next to a convention center resembling a space station. She was going home to change and then to her headquarters. Until she met with her chiefs, it would be better if he didn't accompany her.

"It is delicate," she said. "I need a little time."

"I understand," he said.

She had been up-front with him and brought him back into the case. But he was a foreigner. He wasn't official law enforcement; he wasn't on the team. Her words increased his feeling of isolation and uncertainty.

"Rest," she said.

They gave each other a lingering kiss, the first since the jungle. He savored it while he trudged like a zombie to his room and collapsed.

When he awoke, it was dark outside. He had slept all day. He showered, changed, and turned on the TV news. The lead report described rumblings of unrest in the slums of Paris and other cities. As summer neared, the government feared riots. He understood most of what he heard, and that was a relief. Speaking French would be another matter.

The room phone rang. Fatima Belhaj was downstairs. She steered him to the hotel restaurant and ordered for both of them, looking impatient until the waiter left.

"News?" he said.

"Enormous news," she said. "You were right. Alberto Francisco was Raymond's alias in France. Bravo, Valentín."

"Wow. Is he still here?"

"We do not know. Not only did he live in France, he has been known to the authorities for some time. Not only has he been known, he was *un indic*. An informant."

Still half asleep, he took a while to process the information. He asked, "How is that possible? How are you just now finding out?"

Her eyes flashed. "The things can be very strange in this world. I had an uncomfortable day. A number of colleagues were reluctant and unhappy to talk to me. This is an explosive affair. It had been kept quiet. And Valentín"—she reached to take his hand—"it is completely confidential. I should not tell you any of this."

"Don't worry. I don't tell anybody anything. When did Raymond stop working for you guys?"

"Last year. I am still assembling the narrative."

"Has Ali Baba been identified?"

"No. Tomorrow we fly to the south."

"What's there?"

"Raymond's...*officier traitant.*"

"Case officer?"

"Yes. We are going to see him. He is not happy about it."

"Another member of the Ray Mercer International Fan Club."

14

How Blue Can You Get?

Raymond's ex-handler was known in Sète, his hometown, as the Commandant.

Bruno Esposito had been a police commandant, a midlevel supervisor. His former rank had become his fighting name. The announcer proclaimed it over the sound system, rolling out the syllables: "Bru-no Es-po-si-to: *Le Commandant*!"

Cheers went up from the bleachers, echoing across the sun-splashed canal.

"That's our guy, right?" Pescatore asked. "In the red boat?"

Fatima Belhaj removed her sunglasses. "Yes. The one in the blue boat is called Hercules."

"No wonder. Look at that bruiser. He must weigh three hundred pounds. He's like a whale with arms and legs."

Sète was Pescatore's first real taste of France. It won him over right away. The port city of forty thousand spread around canals and lagoons beneath Mont St. Clair. He and Belhaj had flown to Montpellier and made a short drive to the coast. They sat in a sidewalk café on the downtown waterway lined with palm trees and temporary bleachers. Following Belhaj's lead, Pescatore was drinking a yellow anise-based beverage called pastis.

The liquor and the jet lag accentuated the disoriented fascination with which Pescatore discovered a sporting spectacle he had never heard of: boat jousting. Known as *les joutes,* the aquatic ritual reminded him of bullfighting and sumo wrestling as well as medieval jousting. There was a tournament in full swing on the canal, and the Commandant was participating.

The Commandant glided into view from the right. He went about six two and two fifty, bulky in the shoulders and back and gut, a skull of Easter Island dimensions. He wore the nautical jouster uniform of white pants and a white shirt over a long-sleeved blue-and-white-striped jersey. His left hand held a wooden shield; his right hand raised a wooden spear to salute the spectators. He stood atop a platform at the end of a ramp jutting from the stern of a boat propelled by ten oarsmen. The red-and-white vessel also carried a drummer and an oboist.

The rival boat approached from the left with the opponent and a similar coterie. The musicians played a fanfare. The crowd murmured.

The Commandant planted a trunklike leg and hunched behind his shield, a statue silhouetted against the sun. The boats converged. The spears slammed into the shields with the force of slow trucks colliding. Hercules roared; the Commandant stayed silent. Crouching low, muscles bunching behind his spear, he slowly and inexorably lifted Hercules sideways off his turret, the bigger man's face filling with disbelief. The Commandant finished him with a jab that knocked his shield into his mouth. Hercules grunted, toppled fifteen feet, and splashed prodigiously into the canal. He swam toward a rowboat sent to retrieve him, shaking his head and spitting.

"Damn," Pescatore said amid cheers. "Blood in the water. The Commandant can joust!"

Belhaj rolled her eyes. She didn't have to wait much longer. The ex-cop was eliminated in his next match by a bronzed behemoth known as the Anti-Parisian. Before Esposito hit the water, Belhaj was on her feet stubbing out her cigarette.

"Come on," she said.

Heads turned when she went by: her mane streaming in the breeze, her bare shoulders in the sleeveless top, her straight-backed stride in leggings and ankle-high sandal boots that made her taller. She carried her gun in a purse on a short strap. Minutes later, she and Pescatore found their man in an outdoor restaurant in a small shaded plaza. The tables were filled with jousters: white-clad knights of the waterfront proletariat shoveling down calories, their girth the product of physical labor, hearty food, strong wine. Pescatore saw bruised brows, mashed noses, mangled ears, damaged eyelids.

The Commandant had a scar on his jaw. The ex-cop sat alone at a table positioned, no doubt for their meeting, at a distance from the others. He had changed into a blue jersey of the French national soccer team. He wore a towel around his fireplug neck and sunglasses in his hair, which was wet and thinning. His smile showed slablike teeth and lines around the eyes and mouth. His voice was softer and subtler than his physique.

"Before we talk, we eat," he said. "I have to stay at fighting weight."

The waitress served plates piled with pasta. The dish was a *macaronade,* macaroni with a dark meat sauce. Fatima had said there was history of Italian, Spanish and Maltese immigrants in this region, many of them *pieds-noirs* from Algerian colonial days. Esposito was probably a Neapolitan name, Pescatore thought as he dug in.

The encounter between Belhaj and the Commandant resembled a joust on dry land. They addressed each other with the formal *vous.* Her attitude was politely stern. Esposito made a comment about one of her cases, indicating that he was familiar with her hotshot reputation. But his wary slouch, reminiscent of a sea lion, set the tone.

The Commandant had been based in Montpellier with the

national police division known as Renseignements Généraux, General Intelligence. The RG, as it was called, had its roots in the Napoleonic political police. It had monitored just about everything.

"Labor unions, political parties, students, journalists, casinos," he told Pescatore. "But our most important mission was the threat in the slums: Islamists and criminals. We knew the terrain better than anyone."

In 2008, the RG was fused with Belhaj's agency, which did national security. The result was a new superagency called the Direction Centrale du Renseignement Intérieur (DCRI), the Central Directorate of Domestic Intelligence. Esposito felt that the new arrangement had left him and other former RG officers in a position of inferiority.

"A shotgun marriage," he said wryly. Pescatore thought of the bad blood lingering from the merger of the immigration and customs services in the United States.

About two years after the fusion, the Commandant had recruited a promising informant named Alberto Francisco: an Argentine Muslim convert in a clique of hard-core extremists who worshipped at a mosque in a former automotive plant on the outskirts of Montpellier.

"We had been aware of them for years. Their discourse was radical. They had links to a network that had moved fighters to Algeria and Iraq after the American invasion. This Alberto, or Raymond, as one now calls him, pops up. Out of nowhere. Charismatic. He made an impression at the mosque as a muezzin, chanting the call to prayer. They said he had a voice like the angels."

The Commandant glanced skyward to illustrate the point.

"I don't know," he said. Pescatore noticed he had a habit of using that phrase before showing that he knew quite a bit. "It was strange, a South American in this milieu. But he had Lebanese origins and references from Islamist drug traffickers in

Spain. He took over a splinter group that held private prayer sessions. Many were converts. They tend to be the angriest and most volatile of all. They want to prove themselves. The ones you really have to watch so they don't do some big stupidity."

Belhaj nodded knowingly. Esposito said his unit learned that Raymond was stirring things up. He organized travel to terrorist training camps and combat zones. The Moroccan wife of one of his recruits caught his eye. The recruit soon died in a suicide bombing in Afghanistan.

"The wife was a fire-breathing ideologue. Educated, very tough. The husband was young and not bright. Raymond manipulated him and sent him to his doom to clear a path to the wife's bed. Then he married her."

"Is that the mother of his boys?" Pescatore asked.

"Souraya. Yes. You know the dossier, sir."

Pescatore rested his head on his hand. He remembered Raymond glowing when he talked about his family during the conversation in Argentina. Pescatore wasn't surprised to find out that the seed was ugly.

"The wife's immigration status was problematic," Esposito said. "She was on the blacklist of the Moroccan services because of her radicalism. I pulled in Alberto, I mean Raymond, and had a muscular conversation with him. A cool customer, but the threat of deporting the wife shook him up. We reached an arrangement. Voilà: We were inside the network. Inside the routes to Pakistan, Afghanistan, Mali, Syria. All the theaters. His information helped us and other services. We intercepted jihadis on their way to fight or coming back. We identified foreign training compounds. One camp in Pakistan, perhaps coincidentally, I don't know, got a wake-up call from a Hellfire missile. Everyone was content."

Declining sugar for his coffee, the Commandant asked the waitress for artificial sweetener. He said, "I'm on a diet, dear."

Raymond soon developed a friendly relationship with his

handlers. "Very engaging. Always finding an advantage, a vulnerability. He was full of little gestures. Once, we were in my car with the music playing. I am a fan of the blues. Raymond knew a lot about the blues. He brought me a classic live recording of B.B. King in Chicago: 'How Blue Can You Get?'"

Esposito pronounced the English hesitantly. He stirred his coffee. "I don't know. Perhaps he was too slick for his own good. I told my men: 'Boys, keep an eye on this one. He's not the typical exalted stooge.' Sure enough, we began to see things we didn't like."

The Commandant discovered that Raymond and his gang had rackets on the side. They dealt in hashish and cocaine with Moroccan traffickers in Barcelona, Gypsies in Perpignan, Italians in Nice. They were involved in robberies and shootings.

"Informants double-deal all the time. We didn't do anything about it. But the scale, the audacity, concerned me. He was a full-fledged gangster. At first he wore a long beard, the whole getup, but soon he shaved it. He dressed well, chased women. He told his followers his lifestyle was *taqiyya,* dissimulation to fool the infidels. I got a feeling that he was playing...Pardon me, I must pay my respects to the victor."

The Anti-Parisian, the tanned young jouster who had defeated the Commandant, walked up to greet him. The backslaps sounded like someone hitting an elephant with a baseball bat. Belhaj directed an exasperated look at Pescatore. Esposito sat down when the other man left.

"What a warrior," Esposito told them. "I was a champion in my youth, but I am out of practice. No matter how hard I train, I don't know if I'll ever beat the Anti-Parisian."

"Why do they call him that?" Pescatore asked, breaking his personal rule about keeping his mouth shut when in doubt.

"The reality is that many of us in these parts are not enamored of Paris." The Commandant gulped down his coffee. "I worked there as a young officer in the CRS, the riot squad. I speak from personal experience. Paris is bizarre. Paris is a museum surrounded by a jungle."

Belhaj scowled. She snapped something that Pescatore didn't understand. The Commandant retorted. They yammered at each other, fast and furious. Pescatore caught words: *Franchement, écoutez, épouvantable.* She said Esposito might as well have called her an ape. He responded that it was ridiculous to think his statement was directed at her.

Pescatore realized that he had tossed a hand grenade onto the table. Fatima saw the Commandant as a racist, sexist dinosaur from the provinces who had just insulted the area where she grew up and the power center she represented. The Commandant regarded her as a pushy ethnic female climber sent by chicken-shit bosses. Pretty ironic, Pescatore thought, because Esposito was no doubt the son or grandson of immigrants himself. Maybe that made him resent her even more.

Taking advantage of a diminuendo in the argument, Pescatore intervened. He spoke in the most formal French he could muster.

"It is all my fault," he said, addressing them both. "I should have never asked the question. My most sincere apologies."

His words had a pacifying effect on Esposito.

"Listen, I admit I am bitter," he said to Pescatore, sighing. "I did my duty and I was ignored. I know you are investigating the attacks in Argentina. I deduce that Raymond was involved. This fulfills my worst fears."

In a stony voice, Fatima Belhaj said, "You were saying that he was manipulating intelligence."

"It was worse than that. I suspect him of espionage. And at least one act of political violence on French soil. My analysis is not popular in the intelligence community."

The Commandant bent to his left and reached into a gym bag. "When I was advised you were coming, I retrieved a report

I wrote back then. I would like you to read it, to absorb the information without emotion or bias."

He followed her disapproving gaze from the papers in his hand to his gym bag.

"What? Are you concerned about my carrying a sensitive document in public?" He grinned. "Jousters don't steal. And no one steals from a jouster. Please read it, take your time. Then we can continue."

Giving them no opportunity for objections, he left and went to visit at a table across the plaza. His high-shouldered, prow-chested walk recalled Robert Mitchum or John Wayne.

"I begin to lose patience with the Com-man-dant," Fatima muttered to Pescatore. She pronounced the title with derision.

Unable to think of a safe response, Pescatore pulled his chair closer. She said she would translate the parts he didn't understand. Dated fifteen months earlier and stamped with warnings about confidentiality, the report referred to Raymond as Alberto Francisco. After a preamble, it said:

This informant has helped our unit infiltrate an international al-Qaeda-linked network. The results are well documented (see first attached addendum).

Nonetheless, recent information forces us to reassess the credibility of said informant. Although he plays a central role in a Sunni terrorist network based in the Montpellier region, concern has emerged that he has secret ties to Hezbollah and Iranian intelligence.

Despite the enmity between Sunnis and Shiites, there are precedents. Iranian intelligence used Sunni North Africans for attacks in Europe in the 1980s. Iran sheltered fugitive al-Qaeda chiefs after September 11. The Iranians see the bin Laden galaxy as a weapon against the West, Israel, and Saudi Arabia, one that can create terror and confusion and shield Iran against retaliation.

Three examples of the evidence for this admittedly sensitive thesis:

1. Francisco's group is involved in robberies and drug trafficking. The proceeds fund his luxurious lifestyle, but we also detect signs of cash sent to atypical destinations. A source reports that couriers bring suitcases full of euros to Beirut. Unfortunately, it has been impossible to intercept a cash shipment. But we believe this money could be financing Hezbollah, which is increasingly involved in drug smuggling.

2. Last month, a source recounted a notable experience in Iran (see declaration of Ricard Xavier Vives, addendum two). The source, a Spanish extremist, previously served in the Spanish army. Francisco selected him to go to a Pakistani training camp with a group who traveled via Turkey and Iran to the border of Pakistan, led by a Spanish-speaking militant named Belisario.

3. The Iranian security forces detained the travelers. The Spaniard was taken to a safe house for a separate debriefing. Iranian officers showed knowledge of his military background and offered him money, training, and missions in Europe and South America. He declined and returned home after the incident, which he feels was orchestrated by Alberto Francisco. He has since disappeared. Our hypothesis: Francisco grooms certain promising converts and sends them ostensibly to Pakistan through Iran, where intelligence officers try to recruit them. These recruits could be used as Iranian sleeper agents for eventual terror or espionage in France and Europe.

4. In fact, there are links to the recent murder in Lyon of an Iranian dissident, Leila Shahidi, the daughter of a prominent exile family. The judicial police insist that the young lady died in a common robbery. But my unit persists in the be-

185

lief that it was an assassination motivated by her family's activism against the regime in Tehran. The suspected killer was linked by phone traffic to the entourage of Francisco (see third addendum). Of course, the suspect's guilt has not been proven and he has since died in a motorcycle accident. Nonetheless, Francisco was in a position to organize the murder of the dissident.

The report ended with an urgent request for a full investigation of Alberto/Raymond with assistance from other law enforcement and intelligence services, including foreign ones.

"What do you think?" Pescatore asked.

Belhaj studied a diagram of phone links. Pescatore added excitedly: "Belisario. That's gotta be Belisario Ortega, the ex-cop who was the leader of the attack in Buenos Aires."

"It is the most interesting and solid detail in this," she said.

"Meaning you have doubts."

"Remember, this was written defensively, to explain the loss of control of an informant. It is full of speculation. Many Islamist groups send jihadis to South Asia through Iran. The Iranian services are aware of it, but that does not mean they infiltrate the networks. The war between Shiites and Sunnis in Syria has made the Iranians more hostile to al-Qaeda."

Fatima was right to be hard-nosed; the theory required that Raymond be sneaky enough to run a secret parallel network. Still, Pescatore wondered if her beef with the Commandant might affect her objectivity.

She asked him to bring Esposito back. Pescatore went to the table where Esposito sat laughing with his crew. In a friendly tone, the Commandant asked, "Is the *haute personnalité* from Paris ready for me?"

As they walked, Pescatore asked, "How long have you been jousting?"

"Since I can remember. My father was a jouster. There has been jousting here since the Crusades. The crusaders invented it while they were waiting to sail to the Holy Land."

"Looks like fun, if you don't mind a spear in the face now and then."

Esposito chuckled. He asked Pescatore his first name. When he heard it, he asked him to repeat it. The ex-cop hesitated with a curious expression, but said nothing more.

Belhaj lit a cigarette and asked Esposito to resume the briefing. After he submitted the report, he said, his chiefs called him on the carpet. They lectured him about speculation based on limited proof. Then they bigfooted him. A squad based in Paris took over as handlers for Raymond, who helped prepare an operation to dismantle his own network.

"He went to someone powerful behind my back and made a deal to protect himself and his family. Perhaps U.S. intelligence. The Americans were keenly interested in the case. After all, the militants were traveling and training with the goal of killing U.S. troops. I made strenuous objections. I said we couldn't let Raymond go free. He was the ringleader! He had deceived us. But he convinced everyone that he was indispensable."

The roundup produced a dozen arrests in France, Belgium, Spain and Turkey. Raymond and Belisario were not captured.

"A farce. He threw them bones. They didn't even arrest anyone in Pakistan, because the Pakistani services are on the side of the enemy. The affair left a bad taste in my mouth. It was a question of honor. I retired. Imagine, at forty-seven. A full-time jouster."

"What do you know about Raymond today?" Belhaj asked.

"Nothing. Recently I was informed that you were looking for him, and that he is really an American. It only makes me more suspicious. But your colleagues who took over the dossier are the ones to ask. It is my understanding they have lost track of him. Not very impressive."

Belhaj shrugged, conceding the point.

"Be careful with this guy," Esposito said. A grimace etched lines like cracks in granite on his broad earnest face. "He's a scorpion. He destroys whatever he touches."

Belhaj thanked him for his time. She handed him the report, but he asked her to keep it. He hoped it might still be of value.

"I presume that, like me, you are the first in your family to join the police," Esposito said to Belhaj. He sighed. "It was once a source of great pride for me. But it turned out to be ephemeral. Other things endure."

The Commandant scanned the crowded, boisterous tables around him. *Back home, back in his tribe,* Pescatore thought.

15

Jour de Paye

As the taxi drove toward Paris from Charles de Gaulle Airport the next morning, a fleet of police vans sped by in the opposite direction.

A dozen vans. Lights flashing. Crammed full of officers. The initials *CRS* on the sides: *Compagnies Républicaines de Sécurité.* The riot squad.

"Merde," Fatima Belhaj said. "It begins."

Newspapers and televisions in Montpellier had blared the news as Pescatore and Belhaj were leaving. After weeks of scattered violence in the slums, police nationwide were girding for the worst because of an incident in a housing complex near the Paris airport. Armed with spray cans and bad attitudes, two teenage graffiti artists had tagged the wall of a police substation. Officers gave chase. A boy fled into the path of a bus. He was in a coma.

"If he dies, this area we are passing now will be very hot," Fatima said.

"Are the Islamic networks stirring it up?" Pescatore asked.

"No. They are a separate world, though sharing the same space. The rioters are low-level gangs. Normally they do not respond to politics or religion. They have particular codes, their own logic. Riots happen because of conflict with the police. Especially if someone dies, accident or no."

189

"Not a great atmosphere to be hunting for Raymond. Imagine a terrorist attack now."

"This is what I fear."

The traffic slowed. She pointed out fresh graffiti on the cement wall of the highway.

"You see it?" she said.

The graffiti proclaimed, *C'est le Jour de Paye.* It was the phrase the youth had painted on the police station before the bus hit him.

"'It's Payday,'" Pescatore said.

Fatima had explained that "Jour de Paye" was a song by Booba, a gangster rapper of Moroccan-Senegalese descent with jailhouse muscles and a way with words. The slogan had appeared overnight on walls across the country.

The taxi cruised along the Seine into the heart of the city. Pescatore experienced the splendor of Paris at full blast: the symmetrical stone facades enclosing the river, the boats skimming the water, the elegant frame of the Eiffel Tower. The vista made him feel like what he was: a kid from Taylor Street.

"Nice town you got here, Fatima," he said, lifting her hand to kiss it. "I went from the Paris of South America to the real McCoy."

"I am happy you are here," she said, holding his gaze.

They had slept together at the hotel in Montpellier, making up for the missed nights. He had learned more about her personal life. She got a lot of attention from male colleagues, but warded off serious relationships. She maintained a discreet distance from her family. Two brothers were serving time in prison. People in the neighborhood asked for favors now that she was a big shot. That came with the territory, as did her vigilance for challenges or slights to a Muslim woman who had gone far.

"Like Le Commandant making that jungle crack," Pescatore had said sleepily in bed.

"I feel sorry for him." She lay with her head pillowed on his chest. Her hair smelled sweet.

"You do?"

"He was a good officer. He had a bad experience with a manipulative informant. Yes, I have doubts about his Iranian theory, but he is not dumb."

"I thought you were gonna smack him."

"He probably did not mean to insult me personally. But it was still insulting. I could not let it pass."

"I think he got the message."

The only hint of conflict between them came at breakfast in the hotel when Pescatore broached the subject of obtaining a gun for self-defense.

"Impossible," she said.

"Came in pretty handy in Bolivia."

"In the jungle, an extreme situation," she said. "Now we are in France. It is against the law for you, Valentín. I cannot permit it."

The taxi left her at the Ministry of the Interior on place Beauvau in front of a tall, ornate gate flanked by flags and columns. Her bosses had summoned her to discuss the Raymond Mercer investigation and the terrorist threat. Pescatore checked into a small hotel on boulevard Malesherbes.

The cool June day was great for walking. He wandered from one majestic landscape to another: the place de la Concorde, the Tuileries Garden, the Louvre. The problem was that he kept looking at the terrain through the eyes of a terrorist. Noting a busload of cops parked outside the U.S. embassy, he asked himself if Raymond's network—whoever they were—would go after soft targets in Europe as they had in Argentina. He thought about Raymond's role. During the phone call, Raymond had given the sense that he was a secondary player in the South American plots. Yet the Commandant said that Raymond had run the show in Montpellier.

Pescatore stopped near the place Madeleine to eat at a little lunch spot called Caffè Corto. An Italian named Massimo served him an espresso and a prosciutto sandwich and gave him a piece of intel: your chances of scoring a good cup of coffee in Paris were improved if you requested it *bien serré* (short and tight).

After a second espresso, Pescatore pulled out his notebook. He reviewed what he had jotted down in recent days and decided to put together a timeline of Raymond's movements.

November 2004—Ray arrested in Chicago. Drug informant: Chicago, Miami, Latin Am.

Late 2005—Buenos Aires. Singer/pianist.

2006/2007—Involved with Flo, Kharroubi, Belisario Ortega. Fraudulent docs, human smuggling, cocaine. Conversion to Islam.

2007—aka Ramón Verdugo. Back and forth to Bolivia. Smuggling to Argentina, Brazil, EU, Middle East.

2007—Drug bust in Buenos Aires province. (Still U.S. informant?) Relocates to Bolivia. Busted with Ali Baba (photo taken by Bolivian cops), released.

2008—??

2009–2011—Montpellier, France, aka Alberto Francisco. Boss of extremist cell. Marries Souraya. Recruitment, travel of al-Qaeda militants to Pakistan (via Iran), other jihad areas. French informant.

2012—Postcard from Lebanon to Argentine cousin. Commandant detects double-dealing, drug racket, robberies. Possible drug money going to Beirut. Killing of Iranian dissident in Lyon.

2013—Belisario Ortega with militants in Iran/Pakistan. Commandant reports concern to chiefs about Iran/Hezbollah link. A new DCRI unit takes control of R. (U.S. intel role?) Network busted.

Late 2013/early 2014—Raymond back in Buenos Aires.
    Reconnects with Flo. Spotted at club by Bocha.
2014—April: Infiltrates suicide bombers into Argentina.
    May: Calls Amélie and me about plots.
    La Paz cell dismantled.
    BA attacks.

The exercise helped him organize his thoughts. Pieces were missing: The gap after Bolivia and before France. The extent of contact with U.S. agents. The possible Iranian link. Pescatore wanted to consult with Facundo and check how the surgery had gone. As he pulled out his phone, it occurred to him that Facundo could help with another issue.

Facundo sounded strong.

"The surgery was a success," he declared.

Pescatore gave him an update. Then he spoke in code.

"Facundo, I need help," he said. "I left my copy of *Martín Fierro*"—he emphasized the final word—"and I'd like to get a new one. Do you know where I could do that? I feel lost without *Martín...Fierro*."

Martín Fierro was an Argentine epic poem. The word *fierro* was slang for a pistol.

Facundo understood immediately. "Are you sure?"

"I'm at a point in my intellectual development where I need it," Pescatore said.

"That's a heavy book. A serious commitment. Especially overseas. That kind of reading is easier here."

"I understand," Pescatore said. "But I'm a serious and careful reader. I really think I'll be better off. I wouldn't bother you otherwise."

"Very well. By the way, do you need money?"

"No, I've got plenty left from what you gave me."

"Fine. I'll call you back. Be careful, son."

Within the hour, Facundo called with an address and a name.

Pescatore took the Métro to the Marais neighborhood. He found himself on a subway platform among a group of small boys on a school outing. There were two dozen of them, seven or eight years old. Pescatore noticed that all of the boys, and a male teacher, wore baseball caps. He didn't think the French were into baseball. A boy stopped to remove his sweater with the help of a woman teacher. She held his baseball cap as he pulled the sweater over his head. Pescatore saw the boy was wearing a *kippah*—a skullcap. The teacher replaced the baseball cap carefully over the *kippah*, took the boy's hand, and hurried to catch up with the group.

Pescatore understood. The boys wore the baseball caps to hide the fact that they were Jewish. Facundo had told him about the dangers on the streets of Europe: beatings, stabbings, the occasional murder. Pescatore remembered the terror spree in Toulouse by a French extremist gunman who had killed French Muslim soldiers because he saw them as traitors, then slaughtered children at a Jewish school. Like Raymond's crew, the killer had links to Islamist networks in Pakistan and Afghanistan.

The address provided by Facundo was a shoe store near rue des Rosiers, a charming neighborhood with narrow streets and lots of pedestrian traffic. The contact was the youthful rumpled proprietor, whose name was Moshe. He wore a *kippah* and a sport jacket with rolled-up sleeves. His store was small, cluttered with merchandise and bereft of customers. A bored saleswoman with stylishly short hair glanced up at Pescatore, then returned her attention to her cell phone.

Moshe led Pescatore down a narrow hall and through a courtyard to a storeroom. Once they were inside, Pescatore said he needed a gun he could carry discreetly. Moshe outlined options. Pescatore settled on a Colt .25 automatic and an ankle holster. Moshe put a leather satchel on the table. Pescatore inspected and loaded the gun and strapped it onto his ankle.

"What do I owe you?"

"Please." Moshe waved him off. "We have an arrangement with our mutual friend."

On the subway again, Pescatore brooded. He hated to deceive Fatima. However, he was sick of his limbo status, first with the FBI and now the French police. He considered the prospect that Fatima was not telling him everything, especially about U.S. involvement. Furukawa had said a team from FBI headquarters was on the case. The Commandant had said U.S. intelligence knew about Raymond the year before the Buenos Aires attack. Apparently, they had signed off on a deal to let him walk in exchange for rolling up the Montpellier network. That raised serious questions. Like whether the attack in Argentina could have been averted.

It's no fun being kept in the dark, Pescatore thought. *And it can get you killed.*

The closer he got to Raymond, the more dangerous the situation became. He was a cop; he was going to carry a gun. Better the good guys caught him with it than the bad guys without it.

Back in his hotel room, he watched television. No riots yet. The injured youth remained in a coma. The news showed police vans and kids milling around in front of towers. Waiting for payday.

Fatima called. She gave him an address and told him to take a taxi. On the ride out, he made sure the ankle holster was well concealed. The route led through a long complex of tunnels beneath the high-rises of the outlying La Défense business district. The taxi rolled into the sunset—green hills, shopping centers, leafy streets—then climbed past walled homes and stopped in a narrow cobblestoned plaza with a post office and a café. The community seemed a mix of rich suburb and country village.

Fatima waited at the wheel of a gray Peugeot 407 sedan. She squeezed his hand when he got in.

"You found him?" Pescatore blurted.

She allowed herself a triumphant smile. "His family."

"This isn't the kind of area I expected."

The intelligence agency had tracked down the wife and set up surveillance. The property had been purchased in her name two years earlier. The neighbors often saw Souraya, who wore a head scarf and Muslim attire, and the two sons. There had been a few sightings of a man resembling Raymond.

Belhaj would have preferred to watch as long as possible to identify suspects and hope that Raymond showed up. But her bosses feared that a terrorist attack was imminent. They wanted to swoop in and make arrests to disrupt any potential plot.

Belhaj cruised past Raymond's house. The street meandered up a hillside past a row of large lots. An ivy-covered stone wall with a portico entrance for cars fronted Raymond's property, which was near the top of the hill.

"Nice place," Pescatore said.

"Drug money."

Belhaj drove to a nearby parking garage, where they found six officers from her unit and twice as many SWAT officers. Belhaj got into a van to confer with the chief of the SWAT team. After she got out, Pescatore took her aside.

"I can come along, right?" he asked. "It doesn't create a problem?"

"I am in charge," she said. "I want you there. But please put on this Spider-Man thing when the operation begins. It is protocol."

She handed him a wool ski mask.

A few hours later, he sat with Belhaj's unit in a van parked on the hilltop near Raymond's house. An officer's laptop computer showed several angles of the house from spy cameras. The SWAT officers waited in a second van. At about midnight, a Volkswagen sedan arrived and drove up through the portico. Two North African–looking men with thick beards went into the house. Pescatore heard an officer describe them as *barbus*.

Neither visitor appeared to be Raymond. Belhaj thought one was the brother of Raymond's wife. Their presence complicated the situation.

"It appears something is going on," Belhaj said. "Perhaps they are preparing to help the family leave."

Pescatore toyed with the ski mask. He glanced around at the investigators, who looked rumpled, unshaven and swashbuckling in sweaters and leather jackets. They had accepted his presence nonchalantly and treated him with courtesy and discretion. They probably thought he was CIA. The warm welcome brought back memories of raids he had done on smugglers' safe houses in the Border Patrol. A familiar sensation: anticipation, anxiety, hyperconcentration. Now he felt even more guilty and nervous about the ankle gun. He did his best not to move around and kept his shoes planted on the floor of the van.

"What's with the masks?" Pescatore asked, lifting the one in his hand.

"To protect our identities," Belhaj said. "It is common for police in Europe."

"Yeah, I guess I've seen that on TV."

"Not in the States?"

"Over there, these are strictly for bank robbers. Pretty intimidating."

She grinned. "To terrorize the terrorists."

At four a.m., Belhaj decided it was time. She pulled her curls back into a ponytail and put on her ski mask. The others followed suit.

SWAT officers scaled the wall from the street and entered the backyard from a property next door. Belhaj, Pescatore and her team crouched by the portico. On the other side of the wall, flash-bang grenades went off in the dark. The SWAT team made entry into the house. Pistols drawn, the plainclothes officers loped behind Belhaj up the driveway. As he ran, Pescatore had to restrain the reflex to pull the gun from his ankle holster. He could not show the gun unless he had no choice. Once he did, his little game was over. He charged over the lawn, passing the shadows of a swing set and a trampoline, almost tripping over a soccer ball. Radios echoed with shouted commands, doors banging, women screaming, a child wailing. Lights went on.

The interior had high ceilings and a modern design. A SWAT officer in full body armor stood in the middle of the living room with his foot on the neck of a prone and shirtless man, one of the visitors. Belhaj talked into the radio. A calm voice reported that the house was secure. Pescatore heard a woman in the kitchen. Her snarls and threats reverberated off walls. Voices told her to shut up.

Madame Mercer, Pescatore thought.

The investigators spread out and began a search. The living room was handsomely but sparsely furnished. The walls were bare. A Koran sat in a place of honor on a reading stand. Pescatore hunched over and examined a row of DVDs on a shelf beneath a king-size plasma television. He touched Belhaj's arm.

"Look, *The Battle of Algiers,*" he said. "Ray really liked that movie."

Her mask brought out the beauty of her eyes. She asked, "The politics or the cinematography?"

"Both. Can I look around?"

"Yes."

Pescatore poked his head into an adjoining study. An electric piano. Lots of books in English, Spanish, French and Arabic. A collection of vintage CDs and record albums.

Belhaj called his name. He followed her up the stairs and down a hall past officers. They entered a bedroom.

Pescatore came face-to-face with a miniature Raymond.

The boy was about four. He wore footed, one-piece pajamas decorated with Chicago Bulls insignias. He had his father's distinctive deep-set eyes, his high cheekbones, his thin build. He hugged a large stuffed lion. He looked scared, but he was dry-eyed. Anger glinted in his sidelong stare at the large invaders with masks and helmets and guns.

He's got his old man's attitude too, Pescatore thought.

The younger brother, meanwhile, wailed tragically in the arms of an older woman in a head scarf sitting on a bed. Pescatore assumed she was a nanny.

Pescatore asked Belhaj if he could talk to the older boy. She told an officer to clear everyone else out of the room. Pescatore pulled off his mask, thankful for the cool air on his face, and squatted on his heels.

The boy had taken refuge behind a toy drum set. Glancing around, Pescatore saw nothing Islamic or fundamentalist. There were piles of toys and many posters: European soccer players, NBA players, Disney characters, Muppets. The compact discs included not just children's songs but selections that he could imagine Raymond choosing to start a musical education at an early age: classical music, big band, Santana, the Beatles. In a corner were a xylophone, a mini-keyboard and a guitar.

"How you doing, son?" Pescatore's voice caught in his throat.

Instinctively, he had spoken in English. The boy looked at him intently, eyes wide. Pescatore realized that, without even trying, he sounded like Raymond. No matter what other languages this family used, he had no doubt that Raymond spoke to his sons in English.

The boy's arms were wrapped around the stuffed lion, which was half his size and wore a jeans jacket.

"That's a cool lion," Pescatore said. "What's his name?"

The boy looked down. He mumbled something that sounded like *Roland*.

"I'm a friend of your dad," Pescatore said. "From Chicago. You know Chicago?"

"Bulls."

The boy said the word very softly in accented English, still looking down.

"That's right, the Chicago Bulls basketball team, like your pajamas," Pescatore said. "My name is Valentín."

The boy perked up again, making eye contact.

"Valentín," the boy said, mimicking Pescatore's pronunciation.

"You got it, son. And you?"

"Valentín."

"Right, that's me." Pescatore chuckled. "Now, what's your name?"

The boy's face constricted into a mask of frustration, cheeks puffing out, eyes almost closed. Then Pescatore understood. He remembered the Commandant reacting strangely to his name. He felt tears well up.

In a gruff halting voice, the boy said, "I — am — Valentín!"

16

Champs-Élysées

*G*arde à vue.

  He hadn't come up with a good translation yet. "Police custody" fell short. After twelve hours, he had a solid understanding of the term. French law gave the police up to four days to interrogate terrorism suspects. No defense attorneys. No prosecutors. Just cops firing questions around the clock. Although they hadn't thumped anybody, he believed this was chiefly because they didn't need to: their information was too good. Still, *garde à vue* was a world of shit in which you did not want to live. French law enforcement did not pussyfoot around with terrorists.

  "Once, we put a whole family in jail," Fatima Belhaj had told him during the ride to headquarters. "The son was the suspect. His brother was an accomplice. The father was a radical imam. And the mother, she was detained for criminal association. If they had a dog we would have got him too, but dogs are *haram*."

  It was evening. An investigator placed another cup of coffee in front of Pescatore. He gave up his best *Merci, monsieur*. Luckily, the squad had a Nespresso machine and kept it cranking. Pescatore sat at a back table in the chilly underground room. The officers sat or stood near the one-way glass facing onto the empty interrogation chamber. They swilled coffee, reviewed documents, talked on phones, and worked at laptops.

Pescatore knew more now about Raymond's family. In addition to the house, they owned luxury apartments on France's southwest coast and in Spanish Morocco. The police had found evidence of serious wealth: bank accounts, real estate, luxury vehicles. Raymond's wife, Souraya, was twenty-six and had a law degree from Morocco. The sons were Valentín, age four, and Ramón, age two.

Pescatore was still getting his mind around the discovery that Raymond had named one of his sons after him. Unlike other things Raymond had done or said, the gesture could not be written off as manipulative or deceitful. Then there was his decision to give the second son the Spanish version of his own name. Fatima believed that Raymond looked back on his friendship with Pescatore with a sense of loss. He had tried to re-create a symbolic version of it with his sons. Pescatore was haunted by the image of little Valentín clinging to his lion. He had taken a liking to the kid; he had felt a tug of protective obligation. In the boy's face, Pescatore had seen the solitary awareness that this invasion of strangers was going to change his life in a bad way.

The interrogations up until now had been warm-up acts. Belhaj had watched her team question the nanny, the wife's brother, his associate and the wife, who had said little except to protest that the police had taken away her hijab. Belhaj had announced that she planned to interrogate the wife herself. She had taken refuge in her office, smoking up a storm, to prepare. The investigators hurried back and forth to answer her questions and provide data from the search.

A door opened on the far side of the interrogation room. Two uniformed officers, a man and a woman, brought in Souraya. They sat her down at the table. She was not handcuffed.

Although Souraya was Moroccan, her complexion was

lighter than Belhaj's. Her features were sharper. Under the smocklike garment, her shoulders were high and slender. Her long disheveled black hair swirled around eyes full of fury. There were rings under the eyes; she hadn't slept since the rude awakening of the arrest. Her face was dominated by a wide and sullen mouth. Pescatore remembered Raymond calling her a princess and a lioness.

Addressing her guards and the unseen watchers, Souraya demanded her head scarf.

"It is shameful that you leave me uncovered this way," she said, her strident delivery no doubt polished in university halls and street protests. "It is a violation, a humiliation. You trample my most basic human rights."

In spite of himself, Pescatore experienced a pang of empathy. He recalled his arrest in Argentina: the shirt over his face, the smells of horses and urine, the absolute helplessness. He had a fleeting irrational fear that someone was going to decide he was on the wrong side of the glass.

Belhaj arrived. She passed Pescatore and the investigators and went into the interrogation room. The guards exited, leaving the two women alone. Belhaj's entrance rattled Souraya. She watched in consternation as Belhaj put a folder on the table. Belhaj removed her leather jacket and draped it methodically on the back of a chair. She wore a tight pullover shirt, jeans tucked into boots. Her gun and badge flanked her metal belt buckle. She took her time lighting a cigarette.

"Now we are going to see something," an investigator said. He fanned his knees open and closed suggestively. There were chuckles and comments.

Belhaj's deputy, who was named Laurent, raised his head from his laptop. He was a short man in his forties with neat chiseled features and small round glasses that gave him an air of studious expectation. He made a stern growling noise that put an end to the snickering.

Souraya spoke rapidly in Arabic.

"One speaks French here," Belhaj said.

Souraya switched to French and raised her voice. After some back-and-forth, Pescatore caught the gist. Souraya refused to believe that the DCRI employed a female North African–looking investigator. She suspected that Belhaj was really a Moroccan intelligence officer, an interloper brought in under false pretenses to grill her. Souraya turned to the glass to appeal to the spectators again.

"This Moroccan spy has no jurisdiction here. We are in France. I have my rights!"

"Very amusing." Belhaj shook her head. "A terrorist who wants to destroy France, who despises everything about France, and now she has rights. Because she is in France. I have news for you, Souraya. I am a commander of the French police. Look at the badge. Yes, I am Moroccan too. But I am nothing at all like you. I am not a pathetic fanatical slave. I smoke, I drink, I give orders, I do what I please. And my job is to fuck you up."

Belhaj sat. She crossed her legs and puffed smoke. Souraya stared at her balefully.

"Where is your husband?" Belhaj asked. She used the familiar *tu* form.

"I have nothing to say to you."

Belhaj took a thoughtful drag of the cigarette. "I just met his Argentine girlfriend in Buenos Aires. You know her? Florencia? Fat, old, grotesque. Still, she must do something better than you. He can't get enough of her. He was over there fucking her a few weeks ago. Before the attacks. He sings to her. 'Sophisticated Lady.' Isn't that romantic? Does he sing to you?"

"I have nothing to say," Souraya snapped. But the mention of Florencia had hit a nerve. Her eyes smoldered.

"Perhaps my colleagues were reluctant to spell things out," Belhaj said. "Let me explain your situation. From a preliminary look at the evidence, e-mails, credit cards, et cetera, it is clear that you had prior knowledge of the plot in Buenos Aires. You helped your husband buy plane tickets on the Internet. Those facts in and of themselves constitute terrorist conspiracy in the murders of two hundred people, including two French citizens. Which means, Madame the lawyer, Madame the terrorist, that you are fucked."

Pescatore had never heard her speak so crudely and brutally. She exuded contempt. She was transformed.

"Nonsense," Souraya said.

"You know the law. There is no question we have enough evidence to hold you for trial. A case this complex, international angles, procedure and paperwork, that means four years in pre-trial detention. The number of victims increases the chances of a conviction and a long sentence. If by some remote chance you are acquitted, that's fine: we deport you to Morocco. You are high on the wanted list of the Mukhabarat. They can't wait to get hold of you. They will hang you upside down by your feet to drain the stupidities out of your head. And that will be just an *amuse-bouche.*"

Souraya folded her arms. She repeated her demand for the head scarf. Belhaj got up and paced, her boots loud.

"Enough crap about the head scarf," she said. "Wipe yourself with the head scarf. You are a repugnant hypocrite. You pretend to fight for your brothers and sisters in the *banlieue.* Look at the palace you live in, that stuck-up neighborhood. Pure bourgeois Western decadence. Financed by filthy sinful drug money."

"Don't you dare judge me."

"Natural human weakness, I suppose. You grew up in a stinking slum in Casablanca. Now this man showers you with money. Fine. But don't call yourself an Islamist. Look at how you raise your sons. Pop music, Disney, Batman!"

"I am entitled to provide the best for my sons. They must learn how to live in the West, even if they are not of the West. That is the path to true resistance."

A ripple of reaction went through the investigators. Belhaj had broken through, elicited a response. She dropped her cigarette and ground it beneath her boot as if it were Souraya's face. She laughed savagely.

"Is that how Raymond justifies it? Is that what you tell yourself? You deluded fool. Manipulated first by the Moroccan *barbus,* then this phony American Islamo-gangster playboy. You disgust me. The way you got rid of your first husband. You remember him, no? Bilal? The one who blew himself up in Afghanistan?"

"Bilal is a glorious martyr. You are not fit to utter his name."

"A martyr. A cuckold! Raymond played that boy like a violin. He sent him to die. The guilt must eat you alive."

"Shut up!"

Belhaj stalked up to the table. It looked for a moment as if she was going to slap the prisoner. Souraya reared back. Belhaj opened the folder on the table. She took out a paper: a printout of a color photo.

At the sight of the photo, Souraya let out a wail of anguish and revulsion. The sound echoed in the small room. She turned away, shaking violently, weeping. Pescatore thought for a moment that she would throw up. He saw the officers around him leaning forward.

Belhaj waited for the woman's lament to subside. She let the impact sink in, the silence gather.

"Yes, it is his head," she said softly. "That happens with kamikazes. The body disintegrates, the head flies off intact. Poor Bilal. So pathetic, so inept. His bomb vest malfunctioned. It was a partial detonation, too weak to kill the American soldiers he attacked. Their only injuries came from the spray of his bones and flesh."

"Liar!" Souraya sobbed. She wiped her eyes and nose. "He killed five infidels."

"No. Raymond deceived you. He told you that to make you

feel better. I read the dossier. I have a news story. Voilà. 'No fa-talities except failed bomber.' Your martyr's fiasco rated a few paragraphs. As meaningless as his life. Raymond must have had a good laugh. And of course, infidelity breeds infidelity. You cheated on Bilal. Raymond cheats on you."

Souraya was rigid and livid. Her Medusa-like shock of hair gave her the look of a madwoman.

"Where is Raymond?" Belhaj asked. "What is he plotting? What are the targets?"

"You are wasting your time."

"No. It is you whose time is running out." Belhaj walked around the table. She stood behind Souraya, uncomfortably close. She reached over her to pull another photo from the folder.

"Your boys," Belhaj hissed in her ear. She put her hands on Souraya's shoulders, a sarcastic caress. The woman shook her off, tendons and veins bulging in her neck. "Valentín and Ramón. Not Muslim names. But very cute."

"They have Muslim names," Souraya said in a strangled voice, as if speaking against her better judgment. "Seifullah and Ayman."

"But Raymond gives the orders in your house," Belhaj re-torted. "And they respond to the names he gave them. Take a good look at the boys, Souraya. I have made it my personal mis-sion to ensure you never see them again."

Belhaj walked back around the table. Her voice grew colder. Each word was like a blow.

"Never again. You are an unfit mother: a murderer, a ter-rorist, a drug trafficker, a money launderer, a monster. You are going to prison. Your husband too, if he lives. I have already conferred with the family services agency. We need to split the boys up, of course. Easier that way. We are looking for foster families to take immediate custody. I think nice Jewish fami-lies would be best, don't you? With time and effort, the right cultural—"

"Dirty whore!"

Souraya erupted. She shot to her feet and charged around the table. Belhaj planted herself in a defensive stance with her hands waist-high. She was unhurried; she might have been doing a martial arts warm-up. As Souraya came at her, Belhaj stepped into the lunge and slammed the heel of her hand into the bridge of her assailant's nose. Then she slid sideways and swept the woman's legs out from under her.

Souraya sat on the floor holding her face. Blood leaked through her fingers. Sobs racked her body.

Amid exclamations and toppling chairs, investigators rushed into the interrogation room. Belhaj made a calming gesture. She asked for a towel and a glass of water for the prisoner. Catching her breath, she leaned over next to Souraya.

Pescatore could not take his eyes off Fatima. Her serenity had returned with the speed of someone pulling off a mask.

She's a pantera, he thought, thinking of the term that Facundo used for Israeli commandos and other badass warriors. *I wouldn't want her interrogating me.* He remembered the forbidden pistol on his ankle.

"We are going to get you cleaned up," Belhaj said. "And then, because you love your boys, because Raymond Mercer has destroyed your life, you will tell us everything we need to know."

Souraya ended up talking until midnight.

Pescatore was a bit surprised that she betrayed Raymond so fast. He concluded that she had made the stark calculation that her situation was hopeless. The threat about the children had shaken her. She would do whatever it took not to lose them, to protect what was left of her family. It also had become clear to Pescatore that her relationship with Raymond was tormented. The guilt over Bilal festered. There were accumulated resentments: of how Raymond dictated the upbringing of the boys, of his secrecy, and, above all, of his affairs with other women. She peppered Belhaj with questions about Florencia.

"He has a right under Islamic law to more than one wife," Souraya hissed. "But not to run around with gutter whores and make a fool of me."

The dog gets dogged, Pescatore thought.

Souraya's confession revealed that she was an active player in the network, though Raymond compartmentalized information. In addition to what she picked up from him, Souraya learned a lot through the wives of other jihadis, a circle of informal informants. She said Raymond's group financed itself with drug money. It drew inspiration and training from al-Qaeda but was autonomous. Raymond had gone to al-Qaeda bosses in Pakistan to get their blessing. The "wise elders" in the tribal areas were busy hiding from drone strikes and happy to leave the specifics to him. Souraya showed no knowledge of Raymond's warning calls to Pescatore and Amélie Hidalgo about the plots in South America. She had never heard of Ali Baba and did not recognize the face in the photo.

To Pescatore's surprise, Belhaj asked about drug money going to Lebanon and contacts with Iranian intelligence. She had not dismissed the Commandant's theory after all.

Souraya shook her head disdainfully. Beirut was a destination for drugs and money, she said. But that was business. She doubted that Raymond had Shiite connections.

"The brothers use Iran as a passage to Pakistan," she said. "The Iranian services generally don't interfere. That doesn't mean we have anything to do with the Shiites. They are serpents and heretics. We despise them just as we despise you."

The next stage in Raymond's plan called for simultaneous attacks in Europe, Souraya said. The likely targets were London and Paris. She had not seen Raymond in weeks. He was moving around, making preparations.

"Don't think my arrest will stop the project," she said. "If anything, it will speed things up."

Souraya gave them names and information about phones, e-mail addresses, and documents. She warned that her knowledge was incomplete.

"He has bank accounts, passports, identities I don't know about, allies everywhere," Souraya said. She tapped her temple. "He is smarter than you. You watch: There has not been a major attack in Europe since London in 2005. He will pull it off."

Belhaj asked, "Will he take part personally?"

"It depends on the needs of the network. He is prepared for martyrdom."

I wonder, Pescatore thought. *More like he's prepared others for martyrdom.*

Over the bloodstained towel she held to her face, Souraya's look of pure hatred had not wavered. From what she had pieced together, she predicted the plot in Paris would target public places. She spoke with bitter admiration.

"He's a master of choreography," she said. "The new Carlos the Jackal, the Khalid Sheikh Mohammed of his generation. The idea is to use a world city as a world stage. Iconic backdrops. The Eiffel Tower, the Louvre, the Champs-Élysées. If I were you, I would be very worried about the Champs-Élysées."

17

The Battle of Algiers

Pescatore had seen *The Battle of Algiers* a number of times. He wasn't obsessed with the film like Raymond had been, but it had made an impression on him as a kid. In Argentina, he had seen it again with Facundo, who said the Pentagon used it as a counterinsurgency primer. Pescatore had rediscovered the haunting sound track, especially the opening theme: drum, cello, horns sounding the call to arms while paratroopers swarmed the Casbah hunting Ali La Pointe, hoodlum turned revolutionary.

The melody echoed in his head as he watched the counterterrorism apparatus of the French state rumble into action. He had a privileged vantage point next to Fatima Belhaj in the Peugeot 407, the rolling command post from which she coordinated offense and defense.

The offense was the hunt for the attack cells. After Souraya's interrogation, the French had warned the British and other allies about the threat. Counterterrorism agencies had spent the day casting a net of communications intercepts and border and transportation alerts. They combed through data about Raymond's crew, tracking down cars, phones, and addresses, questioning relatives and associates, kicking down doors. They activated sources in mosques, prisons, eateries, housing projects, martial arts clubs, Islamic bookstores, halal butcher shops, and even black-market rings that raised and sold sheep to fundamentalists for slaughter.

The defense was the protection of potential targets in Paris. Because of the existing fear of riots, the police brass were reluctant to further agitate the public with news of a terrorist plot. And counterterrorism security measures had been in place for months because of conflicts in the Middle East and North Africa. The police quietly augmented the deployments.

"This is one place in Paris where everybody mixes, all races, socioeconomic classes," Fatima said, driving toward the Arc de Triomphe, the traffic flowing in rivers of light into the portal. "We were coming here with my brothers and sisters when I was young. The *cité,* our apartment complex, was ugly and boring. No cinema, nothing to do. We were coming to the Champs-Élysées to walk, see the lights, go to McDo. Like tourists."

The avenue was a magnificent corridor of stone, metal and glass. It glowed like a grounded constellation. Saturday night had brought out crowds. Sightseeing buses disgorged Americans, Europeans and Asians. Spotlights and flashbulbs lit up the bustle at a movie premiere. Families lined up at a crepe stand where an African in a chef's hat worked his spatula with a flourish.

Pescatore saw more faces of immigrant, working-class France than he had seen since his arrival. The youths moved in groups in an international uniform worn with obligatory swagger: hooded sweatshirts, gold chains, baggy low-slung jeans, and basketball shoes. He saw a young man—flattop haircut, sprinter's build, tracksuit in the colors of the Algerian flag—greet a friend. After shaking hands, they touched their hearts. Pescatore thought that was cool. The girls wore tight pants and miniskirts and the occasional head scarf. He spotted ethnically mixed groups; Belhaj used the phrase *black-blanc-beur* (black-white-Arab).

212

"Everybody's pretty well behaved," Pescatore said. "Of course, it's wall-to-wall cops."

The Champs-Élysées was one of the best-policed stretches of pavement in the country. Crime was low, Fatima said, except for petty theft and occasional brawls. Red-and-white patrol cars glided by. Beat cops on foot had been reinforced by a regiment of the CRS, who walked in groups of four. Pescatore remembered that the Commandant had served in the riot squad; he saw jouster-like bulk, bull necks, trousers tucked into laced boots, leather gloves stuck in back pockets, lumbering wide-armed walks.

Belhaj pointed out the undercover officers of the anticrime brigade and her counterterror agency on foot, in cars, and two to a motorcycle. Pescatore put himself inside their heads. Scanning sidewalks and vehicles, mentally rehearsing the quick draw, visualizing a confrontation with a terrorist appearing out of a crowd, imagining their obliteration by a human bomb. They had been staring at photos of Raymond, memorizing his face, forging a psychic bond with their prey.

What a fucking mess you made, bro, Pescatore thought.

He yawned and rubbed his unshaven cheek. He had changed and taken a quick shower at his hotel. Otherwise he hadn't stopped since the night before, when the interrogation had ended and Souraya had been allowed to see relatives and a lawyer.

Belhaj had brought Pescatore to her office and asked him to write an e-mail to Raymond. Although Raymond had not mentioned it on the phone, she believed he had received Pescatore's first e-mail from Buenos Aires. They went over the wording. Pescatore wrote that he was in France and knew Raymond's wife had been arrested. He offered to mediate with the authorities and implored Raymond to make contact before anybody else got hurt. He gave him his cell phone number and the hotel number as well; the last thing he wanted was to miss another call.

I met Valentín pequeño, he wrote. *Great kid. They're taking good care of him. But for his sake, for your family's sake, this is the time to do the right thing.*

Now, Pescatore checked his phone again: no response. Belhaj parked near the place de l'Étoile, the traffic circle around the Arc de Triomphe where a dozen avenues formed a star. She talked on her radio. Her squad was chasing a tip about suspicious characters stockpiling weapons in a storage basement near the airport. Belhaj opened her door, saying she wanted to take a look at security in the Charles de Gaulle l'Étoile station, an underground hub for the subway and the RER, the regional train line.

Riding down on the escalator, Pescatore saw a police officer walk by between uniformed soldiers with rifles. The RER was the main rail line to the *banlieue.* On weekends and during times of urban unrest, intelligence officers monitored outlying stations and alerted downtown units if street gangs or suspected groups of *casseurs,* vandals, were on their way. With the hospitalized "Jour de Paye" graffiti artist unlikely to survive, the police knew that disturbances would break out in the projects sooner or later. But they were determined to prevent the spectacle of cars burning on the Champs-Élysées, which would hurt tourism, political fortunes, and law enforcement careers.

Riots were the least of Fatima's worries. Although Souraya had talked about attacks on landmarks, Fatima was concerned about bombs on trains.

"Nobody wants another Madrid or London," she said as they walked through the crowded station. "The tactic is too easy, too devastating. It has required a lot of work and luck to avoid something like this in France."

They reached a train platform. A row of riot police and canine units stood along the wall. When the train arrived, the officers stepped forward, eyes roving over the emerging passengers, and intercepted selected young males, mostly in groups and mostly minorities. The police checked their identification cards, questioned them, frisked them, and, for the most part, sent them on their way. It was a largely silent, strangely efficient ritual. The other passengers went about their business unfazed. The youths complied with little resistance.

Another train arrived. The riot police stopped a rowdy group. As the officers ordered them against the wall to be searched, a police German shepherd got overexcited. The dog barked and lunged, leaping against a leash held by a canine officer in a blue jumpsuit.

"Careful with that dog!" snapped a young man with a retro Afro and a T-shirt decorated with a map of the island of Guadalupe. His palms flat on the wall, he glanced fearfully over his shoulder. "He's trained to bite blacks and Arabs, right?"

The police released the group. The youths loped toward the escalator. Their chant echoed: "It's payday!"

Pescatore raised his eyebrows at Belhaj. He asked, "So just stop and frisk, no probable cause?"

"The law allows the police to check papers and conduct searches," she said.

"I don't want to sound politically correct and everything, but don't you guys get sued for profiling?"

Belhaj's phone rang. An informant wanted to meet right away. Pescatore took care to keep his ankle holster concealed when they jumped in the car. Belhaj hit the gas, lights and siren. She blazed into the traffic madness around the Arc de Triomphe.

Out of the blue, her eyes on the street, she asked: "You hurt your foot?"

"What?"

"You walk uneven. Like your foot hurts."

Pescatore did his best to play it cool. He wasn't used to wearing a goddamn ankle holster, and it showed.

She's running the biggest manhunt of her career, but she doesn't miss a trick, he thought. *That's what happens when you try to hide something from the cop you're sleeping with.*

"Oh yeah, well, you know," he said. "I pulled my hamstring in the Almacén attack. The back of the leg. It clutches up on me now and then. I hurt it when I was dragging my boss, Facundo, after his heart attack. You never met him, he's plenty big."

His chuckle sounded weak and forced. But she was distracted by a radio call from her deputy, Laurent. Minutes later, Laurent's car swung in behind them carrying more investigators. They sped to the Périphérique, the highway encircling the city, and headed east.

Pescatore decided to stave off further inquiries by asking a question that had been nagging at him.

"Fatima, are you in touch with the FBI and CIA?"

Concentrated on driving, she adopted a mock-wary expression with lowered eyebrows.

"Why?"

"Number one, they're pretty good at finding people when they want to. Especially Americans. Number two, they have questions to answer. What Raymond did for them, why they let him slide last year in Montpellier, like that."

"They do not know where he is. They are not talkative about him."

"Do they know I'm working with you?"

"I suppose. I did not ask their permission. I would only discuss you with them if it is urgently relevant."

He liked that answer. He asked, "Do you buy this idea that Raymond runs the show by himself, like Carlos the Jackal? The Khalid Sheikh Mohammed of his generation?"

She glanced at him, her hand resting on top of the wheel.

"No."

"Me either. Not just because he saved our lives in Bolivia. I'm not convinced he's the mastermind."

"Souraya's perception is inconsistent with facts she does not know."

"Right. I think he exaggerated his role to impress her. If he's the boss, I don't see why he warned about the attacks in South America. And he claimed to me he wasn't. For what that's worth."

They exited at Porte de Pantin past the northeast corner of the Périphérique and zoomed down a boulevard, lights flashing but no sirens.

"I'm looking for motivations," he continued. "He talks the ideological stuff, but I think it's more about money. And juice. Glory. He always acted like he was living in a movie."

"An unusual profile."

"I think he's got somebody behind him pushing."

"*En tout cas,* his level in the hierarchy is academic. There is a plot. We must stop him."

Belhaj's informant was named Adel. He was a former Islamo-*braqueur,* a professional robber of armored cars who had used the loot to finance extremist causes. She had enlisted him to look into the chatter about a terrorist arsenal in a storage locker. The meet was in Buttes-Chaumont Park. Shrouded in darkness now, the sprawling park featured a lake and a kind of urban mountain range with rock formations. Adel waited in a hillside clearing near a gazebo with a view that was no doubt impressive in the daytime. He shook hands with Belhaj, Pescatore and Laurent, touching his heart each time. The other investigators stood in a loose perimeter.

Adel was in his thirties, with droopy eyes and a falconlike profile beneath short crinkly hair. He spoke in a slow voice with a strong Arabic accent.

"*Madame la commissaire,*" he said. "I keep expecting to hear you've been named Minister of the Interior."

"When they make me minister, *habibi,* I'll appoint you my adviser," Belhaj said, her charm turned up high.

"Good idea. Special counselor in charge of relations with *la racaille*."

"Careful using that term in my presence," Belhaj said, glancing around sarcastically.

Racaille meant "thugs" or "rabble." Belhaj had told Pescatore that street guys could use it to refer to themselves, but it became a throw-down insult in the mouth of a cop or politician.

Adel's appearance straddled the line between thuggish businessman and classy hoodlum. He had a wiry build and wore a maroon jacket over a pressed black shirt and slacks. His manner was courtly and deliberate. He reported that he had tracked down a gun dealer who owned a basement storage unit in a working-class area called Stains. Months earlier, the arms dealer had rented the unit to a group of Islamists. They used it to store the assault rifles, pistols, grenades and ammunition that the dealer had sold them. The dealer had provided the storage as part of the sale and kept the keys to the cache in case of an emergency.

"Last night they show up," Adel said. "Four of them. They pull the material out of the *cave,* load it into two cars, and leave in a hurry. Like they had a big score in the works. They made it sound like it was a bank or an armored car. But he thinks it's something else. The kind of thing you folks worry about."

"Why does he think that?" she asked.

"They are not professionals. He doesn't believe they've done a robbery in their lives. One is a Turk, an ex-convict. But the others are *petits blancs.* Students or radical types. Converts, though they don't wear beards."

Petits blancs meant "white guys," as far as Pescatore could tell. Adel gave descriptions of vehicles and suspects. Laurent jotted on a notepad.

"Did you get any phones?" Belhaj said.

Adel made a gesture—head back, chest out, arms widespread—that said the question was beneath her. He squinted at his cell phone and read off numbers. Laurent wrote them down.

"Anything else?" Belhaj asked.

"He heard these mugs talking about an ambulance or ambulances. They said someone was going to need an ambulance."

"Their victims?"

"I suppose, yes." Adel shrugged. "Voilà. I have done my good deed for the day."

They fairly sprinted out of the park. Belhaj had Laurent switch cars and drive for her. Their destination was the home of the arms dealer. She sat in the front passenger seat talking on the phone. They had driven about five minutes when Belhaj ordered Laurent to turn on the car radio.

News bulletins were coming in from London. Reports of shootings and explosions outside Harrods, the luxury department store. Between the radio and Belhaj's phone conversations, the story came together. Men with guns and grenades had attacked pedestrians on Brompton Road, the busy boulevard where Harrods was located. Gunmen had fired from a stolen or commandeered taxicab. Others had attacked the nearby Knightsbridge subway station. The London police, who had been out in force because of the French warning, had responded swiftly and killed or captured the assailants within minutes. But there were civilian casualties.

"They pulled it off," Pescatore exclaimed.

"An iconic target, the street as stage," Belhaj said. "As Souraya said."

Pescatore slumped in the backseat. The London attack recalled Buenos Aires, though these terrorists hadn't stormed the store or used suicide bombers. He could see the chaos: strolling crowds, one of those big black London cabs rolling down the street, gunfire spraying from the windows…

"Fatima!" He grabbed her shoulder. "Fatima! What your informant said. The ambulance!"

She turned in her seat. "Yes?"

"Remember that scene in *The Battle of Algiers*? The guerrillas steal an ambulance and drive around like maniacs with the siren going, shooting everybody that moves. Raymond loved that scene. It was his favorite part. He said the Algerians were getting payback, spreading the pain around. Look how it went down in London. What if they're gonna hijack an ambulance and do a drive-by on the Champs-Élysées?"

Her eyes got even bigger. "They were not joking about the victims. They needed an ambulance for the attack."

"That's what I'm saying."

Belhaj ordered the second car to continue to Stains to find the arms dealer. After telling Laurent to drive them back to the Champs-Élysées, she issued an alert to check ambulances on the streets in the central city and review reports of missing ambulances and extremists with access to ambulances through associates or employment.

The sighting happened an hour later as Belhaj conferred with police brass at a command post at the place de l'Étoile. They gathered around a police radio to listen. A patrol car had spotted an ambulance coming off the Périphérique at Boulevard Malesherbes. The officers verified that the ambulance had been reported stolen from a hospital parking lot the day before. The police sedan followed at a distance, joined by marked and unmarked vehicles, a helicopter, a tactical team. The predatory escort closed in as the ambulance rolled toward downtown.

When the ambulance turned onto a one-way side street, police vehicles and officers on foot sealed the block at both ends. The police used a loudspeaker to order the occupants to surrender. The ambulance crashed into a squad car in an attempt at escape. The fusillade killed the driver and both passengers of the ambulance. The only other injuries were two officers grazed by friendly fire.

The shootout scene was east of the Champs-Élysées in an

area of narrow streets lined with restaurants and nightspots. Belhaj and Pescatore waded through bystanders, camera crews, law enforcement and fire personnel. Pescatore kept expecting someone to put a hand on his chest, demand his credentials, and end his masquerade. But he was with Fatima Belhaj, so the walls of uniforms parted like magic.

Damaged by bullets and shrapnel and the crash, the ambulance glowed in the glare of spotlights, revolving lights, television lights, the neon of a Chinese restaurant and a strip club. A forensic team in white protective suits was at work. Belhaj ushered Pescatore past them to look at the two bodies in the front of the ambulance. The terrorists were slumped in their seats, bloodied and disfigured. He studied the faces, which were freshly shaved in the manner of aspiring martyrs. He didn't recognize them.

They walked down the block about a hundred feet. A ring of chalk encircled a third body covered by a sheet and surrounded by blood, glass, debris, and an AK-47. The gunman had bolted from the back door of the ambulance. He had tried to throw a grenade, but gunfire had cut him down. His grenade had exploded next to him.

At Belhaj's order, a forensic investigator lifted the sheet. Pescatore turned away, fighting down vomit. He took a deep breath. He saw a police helicopter hovering between him and the moon. He had a memory of the young Argentine cop reacting to the aftermath of the shootout in La Matanza. Pescatore had seen too many corpses lately: a gallery of gore.

The body under the sheet no longer had a face. But whoever that torn-to-shit son-of-a-bitch was, his pudgy frame and short legs ruled out the most interesting possibility.

Fatima Belhaj put her hand on Pescatore's shoulder. She leaned her weight into it, a furtive act of affection. He collected himself, looked at her, and shook his head.

No Raymond. But he felt close.

18

Jour de Paye (2)

Half awake, Pescatore ran his fingertips up along Fatima's bare thigh. He traced the high smooth curve of her hip outlined against the faint light in his hotel room.

They lay entwined in a disorder of sheets and clothes. They had crawled into bed late at night. Pescatore had managed to hide his ankle holster under the bed. They were too worn out to do anything but hang on to each other and surrender to exhaustion. They woke up at dawn, made love with slow-motion urgency, and fell asleep again. Now it was time to get back to work, as she had murmured several times without moving.

Pescatore pushed her curls out of her face and gave her a kiss.

"What's the rush?" he said. "You're a hero. You saved Paris. The interior minister ought to come serve you breakfast in bed."

"Breakfast for you too, then."

"Tell him I like my coffee *bien serré*."

She stroked the muscles of his shoulder. "This is not over."

"Aren't you glad how things worked out?"

"Yes. But there are unsolved problems."

The death toll in the London attack had reached twenty-three. The unidentified fourth terrorist in the Champs-Élysées plot remained at large. So did Raymond Mercer—whether he was that fourth terrorist or not. The arms dealer had been shown a photograph of Raymond, but it was no help because the fourth suspect had worn a hooded sweatshirt and kept his distance as they loaded the weapons into the cars.

And the night before, taking second billing to the media frenzy about the Saturday-night jihad on the Champs-Élysées, the hospitalized graffiti artist had died. The news resulted in arson, looting and clashes with police overnight in the slums around Paris. The riots were likely to spread to other cities because of news coverage and rioters bragging on YouTube, Twitter and Facebook. Payday had arrived. Although the events were unrelated, the juxtaposition of the riots and the terror attack was a worst-case scenario for public relations.

"We do not need another 2005, when the American television made it sound like France was burning down," Fatima said as they drove to her headquarters. "An Islamic insurrection."

"That wasn't true?"

"No! They are idiots. In fact, at that time, colleagues from my service were watching a terrorist cell near the airport, the zone of the worst riots. The Islamists had heavy guns. But they did not participate at all. They did not touch the guns. They sat tranquil inside until it ended."

"But now you're afraid of copycat terrorists getting fired up by the Champs-Élysées action."

"Yes." She smothered a yawn, rubbing her eyes at a stoplight.

At DCRI headquarters, Pescatore worried about getting busted with his ankle gun. But she once again took him in through the garage entrance, bypassing metal detectors and sign-in desks; he was a VIP visitor. Her squad received them in a celebratory mood. Though the officers still didn't know exactly who Pescatore was, they had heard that his information helped stop the attack.

Belhaj let him sit in on a briefing. The dead leaders of the attacks had been a Briton of Pakistani descent, in London, and a Frenchman of Turkish descent, in Paris. Both were thought to have trained overseas. The rest were mostly converts unknown to antiterror police. The investigators believed the group had not attempted suicide bombings because of their inexperience and the police pressure, which had forced them to rush the attacks. In London, almost half the victims were Saudi. The stores and restaurants of Old Brompton Road had been full of wealthy Saudis on summer vacation.

"That is a curious detail," Belhaj told Pescatore after the briefing. "It will be interesting to see if the Saudis were targeted intentionally."

"Because?"

"Because it could mean al-Qaedists wanted to strike the kingdom on European soil. Or, if one thinks like Le Commandant, attacking Saudis could be a sign of an Iranian element. After you and the Israelis, that is who the Iranians hate most. In fact, often there are Saudis on the Champs-Élysées in the summer as well."

After they had returned from a quick lunch, Laurent walked into Belhaj's office without knocking. His expression was grim. He put a paper in front of her. She read it, brow furrowing, and looked up at her deputy.

"Where did you find this?"

"A jihadi website," Laurent said.

The anonymous Internet diatribe identified Fatima by name and rank. It accused her of abusing Souraya during her interrogation. It claimed that Fatima and her officers had beaten Souraya, touched her indecently, made sexually offensive comments, threatened to strip her naked, terrorized her sons, torn up her head scarf, and used the vilest possible language to insult Souraya, her family, the Koran, the Prophet Muhammad, and Islam itself.

"'Fatima Belhaj is a servile, hateful, traitorous, apostate repressor of her own people,'" Belhaj read aloud, enunciating with exaggerated precision. "'It is the duty of strong devout brothers everywhere to rise up and avenge the violation and humiliation of sister Souraya, a Moroccan lioness of the faith.'"

Laurent had ordered an investigation. He suspected the writer had been in touch with Souraya's lawyer or her relatives.

"What annoys me is the inaccuracy," Belhaj said. "I said she could wipe herself with her head scarf. Why not quote that? Why invent things? She is an idiot."

Laurent said higher-ups wanted to give Belhaj special security. She said that was out of the question. When Laurent left, Pescatore spoke up.

"Fatima, I gotta say I'm a little worried about your name plastered all over terrorist websites."

"Don't be absurd," she declared, swallowing almost imperceptibly. "They are the ones who should worry about me. I assume you are checking for a response from Raymond?"

"Every other minute."

She swiveled pensively in her chair.

"If he is not the big boss, if he really thinks he can offer a deal, now is the time to come forward."

"You want me to e-mail him again?"

"Not yet. But soon we tell him that if he does not surrender, we will make public his name. That will hurt his ability to negotiate."

Laurent stuck his head back into the office. There was a lead on the missing suspect from the Champs-Élysées crew.

A few hours later, they were in an unmarked van with tinted windows cruising through the damaged landscape of a place known as the Rock.

"You know, in the States that's what we call prison," Pescatore said. "The Rock."

"It is not the real name," Fatima said. "Actually, it was designed by a famous architect. In the 1960s, it was bold, innovative. Perhaps not practical: putting thousands of poor immigrants on top of each other in huge towers, all cement, no grass, no trees, the middle of nowhere."

"I coulda told him that. Shown him the projects in Chicago, saved you some grief."

The Rock was the nickname of a housing project. The futuristic vision had decayed into a ghetto-Jetsons reality. It was a brutalist maze of towers shaped like giant hair rollers and filing cabinets: multilevel plazas, curving elevated walkways, the surfaces smothered in graffiti, the cement cracked and discolored. Pescatore and Belhaj rode with Laurent and a driver; a second van followed. The street entered a tunnel below a building. They passed carcasses of charred cars, pools of water, ash and garbage, a fetid smell of destruction from rioting the night before.

"These aren't Rolls-Royces down here," Pescatore said. "They're burning their neighbors' cars."

She bridged her eyes with her hand, pressing her temples. She had complained of a headache earlier.

"They burned the new pharmacy, the post office, the gym, the nursery school," she said. *"C'est le nihilisme total."*

She knew the turf well. He wondered if that was the result of previous cases or if she had grown up in the Rock. She had talked about the *cité* of her youth without being specific. She was private about certain things, and he didn't plan to ask.

The van drove up a circular ramp and pulled into an open-air second-story parking lot. They had a commanding view of the central pedestrian esplanade, a kind of town square of the housing complex. Garbage cans had been torched and windows smashed. Vandalized light poles slumped like drunken skeletons. Soot and spray paint covered walls. The dominant graffiti slogans were *C'est le Jour de Paye* and *Police: NTM (nique ta mere,* or "fuck your mother"). Kids kicked a soccer ball off the metal shutters of a closed bar. A family walked through the debris in full fundamentalist regalia: the heavyset husband wore a skullcap, chest-length beard, sweater over salwar kameez, the pants cuffed well above the ankle, white tube socks, and gym shoes. He carried groceries. His wife trailed him pushing a baby stroller with her black-gloved hands, a tentlike, burka-style outfit revealing only her eyes.

Young men and teenagers congregated on the esplanade and in walkways between buildings. They wore hoods, caps and scarves to hide their faces and because it had turned unseasonably cold, more like June in Argentina than in France. Many youths rode scooters, motorcycles, or all-terrain three-wheelers. The riders sped through the tunnels and parking lots, rolled in lazy circles on the esplanade, popped wheelies. The police did not interfere. After the night's clashes, the riot squad had pulled back to the edges of the complex. Police and rioters were in halftime mode, letting the civilians do their business, return from work, and get inside before dark fell and the duel resumed.

Belhaj leaned between Laurent and the driver to point binoculars at the windshield. Laurent communicated on the radio.

"Nothing?" she asked.

"Nothing."

An extra layer of law enforcement had deployed in and around the Rock. An anonymous phone tipster had reported that the fugitive fourth terrorist was in the housing project. No details, just a general location. Officers spotted a stolen Renault Clio identified by the gun seller who had armed the would-be Champs-Élysées shooters. The Clio was in an open-air parking lot visible from where the police van now sat. The Clio's windows had been broken and the trunk popped, one of many vehicles vandalized in the unrest. The police used the pretense of a uniformed foot patrol to run an explosive-sniffing dog around the car and glance inside. Satisfied that it was safe, they set up surveillance. Then a phone intercept picked up chatter among local drug dealers alluding to a fugitive hiding on their turf. No mention of terrorism, but a good lead. Belhaj had a plan to pursue it. After dark.

Pescatore adjusted the body armor under his jacket. When Belhaj had given him the vest before leaving for the Rock, he made another appeal to borrow a pistol. He hoped that would let him lose the ankle gun and calm his conscience.

"A vest and no gun, that's a bad combination," he argued. "Remember what happened in La Matanza."

"You Americans and your guns," she responded. End of discussion.

Pescatore's iPhone buzzed: an e-mail from Facundo. It asked him to call as soon as possible. Pescatore wanted to talk to his boss in private, but the operation was too sensitive to propose getting out of the van.

They waited. Fatima took aspirin and rested with her eyes closed. With the exception of when she had been taken hostage in La Matanza, Pescatore had yet to see her rattled. But he believed the Internet attack was bothering her. He watched the sunset glint off a sea of windows in the concrete citadel. He fretted about the threat against Fatima, the message from Facundo, the mayhem that Raymond had spread in his wake.

The evening brought more rioting, which served Belhaj's plan. The wiretap had caught a teenage drug dealer named Bakary mentioning a fugitive in the Rock. Belhaj's crew, joined by twenty riot cops, set up near Bakary's building: a high-rise tower dotted with miniature satellite dishes and shaped like the monolith in *2001: A Space Odyssey*. Belhaj, Pescatore and the rest were given riot helmets and Plexiglas shields to blend into the phalanx of CRS officers.

Fires flared, rioters roamed, motorcycles whined back and forth. Word came over the radio that a group had attacked passing buses with Molotov cocktails and were retreating into the complex. A handful of youths jogged to the entrance of the building. They carried bottles and gasoline cans. The police charged, but slowly enough to ensure that their prey fled inside. Belhaj's plan was to use the chase as camouflage. A visit from the counterterror squad could raise the alarm; hot pursuit by the CRS was business as usual.

Pescatore hung back during the chase, worried about his ankle holster. Hoisting the shield, he followed the throng of cops pounding up the dim narrow stairwell. The air was cold and heavy with odors of smoke, marijuana and cooking. The officers took the stairs two at a time in their Robocop armor, cursing as the fleeing youths dropped bottles, gas cans, knives, lighters and other incriminating objects. The police caught the suspects at the sixth floor. Breathing hard, bellowing commands, they forced the prisoners to put on plastic gloves in order to test their hands for residue from Molotov cocktails.

Pescatore continued, now more slowly, up the stairs with the counterterror unit and a couple of CRS men. At the eighth floor, music boomed from the hallway into the landing: the angry synthesizer chords and snarling rhymes of "Jour de Paye."

As Belhaj climbed, she muttered a verse along with the rapper Booba: *"Dangereux banlieusards, ici c'est Paris, fuck l'OM."*

"What's that?" Pescatore asked.

She grinned sardonically beneath the face shield of the helmet. "The Marseille soccer team. Paris and Marseille rap groups are rivals. Like East Coast and West Coast."

Their destination was an apartment on the thirteenth floor. In the hallway, the officers unholstered their pistols and held them at their sides, pointing down. The uniformed officers banged on the door. A black youth opened it.

"Bakary," an officer said. It was not a question.

Bakary shook his head and said, *"Non, merci,"* waving his arms as if fending off a salesman. A gloved hand planted itself on his chest and propelled him backward. The platoon surged in.

The apartment was small, neat and clean. Family photos, school trophies and African tapestries and figurines adorned

Leabharlanna Poibli Chathair Baile Átha Cliath
Dublin City Public Libraries

walls and shelves. Pescatore saw the word *Mali* on a poster. A plasma television faced an armchair and a couch. The CRS men pushed Bakary into the armchair. The sofa was occupied by two little girls with long braids. They clutched schoolbooks and pencils, staring with giant eyes at the newcomers.

Bakary tried to rise; a riot shield bumped him back down. The intelligence on him was that he led a ring that did lucrative business in hashish and cocaine and avoided drama and violence. He was nineteen and had an athletic build in a white Real Madrid sweatshirt. His bushy hair seemed electrified. He played it stone cold. As he recovered from the surprise, his broad features went blank. He slouched, low and motionless, watching officers fan out into adjoining rooms, calling the all-clear, holstering their guns. One of the girls asked a question. Bakary put a finger to his lips.

The cops removed their helmets. Pescatore did too. Fatima Belhaj shook out her hair and crouched in front of the couch at eye level with the girls. She spoke in a soft voice. Pescatore didn't catch what she said, but it appeared to have the desired effect. The girls nodded solemnly.

Belhaj turned to Bakary. There was an interruption. An African woman hurried into the apartment. Her multicolored turban and elaborately draped wool shawl gave her a wearily regal look. Despite the cold, her legs and feet were bare and she wore sandal-type clogs. A uniform from a kitchen or hotel protruded from her bag. Unlike her son, she spoke French with a strong accent.

"Bakary!" She sounded more indignant than fearful. "What have you done now?"

"It's fine, Maman, it's fine, calm down," Bakary said, rolling his eyes.

The mother dropped her bag, shaking her head, contemplating with disbelief the crowd of law enforcement in her living room. She appeared to be on the verge of collapse. Belhaj intervened. She introduced herself, apologized for the inconvenience, and took the mother aside. She asked the mother to go with the girls into another room so the police could discuss a delicate matter with her son.

After an officer led the mother and daughters away, Belhaj ordered Bakary to tell her about the fugitive terrorist in the Rock. Bakary visibly relaxed; he wasn't the prey of this muscular manhunt after all.

"Terrorist?" he exclaimed in a gravelly voice. "All I know is he's on the run. We have no interest whatsoever in terrorists here. Frankly, they're bad for business."

The fugitive was staying in another tower in an apartment next door to a friend of Bakary's. This had led to the mention in the intercepted phone conversation. The apartment belonged to a woman, possibly a wife or girlfriend of the fugitive. The drug dealers, who had eyes and ears all over the complex, had seen the man arrive Saturday afternoon in the Clio. There was talk that he had an assault rifle and other weapons. Bakary had crossed paths with him briefly in a vestibule.

"What does he look like?" Belhaj asked.

"No beard. Not black or *beur*. Not *gaulois* either."

"Like what, then?" she snapped.

"More Spanish. Gypsy type…" Bakary looked around. "Like him."

His back pressed against the counter of a kitchenette, Pescatore had the disconcerting experience of seeing the youth's finger extend and point at him, followed by the gaze of everyone else in the room. He wished that he had not removed the helmet. Belhaj exchanged a glance with Pescatore. He had told her people tended to think he and Raymond were related.

"He resembles this officer?" she demanded, gesturing at Pescatore.

"A bit, yes," Bakary said. "But taller. Straight hair."

Pescatore's heart, already racing from the stairs and the

adrenaline, thumped harder. He imagined Raymond, desperate and armed to the teeth, hunkered down in the Rock. With yet another woman.

Belhaj showed a photo of Raymond to Bakary. He studied it.

"Frankly, I can't say," he said. "I didn't get a good look at his face."

The clandestine deployment reconfigured around the fugitive's hideout. A SWAT team established a command post outside the Rock. Belhaj left two CRS officers standing guard at Bakary's place to ensure he communicated with no one. Her squad shifted to a spot near the target building. They parked the unmarked vans in a courtyard that was the size of several tennis courts. It was an intersection of four internal lanes of the complex, two for cars and two pedestrian walkways.

Laurent and the driver joined the rest of the unit doing reconnaissance on foot. Pescatore remained in the van with Belhaj. She talked on the radio. Flames flickered in the distance. Faint sounds echoed through the corridors of concrete: the wail of sirens, the growl of motorcycles.

Pescatore asked if anyone had died in the riots so far.

"No," Fatima said. "A lot of destruction. But deaths are rare."

"If you had two nights of this all over the United States, a whole bunch of people woulda got shot by now."

"Because there are so many guns. And the American police shoot back. I do not criticize. But here, the chiefs usually give an order not to fire during riots. It is absolutely obeyed."

"Tough as these projects are, I think American ones are worse. Because of the guns. Plus it looks like the government takes better care of poor people in France."

She sighed. "The government spends money. That is not the problem. The problem is communication. The kids know how to express themselves only through violence. The teachers in the schools don't know how to talk to the kids. The police don't know either. The young officers know one thing: they check papers. My brothers used to complain: they would go to Paris to look for work and get stopped five times, six times. The *cité,* the train, the street. Imagine how they felt by the time they got there to apply for a job. It creates rage."

Pescatore remembered that two of her brothers were in prison. He wondered again if she had grown up in the Rock.

"You know what?" he said. "It's like there's a border between here and Paris. And the police are the Border Patrol."

She raised her eyebrows.

Pescatore's phone buzzed again. This time, Facundo's e-mail consisted of one word: *And?*

It was evening in Buenos Aires. Facundo was getting impatient. Pescatore decided not to wait any longer.

"Fatima, my boss is trying to reach me. I'm gonna call him, okay?"

"Fine."

Facundo answered on the first ring.

"I can't really talk, but I figured it was important," Pescatore said.

"It is." Facundo sounded triumphant. "Ali Baba has been identified."

"By?"

"The *paisanos.* It was not easy. Few photos in circulation. His name is Ali Houmayoun. Iranian Quds Force. A major at the time of the photo in Bolivia. At least a colonel by now."

"Oh, man." Pescatore squeezed Fatima's hand involuntarily. She gave him a quizzical look. He told Facundo, "You were right."

"Modesty aside, yes, I was."

The Commandant was right about the Iranians too, Pescatore thought. He said, "This is huge."

"It fits," Facundo said. "The major helped lead the Iranian expansion in Latin America. A dangerous personage with a long history."

"Do the *paisanos* know anything about Raymond?"

"Very little. But I don't doubt he and Ali are still working together. The Americans know. The Europeans will be briefed."

"So I can discuss this here?"

"Go ahead," Facundo said.

"I'll call you tomorrow. Thanks, Facundo."

Pescatore hung up and told Fatima the news. Her reaction surprised him: understated, almost impassive. She asked him to repeat the Iranian's name, then wrote it down. She shielded her eyes with her hand again, kneading her temples. Pescatore had a twinge of regret; he should have waited until after the raid rather than distracting her.

"I figured you'd want to know right away," he said.

"I am glad you told me," she answered. But she looked mad when she added, "I am curious when the Israelis and the Americans plan to inform us."

"It complicates things, right? If you've got Iranians and al-Qaeda involved at the same time?"

"If that is really what is going on."

They did not have time to talk further. The radio came back to life. Surveillance indicated the fugitive was in the apartment and had gone to sleep. The SWAT commander gave the order to conduct the raid.

The fugitive's hideout was in a building at the other end of a walkway connected to the courtyard where the van was parked. Laurent convinced Fatima to keep her distance during the raid. As far as Pescatore could gather, his reasons had to do with her safety and the Internet threats. She agreed, though she wasn't happy about it. Laurent and the rest of the intelligence officers went in behind the SWAT team. Fatima stayed with Pescatore in the van.

The raiders were not fast enough. When they stormed in, the fugitive shot himself. Holding the radio to her ear, Fatima shook her head. Laurent reported that the dead man was not Raymond.

Pescatore was not that surprised. He should have known better. Raymond liked pulling strings, not triggers.

"We will go see," Fatima said grimly, lifting her phone. "I want to make one call first."

"At this hour?"

"I will wake up someone at a certain embassy and ask why I had to hear about this Iranian *type* through informal channels."

She left a terse message on a voice mail. She and Pescatore got out of the van. When they reached the walkway, her phone rang: her embassy contact returning the call. She answered, but lost the connection. The cell phone reception was bad between the buildings.

Fatima returned to the courtyard, trying to get a signal. She called and started talking. The connection failed again. She walked farther back into the courtyard. Pescatore waited at the edge of the walkway. Fatima's call went through. She had a conversation near the vans, pacing.

Pescatore watched her. She looked tired but lovely in the landscape of broken glass, ruined cars, strewn garbage. Distant fires backlit her supple silhouette: the boots with the jeans tucked into them, the tight waist and upturned collar of the leather jacket, the mane of curls.

He spotted something in his peripheral vision on his right. A motorcycle. Two riders. The motorcycle idled in the opening of the lane that entered the courtyard perpendicular to the walkway where he stood. The riders wore big ninja-style helmets. The lights of the motorcycle were dark. He wondered how long they had been sitting there. It gave him a bad feeling.

Pescatore started into the courtyard. The motorcycle surged forward. He shouted a warning to Fatima over the whine of the engine. He knew the motorcycle would gather velocity, take a hard left, and speed toward Fatima from behind. He knew the rider in back would raise a pistol, straightening his arm to aim at her, even before the barrel glinted.

"Fatima, look out!" he shouted.

Though caught up in every detail, Pescatore wasn't just watching. He was at long last executing the move that he had imagined and anticipated and rehearsed since he had strapped on the ankle gun. He dropped to his right knee, reaching with both hands for the hem of the jean on his left leg. For a nightmare moment, the denim resisted. His fingers tugged ineffectually, the pant leg stuck on the boot and the holster. He yanked hard, and then the fabric was clear, and then he drew the gun.

Fatima reacted, whirling toward the motorcycle. The phone fell from her hand. She scrabbled at her belt as the motorcycle rocketed toward her. She stepped toward the vans, pointing her pistol back across her body. The rider fired; Pescatore fired; Fatima fired. The triangular barrage resounded in the cement box of the courtyard. When the motorcycle was parallel to Belhaj and about fifteen feet to the right, it shuddered, swerved and overturned.

The gunman was launched as if shot out of a cannon. The motorcycle went into a long shrieking skid with the driver hanging on. There was an ugly shearing series of impacts, sparks flying off the pavement. The cycle and cyclist came sliding and tumbling and rolling toward Pescatore at high speed. Pescatore kept firing from his one-kneed stance.

He felt frozen, strangely detached. He was unable to dodge or look away from the hurtling figures. It was as if they were on a screen. He swiveled, tracking the cycle and cyclist with his gun as they flew by on his left. They crashed, finally, into the side of a building. He flinched, expecting an explosion, but there was none.

The cyclist lay inert. The rider had soared headfirst into the hulk of a burned car. His legs protruded grotesquely from the windshield.

Turning, Pescatore saw what he had somehow known to be inevitable: Fatima Belhaj was down.

PART III

19

Going to Chicago

A nother hospital. Another waiting room. Another vigil.
Hours earlier, he had seen doctors and officers hurrying her parents down the hall. The father's solemn bearing and trim mustache fit the image of the man in the stories she had told. The mother resembled a small, stout version of Fatima in a head scarf.

Her vest had stopped three bullets. Three more hit her in the arm, shoulder and upper thigh, the last striking an artery. He saw the shock in her eyes, mirroring his own, when he sat her up against the van and discovered the torrent of blood pumping from the thigh wound. He tried to stanch it. The courtyard echoed with his cries for help, frantic voices on the radio, officers converging on foot and in cars.

The wait for the ambulance was agonizing. She held on to him. He told her he loved her, the first time he had said it. She drifted, speaking semicoherently in French. She said she had lived in the Rock and didn't want to die there.

He drowsed in the waiting room, arms folded, chin on chest. The sense of devastation was worsened by the fear that he was once again to blame. In Argentina, he had missed the opportunity to prevent Raymond from unleashing calamity. He had been a step too slow since then. The Commandant had called Raymond a scorpion who destroyed whatever he touched. Pescatore knew the danger better than anyone else, yet he could not stop the scorpion's sting.

"Monsieur Pescatore."

Belhaj's deputy, Laurent, was standing in front of him. As the ambulance left the scene of the shootout, Laurent had comforted Pescatore, patting his back while gently relieving him of his pistol.

"What do the doctors say?" Pescatore asked.

"Her condition is grave. She lost much blood. But she is out of danger."

"Gracias a dios." He inadvertently spoke in Spanish.

"Yes. You are very tired. But it is necessary to talk in private."

He rose unsteadily and followed Laurent to an empty doctor's office. Laurent sat behind a desk. He studied Pescatore through his small, round glasses. Although Laurent was unshaven, his gray eyes and chiseled features exuded energy. He expressed thanks on behalf of his agency for Pescatore's actions in the gunfight and afterward.

"All of us have admiration and respect for Commissaire Belhaj," Laurent said. "In this service we take care of our officers and those who aid our officers. We are grateful."

Pescatore said he was honored. He asked about the attackers on the motorcycle. One was dead, one was in a coma. Both were ex-convicts from the Rock. The police had found a total of twenty-five thousand euros in cash at their homes. Investigators had not yet linked them directly to the Paris terrorist cell. Nonetheless, the theory was that they had been hired to kill Belhaj and that the tip about the fugitive had been part of a scheme to lure her to the housing complex.

"Why wasn't he with the Champs-Élysées crew?" Pescatore asked.

"He was a logistics person, a secondary figure. And he apparently did not know about the trap for Commissaire Belhaj."

"So the network sacrificed him to ambush her?"

"That is the hypothesis. Of course, the denunciations of Fatima on the extremist website could have motivated a separate group. But it is less likely."

"Who do you think ordered the hit?"

"One possibility is Souraya's entourage," Laurent said. "Carrying out an instruction from her or interpreting her wishes."

"Really? What about her kids? It's so self-destructive."

"I do not know if you have encountered many Islamic extremists, Monsieur Pescatore."

"Not till lately."

"One finds that pure ideology overwhelms everything. She is fanatical, as you saw, and vengeful. Her family as well. Her confession was revenge against Raymond Mercer. Similarly, I think she was determined to retaliate against Commissaire Belhaj. The Internet message shows that. Obviously Souraya is in custody, so her communications have been limited. We will find out soon if she gave the order."

"I think Raymond had a photo of Fatima. Based on something he said when he called me in Bolivia. He knew what she looked like."

Laurent scribbled in a notebook. Pescatore asked the question that he had been wrestling with: "Is Raymond a suspect too?"

"Of course."

"The reason I ask: I think the hit men waited until I was out of the way and they had a shot at Fatima alone. It's a weird thing to say, it's disgusting and makes me ashamed, but I think Raymond still looks out for me."

"If he gave the directives, it was from somewhere else. We do not think he is in the country."

Laurent shifted his compact frame and tightened his jaw. Pescatore thought, *Now we're gonna get down to it, whatever it is.*

After praising his bravery again, Laurent said that certain aspects of the situation were delicate. A U.S. civilian with an illegal gun had participated alongside counterterrorism police in a gunfight in the middle of a riot zone. An explosive scenario if it became public.

"So far, we have kept your presence secret. That may become impossible. The ballistics will show the assailants were shot by someone in addition to Fatima. Residents"—he spoke the word as if it were an epithet—"no doubt saw the incident. Perhaps someone videotaped you."

"Hope not."

"The potential repercussions are grave because of the tensions in the *cités*. I must ask you some questions."

"Sure."

Laurent asked him to describe the shootout step by step. Pescatore did that.

"Did Commissaire Belhaj authorize you to carry the weapon?"

"Absolutely not. She told me I couldn't, it was illegal. I hid it from her."

"Where did you procure the pistol?"

"Through a South American guy."

"And I assume this South American has left France and would be very difficult to find?" Laurent held his pen in a pose indicating that he would move on when he received an answer.

"Exactly."

Laurent asked him about his affiliation with the U.S. government and how he had become involved in the case. After Pescatore answered, Laurent pursed his lips and said, "Forgive me, but what is the nature of your relation with Commissaire Belhaj?"

Pescatore considered the possible repercussions for Fatima if their romance came to light. Intelligence services tended to have strict rules about intimate contact with foreigners.

"I'd say we're good friends," he said slowly. "We've worked closely together. We've been through some dangerous situations. There's nothing inappropriate about the relationship, if that's what you mean."

Laurent nodded. He reached the bottom line: He wanted Pescatore to leave France. The powers that be had decided his departure would keep things quiet and reduce complications if his role in the shootout came out. An evening flight to the United States had already been reserved.

Pescatore couldn't argue with the logic. Still, he wanted to stay close to Fatima. He was sick of people taking guns away from him and kicking him out of countries. He protested, reminding Laurent that he was a conduit to Raymond.

"He has communicated with me several times," Pescatore said. "Fatima believed he'd do it again, maybe to surrender."

"The American authorities will be your interlocutors. They will meet you when you arrive home."

"Where are the American authorities? I'm surprised there's no one from the embassy poking around by now."

"They are aware of developments," Laurent said, hunching his narrow shoulders. "But everyone is in agreement that your situation is best handled outside of France. Because of the delicate aspects."

"I found out last night that Raymond dealt with Iranian intelligence when he was in South America. A Quds Force officer. Are you familiar with what I'm talking about?"

Laurent nodded, lips pursed again.

"Well?" Pescatore continued. "Is there an Iranian element to these plots in Europe?"

"That, I am afraid, is not something I can discuss."

"How you figure that? I've been working with Fatima. I've been sharing everything with you guys. I've gotten shot at. And now you can't discuss the case with me? Me of all people?"

"It is classified."

With effort, Pescatore restrained his temper. The important thing was that Fatima was going to survive.

"Listen, Laurent," he said. "Can I see her?"

"Believe me when I say it is not possible." Laurent removed his glasses and rubbed his eyes. "Her family is in the room. There are visits, superiors from the Interior Ministry, the police hierarchy. It is problematic. And she is in a heavily medicated state."

"Just for a minute?"

"*Désolé,* Valentín."

Pescatore absorbed the reply. He looked down for a moment. "When you can, please tell her I'm thinking about her."

"I will."

"You said you reserved a flight for me? Where to?"

"Chicago."

Back at his hotel, he functioned in a daze beyond exhaustion and sadness. He stuffed his blood-drenched pants into the trash. He packed, putting on his black fatigue vest over a pullover sweater with a zippered collar. He went downstairs with his suitcase and paid his bill. In the lobby lounge, he sank into an armchair and ordered a sandwich and a rum and Coke. Alcohol was as necessary as caffeine. Laurent was sending a car to take him to the airport at six. He had an hour.

Going to Chicago. As far as he could tell, they had chosen the destination because it was the birthplace on his passport. Fine with him. Not much difference at this point. He wasn't sure Chicago was home anymore, but nowhere else was.

He put his phone on the table. He wanted to report to Facundo, but he was having trouble working up the energy. It seemed futile. He leaned his head back and closed his eyes.

When a polite tap on the shoulder woke him, it took him a moment to remember where he was. A squat man with a blond buzz cut excused himself and asked if he was Monsieur Pescatore.

"Yes, sorry, I was beat," Pescatore said, rubbing his eyes.

The man stood in a dutiful pose with his hands crossed in front of him. His right hand held an envelope. His torso strained a tan sport coat. Unlike the investigators in Belhaj's unit, he wore a tie, his powerful neck spreading behind a Windsor knot. Not a surprise that they would send a muscle guy as a chaperone/bodyguard.

"We're going to the airport already?" Pescatore asked.

The blond man blinked and nodded.

"Yes, at your service," he said in a thick French accent. "Much traffic."

Twenty minutes early, Pescatore thought. They want to make damn sure I catch that plane.

"Okay," Pescatore said. "I guess it's better waiting there than here."

The car was a Peugeot sedan. Moving with a slight limp, the blond man loaded Pescatore's suitcase into the trunk and opened the door for him. Pescatore slid into the backseat, eager to resume his nap. The driver was a tall and light-skinned black man. His shaven head bobbed in greeting behind sunglasses.

"*Aéroport,*" the blond man said as they pulled away.

The car entered the Périphérique highway and picked up speed. Pescatore started to doze off. The blond man turned around in the front passenger seat and handed Pescatore the envelope.

"*Pour vous, monsieur.*"

As he opened the envelope, he was vaguely uneasy. The guy was still watching him. When he began to read the note, he understood why. Fright and disbelief froze him. The printed note said,

Cuate,

First of all, don't freak out. My guys aren't going to hurt you. I vouch for them.

Second, you are the one person in the world I trust right now.

You were right, we need to have a conversation. I'm counting on you to step up, as usual.

So here's the deal. If you want to meet, just stick with my guys and they'll take good care of you and make it happen. If you don't, tell them that. And that's the end of it.

It's up to you, homes.

Abrazo, R.

Slowly, Pescatore looked up into the steady blue eyes of the hardass in the front seat who, he knew now, was not a cop. He had made a classic mistake. He had dropped his guard and assumed the blond man was with the Interior Ministry. Raymond's emissary—whose initial plan had probably been to hand him the letter in the lobby—had jumped on the opportunity. Better to deliver the message in private to a captive audience.

Pescatore remembered an anecdote about a Spanish executive who landed in Buenos Aires, walked into the pack of hustlers hawking taxi services in the airport terminal, and inquired in a loud, haughty voice: "Who is here for Señor Sosa de Olivares?" A sharpie stepped forward immediately to say that he was there for Señor Sosa de Olivares, welcome to Argentina, did you have a good flight. A few miles from the airport, the driver and an armed accomplice robbed the executive of his every cent and possession. Pescatore recalled laughing when he heard that story. Because he was so streetwise, so alert, so down, that you'd never catching him acting like such a lame chucklehead moron. Not in a million years.

The blond man stayed in a seemingly casual pose with his left arm draped on top of the seat. Pescatore couldn't see the right hand, but he had to think it held a gun. The driver was watching him in the rearview mirror. Pescatore lifted his chin, eyes wild. The idea that Raymond had tricked him and taken control again filled him with rage. He thought about Laurent's comment that Raymond might have ordered the hit on Fatima.

He considered attacking. He would take a bullet in the face before he'd unbuckled his seat belt. Unless Raymond had given strict orders not to kill him. The blond guy might hesitate. Pescatore might have time to go for the gun or the driver's neck, hoping to cause a crash. At which point they would shoot him for sure.

"Well, monsieur?" the buzz-cut blond said. "You are free to reject the invitation."

"Invitation?" His voice shook. "Is that what it is?"

"Of course. If it is not acceptable, we drop you where you like."

Oh yeah? he thought. *How about police headquarters?*

He told himself that Raymond had identified his hotel because Pescatore had put the phone number in the e-mail he had sent him. These guys were not deranged holy warriors. More like sophisticated gangsters: slick and brazen enough to have monitored him, maybe with the help of sources at the hotel or even in law enforcement. They had slipped in ahead of the police to engage him and then improvised on the fly.

Paralyzed, avoiding the blue-eyed gaze, he reread the note. Raymond's offer was risky, outrageous, and completely characteristic of him. As the initial impact wore off, Pescatore told himself they were unlikely to hurt him. Raymond had passed up a chance to whack him in Bolivia and—if Raymond had been involved in the ambush—another one in the Rock. What would he gain now? The gambit was consistent with Raymond's previous behavior: whether out of friendship, self-preservation, or both, he intended to keep Pescatore alive and well. Perhaps he had decided that the time had come, once again, to try to cut a deal.

Pescatore wanted answers. He wanted payback. Now he was being handed a chance to confront Raymond one-on-one.

The gaze of the blond man had not faltered. Pescatore looked him in the eye. He thought, *It's up to you, homes.*

20

This Masquerade

Stepping out of the car, he saw the low hills across the water. The sight of the coast of Morocco made him think of Fatima. A warm wind ruffled the palm trees. The shaved-headed driver, whose first name was Murphy, carried Pescatore's suitcase. The thickset blond man, Jérome, limped ahead to open a front door covered with grillwork. The white-walled villa was on the southern coast of Spain. A winding road led to the property in a residential enclave behind walls, gates, cameras, guardhouses, and the yellow armored truck of a security company.

The trip had lasted overnight and through the morning. Murphy and Jérome had been efficient and silent. After Pescatore agreed to go along for the ride, they went into countersurveillance mode. Leaving the Parisian highway, they sped to a garage, patted him down, and took away his phone. They changed vehicles and drove to a small airport north of Paris to catch a private jet. It landed at a lonely airfield in the pitch-black flatlands of central Spain. The drive south was interrupted by two stops at safe houses to change cars. The geography and methods led him to think he was traveling, in reverse, along a drug-smuggling corridor.

In the villa, their footsteps echoed on marble. He caught a glimpse of a piano in an atrium-like living room, floor-to-ceiling windows with a view of the water, a spiral staircase with an ornate iron railing. Murphy and Jérome stepped aside, but not far. Raymond hurried down from the second floor.

"My mean main man. You're here!"

Raymond looked as if he'd just taken a dip. His hair was wet. A sleeveless V-neck shirt displayed his tanned, lean build and long, corded arms. He wore warm-up pants and loafers. His smile was exuberant.

"Hey man," Pescatore said.

Raymond gave him a palm-slapping handshake and leaned in for a brief hug, as if not wanting to come on too strong.

"Great to see you, Valentín. Thanks for coming. I hope the fellas didn't spook you too bad."

"Nah."

"I likes that in you. Come on, *fiera,* check out the view."

Raymond led the way to the large square balcony, which had blue and white ceramic tiles. The balcony overlooked a cliff that dropped to a rocky cove. To the right, a pool deck was built into the side of the cliff. Steps descended to a dock, where a big, fast-looking boat was moored. The cove opened onto the luminous expanse of waves and sky.

"What a spot, right?" Raymond said. "That's Africa across the strait."

Pescatore lifted his face to the warmth of the sun. He heard amplified music from the pool area. A swimmer cleaved the surface: a young woman. She propelled herself out of the water onto the pool deck. She had cascading tresses and a lithe brown body. She could have starred in an ad for the joys of the Costa del Sol. Raymond blew a kiss down at her. She mustered enough energy to raise a hand, holding it high to display herself at full taut extension, then tumbled languidly into a lounger.

"A bona fide *andaluza,*" Raymond murmured. "Twenty-two. Fucks like a rabbit."

That was when Pescatore experienced an impulse to throw

him off the balcony onto the rocks below. Pescatore had chased him across land and sea through terror and bloodshed. Pescatore had killed people; people he loved had come close to dying. And here was Raymond showing off his beach palace and latest babe as if Pescatore had dropped in for a fun-in-the-sun vacation. It was surreal, obscene, psychotic.

He resisted the urge. He could not deny the conviction that Raymond had protected him repeatedly, from Chicago to Paris. During the overnight trip, he had made a decision: he would play Raymond the way Raymond played everybody else.

"Damn," Pescatore said. "Looks like an actress."

"*Y tanto.* You hear that tune, man?"

Pescatore listened to the suave virtuoso interplay of guitar and voice drifting from the pool deck. He knew it word for word, note for note.

"I sang 'This Masquerade' for her," Raymond said. "Now she listens to George Benson all day."

"You always said he was one of the best."

"Nobody else scats along with the guitar like that."

"So this is where you been?" Pescatore demanded. "Bodies dropping like flies, you're chilling in your little supervillain hideout. That's fucked up."

"No, man, I just got here. I barely use this place. Look, Valentín, you had a brutal trip. You want to rest awhile? Want to change? Murphy, *coup de main,* get my *cuate* an espresso!"

Pescatore accepted the espresso and the offer to clean himself up. When he returned from upstairs, the rustic wooden table on the balcony was covered with food: a potato omelet; platters of shrimp, octopus and mussels; ham and chorizo; fresh bread; gazpacho. Raymond popped open a bottle of champagne.

"Serious spread," Pescatore said.

Raymond sat with his back to the railing. The henchmen and the Andalusian girlfriend were nowhere to be seen.

"*Figli maschi,*" Raymond said.

They raised glasses. The toast reminded Pescatore of their dinner in Buenos Aires and of Raymond's sons.

Raymond asked anxiously, "You saw my boys?"

"At a police station."

He didn't plan to disclose that Fatima had given him inside access to raids, much less mention his romance with her. Or the ambush.

"How were they?"

"Ramón was squalling up a storm, poor little guy."

Pescatore spoke more gently than he had intended. Tears brimmed in Raymond's hooded eyes. Despite his vigor and swagger, he looked tired. The cheekbones seemed more pronounced. He hunched in his Springsteen-album pose, fingers at his mouth, one leg jiggling.

Pescatore continued, "Now Valentín, he showed some heart. I talked to him a minute. He's a Bulls fan."

"He's crazy about basketball, soccer, all sports." Raymond's voice quavered. "He's strong and fast for his age. Got an ear for music too."

Pescatore nodded. The octopus was cooked to the right chewy consistency. The ice-cold champagne took the edge off his headache. The wind tempered the heat. It occurred to him that nobody else knew his location. He was off the grid, under the radar, outside time.

"What did they do with the boys?" Raymond asked "Where are they?"

"With relatives of your wife. I think."

Pain tightened Raymond's face. "I'm so worried about *mis gorditos*. They need me, they're alone, and I can't do anything about it."

Pescatore nodded, unsure how to respond.

"And my wife?" Raymond asked.

"What can I say, man? She dropped a dime on you."

"I knew it."

"Way I heard, she identified you as the big boss."

"Some nerve. She's in deep. That French lady detective who got shot? My wife's people did that. I had nothing to do with it."

Pescatore stared at him. He rode another wave of homicidal fury. He didn't buy Raymond's story. Raymond was far more capable than his jailed wife of engineering an assassination. Pescatore had a flashback of sprinting to Fatima after the gunfight in the Rock, her body crumpled amid broken glass. He shook his head to dislodge the image, trying to look unruffled.

"When Souraya gets mad, it's over, *che,*" Raymond said. "You know her problem? Her father was a famous imam. They pounded that jihadi shit into her head when she was growing up. And she takes it seriously."

"What, you don't?"

"I mean, I do to a point." Raymond rolled his eyes. "As a tool, a means to an end. It's not like I want to go back to the seventh century."

That probably explains why you're eating chorizo, Pescatore thought. He said, "Souraya told the French police you're the new Khalid Sheikh Mohammed."

"*Qué hija de puta.* Man, I'm like a lieutenant at best. A facilitator. Not the fucking mastermind. The *mero mero,* he's—" Raymond was at full speed, words spilling over each other. He grinned slyly. "Actually, you've seen him. You got his picture in the Chapare. They called me middle of the night. I had to stop the Bolivian cops from carving you up. Don't you know who the dude in the photo is? Didn't the French tell you? Or the Americans?"

Pescatore sipped champagne. He wiped his mouth carefully. He rested his elbows on the wood and interlaced his fingers.

"I'm not here to answer questions, Ray," he said. "I'm here because you sent for me. I want to hear the whole story, start to finish. And spare me the bullshit."

"Of course, of course." He opened his arms magnanimously.

Raymond started with Buenos Aires: his plunge back into criminality, his conversion. He had taken the religion very seriously at first, tormenting himself when he went astray. He changed perspective under the influence of his Arab-Argentine associates.

"Ortega, the cop, he was a convert like me. Hard-core. One thing I learned fast: a convert is like a guided missile. But Kharroubi and the other *turcos* were more interesting. They talked the Islamic talk, but for them it was really a nationalist, anti-imperialist cause. That made sense to me. More than rubbing your forehead on the floor every five minutes. I'm Sunni, but I could care less about Sunni-Shiite beefs. They liked to live large; so do I. I got them to push into Bolivia, go to the coca source, take the business to the next level."

Using plates to represent continents, Raymond traced out the empire he had built using Florencia's border contacts and fraudulent documents and Kharroubi's smuggling racket. He had joined forces with a Lebanese-dominated web of drug traffickers and money launderers. They were all over: Latin America, West Africa, Europe, and the Middle East. Whether Shiite, Sunni, or Christian, true believers or pure businessmen, they got with the program dictated from Lebanon and kicked back part of their profits to Hezbollah.

"Hezbollah needs nonstop cash, bro. They got an army to pay for, covert ops overseas, a political party at home, hospitals, charities, welfare. And they're getting rich off dope: sheikhs in Lebanon, Iranian generals along with them. If you hurt the decadent drug-addicted infidels in the bargain, all the better. You make allies with cartels and guerrillas, fuck up Uncle Sam in his backyard. Asymmetric crime warfare."

Iran, Hezbollah's sponsor, had pressured the Lebanese militia to crank up the cocaine business for financing, he said. Clerics had issued fatwas justifying the drug trade as a covert jihad.

"Hezbollah brothers introduced me to the dude in the photo," he said. "Ali Houmayoun. Back then, he was a major in the IRGC. Iranian Revolutionary Guard Corps. Did South American ops for the Quds Force, their external unit. A badass. The Mossad once tried to whack him in Istanbul. Killed his brother: mistaken identity. He hates those Israeli fuckers with a passion. We made him a partner, helped him develop sources for documents, laundering. But I ran into trouble with U.S. agents."

"You were still a cooperator?"

Raymond popped open another bottle of champagne. "My status was fuzzy."

In Argentina, he retained informal contact with the Miami antidrug task force for which he had worked. He took advantage of relationships he had developed with law enforcement and intelligence agencies. Raymond claimed he had learned to manipulate them as much as they manipulated him.

"You know the feds," he said. "You play them against each other, exploit rivalries. They were hot for dope and terrorists. I threw bones to my old handlers now and then, off the books. Sometimes one agency, sometimes another. I ratted out competitors. Then the task force started sniffing around my Hezbollah connects. Intercepts made them curious. I needed to protect Ali. So I sacrificed a truckload of coke in Buenos Aires Province. Satisfied the gringos, but I had to relocate to Bolivia."

"Some drama up there too."

"Straight-up gang war, homes!" Raymond mimicked firing a tommy gun. "Like Cagney and Bogart. The worst part was when the major and I got busted with a load in the jungle. A cop took that photo. Ali was furious. He hates cameras. I was like, 'Hey, *boludo,* focus on the fact that these Bolivian cops are arguing about whether to kill us or not. And your diplomatic passport doesn't impress them.' I've talked my way out of jams, but nothing like that night in the Chapare. Saved our asses. It made us brothers forever."

Pescatore saw a glimmer of an offer in the making. *If Raymond calls him his brother,* he thought, *he's probably sizing him up to fuck him over.*

Raymond moved to Spain, the gateway to Europe for cocaine and hash, to consolidate his drug ring with the help of Ortega, who shuttled back and forth from Argentina. Major Ali was still their partner, but he returned to Iran. He rose to colonel and brought Raymond to Tehran. Raymond underwent training: survival, self-defense, tradecraft, urban and rural combat, surveillance and countersurveillance, Arabic and Farsi lessons. He became a spy.

"I loved that shit. I guess I've been doing it all my life, one way or another. They told me I was a natural."

No doubt, Pescatore thought. He noted that Raymond had filled in the crucial gap in the timeline Pescatore had assembled.

"What about being a true-blue frontline holy warrior, sacrificing yourself for your Muslim brothers and everything?" Pescatore asked.

"I'm still a soldier, man. It's still a holy war. But I'm in the command post. I'm not some little grunt."

A Latin American woman in an apron came onto the balcony and cleared the plates. She set out fruit, desserts and a bottle, which Raymond hoisted delightedly. Cardenal Mendoza brandy.

"El Cardenal, baby. I wouldn't fail you." Raymond got up with a snifter of it and paced. Silhouetted against the view, he looked as if he were onstage.

Raymond painted the Iranian security forces as a state within a state, a swarm of mafias. Once renowned for bombings, assassinations and hostage taking, they had grown corrupt and sloppy. Thanks to his talent and wealth, Ali was a powerhouse. Raymond was his star agent.

"Ali's a brilliant strategic thinker. He put together his own unit. He was sick of Israel and the U.S. killing Iranian scientists, sabotaging the nuke program, all the sanctions. And Iran kept fucking up the retaliations. His idea was to infiltrate al-Qaeda and use them. Beauty of it is, you have an existing structure, a known brand. Hungry jihadis. Give them direction and resources and point them at the target. Your enemy isn't sure who hit him."

"False-flag attacks."

"Right. It puts the heat on fucking al-Qaeda, which is killing Iranian and Hezbollah fighters in Syria, and Shiites all over."

"I thought Iran was trying to get along with us, calm things down."

Raymond affected a worldly look. "Maybe the politicians. Not Ali's crew in the IRGC. They don't believe in that make-nice-with-the-West shit. And they want the nuclear bomb, sooner or later. A lot of enemies in their neighborhood."

Raymond's new mission was aided by debriefings with al-Qaeda veterans who had fled to Iran and been detained. Iranian intelligence kept their useful Sunni rivals in a reasonably comfortable limbo, guesthouses rather than jails. The holy warriors gave him guidance and contacts in the terrorist underworld. Basing himself in Montpellier, a city he knew from drug trafficking, he infiltrated an al-Qaeda-connected network for his Iranian handlers.

"I incorporated my dope organization too. I told Ali: We've got a recruitment pool here. We find radicalized brothers. Criminals from Muslim backgrounds. Or converts, former military, dirty cops like Ortega. Professionals. They'll be the point men. Back them up with cannon fodder. Kleenex terrorists."

Chuckling, he produced a folded Kleenex from his pants pocket and opened it, revealing a joint. He lit it, leaned against the rail and took a hit, then offered the joint to Pescatore.

Pescatore had expected and dreaded this. He hadn't smoked marijuana since his informant work with the Patrol. It made him stupid and sluggish. But for the role he was playing now, he needed to come off as weak. He hesitated. Raymond's arm extended insistently across the table.

"For old times' sake," Raymond said.

They smoked. Raymond said his wife had helped lead the group but knew nothing about his Iranian ties.

"So the marriage was just part of the scam?"

Pescatore spoke with calculated scorn. He wanted to keep the guy off balance. Sure enough, Raymond looked hurt. His eyes glistened.

"No, *cuate*. How can you say that? I fell for Souraya like nobody else. She's the mother of my sons. Devout, fearless. A Muslim wife *como dios manda*. It's my own fault she hates me now."

Pescatore would have found the sentimentality more convincing if it weren't for all the cheating and the snide comments earlier. Raymond took a long hit. Resuming the story, he said everything went smoothly until his run-ins with the Commandant and French intelligence.

"That big French mug nearly messed up everything. A real *fregón*. First he used my wife's immigration problems to lean on me. It got complicated running my network and feeding him at the same time. Then he figured out we'd popped this Iranian dissident in Lyon. Special assignment from Tehran. Esposito was breathing down my neck. But I had an idea. I reached out to a U.S. boss I had worked for. A counterterror supervisor Stateside. His career was tanking: divorce, alcohol. He needed a score. And I knew some embarrassing shit about his drinking. I told him, 'I've got the goods on an al-Qaeda group in Europe.' I gave him expendable fighters, gift-wrapped. He went to the French at a high level. He got his terrorist bust, his Brownie points. My problem went away."

"They blew off the Commandant's suspicions about the Iranians?"

"There was a dustup. I guess some agents wanted to look into

257

it, some didn't. Bottom line: they let it slide. But they all told me I was dead to them. They'd had enough of me. I said, 'Fuck you, *maricones*. It's not like you pay my bills.'"

Raymond sucked on the joint, his face feral and hungry behind the ember. Pescatore marveled at the seascape. It gave him vertigo. The wind deployed cloud formations. The sun seared the Moroccan coastline. He had read a line once about "the lion-colored hills of Africa." Were they lion-colored? What color was a lion exactly? The champagne and weed had gotten all up on top of him.

"Ray," he said. "The Buenos Aires airport. Was that real or a scam?"

The bleary eyes lowered. Pescatore thought, *As far as I can tell, you've been pretty truthful so far. Don't lie to me now or I will throw your ass over the side.*

Raymond said, "I didn't run into you by accident. But a few days before the airport, I really did see you out of the blue. I was walking near Recoleta Cemetery. You went into that café, La Biela? I couldn't believe my eyes. I had my Argentine guys look into what you were doing in BA. They shadowed you, found out you were taking a client to the airport, and I made the approach."

"Why?"

"I needed help. The train was going too fast and I wanted to jump off."

"You didn't mention anything that night at dinner."

"I had to be sure I could count on you. Besides, Ali hadn't given the green light yet."

Ali had been promoted to brigadier general. He launched the terror campaign to impress his hard-line political patrons. He started in South America in order to use Raymond's infrastructure, cause strife in the region, and hurt Israel and al-Qaeda in one masterstroke.

"He wanted to hit the Jewish school in Buenos Aires," Raymond said, chewing a pastry stuffed with *dulce de leche*. "He said we'd kill the children of Shin Bet and Mossad officers. It had to be a purely Jewish target. El Almacén was a double target: Argentine and Jewish."

"You helped choose targets?" Pescatore couldn't hide his disgust.

Raymond didn't appear to notice. "Brigadier Ali respects my opinion. He says I have a knack for this stuff. A terrorist act is essentially an act of communication. Like a song, a performance. Narrative, images, symbols. Choreography."

"I don't understand," said Pescatore, who understood perfectly.

"I told Ali, 'We need to kill a lot of people. Major casualty count. Dramatic images. Otherwise, the media doesn't give a shit about Argentina down in the middle of nowhere.' That's why we used suicide bombers. Psychosocial impact. We had to bring in two guys. We weren't sure our Argentine *pibes* would go boom. If the car bomb had gone off at the school, we could have got five hundred easy."

Pescatore's headache had returned with a vengeance. He gritted his teeth. "Why did you call me?"

"I wanted to stop it," Raymond exclaimed, voice anguished. "I really did. Everything was set. I was going to Beirut to watch the fireworks from there with Ali. I stopped in France to see my family. One afternoon I was kicking the ball around with Valentín. I freaked out. Shaking, hyperventilating. I couldn't go through with it. I called Amélie Hidalgo in Bolivia with a throwaway phone. I'd set up the cell in Bolivia mainly as a decoy anyway. Ali had told me I could give those guys up if it would improve our chances in Argentina. That was within the plan."

Raymond sagged against the rail.

"Then I took a huge risk and called you," he said morosely. "There was no one else. I knew you were still my *cuate*. I could trust you with my life. If I burned the brigadier, someone had to bring me in. I was ready. I called three times. But you didn't answer your phone. I had to catch a plane. Ali was expecting me. My wife was all gung ho about the attack. And she was in my face about family stuff: was I seeing women on the side, why didn't I spend more time at home. She made me take her to buy furniture at fucking Ikea, which is more crowded than hell. I ran out of time."

Pescatore rose, unable to sit still any longer. Raymond's excuse for failing to stop a terrorist attack was his unruly domestic life. Pescatore paced back and forth on his side of the table.

"Why didn't you warn someone else?" he asked. "Or figure out a way to reach me? How hard could that be?"

"I was torn." Raymond's voice hardened. "The plot was a masterpiece. I was proud of it. I believed in the cause, even though I got cold feet. I was ashamed of my weakness. The attack had a momentum of its own. It was meant to be. Like the Arabs say: *Maktub*. It was written."

"It was written?" Pescatore roared, straining his throat. "What kinda bullshit is that? You selfish crazy coldhearted motherfucker!"

His head spun. He looked around wildly. He grabbed the nearest object, the bottle of Cardenal Mendoza. Raymond flinched. Pescatore wheeled and whipped the bottle as hard as he could at the doors of the balcony. The impact of glass on glass was spectacular.

There were exclamations in the house. Within seconds, Jérome appeared holding a pistol with two hands, pointed down. A shirtless Murphy ran up slapping a clip into his gun. They stared out onto the balcony through the jagged remnants of the door. Glass tinkled.

Pescatore stared back at Jérome and Murphy, a firing squad in the making. He saw Jérome edge to the right to remove Raymond from the line of fire. Pescatore was in a bad spot. His follow-through had left him away from the table and any semblance of cover.

Pescatore looked at Raymond, who had taken refuge in the far corner of the balcony. Their eyes locked. Raymond hesitated. His expression went from scared to sad to resolute.

Raymond raised a hand.

"Easy, easy, everything's all right!" he shouted.

Speaking in French, he ordered Jérome and Murphy to get lost. He said they could clean up later. He used profanity. Finally, reluctantly, they obeyed.

Pescatore collapsed into his chair. He was breathing hard and sweating as if he had run a sprint. He stared into the distance.

Raymond patted him on the shoulder. He hovered awkwardly for a moment, then walked back around the table and sat down.

"I understand," Raymond said. "Of course. You feel like I made you part of it. You feel guilt. You feel—"

"Ray," Pescatore said hoarsely. "Do me a favor. Don't explain to me what I feel."

When the glass shattered, Pescatore thought his improvised mission had crumbled along with it. He had lost control and perhaps earned a bullet in the head. Now he realized he was wrong. In fact, he had been playing it too cool. His outburst was what Raymond had expected, totally in character. It had set the stage. He waited.

"I have a proposal," Raymond said.

"I'm listening."

"Europe was phase two. We hit prime-time. Yeah, the London attack could've been bigger. Yeah, Paris didn't work out. Doesn't matter. We racked up a body count and scared the shit out of everybody. Islam two, Infidels zero. Now Ali wants to do a strike in the U.S. We're developing a project to launch from Latin America. Another false flag."

Raymond paused for effect.

"You and me have to go to the FBI and the CIA," he continued, more animated. "I told you Brigadier Ali is Mr. Most Wanted. He's security-conscious, careful about travel. But the U.S. plot is so important he'll run it personally. He'll take risks. He trusts me. I can deliver a bona fide terrorist general. Now that's a coup."

I knew it, Pescatore thought. *The Big Backstab.*

"How?"

"We've run into obstacles," Raymond said excitedly. "We need operatives with narco profiles. And a way to get them into the U.S. A while back, two of our Lebanese guys tried to hire a smuggler in Mexico to bring them across the border. Some *cabrones* took a hundred grand from them, then slit their throats in Matamoros. *Mataron a los moros.* That really discouraged the planners back in Iran. Ali's looking for a southwest target. San Diego, LA, Houston. Right on the border, if we can find a good venue. The attack fuses the Islamic threat and the border threat. A fucking Fox News fascist redneck nightmare come to life."

The idea had Raymond's imprint. Pescatore could imagine him pitching it with the same excitement he showed in selling the betrayal.

"Just get me in front of the feds, a chance to talk to them," Raymond said. "Let me do the voodoo that I do so well."

"Where are you going with this?"

"Listen. I know how to hook Ali. I say I've got a specialist he has to meet. A guy who's the key for this plot because he's wired in Latin America and the States. A guy who knows the border inside out: U.S. and Mexican cops, smuggling, the security structure. The bait is the guy."

"And the guy is…"

"You."

21

Ya No Me Acuerdo

After his second attempt at knotting the necktie, he gave up. He hated ties with a passion. It wasn't like he had a job interview. Although the others would probably be in workday embassy attire, he doubted that his wardrobe would be an issue. The blue sport coat and jeans would do fine.

The suite was sleek and comfortable, steel gray and beige. The minimalist style contrasted with the stone exterior and grounds of the hotel, once a duke's manor. Facundo had recommended the place. He said Pescatore deserved a nice stay in Madrid after what he had been through and what awaited him.

Sitting at a small round table, he turned on his iPod. He wanted to hear the song again before she arrived.

I don't remember anymore
If your eyes were brown or black
As the night
As the day
We broke up

The ballad was by Estopa, a duo of brothers from a factory town outside Barcelona. It was tender and melancholy. In Argentina, he had listened to the song when he thought about

263

Isabel Puente. When he wondered if she felt as alone in Washington as he did in Buenos Aires, if she suppressed the same urge to call, write, or catch a plane and break the silence and solitude. The lyrics haunted him with the idea that he would gradually forget what she was like. He couldn't imagine anything bleaker.

Recently, he had begun listening again to "Ya No Me Acuerdo." He was in Spain. He missed Fatima. And now he was about to see Isabel Puente, his former fiancée and a current big shot at the Department of Homeland Security, for the first time in a long time.

She knocked on his door at ten a.m. sharp. They hugged with limited contact, as if over a fence. It was strange to stoop to Isabel; Fatima was about his height.

"Isabel. How are you? How was your flight?"

"Fine. Good to see you, Valentine."

It had been a while since anyone had called him Valentine. He and Isabel always spoke English, interspersing Spanish words. She always called him by the name with which he had been inadvertently rechristened by the U.S. federal government.

"Come in," he said. "Have a seat. Here, at the table."

"Nice room."

"I'm living large, right?"

Never mind the song. There was no way to forget Isabel. The feline Cuban features, the compact curves and sure-footed padding walk. There was no way to forget the slight trace of an accent, a melodic echo of Spanish. She looked a bit paler, a bit thinner—no doubt the result of long Washington office hours. Her embassy-appropriate outfit was a belted black dress beneath a silver summer blazer. Sunglasses nested in her hair, which she wore pinned back and hanging to her shoulders.

"You look good," he said.

"You too. But tired. *Esas ojeras.*"

When they were living together, it had been a ritual. She would comment on the circles under his eyes and reach out to trace them with a finger. He instinctively anticipated her touch; it didn't come.

"I haven't slept for a month," he said.

"You've been busy."

Her smile was steely. Their last face-to-face conversations had been epic screaming matches or terse exchanges about the logistics of breaking up. Now she came off livelier than he'd expected. He understood why. She had returned to the mind-set in which she was the handler and he was the informant.

"I saw Leo Méndez a few months ago," she said.

"My man Méndez. How's he doing?"

"Good. He started a newsmagazine. He's living between San Diego and Tijuana, depending on who gets mad at him. You know Leo: cop or journalist, he's always sticking it to the man."

"I likes that in him," Pescatore said. "What're you doing exactly at DHS-HQ? I figure you pretty much run the show by now."

"My title has the words *assistant* and *deputy* in it, for what it's worth. Basically, I oversee national security issues. Coordinate major cases. Terrorism, counterintelligence, arms trafficking, smuggling. Most national security cases have a border component."

"You're up to speed on what's going on? I got the idea when I called that you already knew a lot."

She stayed impassive. "As a courtesy, a colleague did advise me your name popped up after the attack in Argentina."

"An FBI agent told me there's a big-time internal investigation."

"Since he told you that already, I can clarify there are two inquiries: the internal review and a CT investigation. The counterterrorism investigation takes precedence after London and Paris. And your new lead."

"Well, I appreciate you zooming over here. You're the…only one I can trust right now."

He had hesitated because he sounded to himself like Raymond. At the villa two days before, he and Raymond had conferred until late. Murphy and Jérome had driven him to the Málaga airport and returned his phone. His first call was to Facundo, who was at home convalescing. They decided it was time to bring in the heavy artillery: Isabel. When Pescatore called, she listened calmly. Her reaction stoked his paranoia. As if she had been expecting to hear from him. She told him to make the quick flight to Madrid. He had thought she would put him in touch with U.S. agents there. Instead, she hurried over in person.

He rose. "I must've mislaid my manners. Can I offer you something to drink or eat? Room service?"

"Better not to have foreign nationals coming in and out right now," she said. "Water is fine, thanks."

He set out glasses, ice and bottles, water for her and Coke for himself. He took her through the story of the meeting with Raymond.

"I guess Brigadier General Ali is a great big deal," Pescatore said.

"That's accurate. He has American blood on his hands, military and civilian, going back to the nineties. Not to mention Israeli and European."

"The baddest terrorist the public never heard of, according to Raymond."

"He is dangerous and active. Apparently he has a lot of autonomy from the Iranian leadership."

"A serious bargaining chip, then."

"What did Raymond ask for?"

Raymond had made his case like a lawyer delivering a closing statement. He paced on his balcony as the sunset painted slashes of orange and purple. In exchange for the extraordinary service he intended to render, he wanted to avoid prison. And he wanted custody of his sons.

"But the kids are French citizens, aren't they?" Isabel asked.

"Yep. I told him it sounded unrealistic to walk away with no time. He said he'd consider doing a couple years, at most, in a country club–type minimum-security facility. He hasn't killed any Americans that he knows of, he said."

"That he knows of." Isabel shook her head. "What a piece of work. Four or five countries would want to prosecute him. By his own admission, he's played a major role in several terrorist conspiracies resulting in the deaths of more than two hundred twenty-five people."

"Buenos Aires, London, Paris, the Iranian activist in Lyon, his own guys. Yeah, that's about right."

"Don't forget the terrorists he sent to Pakistan and Afghanistan and wherever else. They killed people, probably U.S. military personnel. If he doesn't think he's going to do hard prison time, he's crazy."

"He always cut deals before. He flipped and it worked."

Pescatore thought back to Raymond's performance on the balcony. When Raymond believed something, he had a way of making you believe it too. Even if you knew what the odds were, what an operator he was.

"Not this time. No matter what he offers, this is as bad as it gets. He has to turn himself in, negotiate face-to-face and hope for the best."

"He's too cagey."

"Why does he want you to go to Iraq?"

"Well, Iran's not an option. Lebanon could be, but the brigadier feels safe in Iraq. The Iranians are wired up with the Shiites in the government. The brigadier knows Iraq; he used to run guns and train Shiite militias. He has investments there. He thinks nobody can get at him in Iraq. Raymond feels safer there too."

"It's not a country where we could arrest them ourselves. The Iraqis aren't going to cross the Quds Force."

"This would be a get-acquainted meet. We're hoping Brigadier Ali buys it and brings me into the project."

"And he's going to trust you to the point he's willing to meet you again somewhere like Latin America, so we can grab him?"

Her widely spaced eyes raked him like searchlights. She sat with a leg beneath her in an alert pose. Isabel never quite kept still. Her hands toyed with each other and her glass and her hair.

"Yeah. Raymond thinks the general would come over to Central America or someplace to run things when the plot develops. Raymond says if he vouches for me, that's half the battle. They're tight from way back."

"Does he know there are newspaper articles about how you went undercover in a Mexican cartel that had indirect links to Hezbollah cells at the Triple Border? For the Iranians, that's not the best thing to have on your résumé."

"Raymond's got that covered. After all, he was a U.S. informant too, and the Quds Force knows it. If he says he's known me since we were six and trusts me with his life, which he does, I'm cool. They're all excited about this attack in the U.S. They need a specialist to make it happen."

"Explain to me why an IRGC general is supposed to think Valentine Pescatore is the man for the job."

"Hey, I had the same reaction. But now I'm convinced. With my Patrol experience, I do have a profile to help smuggle in terrorists and do recon. These guys might be superspies and everything, but Mexico's a long way from home. They don't really have a clue how to operate at the Line."

"I'm still concerned about the scenario of bad guys killing you in Iraq."

"Raymond's had chances to kill me already. He cares about me. The attacks in Europe burned him. He can't travel. He's wanted. I'm a new asset, I compensate for that. He needs me to impress Brigadier Ali, to cut this deal with you guys. He's on borrowed time with the Iranians. Sooner or later, they'll find out he tried to drop a dime on them about Buenos Aires. Raymond's rich as hell, but his life reminds me of that expression in Spanish. Escaping all the time? Fleeing forward?"

"Huyendo hacia adelante," she said drily. "I'm familiar with the term."

She was insinuating that the phrase could apply to him. *Point taken,* he thought.

She added, "I'm not convinced this is wise or feasible."

"Listen, Isabel." He paused and ran a hand through his hair. "It's good we're talking just the two of us. I want to make something clear before we go to the embassy. I'm not asking permission. I'm gonna do this. I'm gonna go to Baghdad, meet these guys, and do my best to lure out this Ali. If it works, I hope somebody is gonna scoop him up before it's too late."

Isabel's thumb rose to press against her teeth. Not a good sign. Battle stations.

"Is this an offer or an ultimatum?" she asked.

"A proposal."

"You propose a freelance op in a hostile zone out of the blue and everyone's supposed to jump on board. On your terms."

Her tone had turned flat and officious. They had fallen into a familiar dueling rhythm, building toward the flash point.

"Raymond dragged me into this," he said. "I feel responsible."

"Don't blame yourself. It's not noble, it's dumb."

"I'm not the only one to blame. I think the U.S. government shoulda known years ago Raymond was a liar playing all sides. He kept messing up, setting off alarm bells, and agencies kept letting him skate. When you get right down to it, I don't understand how the CIA or FBI or somebody didn't find out what he was up to and stop the attacks in Buenos Aires. It's outrageous."

"Maybe. That's why there's an internal review. But it's easy to say, after the fact, that we should have known about a plot. It's not realistic, Valentine. Especially if the target isn't American."

"Raymond's American, though. And he was an informant."

"Don't rule out the possibility that the intelligence community knew more than you think. They may not have seen the act was imminent."

"Or maybe they didn't care if it was just South Americans dying. Maybe Raymond was still useful."

"Look." She leaned forward with her small palms pressed on the table, as if pouncing might become an option. "Once you're inside the system you see how big it is, how much information there is, how many players. That's usually the explanation, not conspiracies. Sometimes—"

His phone rang. He started to shut off the ringer when he saw, his heart leaping, that Fatima's number was on the display. He had spoken the day before with Laurent. The French were fuming about the stunt pulled by Raymond's men in Paris. Laurent had sent investigators to Spain. They believed Raymond had used a false identity to leave the European Union, perhaps via Morocco. Pescatore had asked to talk to Fatima, but Laurent had told him she was still too weak.

"Excuse me, I'm sorry," Pescatore said to Isabel.

She nodded. He took the phone and went into the bedroom, which had two sliding panels rather than a normal door. He pulled shut a panel one-handed, got flustered, and retreated to a corner with the phone. Bad timing. But he couldn't wait any longer. He sat on the bed and answered, keeping his voice low.

"Fatima?" he said.

"Valentín," she said. *"Mon amour.* Where are you?"

Her words melted something inside him. Her voice sounded thick, dazed, even throatier than usual. She drifted between Spanish, French and English. She told him she was pumped full of painkillers.

"That's okay, beautiful," he said softly. "I'm in Madrid. Worried sick. I'd be right there with you, but your boy Laurent kicked me out of France."

"You Americans and your guns," she said.

"I'm sorry I hid that from you."

She said something unintelligible. He hunched forward to listen, covering his left ear.

"Fatima? You there?"

"Valentín," she said, disoriented. "I had a bad dream."

"You did?"

"I dreamed you were singing to me. In the jungle. A funny Italian song. It was raining. Then I woke up, in the dream. I saw it was Raymond singing. By my bed. Very bad dream."

The image chilled him.

"Don't you worry," he said. "I'm the only one who sings to you."

"Très bien." He heard hospital noises. Voices echoed, saying her name. "I must go. I wanted..."

She trailed off. He said hurriedly, "I'm glad you called. I'm glad I heard your voice. You take care of yourself, Fatima. I'll be there soon as I can."

"Je t'aime," she said.

And he said it right back.

He returned to the living area and sank into his chair. Isabel eyed him.

"What happened?" she asked. "Are you all right?"

"Yeah. Sorry." He sat up and cleared his throat. "That was this French investigator who got shot the other day. I was there."

"I heard. How is she?"

"Hurt bad. But she's recovering."

"Good."

"Isabel." He looked down. "I should tell you...this French investigator. Fatima. We've been working together. We're close now. I care about her a lot. She's the first person since you and

271

me broke up that I care about like that. It feels strange. I'm sorry to bring it up now, but…"

She reached out and put her hand on his. "I'm glad for you, Valentine. I want you to be happy."

Her smile was tinged with melancholy. The tension had dissipated; combat had been averted.

"We should get going," she announced.

After they walked across the hotel courtyard and out the gate, Pescatore asked: "Who's gonna be at this meeting?"

"All the relevant federal players," she said. "Be ready. We'll probably bring in the British, the French. The Israelis are interested. Everybody you can imagine who wants a piece of Raymond and his friends. It's going to be complicated."

He saw that Isabel would play the role she had in the past: protector, spokesperson, intermediary.

"Jeez," he said, shaking his head. "All these countries and agencies bumping into each other. Like they say: Bureaucracy is the new geography."

"Who says that?"

"It's a line in a book."

"Which book?"

He hesitated, embarrassed now. "It's called *Are We Rome?* About whether the United States is going down the tubes like the Roman Empire."

She stopped on the sidewalk. Her sunglasses glinted up at him. Her stance was playfully incredulous.

"Since when do you read books?" she demanded.

"You always said I should finish college. I decided you were right. I couldn't study in Argentina, so I started reading on my own. Mainly about terrorism, law enforcement, international issues."

"Good for you."

"Raymond never went to college, but he read books nonstop. And he's one of the smartest people I ever met."

"I hope he's smart enough to pull this off."

The walk to the U.S. embassy took them down an incline and across the Paseo de la Castellana, a tree-lined boulevard with six lanes and two pedestrian walkways. The sky was an immaculate blue. The air was hot and dry and tinged with smells of food and exhaust fumes. Madrid reminded him of a cleaner, more elegant version of Buenos Aires. He and Isabel walked slowly and close together, elbows and shoulders brushing.

"Isabel, remember we used to talk about a honeymoon in Spain?"

"Of course."

"It woulda been a blast. I took a walk last night. Two in the morning, it felt like two in the afternoon. Traffic. People on the street: families, old folks on benches. The bars and restaurants were full, everybody carrying on. Hard to believe there's an economic crisis."

"Maybe they should shut up, get some sleep, and fix the mess."

The U.S. embassy was a tall concrete slab wedged among prime office buildings and stately apartment houses, boutiques and restaurants. Security had been beefed up after the terror strikes in Paris and London. At the fenced back of the compound, two armored vehicles idled at barricades manned by officers of the Guardia Civil in three-cornered hats.

Pescatore had his hands in his pockets, his head down. To his surprise, Isabel slipped her arm through his. The sensation was familiar and comforting. He glanced at her. She removed her sunglasses.

"Valentine. How long were we together, three years?"

"Three years."

"As close as we were, as much as we shared, how is it possible you never mentioned Raymond Mercer? I've read the files. I talked to Facundo and Agent Furukawa. I listened to you talk about him. I see what a big impact this guy had on you. It's like finding out you had a secret brother."

He came to a stop. Her stare was making him nervous.

"I don't know about all that," he said. "We were close when we were kids. When we got older, I figured out he was bad news."

"Still. I can't believe you never once told me about him."

He shrugged. "Isabel, you knew I got in trouble in Chicago. You knew the kind of crowd I ran with. I've always been honest with you."

"You don't lie. But you keep secrets. You lock things away inside."

He thought about that. He thought about how he had concealed the gun from Fatima.

"You always said I was a natural at undercover work," he said.

"Do me a favor and let's go for full disclosure from now on. The stakes are too high. I'm really, really worried about this Iraq thing."

"I'm gonna be fine."

"I'm trying to understand: Is Raymond still your friend? Do you really trust him?"

"I don't know what he is anymore. I trust him because he trusts me."

They resumed walking. He was taken aback by her public display of affection. Isabel was not exaggerating. She thought there was a good chance he was not going to return alive.

22

My Rifle, My Pony, and Me

I t would have been easier, faster and safer to fly into Baghdad. But Raymond had orders from Brigadier General Ali Houmayoun. The Iranian spymaster was intrigued by the idea that Pescatore might hold the keys to the kingdom as far as striking the Great Satan was concerned. Ali had convoked a sit-down. In order to conceal Pescatore's trip to Iraq, Ali and Raymond decided he would use a real-fake Argentine passport from Raymond's stash and enter by land from Jordan. Raymond had used the route to move foreign jihadis in and out of Iraq.

Pescatore had spent a week in Spain after Isabel's arrival. The meetings took place at the embassy, hotels and a U.S. military base. The final days were dedicated to strategy sessions, preparing gear, and making arrangements by e-mail and phone with Raymond. Pescatore updated Facundo regularly and talked several times with Fatima. He kept the phone conversations cheerful and did not tell her about Iraq. She was improving slowly and did not need stress. Meanwhile, against all expectations, he and Isabel had become friends again. She worked tirelessly. She steered him through a gauntlet of cops, spies, soldiers and diplomats. When they hugged good-bye, she said repeatedly, almost threateningly, "*¡Cuidate!*" (Take care of yourself!).

In Amman, Pescatore met Mustafa, an Iraqi smuggler. He looked disconcertingly Mexican: bowlegged, sturdy, Emiliano Zapata mustache on a round face. Pescatore remembered hearing the comedian George Lopez joke long ago that he worried about certain male relatives during hostilities with Iraq. "I've got an uncle who looks just like Saddam Hussein. Don't you?"

Mustafa was at the wheel of a Chevrolet Suburban, a grimy white war wagon speeding through the dark. They had left Amman at midnight in order to cross the Jordan-Iraq border in the early morning. The faster the Suburban went, the more contentedly it hummed. Mustafa hummed too. To Pescatore's alarm, Mustafa performed multiple tasks in addition to driving. He sent text messages. He had gesticulatory phone conversations. He inserted earbuds to listen to music. He poured two cups of tea from a thermos, passed one over the seat to Pescatore and drank the other. As they approached the border crossing, Mustafa reached back to give him an envelope with the Argentine passport that had been prepared by Raymond using photos sent by express mail.

"You now," Mustafa said, pointing at the passport and him.

"I got it, thanks very much," Pescatore said, looking at the windshield in hopes that Mustafa would get the message and keep his eyes on the road.

Mustafa asked for Pescatore's U.S. passport, which he would keep hidden. Pescatore handed it over, feeling bereft. He opened the Argentine document and saw that his new name was Marco Antonio Martin. No doubt a mix of Marc Anthony and Ricky Martin. The envelope contained business cards and a letter on official stationery identifying him as a representative of a Buenos Aires firm that exported halal meat to the Middle East. Raymond had created the firm as a front. A good cover because Iraqis didn't know much about Argentina other than its soccer stars, he said.

It was ironic. A proud U.S. Border Patrol veteran was about

to sneak into a country using fraudulent documents. Pescatore had known Customs and Border Protection officers who had done tours of duty in Iraq training the border police to defend the very port of entry that he intended to breach. He hoped the trainees hadn't done well in the class on spotting phony papers.

The port of entry appeared: a low huddle of structures and floodlights. A line of vehicles waited behind a fuel truck with rust-eaten tanks. Mustafa made short work of the Jordanian bureaucracy. On the Iraqi side, he directed Pescatore to a gloomy waiting room. Pescatore leaned against a pillar watching Mustafa bustle between counters where officials stamped papers, the impacts echoing. Travelers sat listlessly on plastic benches. Fluorescent lights painted them in unhealthy hues.

Pescatore noticed a machine against a wall behind empty desks. It seemed familiar. He sidled closer. Sure enough: a state-of-the-art X-ray machine of the kind used by inspectors in the United States to scan luggage. He knew that CBP had donated a shipment of X-ray scanners to Iraq; his colleagues had trained Iraqis in their use. The multimillion-dollar piece of high-tech equipment stood next to a garbage can, unplugged. Hangers holding uniforms and civilian clothes were hooked at the top of the scanner. It had become a garment rack.

Mustafa conversed with an unshaven official in a blue uniform with rubber shower thongs on his feet. They talked a few yards from Pescatore but did not speak to or look at him. The two of them retreated abruptly into an office. This did not strike him as positive. He had assumed Raymond knew what he was doing. He started to worry. Was his cover going to work? What kind of dumbass Argentine meat importer would do business here anyway? He wondered if the mission would fail before it began. He tried to imagine the penalties for illegal entry. If they charged him with espionage, in most two-fisted nations the punishment was death.

Minutes later, Mustafa emerged from the office. Beaming.

The Suburban plunged back into blackness. Mustafa waved, panoramically and mournfully, at the desert rushing by.

"Iraq," he declared. "*Harb* all the time."

Pescatore had learned enough Arabic to know that *harb* meant "war."

"I know what you mean, brother," he said. "Too much *harb*."

They pulled over onto the shoulder of the highway behind a parked SUV. Raymond appeared out of the darkness carrying a duffel bag. He climbed into the Suburban with a burst of welcoming chatter. Pescatore gave him a high-five; he didn't have to fake being happy to see him. The Suburban roared off again. The SUV followed, carrying guys who would ride shotgun as far as Baghdad.

"Whaddya hear, whaddya say, *cuate*?" Raymond said. He wore dark clothes and a red-checked kaffiyeh. His incipient beard recalled his Pacino-as-Carlito look from ten years before in Chicago.

"*A todo dar,*" Pescatore said.

"I see you followed my grooming instructions. Looks local, doesn't he, Mustafa?"

Mustafa smiled over his shoulder. "Like a Samarra man."

Pescatore hadn't shaved for three days. A U.S. attaché in Madrid who had served in Iraq helped choose his outfit: black pleated slacks, a striped short-sleeved shirt with a wide collar, and a black-checked kaffiyeh. He also wore his black travel vest. The attaché said he might blend in if he kept his profile low and his mouth shut.

"Remember," Raymond said, reaching into the duffel bag. "No seat belt. Or sunglasses. You might as well wear a sign that says *American CIA Jackass*."

Raymond gave him a semiautomatic Beretta, a belt holster, and ammunition. Pescatore strapped up.

Another country, another gun, he thought. Raymond showed him two M4 carbines in the duffel bag.

"You can handle one of these bad boys if necessary?"

"I carried one on detail in Nogales."

"Nogales was nothing, homes," Raymond hooted. "This is the Wild West right here! Anbar Province."

The ride would take them through a hotbed of al-Qaeda militants and other gunslingers, Raymond said. "This country is *puro desmadre*. A nonstop brawl. Sunni versus Shiite versus Kurd versus Christian. And all the factions and tribes. Angling and maneuvering and sniffing at you, trying to figure out if they should shoot you and how many *cabrones* on your side will hunt them for the rest of their lives if they do."

"Kinda like Chicago."

"That's why they call it Chi-raq, homes."

"Keep the rifles handy."

"My rifle, my pony, and me. When was the last time you saw *Rio Bravo*?"

"Oh, man. Been a while."

Raymond repeated his oft-made assertion that *Rio Bravo* was the best movie in the history of the universe. Although, he added, like all Westerns, it had an imperialist-fascist-racist worldview.

"Nobody wants to hear that radical bullshit," Pescatore retorted. "You leave *Rio Bravo* alone."

Raymond grinned. He leaned back and sang "My Rifle, My Pony, and Me," the song from the movie. His imitation of Dean Martin's mellow ginzo-cowboy baritone had only improved with time. Pescatore recalled the scene: Dude slouched on a cot in the jail, hat over his eyes, feet propped up, holding a cigarette as he crooned.

Road signs flashed by. The names were redolent of rage and gore: Ramadi. Fallujah. Baghdad. The Suburban was rolling through the badlands. Raymond was behaving as if it were all a big movie. Typical.

The song put Raymond in a nostalgic mood. He reminisced

about gigs, girls, games, friends, fights, crimes. Pescatore, his face in his scarf, drifted between sleep and wakefulness. Dawn brought a sandstorm. The world turned brown: sky, desert, minarets, flat-roofed buildings, war ruins. People bent into the gritty wind; palm trees bent away from it.

They entered Baghdad at midday. A pall of pollution darkened the sandstorm. He was surprised by the snarls of traffic, the sprawl of expressways, boulevards and overpasses. A gas-guzzler city. He saw blast walls, barbed wire, barricades. The Americans had left; the conflict remained. The streetscapes looked familiar from countless media images. The crowds, menace and casual disorder reminded him of Latin America. Except there were few women on the streets. And even fewer women showing hair, let alone skin.

Their destination was an apartment-hotel behind a checkpoint manned by heavily armed civilian guards. The two-bedroom unit was spacious and dingy, a 1980s decor gone stale. The air-conditioning whined in harsh harmony with a generator. Pescatore asked Raymond if this was where he lived now. Raymond's answer was evasive.

Pescatore took a nap. He was awakened by the evening call to prayers echoing among buildings; he found it soothing. In the kitchen, Raymond poured Turkish coffee and was amused by Pescatore's rictus when he drank it. They discussed strategy for the sit-down with Brigadier Ali. Raymond said the important thing was for Pescatore to be himself.

"It'll be fine," Raymond said. "He likes serious, respectful guys. Guys who've worn uniforms and taken orders. He thinks I'm too wild sometimes. Can you believe that?"

Pescatore laughed. As Raymond talked, Pescatore looked for some sign that he had qualms about plotting the betrayal of a man who had been a close friend and an influential figure in his life.

Raymond changed gears. He asked about the U.S. government's reaction to his hopes for a deal. Pescatore had rehearsed his response.

"They're definitely interested in the brigadier. The plot against the homeland got everybody's attention. But they don't trust you. At some point, you need to hire a lawyer, sit down with them, and work it out. Using me as a go-between isn't gonna fly."

"Fair enough," Raymond said.

"Before anybody does any negotiating, they want to see what you deliver. If you really get us a sit-down with the brigadier."

"That's why we're here."

"Frankly, they're worried I won't come back in one piece."

"Of course you will. I guarantee it."

"I'm counting on you not to make me look bad. And keep me alive."

"Well, I'm counting on you too."

"Good."

"Hell of a team, *cuate*."

They ate a room-service dinner in the living room in front of the television. Reclining in a fuzzy green armchair, Raymond accompanied his channel-surfing with stream-of-consciousness commentary: the relative merits of Shakira versus Jennifer Lopez, the Barcelona-Madrid soccer rivalry, the latest wave of bomb attacks in Iraq. He drifted into a monologue about the future. He had plenty of money, investments and properties that he hoped the feds would never find. Or if they did, maybe they'd let him keep some of it if he served up Brigadier Ali. Once this mess was behind him and he got custody of his sons, he planned to settle down somewhere peaceful and raise them right.

"Academics, sports, music. It's all about discipline. If I could find a military school combined with a conservatory, that'd be perfect. A father has to make rules and set limits. Like your *viejo*."

"I'm not sure my dad's the best parenting model, tell you the truth."

"You turned out good. You know right from wrong."

"It's not that complicated."

"If you'd grown up in the environment I did, the value system in my house, you'd know that's not necessarily true."

"Oh, really?" The tension and weariness got the best of Pescatore. "Here's an example. Killing two hundred unarmed defenseless people minding their own fucking business in a mall, that's wrong. Blowing up kids at a school, that's wrong too. Wrong as hell."

Raymond's eyes narrowed. "Maybe you're ignoring structural issues. Like the hundreds of *thousands* of kids and adults who've gotten killed and victimized every day for years. Palestine, Lebanon, Afghanistan, Iraq. Maybe the people at that school, and that mall, and fucking Harrods in London, weren't innocent. Because they're part of a system that destroys the Muslim world. Thanks to that so-called democracy you're so patriotic about."

Pescatore said, "I hate to think what the world would be like if the guys you work for were in charge. You chose the wrong side, bro."

Raymond extended the footrest and reclined full-length in the armchair. "Never too late to change sides."

"Is that what you think?"

"Shit, I learned that back in Chicago." Raymond turned his head to stare at him indolently. "As long as you got something or someone to offer, you can always convert."

"I wonder."

"Relax, man. By this time tomorrow we'll be done and have you on your way."

Pescatore went to bed early. In his room, he used his phone to send a brief e-mail in code to Isabel at a cover address set up for that purpose. He slept with his door locked, a chair wedged under the knob, and his keys on the chair. His hand gripped the pistol under the pillow. If terrorists or kidnappers struck in the night, he didn't have any illusions that he'd blast his way out of it. He just wanted control over the time and manner of his demise. Like Rodolfo Walsh, an Argentine writer he had heard about. When a death squad tried to abduct Walsh during the Dirty War, he drew a pistol, forcing them to end it right there. He spared himself getting tossed out of a plane into the Rio de la Plata or something equally undignified. Pescatore didn't plan on starring in anybody's jihadi-porn beheading video.

The sandstorm relented. The morning was dusty and punishingly hot. He put on his vest over his holster. Raymond announced at breakfast—bread, dates, more nasty Turkish coffee—that a rendezvous was set in a Shiite neighborhood with the brigadier's security people, who would escort them to the meet. The Quds Force moved quietly in a web of safe houses, secret bases, and front companies. Iran wielded great influence, but the relationship with Iraqi Shiites was complex.

"Even though they're all Shiite, there's the Arab-Persian thing," he said. "The Iranians see themselves as the great ancient empire. The Iraqis think they're uppity pains in the butt."

With Mustafa at the wheel, the Suburban rolled through crowded streets past sand-colored walls. Posters of martyrs and ayatollahs adorned markets and billboards. People wore black. The neighborhood, the site of a Shiite shrine, was poor but vibrant. Traffic caused the Suburban to reduce speed. Raymond talked on the phone. Pescatore caught glimpses of the golden domes of the shrine above the rooftops. It looked shiny and unreal, like a giant toy palace.

The Suburban turned onto a street choked with cars and pedestrians. They slowed to a crawl. Raymond cursed. He was complaining to the driver when the explosions went off.

Three blasts. Loud, but not deafening. Reaction rippled through the crowd. Gunfire rattled faintly. People stampeded around the vehicle. Police in berets and fatigue uniforms ran by. Mustafa tried to advance, then to back up, but it was hopeless. They were hemmed in.

Mustafa conferred with someone through the window. Sirens approached. They learned there had been an attack inside the shrine. Suicide bombers. Emergency vehicles rolled up, further blocking the street. The Suburban sat motionless in the hubbub. Raymond hollered Arabic into the phone. His eyes darted back and forth.

"Listen, man," he said to Pescatore. "We're jammed up here. Our guys are a few blocks away. We'll find them on foot. Okay?"

"You're the expert."

Mustafa watched them go, torn between protecting his clients and remaining with his marooned vessel.

After the air-conditioned cocoon of the Suburban, it seemed hard to breathe in the heat and dust and tumult. Pescatore followed Raymond at a fast walk past a group of women in black veils and robes who wailed and thumped their chests in lamentation. Raymond and Pescatore rounded a corner into a boulevard, a pedestrian zone from the look of it, that ended in the shrine. There was a melee of people, vehicles and flashing lights. He didn't see damage; the blasts must have been relatively small. Militiamen helped clear the way for ambulances and fire trucks. He avoided eye contact, feeling conspicuous and exposed.

Raymond said they needed to work their way around the shrine to meet the brigadier's operatives. Trouble surfaced. A group of men detached themselves from a wall and hurried through the crowd, on course to intercept.

"Thugs at ten o'clock," Pescatore muttered.

"I see them," Raymond said. "They made us for outsiders."

"What do we do?"

"Stay cool. Follow my lead."

The half a dozen men blocked their way. They seemed to be unarmed. But in the phantasmagoria of the street, their leader had the face that Pescatore would have least preferred to encounter. Gaunt, sallow, predatory: a land pirate. A black headband encircled sweaty unkempt hair. A scar twisted down out of the headband to the left cheek. The pirate was whip-thin, twenties, dressed in black. Long sleeves on long arms despite the heat. He looked twitchy, like a heroin addict.

The pirate went jaw-to-jaw with Raymond. It sounded like he was demanding that Raymond prove he was not the enemy. A crowd gathered. People jostled and chattered. Sirens wailed. Raymond's tone in Arabic was earnest, respectful and aggrieved. He put his hand on his heart. He flashed a smile at the circle of faces. Even in this moment of tension, the smile said, he saw absurd humor in the fact that he was perceived as a threat. The smile conveyed confidence that his listeners would come to their senses. And they would all share a laugh.

The pirate switched to English. "Where you from? English? *Amriky*?"

"Argentina!" Raymond declared. "Messi!"

"That's right," Pescatore said. "Argentina. Maradona!"

He pantomimed kicking a ball and raising his arms to celebrate a goal. A spectator next to him delivered a burst of words. The young man wore mechanic's overalls and yellow plastic gloves that were stained, like the rest of him, with grease. He pointed at Pescatore and said, "Maradona."

Pescatore wasn't sure if he was saying that he reminded him of Maradona, or was expressing admiration for Maradona, or was mocking him. But he responded in English, "You got it, man. Maradona. Argentina!"

The pirate glowered. Raymond raised his phone, indicating that he could resolve everything with one call. The pirate shook his head. His men deployed around Raymond and Pescatore. The crowd parted. Raymond and Pescatore were walking briskly again; now they had an escort. They conferred side of the mouth in Spanish, surrounded by the pirate and four more toughs.

"Who are these guys?" Pescatore asked.

"Like a neighborhood watch. He says they're taking us to a command post for questioning. Because of the attack."

"You believe that?"

"No. They're *chorros*. They're looking to rip us off."

The pirate led the way across the sunbaked boulevard. He strode toward one of the side streets in the row of storefronts, cafés and vending stands. A man rushed by carrying a little girl in a pink dress. Her hands and head were wrapped in bloodstained strips of cloth. Her sobs made Pescatore wince. People congregated to help. A merchant swept wares off a sidewalk display table to make room for the girl. An old woman gave her water from a bottle and dabbed at her face with a rag.

The place is full of stand-up citizens and we get hijacked by the lowlifes, Pescatore thought.

Raymond appealed to the pirate, who retorted over his shoulder.

"He won't let me call my guys to vouch for us," Raymond murmured.

"They're gonna jack us."

"Listen, I'm gonna do him just like that Croatian who called you a taco. We hit and run like hell."

"No *cuetes*?"

"Hell, no. Not unless someone else pulls one. We'd get lynched."

Although Pescatore was itching to draw his Beretta, he understood. The narrow street curved left. A tangle of electrical cables hung overhead. They went by barred windows, a barbershop decorated with a poster of Imam Ali, handsome, bearded and backlit like a movie star. The street was dark, cool and quiet. The frenzy seemed far behind them. Pescatore could taste the adrenaline, the inevitability of combat.

"Now's the time," Raymond said impassively.

He had been serious about repeating the incident on the soccer field in Chicago. He did a stutter step, spread his arms, and slammed his hands against the ears of the pirate, who had his back to him. The move was as ruthless and effective as it had been years ago. The pirate toppled as if his bone and cartilage had liquefied.

A big guy lunged at Raymond. Pescatore hit him as hard as he could in the kidney and, when the head descended, tagged it with a left and a right and a left. That ended the boxing phase of the encounter. It became a sloppy brawl. They battled in workmanlike silence except for grunts and impacts. Pescatore saw Raymond deliver a kick to a kneecap while fighting off a smaller man climbing his back. An assailant swung a length of pipe at Pescatore, landing a sharp blow on the left shoulder. Pescatore used a forearm to the throat to drive him up against an air conditioner jutting out of a ground-floor window.

He found himself next to Raymond, their backs to the rusty shutters of a shop, facing three opponents. The pirate and the big man were horizontal.

"We need to get the fuck out of here," Raymond gasped.

"Let's shoot these *comemierdas*."

The murderous instinct bubbled up along with a premonition. The gunfire would bring a horde of militiamen, police and soldiers, who would mow them down. Pescatore would die without even getting within range of his target.

Then a voice echoed. A grizzled, rotund man stormed into the fray. He wore a dishdasha, the gownlike garment favored by Iraqi men, and a knit skullcap. He delivered a tirade in Arabic. He held rank; the Iraqis dropped their eyes and fists. The newcomer marched over to the pirate, who was on all fours shaking his head as if he had water in his ears. The older man put his hands on his ample hips and spewed words. The pirate responded balefully from his knees. A woman in an abaya appeared behind the older man and joined the argument, hovering in the hooded garment like an aerial creature, her tone melodic and indignant. Voices echoed from windows and doorways. The seemingly empty street had come alive with witnesses, and they had opinions. The assailants glanced around uneasily.

"What the fuck?" Pescatore whispered.

"Apparently this gentleman's a local sheikh," Raymond whispered back.

"A what?"

"Like a precinct captain, an alderman. He's tearing them a new one. Bad Muslims, messing with visitors, disgracing the neighborhood."

The sheikh concluded his remarks with a grand dismissive gesture. No translation needed: *Beat it, get the hell out of here.* The gang helped their chief to his feet and slouched away.

The sheikh turned back to Raymond and Pescatore. He extended his arm full-length, palm down, and flapped the fingers as he spoke. The woman repeated the motion, her hooded head bobbing. Raymond answered appreciatively and pressed his hand to his heart.

Sotto voce, he told Pescatore, "Follow the sheikh."

The sheikh's name was Raheem. He and his wife, who was a good twenty years younger, took them down an alley to their home, a boxlike edifice behind a high cement wall. In the doorway, Raymond removed his shoes and told Pescatore to do the same. Pescatore unlaced his black Timberlands reluctantly, worried what would happen if they had to run.

The Arabic word for "thank you" was *shukrun*. Pescatore uttered it repeatedly during the next half hour. He put his hand on his heart as often as a man with chest pains. Sweaty, aching, fists clenched, he sipped tea and slumped in a red velvet armchair. Three identical armchairs were occupied by Raymond, the sheikh, and his eldest son, a lupine man in sweatpants with a pencil mustache. The son clutched a book, an old paperback English version of *Doctor Faustus*. Perhaps he had been reading the book when company dropped in. Perhaps he had pulled it off a shelf as a conversation piece with foreigners. Eight or nine other teenage and adult males sat or knelt on the crimson carpet, an attentive audience.

Raymond translated bits and pieces. Sheikh Raheem and his wife had been on their way to help the victims at the shrine when they came upon the fight. The assailants were incorrigible neighborhood hoodlums known to prey on outsiders, especially foreign pilgrims and journalists. His hands folded on his belly, the sheikh explained that he had invited them to his home so they could recover from the unpleasantness and he could apologize in the name of a pious, hospitable community. Raymond thanked him. He said he and Pescatore were Argentines of Lebanese descent in town for business. They had decided to visit the shrine at precisely the wrong moment.

"You are welcome," the sheikh said in labored English, patting Pescatore's knee. He had merry eyes above a scraggly gray beard. "Most welcome."

"Really appreciate it, sir," Pescatore said.

He was hyperconscious of his body language. The CIA officers in Madrid had drilled him about Iraqi customs. Don't show the soles of your feet, they had said. He kept his socks flat on the floor. Don't give the thumbs-up, that's like the middle finger for us. He had refrained from using the gesture twice in the past ten minutes. Don't eat or touch things with your left hand, that's the one they wipe with. He was safe because his left arm was numb with pain. Don't look at, talk to, or ask about the women. Not a problem — the wife had disappeared. The young men served the tea.

The sheikh excused himself and left the room. Raymond

had brief conversations on the phone with Mustafa and the brigadier's security men.

"The sheikh is going to bring us to the shrine," Raymond said to Pescatore. "We'll meet our guys there. You okay?"

Pescatore nodded. He noticed that Raymond had a black eye. Raymond smiled. For a moment, he seemed much younger.

"Hell of a scrap, man," Raymond exclaimed. "You kicked ass. I likes that in you."

"You threw hands like a pro," Pescatore said.

They bumped fists. This Western cultural interaction elicited interest and amusement in the audience on the carpet.

The sheikh returned wearing a wrinkled gray blazer over the dishdasha. A new expedition set off: Pescatore and Raymond accompanied by the sheikh and his boys.

The sun inflamed the domes and towers rising in fairy-tale splendor over the chaos. In the street market outside the walls of the shrine, Pescatore stepped over pools of blood mixed with water from the fire hoses. Many of the ambulances had departed with the dead and badly injured. Medics and volunteers tended victims with minor wounds in the street or on tables of the market. The sheikh led them to an entrance of the shrine. Police and militiamen greeted him, stepping out of his way. He turned and spoke solemnly to Pescatore and Raymond.

"He wants to show us what happened," Raymond translated. "He wants us to know the tragedy of his country. Let's humor him."

That's a pretty disrespectful way of putting it, Pescatore thought.

The marble surface of the courtyard was littered with shoes. One of the blasts had gone off near the racks where worshippers stored their shoes for prayer. The bombers had waded into a crowd of congregants, forming a deadly triangle. The twisted wreckage of an oak door resembled a battered raft; it had been blown off its hinges. The starbursts of glass in the expanse of debris were the remnants of ornate chandeliers like the ones still hanging in archways farther away. Intricate designs covered the tiled walls.

Few casualties remained in the shrine. Police did investigative work. Militia fighters—who apparently had as much clout as cops in this area—helped the bearded, turbaned clerics clean up. With rags, mops and pails, fighters and clerics pushed the debris into piles. They paused now and then, looked up and thumped their heads and chests in sorrow.

The sheikh joined the lamentation. He turned in a dismayed circle, taking it all in. He tottered suddenly. Pescatore gripped his fleshy arm to steady him. The sheikh pointed.

It took Pescatore a moment to comprehend that he was looking at a heap of human remains.

"People," the sheikh said, grimacing.

"God rest their souls," Pescatore said.

He was beyond shock, beyond nausea. Carnage followed him. Or worse, he brought it with him.

Pescatore turned to Raymond. But Raymond wasn't paying attention. He was on the phone, talking fast, ready to move on.

23

Adam Raised a Cain

The safe house was on the eastern outskirts of Baghdad.

The vehicle carrying the brigadier's men took a circuitous route. The Suburban followed. Eventually, Raymond and Pescatore switched from the Suburban to the lead vehicle. Pescatore was told to leave his cell phone with Mustafa, the driver, who would wait at a distance.

They arrived twenty minutes later. The residential street was lined with high walls and palm trees. A chubby teenager opened a gate. Guards with rifles appeared in the driveway. The two-story house had a pastel Southern California look—except for the lack of paint and repairs. The lawn was a wilderness of weeds. A well-to-do Sunni family had abandoned the home when sectarian combat turned the area into the fiefdom of a Shiite militia. Brigadier Ali had commandeered the property to use it as an occasional base.

"He could operate out of the Iranian embassy if he wanted," Raymond said. "The ambassador was in the Quds Force with him. But this is discreet."

Pescatore counted nine gunmen, including three in the vehicle. Civilian clothes, but they carried themselves like soldiers. Raymond turned over his pistol to a guard and Pescatore followed suit. The guard gave Pescatore a quick pat-down—and near heart failure. It was not an aggressive frisk, however. His being with Raymond ensured respectful treatment. Raymond waded into a flurry of handshakes, backslaps, heart-touching, *salaam alaikum*s and *alhamdulillah*s. Pescatore wished he would turn the volume down. Pescatore had gone from jaw-grinding tension to subdued anticipation. He smoothed his clothes and centered his belt buckle.

The guards said the brigadier had not yet arrived. Pescatore and Raymond waited on a raised veranda.

"Shouldn't be long," Raymond said. "How you doing?"

"Slow motion."

"Hey, Ahmed, is that a soccer ball?"

Raymond jogged down the three steps. A guard was poking his foot at a black-and-white ball half hidden in the weeds. The guard kicked the ball to Raymond. He spun it up on his foot and passed it back. They began kicking the ball back and forth, moving into the driveway.

"Ahmed Zidane!" Raymond declared.

The youthful guard grinned. He clung to the rifle strapped over his shoulder as he lunged to trap a high pass. With his leonine hair and beard, he resembled a cross between Imam Ali and a Bee Gee.

"Valentín, come on," Raymond called, waving at him. "A little keep-up drill."

The last thing Pescatore wanted to do was play soccer. But he'd look bad if he declined. He joined the three-way game. The objective was to keep the ball in the air. When they were kids, Pescatore and Raymond had done this for hours. Raymond had been a wizard. He had put more energy into juggling—a good way to impress girls—than he did into games. His moves now were masterly. He clowned and danced. He delivered commentary in English, Arabic and Spanish. He engaged Pescatore in a short-range volley of head passes. Pescatore was rusty; he lost the ball several times and had to run into the high weeds to retrieve it. The guards moved closer to watch. Pescatore spun to fire a back-heel pass.

"Dale, maestro!" Raymond said. "Puttin' on a show!"

Raymond caught the ball on top of his right foot and balanced it there. He went into a joyful exhibition: foot to foot, thigh to thigh, low balls, high balls. He ducked forward and hunched his shoulders, forming a cradle to catch the descending ball on his neck. He held the ball there behind his head, arms wide like a statue of a soaring man. Maintaining the stance, he let out a triumphant whoop. The guards cheered. Pescatore joined in.

The guards stiffened. Raymond's sudden pass whizzed by Pescatore's head. He jogged onto the lawn in pursuit of the ball, then surveyed the scene from the weeds.

Brigadier Ali had materialized on the veranda. Two gunmen flanked him. Ali had his lips clamped on a thin cigar. He raised his hands and clapped with a kind of sardonic benevolence.

The Iranian general must have entered the compound on foot. Either that or he had already been inside the house. Probably watching from a window.

If Raymond was embarrassed, he shrugged it off. He gave Brigadier Ali a hug and kisses on the cheek. Pescatore tossed the ball aside. He approached the veranda and stood at attention.

"General, it is my pleasure to finally introduce my friend Valentín, about whom you have already heard so much," Raymond said ceremoniously.

Pescatore went up the steps. They shook hands. Brigadier Ali gripped his left biceps, as if gauging his strength. Pescatore said it was an honor.

"The honor is mine." Ali spoke accented English. His smile was brief.

He led them into the house. The two gunmen followed them upstairs into a smell of dust and intermittent use. The gunmen opened a door to a study and took up positions in the hall outside. In the bare and dimly lit study, the Iranian sat in a high-backed leather chair behind an oak desk which had a laptop computer and two cell phones on top of it. A picture window overlooked the lawn and driveway. The air conditioner was not doing much.

Pescatore had spent hours reading and listening to briefings about the brigadier. The combined might of several spy agencies had produced few pictures. None was more recent than the photo in Bolivia six years before. Ali was fifty-three now. His shoulders and neck were meaty and powerful in a collarless shirt of gray silk. He had a slight and solid belly. His short, well-groomed beard had acquired tinges of gray. His hairline had receded farther, a narrow rampart cresting above the middle of his forehead. He had thin hard lips bracketed by indented lines descending from his nostrils. He wore a designer watch. When he stared intently, he lowered his narrow chin, raised his eyes, and tilted his head—the coiled pose of a world-class chess grand master who played on a board piled with corpses and cash. A high-rolling gangster general.

For once, Raymond didn't talk. A bodyguard poured tea and left.

"You are very young."

The voice had a coiled quality too. Brigadier Ali said the words with a hint of surprise and disappointment. Pescatore took it in stride. People tended to think he was younger than he was. The brigadier had started with a challenge to test his mettle. He reacted as if it were a compliment.

"Thank you, sir. Actually, I'm only a year younger than Raymond."

"It's true," Raymond said. "He knows how to handle himself. You should have seen him today. We had a problem near the shrine."

Raymond told the story of the bombing and the brawl, displaying his black eye. Brigadier Ali shook his head indulgently, paternally. Pescatore remembered Raymond saying Ali had four daughters. Raymond wasn't just the protégé and partner in crime. He was a proxy son, brash, charismatic and spoiled.

Raymond crowed about how Pescatore had dropped a larger opponent.

"No big deal, I used to box," Pescatore said, lifting his fists. "Did some wrestling too."

The brigadier's smile lasted longer this time. He said he had been a military wrestling champion many years ago. Pescatore knew this from a briefing, which was why he had mentioned wrestling in the first place. In reality, his experience with wrestling was limited to high-school gym class.

"You see it here and here." Brigadier Ali touched his own nose, which was flat and slightly dented, and a misshapen right ear. "These are not sports for pretty boys."

Raymond chortled with gusto. Brigadier Ali asked about Pescatore's background and family. He answered with the truth. This wasn't exactly undercover; he was playing a modified version of himself.

The general's chin went down, the eyes went up, and the head tilted.

"I am curious why you are here, what motivates you," he said quietly. "Have you become one of us? Do you believe there is no God but Allah, and Muhammad is His Prophet?"

"No, sir. No, I sure don't. I used to be Roman Catholic, but I got disgusted with the priests and everything. That turned me off religion."

"What are your views on the Islamic Republic of Iran?"

"I don't have strong opinions one way or the other. No, sir, I'll be straight with you. My motivation is money. The more, the better."

"That is all?"

"There's another thing," Pescatore said, putting rancor in his voice. "I really dislike the U.S. government. They treated me very badly. I'm sick of their shit and they deserve what they get."

Ali nodded knowingly. "How long were you a border police-man?"

"Six years."

It had actually been closer to five. He chided himself; details like that could be checked. He sipped tea. Sweat pooled at the back of his neck and on his upper lip. The room was stuffy; the cigar smoke didn't help. He described his career in the Patrol. He painted a portrait of a resentful agent who felt used and abandoned. A distortion built on a kernel of truth.

"I've done TDYs—temporary missions—in California, Texas, and Arizona. I've investigated smuggling, so I know the networks that move migrants. I have sources in Mexican law enforcement and the drug cartels, which overlap, as you know, sir."

"*Los narcos mexicanos son los más fuertes,*" Brigadier Ali said. He spoke decent Spanish with a Caribbean inflection.

"*Afirmativo, mi general.*" Pescatore widened his eyes amiably. He saw Raymond nod in approval. Raymond's leg was jiggling nonstop. It was making Pescatore even more nervous.

"We find it difficult to operate in Mexico." The Iranian frowned. "Troubles with Mexican intelligence. Very aggressive."

"Yes, sir. I'm not surprised. You might as well be flying into Miami. U.S. agents are right there with the Mexicans at the airports. They do targeting of passenger manifests for threats. The CISEN, the Mexican intelligence service, they're tough. They work with the Americans tracking SIAs, special interest aliens, from countries with a terrorist or hostile intelligence presence. You, sir, would be considered an SIA. And an OTM: other than Mexican. The Mexicans make SIAs available to the CIA for questioning, in person or by videoconference."

He was tossing out acronyms to enhance his expert status and because he was on edge. The soldier digested the terms, filing them in his head. He gestured at Pescatore to continue.

"The bottom line is, General, the Mexicans—cops and narcos—know U.S. psychology. They want a good business environment. They help the Americans on anything related to Islamic terrorism. They understand no one cares if the narcos massacre seventy Central American migrants. But if a Pakistani crosses the Line from Tijuana and shoots five Americans in the Horton Plaza shopping center in San Diego, and it traces back to training with al-Qaeda, then the shit hits the fan."

"A disaster," Raymond explained. "A political uproar."

"Congressional committees, media frenzy, bosses getting fired. It would hurt commerce and Mexican-American relations."

"*Un tremendo lío,*" Brigadier Ali said, showing off his slang.

"*Exactamente, mi general.* Like that case a couple of years ago when your guys tried to hire the Zetas cartel to kill the Saudi ambassador in Washington. Big mistake. The op was doomed from the get-go. The Zetas associate that your man contacted damn near broke his leg running to tell the DEA. Why in the world would a Mexican drug cartel, which makes millions of dollars a day, want to get involved in Islamic terrorism? Why would the Zetas want to bring down the U.S. military on their heads? Crazy. I'm surprised the Quds Force was that unsophisticated."

Although he had feared coming off as disrespectful, his candor was rewarded. The general waved the cigar dismissively in a flurry of smoke. "This was amateur. My group is functioning at another level entirely."

"I sure hope so." Pescatore scowled, playing the hard-ass professional to the hilt now. "What you have to do is hide your fingerprints. You need an intermediary who isn't Middle Eastern. A Spanish-speaking American like me who can recruit, pay bribes, facilitate."

"What is the best way to infiltrate a team into the United States?"

Brigadier Ali leaned forward, his heavy hands extended on the oak. Pescatore sipped tea to slow himself down.

"Well, I hate to take money out of my own pocket, sir. But really the best thing would be to send them in legally through an airport, with clean passports from a visa waiver country. Europe, Australia, someplace like that."

Ali nodded, acknowledging his rigor. "No, the Mexico border."

"Then it depends on who the team are. If they're Latin, it's easier."

"Assume they might or might not be," Raymond said.

"Either way, they should have Latin American passports. They could fly into Central America, maybe from Ecuador or Venezuela, which are wide open border-wise and friendly to you guys. If the operatives cross illegally from Guatemala into Mexico, we find smugglers with Mexican police protection, specialists in clients like Indians and Chinese who pay fifty thousand a head. That's why they don't get robbed and raped and kidnapped as much as the Central Americans. The Mexicans need to think your guys are VIP illegal immigrants, not terrorists."

"Do you know smugglers?"

"Yes, sir. At the U.S. line, sir, you have two choices. The ports of entry are easiest if we have a connection. We pay off a CBP field operations inspector and he just waves a vehicle past his booth. The downside is, there are a lot of eyes at a port. The other way is through open land: the desert or the mountains. It takes longer, it's physically demanding, dangerous. Allies inside the Border Patrol could help."

"Good." Ali put down his cigar. "What were you doing in Argentina?"

That caught him off guard. The conversation had been clicking along as he had envisioned it. But Raymond had warned him: Ali is a *cabrón*. He changes topics like a prosecutor. He messes with your head. Be ready.

Inadvertently, Pescatore wiped sweat from his upper lip. "Argentina?"

"Yes." The stare was a laser. The smile had vanished.

This was a vulnerable aspect of the cover story. Raymond had said the Iranians didn't know about Pescatore's work for Facundo. If they did, that was a problem. If they had found out the Argentine police had arrested him as a suspect, that could reveal Raymond's attempt to warn him and might end up with both of them dead.

"Well, sir, officially I went there to see friends and family and do security work. Bodyguard. Unofficially"—he offered a roguish Raymond-style grin—"I was interested in the dope business. Smuggling drugs."

"Did you?" Brigadier Ali asked.

In Pescatore's peripheral vision, Raymond's leg jiggled faster. He couldn't remember when he had seen Raymond more agitated.

"Little bit. I've been kind of lazy, tell you the truth. Enjoying the nightlife. Until I ran into Raymond and he mentioned this project."

"Have you had contact with the U.S. embassy in Buenos Aires?"

More uncomfortable terrain. Pescatore wondered if someone had seen him with Furukawa. He had to trust Raymond.

"Got my passport renewed there. That's about it."

He felt as if the eyes beneath the low brow were scouring his skull. He wished someone would turn up the air or open a window.

"Should we talk about targets?" Raymond interjected, smiling.

The conversation turned to attack scenarios. A minefield.

Pescatore wanted to show he had inside intel without giving any pointers. His U.S. handlers had outlined areas in which they knew the Quds Force and Hezbollah had already done surveillance or had gotten access to information. Ali and Raymond discussed Jewish targets in Los Angeles.

Pescatore's goal was to heighten his value by emphasizing obstacles. He said, "Remember, you'd have to get to Los Angeles first. There are Border Patrol freeway checkpoints. It's like a second border."

Brigadier Ali cleared his throat. "I have seen, on television, long lines of traffic at the Mexico border. Many cars and trucks. This seems full of possibilities. A, eh, target-rich environment."

"That's what I was talking about, Valentín," Raymond said "Hit a border station. Symbolically, the strike combines the U.S. and Mexico, government and commerce. A lot of the crossers are U.S. citizens, right?"

"Sure. And green-card holders. U.S. residents."

"The drug traffickers have shot at border crossings, haven't they?"

"Yeah. In Arizona, retaliating for a drug bust. A sniper in the hills on the Mexican side fired at the port of entry."

"Can you imagine, Ali?" Raymond enthused. "A well-organized sniper attack on the border traffic. Or close-range shooters. Combined with a truck bomb? San Diego and El Paso simultaneously? A real spectacular."

The brigadier raised black eyebrows. His forehead was dry despite the heat. "What do you think, Valentín?"

"It could do damage, that's for sure, if—"

"Also, you eliminate the whole problem of the team crossing the border," Raymond exclaimed, talking loud and fast. "The real line is a couple hundred yards south of the port, so you'd technically strike in the United States. Isn't that right, Valentín?"

Slow it down, bro, for the love of God, Pescatore thought.

"That's correct," he said gravely. "In all these scenarios, the issue is operational security in Mexico. U.S. agencies have a major intel presence south of the border: human sources, communications intercepts. The bigger the plot, the more likely the Mexican police or traffickers are going to hear something. The mafias have *halcones,* lookouts, everywhere: gas stations, hotels. They even run their own highway checkpoints."

Brigadier Ali shook his head. "Remarkable."

"I'm the guy who's going to improve your odds, who can overcome those challenges," Pescatore said.

The general asked about ports of entry, the internal workings of border agencies and smuggling groups, countries in South and Central America. Pescatore gave succinct answers. He was starting to worry that this was beyond the brainstorming stage. He wondered if an attack team was already formed, if the brigadier had consulted others. They might be ready to pull the trigger sooner than he had thought.

The general swiveled to Raymond and spoke in Arabic; Raymond's Farsi was weak. Pescatore rested his hands on his belt buckle. As he watched and listened, he began to get angry. Raymond was dangerous, but alone he was ultimately a hustler, a medium-size kingpin. Brigadier Ali had imbued him with skills, focus and resources. He had transformed him into a killing machine. He was the puppet master behind the puppet master.

If you were a man, Pescatore told himself, *what you'd do now is dive over the desk and waste this fucker. Snap his neck. Choke him out. He's in okay shape, former wrestling champ and whatnot, but you could take him. The lives you'd save. The deaths you'd avenge. It would be a public service. A victory worth dying for. The question is what Raymond would do. Lend you a hand? Defend Ali? Sit there with his mouth open? You're probably the one guy he would risk his life for if you pulled a stunt like that.*

Sweating, feverish with hate and fear, Pescatore imagined

the sequence of violent events. The tangible possibility of it made him dizzy. Even if Raymond followed his lead, even if he finished Brigadier Ali quickly and quietly, there were a dozen gunmen in the compound. For the sake of argument, say he and Raymond succeeded in overpowering the two guards inside and grabbing their rifles. Two more down. By then, however, they would have made noise and lost the element of surprise. And Raymond hadn't signed up for a suicide mission.

Pescatore shook his head. *Get a grip,* he told himself. *The real world doesn't work like that. That's some grade-Z Hollywood bullshit. Martyrs are either real brave or real stupid. You're not brave or stupid enough. Stick to the plan.*

"Yes?" the brigadier said, looking straight at him. In a panic, Pescatore saw that the man thought he wanted to speak.

"No, sir, I was just going over something in my mind. Not important."

"You have not asked about money," the general said, taking a long puff on the cigar with his hand over his mouth.

"No, sir."

Pescatore held the stare until the Iranian allowed himself a smile.

"I will ask you, then," Ali said. "What is your price?"

"Honestly, it depends what I end up doing." Pescatore spoke earnestly while going for a sharklike edge. "This is the biggest, hardest target there is. You need top-quality services. That's what I intend to provide. If I work for you on the ground, surveillance and recruiting smugglers and everything, that could get me killed any number of ways. So we're talking about two hundred fifty thousand dollars. If it's more like just consulting, one hundred fifty thousand. Plus travel and expenses."

"Not cheap."

"No, sir. I think I'm worth it. And I think the expense is worth it to you."

Ali nodded. His body language indicated that the meeting had come to a close.

"I'm so glad that my two favorite people are now friends and allies," Raymond declared. "We will do great things."

"You are young, but you are intelligent and strong," Brigadier Ali said to Pescatore, beaming. "I think we will be working together."

"That's a real honor coming from a great and wise soldier like yourself, sir. I look forward to it."

The general raised a finger. "Remember, with this honor comes responsibility. Raymond says you are his brother. This means you are now my brother."

Pescatore pressed his hand to his heart and lowered his eyes. Brigadier Ali continued: "Two things now. Absolute discretion. And being ready. We will communicate soon. You must be ready."

"I am, sir."

The Iranian rummaged in a desk drawer and pulled out an envelope. He placed it on the desk in front of Pescatore. It was stuffed with U.S. currency. *A tip for the new henchman,* Pescatore thought.

"A token of appreciation," Ali said.

They stood. The general glanced at one of the phones on the desk. Pescatore thought, *Last chance. Now's the time. Tell him where he can shove his money, then hit him in the throat to shut him up, then kill his ass.*

Pescatore murmured thanks and slipped the envelope into a vest pocket.

"There may be obstacles, but money is not one," the Iranian said.

"Good. Money is usually an obstacle if you don't have it."

Brigadier Ali emitted a short sharp laugh. They shook hands. The brigadier gripped Pescatore's left biceps again. He spoke in Arabic to Raymond. Raymond and Pescatore passed the sentries and went downstairs. Raymond kept his hand on Pescatore's shoulder, pounding it softly.

"It went great it went great it went great," he exulted.

There was no shade left on the veranda. Pescatore felt unsteady on his feet as they conferred.

"You think so?" he asked. "He wasn't too concrete about a follow-up."

"The meet was about the feel, *che*. About you giving him a good vibe. And that's what you did. He leaves the details to me. The important thing is you handled yourself just right. This will move fast now."

"Good."

"Everybody needs to be ready." Raymond raised his eyebrows for conspiratorial emphasis.

Pescatore noticed a green Nissan Pathfinder in the driveway. Ahmed—the Bee Gees–looking guard who had played soccer—stood by it with his rifle. He exchanged words with Raymond. His hand still on Pescatore's shoulder, Raymond turned so their backs were to the driveway.

"Listen, man, change in plans," he said. "Ali wants me to stay. He wants to go over our project. Other stuff, too. There's a meeting tonight. Then he leaves town and I'll be done."

"I don't understand. We're done. You're supposed to take me to the border right away."

"I know, but—"

"You said I'd be in Jordan ASAP."

"Sorry, he's the boss. He changed schedule on me." Raymond's voice was urgent and soothing. "Ahmed will take you to Mustafa, Mustafa will take you to the hotel. Chill out, eat something, watch TV. I'll be back late. Or in the morning. We leave tomorrow for sure."

"I don't like it."

Pescatore glanced back at the driveway. Two more guards

had appeared near the SUV. Others stood ready at the gate. Ahmed smiled at Pescatore. A broad, telegenic smile.

Pescatore looked, finally, at Raymond. He was smiling too. His hooded eyes were intent.

A coldness welled up in Pescatore's chest. *Goddamn it,* he thought. *You got me. I thought that was the one line you would not cross. The scorpion strikes again.*

"Come on man, everybody's waiting, this is starting to look weird," Raymond whispered.

Pescatore wiped sweat from his forehead with a sleeve. He mustered a grin. He put a hand on Raymond's shoulder, presenting the onlookers with a pose of old friends sharing a confidence before they parted.

"Raymond," he said in a light offhand voice. "I really think we should stick with the plan. I really think you and me should go back to the hotel now, together, and get me out of the country like we agreed."

"I can't. If the boss says jump, I jump. You'll be fine. A minor adjustment, that's all."

Pescatore exhaled. The suspicion had taken wing: the brigadier had seen through the scam and told Raymond to get rid of Pescatore. Or Raymond had turned triple agent and revealed all. It had been a charade to lure Pescatore into their clutches and take an American scalp. He imagined a videotaped decapitation after a torture-induced confession denouncing the U.S. spymasters who had dared to fuck with Brigadier Ali. Pescatore cursed the day the foolish idea had entered his head that he was slicker than Raymond. He was about pay for it big-time.

Very softly, he said, "I'm getting a bad feeling about this."

Playing for their audience, Raymond burst into laughter, giving it a lot of shoulder and head movement.

"That's ridiculous," he muttered through his teeth. "We're in this together, all the way. I'm always straight-up with you. I know you got heart. Don't punk out on me now."

Pescatore squinted against the sun. He had doubts about his doubts. If they were going to kill him, the safe house was perfect. Surely it was equipped with rooms for interrogations and wet work. Why take him anywhere else? Moreover, Pescatore was willing to admit that Raymond had hoodwinked him. But he believed that, if this was true, he would see the betrayal in Raymond's eyes. And he didn't. Maybe that was ridiculous, but his instincts hadn't been wrong up to now.

Nevertheless. Even if Raymond was sincere, even if Pescatore was not in danger, the bottom line had not changed. It was still imperative that Raymond follow the original program and leave with him right away. Pescatore had to get that across, but not too obviously.

He was aware of multiple eyes on him. Perhaps Brigadier Ali was watching from his study. Pescatore stalled by adding a little pugilistic horseplay to the farewell scene. He bobbed, weaved, and threw a fake punch at Raymond's midsection, talking under his breath as he did so.

"I know all that, man," Pescatore said, "but I'm telling you I'd feel a lot better if we stuck to the plan and you came with me now."

Raymond responded with a playful rope-a-dope defensive stance, his fists together at his brow, elbows at his midsection.

"Trust me, *cuate,*" he said.

Pescatore wasn't sure whom he was trying to save. He couldn't push any further. He gave Raymond a hug and thumped his back twice.

"See you soon," Pescatore said. *"Cuate."*

Raymond cocked his head, as if examining the problem from a different angle. He gave Pescatore a long, searching look. His eyes shone.

In the Pathfinder, Pescatore was sweating so much that his clothes stuck to the seat. Ahmed sat next to him, two gunmen in front. Pescatore remembered the Arabic word: *Maktub*. It was written.

During the ride, Pescatore watched his escorts from the corner of his eye. He slouched against his window, but his muscles were on a hair trigger. Soon they stopped next to Mustafa's white Suburban. It was parked in the shade beneath an expressway interchange in a landscape of junked cars. Dogs rooted in trash in a vacant lot.

Ahmed handed over the Beretta. Pescatore holstered it. Ahmed flashed the million-dollar smile. Pescatore smiled back. He put his hand on his heart.

His legs ached with accumulated tension. He closed the door behind him.

Looks like Raymond told the truth after all, he thought. *Too late.*

Mustafa greeted him. The driver gave Pescatore his iPhone. It was the weapon he needed the most right this minute. He told Mustafa to take him to the hotel. His sweaty hands shook as he worked the keyboard of the phone.

He wrote a four-word e-mail: *"Adam Raised a Cain."* It was the title of an old Springsteen song and the code phrase he had chosen.

The response arrived immediately.

Please confirm song request: "Adam Raised a Cain."

Affirmative, he wrote. *Can't wait to hear it.*

The Suburban neared downtown. He saw high-rises. He saw bridges across the Tigris River, a steel sheet in the heat. He didn't spot a tail. But he had been the subject of a fullfledged surveillance deployment since Amman. Agents under U.S. command with the aid of MI6, the French DGSE, the Mossad, and the Jordanian Mukhabarat. They had outfitted him with two tiny GPS-tracking devices. One was embedded in his belt buckle. He had secreted the other device in the weeds at the safe house while retrieving the soccer ball.

"Checkpoint," Mustafa said over his shoulder, sounding perturbed.

Two pickup trucks full of Iraqi soldiers blocked the street ahead. Pescatore could see why Mustafa was uneasy. The checkpoint had the look of a special operation; the soldiers wore commando-style uniforms and were poised and fierce. They swarmed the Suburban. Mustafa stammered at the gun barrels in his face. Soldiers hauled out Pescatore and hustled him away. He did not resist. He jogged amid the soldiers, matching their pace, their hands propelling him by the back and shoulders.

When he saw the Americans, he knew he was finally safe. The warrior duo consisted of a dashing and brawny black guy in his forties and a shorter, younger white guy with helmetlike hair and a farm-boy frame. They introduced themselves as Malone and Stockton. Both wore cargo pants, body armor, wired earpieces, wraparound shades, and pistols. They steered him into an armor-plated mini-truck with tinted windows. As Malone started to close the door, an Iraqi commando reached in and handed him something. Malone passed it to Pescatore. His U.S. passport, retrieved at gunpoint from Mustafa.

"All good?" Malone asked.

"All good."

"Where's the other client?"

"He didn't make it," Pescatore said. "The plan's the same."

"Roger that."

The meetings in Madrid had quickly discarded Raymond's proposal to lure Brigadier Ali into a capture. Raymond wasn't reliable. Brigadier Ali was too slippery. There was no guarantee he would venture into harm's way to oversee his plot. Even if he did travel closer to the target zone, he might remain safely out of reach in Venezuela or Cuba.

At the same time, another point had become clear: Brigadier Ali was an urgent threat. Independent intelligence confirmed Raymond's account of Ali's project to strike the homeland.

Sources warned that the general had more than one U.S. plot under way. He functioned with alarming independence. He had to be stopped. After years stalking him, the Israelis said that this was a unique opportunity, and the British and French agreed. The spies took over, though Isabel remained as Pescatore's minder. It turned out that Brigadier Ali had earned a distinction: he was on the kill list of terrorists designated for assassination.

The U.S. embassy in Baghdad was the biggest in the world. The fortress complex had housing, shopping and recreational facilities and internal street signs. Malone and Stockton led him from a garage to elevators, through secure hallways and sealed doorways with prominent warnings about secrecy and safety. The destination was a conference room with a view of Baghdad wreathed in the afternoon heat haze.

The three of them sat down at a table. There were plastic cups and a large bottle of water. Pescatore drank like a man who had been crawling through the desert. They were sitting and drinking in silence when they heard an explosion in the distance. They felt it too: a low resounding thump.

Pescatore closed his eyes.

"Hel-lo," Malone said.

"Hello, Hellfire," Stockton said.

Pescatore opened his eyes. Malone and Stockton bumped fists. Malone extended his arm across the table. Mechanically, Pescatore bumped the big fist.

On the edge of the city, a plume of smoke rose toward the sun.

The planners had counted on the fact that the Quds Force simply did not believe the U.S. government would do a drone strike in Baghdad. Too politically delicate, too diplomatically volatile. Although the Iranians were correct in theory, Brigadier Ali was a special case. He had crossed too many red lines. Washington had decided to send a message. If the Iraqis and the Iranians didn't like it, tough shit.

Another crucial premise: the brigadier trusted Raymond. And Raymond trusted Pescatore. Raymond was told nothing about the real mission. Pescatore's orders were to act as if they were laying the groundwork for an eventual arrest. He would secretly pinpoint Ali's location and drop a tracking device to mark the kill zone. When he and Raymond left the meet, he would signal for the air strike. A trusted Iraqi military unit would scoop them off the street. At the embassy, Raymond would be told the truth. The plan was to give him a choice: accept removal from Iraq in U.S. custody or remain on the turf of the ruthless spy agency that he had so colossally betrayed. Once back on home soil, he could haggle. Isabel Puente had predicted that the prosecutors would offer little more than a promise not to seek the death penalty. Pescatore hadn't been so sure.

An hour later, Isabel arrived from a command post. Malone and Stockton left her alone with Pescatore. She said preliminary reports from sources and witnesses indicated that Brigadier Ali was dead. A television news crew had filmed his body being pulled from the rubble. No one in the safe house had survived.

Pescatore told her what had happened. He had decided to take the shot while he could. He had sacrificed Raymond.

Isabel nodded sympathetically.

"You had no choice, Valentine," she said. "You did good."

"Maybe," he said. "But I feel bad."

Leabharlanna Poibli Chathair Baile Átha Cliath

 Dublin City Public Libraries

Epilogue

Manteca

*F*acundo said he was reminded of a joke.
    The old joke about the bear hunter, he said. He sipped tea with a wistful glance at Pescatore's espresso.

    A guy goes bear hunting. He's in the woods with his shotgun. Someone taps him on the shoulder. A large bear. The bear says: "Uh-oh. What are you doing with that gun? Don't do that." As punishment, the bear has forcible sex with the guy. The next year, bear-hunting season arrives. The guy shows up again. Someone taps him on the shoulder: the bear. The bear says, "You again? I warned you." And the bear has forcible sex with him. Same time next year, hunting season begins. Sure enough, the guy returns to the woods. The bear taps him on the shoulder and says, "You don't come here to hunt bears, do you?"

    Pescatore laughed. He was happy to be back in Buenos Aires at La Biela on a nice September Friday. He had arrived from France a few days earlier. It was the first time he had seen Facundo in three months. His boss was in good form. He had lost weight and gained color. His basso profundo voice had recovered its verve.

    "Pretty good." Pescatore said with a chuckle. "I'm not sure how it relates to my situation, though."

    "It does, in a way." Facundo grimaced apologetically. "Perhaps it was not the most appropriate metaphor. What I mean is, there

are situations in which one perseveres no matter how much one gets banged up, how crazy and traumatic it is. Does that make sense?"

"Not completely as far as the scenario with the bear."

"The point is, son, I could not be prouder of you or more impressed with your achievements on this case. Not to mention the goodwill and positive image we have gained with several intelligence services."

"Thank you. I was mainly just hanging on for the ride."

"What was it like to be a Parisian?"

"Great. I got pretty comfortable."

"I was worried you would not come back. By the way, I had a frank conversation with an interlocutor. The federal police no longer bear you a grudge."

"Good news for me."

"How is your French friend?"

"Better. Her doctors let us go to Bretagne for a week. She's on light duty now. She wants to visit soon."

"Promising, no?"

Pescatore grinned. "I don't know, Facundo, to be honest. I'm American. She's French. Her life is in France. But I can't wait to see her again."

"And Isabel?" Facundo asked.

"We're close again. I'm amazed."

"Ay. I wish I had your youth and your problems with women."

"She's just a friend."

They talked about work. When Pescatore got settled, Facundo wanted to send him on a foreign assignment. In fact, he had enough international business that he had thought about setting up an office in Miami or Washington. It had occurred to him that Pescatore could be his company's U.S. representative.

"Exciting," Pescatore said.

"No rush. We'll discuss it calmly."

Facundo signaled the waiter for another tea and espresso. He *folded his massive hands and lifted his round shoulders. He lowered his voice.*

"I had a long talk with a paisano the other day," Facundo said. "The best insight I have had into the case. Especially the Iruqi aspect."

"Anything new?"

"The Israelis and Americans obtained a detailed report from Iraqi sources about who and what was found at the site of the missile strike."

Pescatore remembered the television images of the devastated house. The pulverized bodies. The fleeting footage of the brigadier on a stretcher, his face swollen and sooty.

"Although there was little doubt, the DNA confirms absolutely that Brigadier Ali met Allah," Facundo rasped.

"How did they get a match?"

"The Mossad cleaned the general's brother in Istanbul years ago."

"Oh, yeah. Raymond told me that."

Facundo said the report had identified other casualties: three Iranian soldiers, five Iraqi Shiite militants, three Lebanese Hezbollah fighters. However, questions had arisen about the identification of Raymond Mercer, aka Ramón Verdugo, as one of the dead.

"How can that be?" Pescatore asked. "At the embassy, they said a source established visual confirmation of Raymond's corpse. They heard chatter about him being dead."

"Yes. Well. That was sloppy. There has been a development." *Facundo's bushy eyebrows knit.* "Weeks ago, in Dubai, a man withdrew seventeen thousand dollars from a bank account linked to Raymond Mercer. His only account that was not frozen yet. A security camera recorded a clear image."

Pescatore rocked back in his chair. "So you're saying..."

"He is alive. The chorro."

Pescatore looked out the window. The sun shone. The outdoor tables were crowded. He took a breath.

"That's quite a bomb you just dropped on me, Facundo."

"I know, son." He inclined his bulk over the table, his face grim. *"Look, he might as well be dead. Everyone is hunting him. And there is a good chance of an, eh, extralegal resolution. For the Iranians and Hezbollah, he is a repugnant traitor. They want to make a memorable example of him. The Israelis too, for different reasons. The French. And the Americans are hot on his heels. Not just the FBI, the clandestine side."*

Pescatore nodded. "They don't want him talking about all those years he was an informant. Or how they almost wasted a U.S. citizen in an air strike in Iraq. Even though that's my fault. It wasn't the plan."

"The official story remains that a militant arsenal exploded. Of course, in Iraq, people think every explosion is really an American air strike."

"Do they have an idea where he is?"

"Africa or Latin America. Don't worry, someone will find him. He will talk on the phone, leave tracks on the Internet. One of the scoundrels he has screwed will screw him back. The death sentence has been imposed. The execution will be a formality."

Pescatore had struggled to come to grips with his actions in Iraq. For his own sanity, he had buried Raymond Mercer and his memory in the rubble. Now, he did not know what he felt. Anger? Dread? Relief?

The waiter appeared and deposited the drinks on the table. Facundo drew a merciful curtain over the topic. He reminded Pescatore about Shabbat dinner that evening. He asked when Fatima planned to visit.

"End of October," Pescatore answered. "I thought I'd take her to Punta del Este. It will be pretty slow then, no?"

"Yes. Until December. Do you know the joke? If the Apocalypse comes, move to Uruguay. Because everything there happens fifty years later."

Pescatore paused with his cup halfway to his mouth. He put the cup down. He picked it back up and drank.

"Yes," he said. "I've heard that one."

Dinner at Facundo's that night had the feel of a homecoming. Pescatore took refuge in the rituals at the table, the family banter about Facundo's diet. He had fun reading The Cricket in Times Square *to David. He left early, saying he still had jet lag.*

Pescatore awoke at dawn. He packed clothes and his hunting knife. He took a hydrofoil across the river to Colonia del Sacramento, Uruguay. A bright windy day: the river was choppy, the ferry half empty. In the port, disembarking passengers were greeted by the sight of a gourd for mate *tea standing atop an unmanned immigration counter. The Uruguayan border inspector showed up minutes later, dignified and unhurried.*

In the museumlike silence of Colonia, a town of cobblestone streets and nineteenth-century Portuguese architecture, he rented a Chevrolet Vectra sedan. He drove fast toward Montevideo.

Florencia had said that Raymond loved this coast. He had told her he'd be happy to wait for the Apocalypse playing piano in a joint by the beach.

Pescatore had done an Internet search for clubs, restaurants and hotels with live music. He started looking in Piriápolis, a genteel and dilapidated resort sunk in off-season somnolence. The wind swept a chipped and empty boardwalk. Whitecaps gleamed on the horizon where the river met the ocean. Palm trees swayed. Locals strolled carrying mate *gourds. Vintage cars chugged by. Uruguay was an automotive dinosaur paradise roamed by lovingly maintained Packards, Bugattis and Model Ts.*

He spent the weekend searching in and around Punta del Este, the flagship resort city. Quite a few places were still closed. On Monday afternoon, he got lucky. He was near the town of La Paloma, which in the summer was a sedate alternative to the glitz and crowds of Punta del Este. He asked a cashier at a grocery store where he could find a fine cup of espresso. The cashier suggested the Hotel Viento Dulce, a new inn on a narrow peninsula.

He was the only customer in the hotel bar. The long room had ceiling fans and an adjoining terrace with a panoramic view. He noticed a piano in a corner. He gathered intelligence from a svelte tanned waitress with spiky, sun-streaked hair. As a matter of fact, the bar did have a pianist. An Argentine named Dino. A real charmer. And quite a voice. Funny story: He had showed up a couple of weeks ago and convinced the owners to give him a gig. Dino was off Mondays. He usually came in to practice in the morning when the bar was closed. She didn't know where he lived.

Pescatore prowled the area until evening. He roamed businesses, cruised residential streets in the fading light. He spent the night at the hotel. His dreams were troubled.

The next morning, he tucked the sheath of his hunting knife in his belt at the small of his back. He put on a denim jacket, went downstairs and made his way to the terrace. Above the sounds of the surf, he could hear the piano playing. He used the shelter of a hedge to approach the tall windows. The glare on the glass made it hard to see inside. The French doors he had scoped out the day before were still unlocked.

Raymond sat at the piano in the corner. His back to the terrace, a wall on his right. He was playing a Latin jazz melody. Pescatore had heard it before. Raymond bent over the keyboard, teasing out a syncopated riff, repeating it slowly. He was alone. The bar was dark. The plants and tables were shadows. The only light came from the terrace.

Pescatore padded closer. Raymond was lost in the music. He wore a hooded sweatshirt, jeans and flip-flops. His hair had grown long. The bangs dangled toward the keys. Pescatore stopped ten feet away. He had his arms at his sides, knees slightly bent.

"Dino," he said.

Raymond whirled. He lurched to his feet, banged into the piano, and dropped back onto the stool. His hair fell across his face, which twisted with terror. Seeing that Pescatore had blocked his path of escape, he cringed in the corner.

Pescatore advanced, right arm back near his knife. He saw no weapons, no aggressive moves.

"Motherfucker," Raymond sobbed. "Motherfucker, what are you gonna do? Por el amor de dios."

Raymond's chest heaved. He pushed his hair out of his bloodshot eyes. He looked haunted. Pale, puffy, stubble around a goatee.

"Easy, man," Pescatore snapped. "Easy."

He spoke in the command growl he had used in the Border Patrol for controlling groups of aliens solo. He waited for him to catch his breath.

"You scared the shit out of me," Raymond said in a strangled voice.

"Uh-huh."

Raymond's back remained against the wall. He was shaking.

"What are you going to do? What do you want?"

"I wanna talk. We didn't really get a chance last time."

Pescatore pulled a chair from a nearby table. He turned it around and sat, his chest against the seat back. Raymond watched like a witness to an alien landing. He glanced at the shadows and the windows.

"You broke my heart in Iraq, man," Raymond blurted. "We were a team. I worked with you, risked everything. You broke my heart."

"Isn't that a fucking pity."

"You figured out I sent those shooters after your French chick. That's why you set me up to die."

Pescatore had already concluded that Raymond was behind the ambush of Fatima. He felt conflicting emotions. He was relieved that Raymond was alive. After all, he had betrayed Raymond in Iraq, not the other way around. Still, he had no illusions. He knew what had to be done. He knew it with absolute clarity, as if a fog had lifted once and for all.

"See, that right there tells me a lot," Pescatore said. "You say I'm your oldest, dearest friend, you'd give your life for me and all that shit, but you don't understand me. That's one of the things we need to work out."

"How did you find me?"

"I know you." Pescatore shrugged. *"I remembered something someone said and put it together from there."*

"Who?"

"A woman."

Raymond sighed.

Pescatore said, *"I haven't hurt you yet. So give it up. Explain to me how it is you're alive and sitting here playing piano."*

Raymond reached down — Pescatore tracked his hands — and retrieved a bottle of beer. He drank, spilling a little. He wiped his chin.

"Actually, it's a pretty good story." His voice lacked affect and energy; a dull echo of a voice. *"I'll give you this: You did try to convince me to leave with you that day in Baghdad. Took a while for it to sink in. Thank God you fucked up at the last minute."*

"How?"

"You called me cuate.*"* He managed a weak smile. *"I've been calling you* cuate *for years. I never heard you say it back. Not once. You acted so hinky. I thought you were worried I was setting you up. Then you called me* cuate. *That's when I knew you were the one pulling something."*

Cuate *meant "twin." Mexicans used it affectionately to mean buddy or pal. Pescatore had never liked Raymond calling him that. The more ambivalent he had grown about their friendship, the less he had liked it.*

"I'm not as good at lying to people as you are," Pescatore said.

"I think you did it on purpose, to send me a signal."

"Huh."

"Maybe without even realizing it. That's what I think."

"Interesting theory."

After Pescatore's departure from the safe house, Raymond explained, Brigadier Ali's men took a break for lunch. Raymond was tense. He replayed the conversation with Pescatore over and over in his mind. He noticed that the chubby teenager who worked as a flunky at the safe house was being sent to pick up food for the brigadier and his men. He improvised a fictitious errand and got in the kid's car.

"*Total survival rush, man. I had to get out of there. I had to think. We were like three blocks away when the missile hit. My ears hurt for days.*"

Raymond and the kid returned to the scene. Minutes later, Raymond melted away in the crowd. The Quds Force zeroed in on him as the obvious suspect. Dodging a manhunt, he traveled overland to Turkey. He eventually reached Dubai, where he took the risk of emptying his last surviving bank account and retrieved an unused passport. He flew to South Africa and Brazil, then made his way to Uruguay.

"*You rooked me good.*" Raymond stared at the keyboard. "*My money, my houses, cars, women, connections. My family. I don't have shit.*"

"*You got the music. This nice spot.*"

"*Not for long.*"

"*True. I found you in three days. All kinds of hard-asses are looking for you. Like a race.*"

Raymond surveyed him bitterly. "*Are you getting off on this?*"

"*Nope.*"

"*I changed sides for you, Valentin.*"

"*For yourself. As usual. Because your back was to the wall.*"

"*I was a loyal friend. Protected you no matter what.*"

Pescatore experienced a physical pang of regret. He let it subside. He spoke as if to a child.

"*Here's the thing, Raymond. Let's say you have a dog. A real mean dog. A menace. It attacks everybody. Even people you love. But it's totally faithful to you. You probably love it back. Sooner or later, though, you have to do something about the dog.*"

"*Now I'm a dog, huh?*"

"*You're smart, talented, funny. I learned so much from you. You had a big impact on me, you're part of where I come from. But you're a monster. You said I did what I did because of Fatima. How did you know we were together, anyway?*"

"*I know you,*" Raymond responded mockingly. "*My people*

watched you in Bolivia. I could tell just by the way you looked at her in the pictures they took. I thought she was American at first. I got more info later, identified her, put her on a list of targets. After the brothers fucked up on the Champs-Élysées, I needed results. And I needed to calm my wife down. I felt bad, but I had to try to whack Fatima Belhaj. I outed her on a website and arranged for the shooters."

"Well, I was mad as hell. But it wasn't the only reason. I was hoping you'd show some sadness about all the lives you took. France. London. Buenos Aires, for God's sake. Where our families are from. I was praying for remorse. Nothing. You were disappointed the car bomb didn't go off at the school. Coulda got five hundred easy, you said."

"We've been over this. I was a soldier. I was fighting a war."

"Fuck that. You're a Nazi. If this was 1939, you'd sign up to run a concentration camp. Shut up and let me finish. In Iraq, I had to operate like you. Scamming, backstabbing. I didn't want to kill you. I'm sentimental. But I couldn't let the brigadier get away. He was a bigger monster. The worst thing was being sneaky. If I had to pull the trigger, I wanted to do it face-to-face."

Raymond was absorbed in the conversation. He had leaned back on the bench, his hair matting against the wall. Now he sat up. Fear flared in the small caverns of his eyes.

"You came here to finish the job," he whispered.

Mr. Drama, *Pescatore thought.* Living the movie to the end.

"Not unless you jump me. I'm here to make an offer."

"Representing who?"

"Me."

Raymond cocked his head and waited. Although Pescatore hadn't discussed the idea with anyone, it had been taking shape over several days.

"My offer is, you surrender to me. I turn you over to a senior U.S. fed I trust. Aboveboard, official. You confess publicly in a written statement and lay the whole thing out. Every crime in every country,

*every terrorist shot-caller, every sleazy snitch relationship, everybody
who let you skate. Let it all hit the fan."*

"You're thinking I could score some kind of deal?"

*The lights flickered on overhead. Both of them jumped. A uni-
formed cleaning man appeared by the bar pulling a mop and a
bucket. He waved at Raymond, who slowly raised a hand in response.*

Pescatore turned back to Raymond and continued in a low voice.

*"Hell, no," he declared. "No deal. I've got some press contacts."
He thought of Leo Méndez in Tijuana, who was wired with journalists all over. "They'll put the pressure on. That'll keep you locked
up and alive. You'll be prosecuted somewhere: Britain, France, the
U.S. I'm thinking you'll spend the rest of your life in prison."*

"So what do I get out of it, exactly?"

*Raymond's eyes narrowed. His voice had regained petulance. It
almost made Pescatore nostalgic. It almost comforted him. He resisted an impulse to stand up and leave.*

*"If I have to spell it out, it kinda defeats its own purpose," he
said, frowning. "You'll be alive, Ray. Maybe your sons will visit you.
You'll pay for your sins. The victims and survivors will get information, closure. A little justice."*

*Raymond used both hands to sweep his hair back. He looked side-
ways with his fingers at his mouth. The pose of a young shaggy
Springsteen. Finally, he shook his head.*

"That's not me. But thanks."

*Pescatore wasn't surprised. He had learned to have high hopes
and low expectations.*

*The adrenaline had faded. They sat in silence, not quite looking
at each other.*

*The cleaning man advanced. The mop squeaked. Furniture
scraped.*

"So what kind of stuff you singing here?"

"Standards. Tango. A little jazz."

"Nothing wrong with old school."

"I'm doing more instrumentals. Not just getting by on the voice, you know?"

"Yeah. Sounds good, Ray."

After a moment, Pescatore got up. He said, "All right, then."

He started toward the door to the lobby. A memory came to him of the wind in the tunnel in Chicago. He walked faster.

"I'm not running," Raymond said. "I'll be right here."

"Won't be long now."

The story appeared in the Argentine press the next week. Murders were uncommon on the Uruguayan coast, so it caused a splash. Reporters and headline writers came up with variations on the phrase shoot the piano player. *Two helmeted gunmen had arrived on a motorcycle one morning. They went directly into the bar of the hotel. They used silencers.*

The police speculated about a stickup gone wrong. No one took that seriously. The crime had the hallmarks of a professional hit. The victim carried an authentic Argentine passport with an invented identity. The investigators wanted to know who he really was.

Pescatore had not told anyone, not even Facundo, about finding Raymond. He knew nothing beyond the press reports. The articles lacked detail. It was not clear what Raymond had been doing, where he had fallen.

The way Pescatore imagined it, though, he had been at the piano. He liked to think Raymond had been playing the song that he had been practicing when he saw him for the last time: "Manteca." The mambo classic by Chano Pozo, the ace drummer, the Santeria zealot who hit the big time for a while. The wild man who was dancing alone to his song in a bar when his past caught up with him.

Acknowledgments

I want to give heartfelt thanks to many men and women in law enforcement, intelligence and diplomatic service in many countries who have been my patient teachers and generous guides over the years.

Many thanks also to Asya Muchnick and Liana Levi and their teams. Also to Valeria and Carmen; Carlo and Sal; my parents; family near and far. And to Andy for the jokes.

About the Author

Sebastian Rotella is the author of *Triple Crossing,* which the *New York Times* Sunday Book Review named favorite debut crime novel of 2011, and the nonfiction book *Twilight on the Line*. He is a senior reporter for ProPublica, a newsroom dedicated to investigative journalism in the public interest. He covers international security issues. He worked for twenty-three years for the *Los Angeles Times,* serving as bureau chief in Paris and Buenos Aires and Mexico border correspondent. His honors include a Peabody Award, Columbia University's Dart Award and Moors Cabot Prize for Latin American coverage, the German Marshall Fund's Weitz Prize for reporting in Europe, five Overseas Press Club Awards, The Urbino Prize of Italy, and an Emmy nomination. He was a Pulitzer finalist for international reporting in 2005.

You've turned the last page.

But it doesn't have to end there . . .

If you're looking for more first-class, action-packed, nail-biting suspense, join us at **Facebook.com/ MulhollandUncovered** for news, competitions, and behind-the-scenes access to Mulholland Books.

For regular updates about our books and authors as well as what's going on in the world of crime and thrillers, follow us on **Twitter@MulhollandUK**.

There are many more twists to come.

MULHOLLAND:
You never know what's
coming around the curve.

www.mulhollandbooks.co.uk

HODDER